Ryan g...
rearview mirror

"We're not going to get away," he shouted grimly.

"We have to," Mildred answered, then shrugged and dropped her heavy med kit. "Heave the supplies! Lose everything!"

Stunned for a moment by the incredible act, Ryan resolutely reached behind for his backpack. Mildred knew her stuff, and whatever it was that was after them, he didn't want it to reach them for the sake of a few pounds.

With the motorcycles moving at top speed, the companions raced through the forest in a nightmare of dodging trees and crashing through bushes.

Unstoppable, the death wave from the Kite swept onward, getting closer and closer with each passing moment....

Other titles in the Deathlands saga:

JAMES AXLER

DEATH LANDS®

Gaia's Demise

THE BARONIES TRILOGY
BOOK II

A GOLD EAGLE BOOK FROM
WORLDWIDE®

TORONTO • NEW YORK • LONDON
AMSTERDAM • PARIS • SYDNEY • HAMBURG
STOCKHOLM • ATHENS • TOKYO • MILAN
MADRID • WARSAW • BUDAPEST • AUCKLAND

As always, for Melissa

First edition October 1999

ISBN 0-373-62547-2

GAIA'S DEMISE

Copyright © 1999 by Worldwide Library.

Printed in U.S.A.

...for when all the strong elements, military and feudal, were unhinged, mighty forces became adrift, and the void was open. And after a pause, into the void strode a maniac of ferocious genius, the repository and expression of the most virulent hatred that has ever corroded the human heart. The door of opportunity was open, the dreadful time was at hand, and God help us, it was all about to begin once more....

—Sir Winston Churchill,
The Hinge of Fate, 1938

THE DEATHLANDS SAGA

This world is their legacy, a world born in the violent nuclear spasm of 2001 that was the bitter outcome of a struggle for global dominance.

There is no real escape from this shockscape where life always hangs in the balance, vulnerable to newly demonic nature, barbarism, lawlessness.

But they are the warrior survivalists, and they endure—in the way of the lion, the hawk and the tiger, true to nature's heart despite its ruination.

Ryan Cawdor: The privileged son of an East Coast baron. Acquainted with betrayal from a tender age, he is a master of the hard realities.

Krysty Wroth: Harmony ville's own Titian-haired beauty, a woman with the strength of tempered steel. Her premonitions and Gaia powers have been fostered by her Mother Sonja.

J. B. Dix, the Armorer: Weapons master and Ryan's close ally, he, too, honed his skills traversing the Deathlands with the legendary Trader.

Doctor Theophilus Tanner: Torn from his family and a gentler life in 1896, Doc has been thrown into a future he couldn't have imagined.

Dr. Mildred Wyeth: Her father was killed by the Ku Klux Klan, but her fate is not much lighter. Restored from predark cryogenic suspension, she brings twentieth-century healing skills to a nightmare.

Jak Lauren: A true child of the wastelands, reared on adversity, loss and danger, the albino teenager is a fierce fighter and loyal friend.

Dean Cawdor: Ryan's young son by Sharona accepts the only world he knows, and yet he is the seedling bearing the promise of tomorrow.

In a world where all was lost, they are humanity's last hope....

PROLOGUE

A hundred years ago, a rain of nuclear bombs obliterated civilization in a few minutes of blazing horror. It was the end of the world. Doomsday. Skydark.

The great cities were gone in a blinding flash, replaced by bomb craters whose deadly glow illuminated the nighttime sky. Mountains rose and fell, valleys slammed shut and lakes boiled under the atomic bombardment, permanently altering the topography of North America. Burning clouds of isotopes and poisons filled the sky in an endless, raging hurricane, and acid rain pounded the lush farmland and forests of the continent into sterile desert.

With the first nuclear explosion, the tissue-thin tapestry of civilization was ripped apart. The rule of law was replaced overnight with the somber, draconian edict of survival of the fittest. Cannibals hunted prey, coldhearts brutally raided farms and slavers seized anybody they could as chattel. Plus, lost in the wilds of the new world were functioning predark war machines. Shielded against the onslaught of the atomic holocaust, the computer-operated juggernauts were patiently waiting to continue a war that was long finished, and death was almost always the reward for the person who foolishly awoke one of the terrible sleeping giants.

In crumbling ruins, ragged people fought to the death over a dented can of food or a single precious bullet.

Any type of gun was more valuable than gold, defense against the horrible swarms of muties, twisted abominations that arose from the nuke craters and feasted on the flesh of humanity.

Slowly, over the long decades, civilization of a sort was returning to the world. Crude walled cities were rising from the ashes of the past. The populations of these villes were ruthlessly governed by self-appointed barons, each ruler backed by a private army of brutal sec men. Whips and chains kept the people inside, while barbed wire and blasters kept the muties out.

Electricity was seldom seen, starvation universal, rape a daily event, death the only known means of escape. This was America in the late twenty-first century. Welcome to the Deathlands.

But one small handful of people refused to surrender hope. Ryan Cawdor and his companions traveled the continent searching for someplace where they could settle down and live in peace. Armed with functioning predark weapons, the companions killed only when necessary, and preferred trading for supplies rather than stealing. In a world gone mad, these simple acts of dignity nearly made them legends.

In addition, Ryan Cawdor and the others knew the greatest military secret of the predark world: the redoubts.

Hidden across America, these often huge underground bunkers were built by the government to withstand direct nuclear hits. Powered by the near limitless energy of nuclear reactors, most redoubts were still intact after a century, incredible havens of safety with fluorescent lights, air-conditioning and drinkable water. Originally, the subterranean bases were stockpiled with everything needed to rebuild the country after the coming apocalypse—weapons, tools, military vehicles, fuel and medicine. Those countless tons of supplies were long gone, with only a few forgotten boxes of dusty weapons and dehydrated food packs remaining. However, these meager scraps from the past were more than enough to give the companions a fighting chance to stay alive. And sometimes they came across a major prize.

Yet even more importantly, the redoubts were linked together by the incredible mat-trans units. These amazing machines depended on technology advanced almost beyond understanding. The mat-trans units could transfer a living person from one redoubt to another in only seconds, which allowed the companions to quickly leave a dangerous area, hunt for food and continue their search for a permanent home.

Unfortunately, it now seemed possible that others might also know the vital secret of the redoubts.

A few days earlier, a stranger named Overton had attacked Ryan's home ville of Front Royal with an army of sec men. The troops were wearing impossibly clean blue shirts and were armed with predark weapons in mint condition. Overton's goal was to conquer Front Royal by any means available, then physically link it with two neighboring villes in Virginia, creating a single massive walled city, a gigantic metropolis the likes of which hadn't been seen for more than a century. The would-be usurper was finally neutralized by Ryan, but the reasons behind the insane plan were lost in violent death, and the mysterious origin of the weapons was never resolved.

Had Overton been working alone in his plan to seize control of those three East Coast baronies? Or was he a vanguard, an advance agent paving the way for somebody else? Was creating a new metropolis in Deathlands the final goal, or only the first step of a much larger plan? And was the secret of the redoubts' existence still safe?

A dying man had said the answers to these questions could be found in a distant ville called Shiloh. While the baron at Front Royal started to rebuild the badly damaged ville, Ryan Cawdor and the companions left on a perilous overland journey to try to discover if the brutal war for the baronies was indeed over.

Or only just beginning…

Chapter One

"Black dust!" the man screamed, pointing toward the horizon. "What the hell is that?"

A dozen people at the campsite stopped whatever they were doing and turned to look in the direction indicated. Cresting a hill far down the road was a wag of some sort—no, it was a rolling box of metal, with a stream of faint bluish smoke coming from its rear. The sides were sloped at sharp angles, no windshield or windows were visible and it had numerous big black wheels. There wasn't a single visible piece of wood in the whole contraption.

"A wag," a teenager murmured, wiping his mouth on a dirty sleeve as he placed aside his plate of stew. Standing, the teenager grabbed a longblaster from the top of a woodpile and worked the bolt, chambering a round. He licked dry lips as a soft wind ruffled the thin rags that were his clothing.

Another man stood and pulled a crossbow into view from his nest of clothes, "A metal wag. I never seen one dat moved before!"

Leaning heavily on a repaired crutch, an elderly man glanced over his shoulder to a nearby grassy field. A crude wall of thickets and sharp sticks formed a defensive barrier around the clearing, and in the middle stood a faded yellow school bus, its many windows heavily patched with gray tape and bits of plastic. The wheels were sunk into the hard ground, and a tilted stone chimney rose from the back. The rusted remains of a few other wags doted the field, the grass thin enough in spots to see the cracked black material underneath. Way off by itself, the rounded shell of a beetle-shaped vehicle was surrounded by weeds, the open front door showing that the interior had been completely stripped except for a cushioned seat that had a hole cut in the bottom. The opening continued through the chassis and deep into the ground. Fat flies buzzed around the battered wag, and for an unknown reason, a half moon was painted on the door.

"A working wag," Tant breathed excitedly. The young man drew a bulky revolver from the belt holding his buckskin jacket closed, and lovingly ran his hands over the Parkerized finish of the big-bore weapon. The wooden handle had been replaced with bone long ago.

"Must be some baron," a pretty blonde suggested, and she pulled a long carving knife from her sleeve.

"Or slavers," another man grumbled, touching a ragged scar that completely circled his thick neck. In his massive hands, he held a metal rod tipped with a razor-sharp radiator fan. The ends glistened, mirror bright in the morning sun. "They got wags. Well, sometimes."

"We best leave it alone," an old woman stated. She hobbled a bit closer to the roadway but didn't cross onto the gravel of the berm. She knew her place. That honor was for menfolk only.

"Let them leave without a toll?" an old man snapped angrily, watching the wag come steadily closer. His face was deeply lined, but not from hunger, and a puckered star on the right cheek marked where he had been shot in the face at close range. His boots were patched, his jacket was lined with the fur of mountain lion and a brace of oiled revolvers jutted from his wide leather belt. "Black dust, what for, woman?"

Her weak eye wandering aimlessly, the old woman scowled down the road and gestured at the strange vehicle. "Are ya daft, Spector? That ain't be no civvy wag. That's a war wag, a tank!"

Raising a hand to strike her, Spector held his anger at the outburst, knowing she was only doing so for the good of the collectors. Dimly, he recalled hearing the word before from Grandda. His father's father had been a great leader of the collectors, siring fourteen children before dying. A mutie had leaped from the belly of a deer they killed one winter and tore off his arms before the others could bludgeon it to death.

Drawing a blaster, Spector squinted against the distance. Naw, couldn't be a real tank as the wag didn't have those metal belts on either side that chewed up the streets. It had whatyacallems.

"Tires," Tant said, loading a massive crossbow. The quarrel was of green wood, but the barbed tip was steel, lashed into place with human hair.

"Blasters," he added, scowling. "Them there be fancy autoblasters on its top!"

"Autoblasters?" asked a pregnant girl brandishing an ax, a naked child hiding behind her voluminous skirts.

"Fire more slugs than a hundred sec men at once!"

A young man with only the wispy hint of a beard on his jaw curled a lip. "Horseshit," he declared.

"It's the truth."

"Let it pass, Da," a redheaded boy suggested, the glass bottle in his hands sloshing slightly. The whiskey bottle with its burning rag of a fuse was actually only filled with urine, but most folks thought it to be a Molotov and steered clear of the pretend firebomb.

Pushing back his cap, Spector stood firm before the steady advance of the war wag. "Anybody can pass," he stated, shifting his grip on his wheelgun. "Long as they pays a toll. This be our road, child! Don't we sweep away the leaves in the fall and fill in the holes after the snows? Our grandies guarded this here road for the eagle god, and so do we. Ain't nobody pass 'less they pays a toll. One can food, one bullet or a day of work."

The group took heart from the ancient words and formed a line across the long expanse of concrete. Only the faintest suggestions of ruins marked where the mighty booths stood, but those had been destroyed in skydark. There were cracks in the surface, but those had been carefully patched. Every weed was pulled, the loose gravel along the east side raked into neat order and the grassy strip to the west trimmed neatly. Beyond the strip lay the broken remains of shattered concrete, trees growing wild from the cracks, and most of the surface masked by decades of grass and vines. But that wasn't their side. That was the north, and they were the southbound. The war between the two rival gangs had ended many winters ago in a bloody fight still referred to as Death Day. Now only the south remained to rule the great road of exit that stretched from the mountains to the terrible ocean.

The big wag was a lot closer now, its speed unchanging. Spector could see it was a lot bigger than he'd first thought, and the body was made of different colors, not painted camouflage like hunters did to hide in the bush. No, sir, the metal itself was a clean green in one area, and blackened with fire damage in another, as if the machine were pieced together from a dozen damaged wags. Surprisingly, it made excellent camouflage. Once in thick bushes, the machine would be damn difficult to spot. Big cans and bags were strapped to the sides under layers of fishing nets.

"Loot," Tant said greedily, releasing the safety lock on his crossbow. "Look at it! They got so much they can't keep it all inside!"

Spector stepped between the man and the approaching wag so that the needle tip of the quarrel touched his chest. "We ain't be thieves or coldhearts," the older man stated. "This be our road, and we take tolls. That be all. No raping the women or taking more than usual. Understand?"

Tant felt a rush of heat to his face, partly from shame but the rest from anger. His hands tightened on the stock and trigger of the crossbow, the muscles in his arms hardening as he fought conflicting emotions. Spector stayed motionless, letting the younger man decide the matter for himself. A good leader didn't always command, but sometimes listened. The engine noise of the war wag was discernible when the younger man finally relaxed his aggressive stance.

"Sorry," he apologized, and fired.

At point-blank range, the shaft went completely through the old man's chest. Staggering backward onto the road, Spector fell to his knees and Tant swung the stock of the crossbow like a club. Spector's head broke apart, one eye flying off into the wood, bones and brains spilling onto the pale concrete.

Retrieving the blaster from the dead man's clothing, Tant turned to face the rest of the collectors. The butt of the weapons were still warm from the dead man, and somehow that gave the killer a rush of courage.

"Now I am in charge!" Tant shouted, thrusting a blaster into the air. "And I say we take everything from everybody who tries to pass! Why should we starve when food comes to us by itself?''

Eagerly, the rest of the family took up the cry, and several stepped closer to spit on the sprawled form of Spector. Only a few of the older women and younger children didn't join the rally against their fallen leader, and quickly moved away from the others. Their brethren seemed like outlanders to them, strangers drunk on the freshly spilled blood.

"Rules, reg'lations," one man slurred, brandishing a glass-tipped spear. "What mean they? The strong take, the weak die. That be the rules here!"

"So speaks Ben, my new lieutenant," Tant shouted. "For I am the leader now."

The collectors roared their approval, and Tant threw his crossbow at the man. The weapon landed at his feet, which were swaddled in plastic and rags in place of boots. Passing his spear to a man with a club, Ben knelt before his new leader and lifted the gore-smeared weapon with a grim reverence.

"Death to the outlanders," Ben said, bowing his head.

"Death to all!" Tant shouted, staring hatefully at the wag coming straight toward them. The vehicle hadn't attempted to swerve into the trees or stop and turn. More fools they, for this was where they would die, and that machine become his to command.

"Positions!" Tant ordered, cocking both hammers on his warm blasters.

The collectors scrambled to their pits and dropped out of sight as Ben raced into the bushes to kick at a block of wood half-hidden amid the greenery. With the block gone, a weight dropped out of sight into the ground and from the trees a barrier swung into the sky on squealing hinges and slammed down hard across the roadway. The heavy beam was a chiseled tree trunk, bristling with rusty nails and bearing the eight-sided metal disk of the tribe painted the magic colors of red and white. All travelers stopped at the sight of the sign of power.

"Hold for a toll!" Tant shouted with an amiable smile, tucking one blaster into his belt.

The wag didn't slow.

"There be muties ahead!" he added in warning, his smile dropping into a sneer. "Much danger! Death everywhere!"

As if in reply, brilliant headlights flashed into operation, the beams temporarily blinding the collectors. Cursing in rage, most dropped their blasters to cover their eyes. Only a few managed to wildly fire their weapons at the invader. Fletched arrows struck the side of the vehicle, the wooden shafts shattering on the armor. A spear smashed on the turret, the glass tip exploding into glittering sparkles. Homemade bullets musically ricocheted off the chassis, leaving gray smears, and the one round that hit a tire simply sank into the resilient material and disappeared, doing no visible damage.

Then the powerful engines of the war wag revved louder, and it surged forward with renewed speed, covering the last fifty yards to the gate in only seconds. The wag smashed into the stout barrier headfirst, and the wood exploded into splinters, a rain of nails spraying from the impact.

Baring his teeth in rage, Tant stood firm and steadily fired his revolvers at the looming wag until they clicked on empty chambers. For the briefest flicker of time, Tant saw a single eye looking at him through a tiny slit in the metal hull of the incredible machine, an eye of icy blue. That was when his resolve broke, and the killer dashed for the safety of the berm, but it was already too late.

The great machine leaped forward in a surge of speed, and the prow slammed into him with the force of an avalanche. Pain filling his world, Tant dropped to the roadway and went directly underneath the juggernaut.

For an electric moment of time, he waited to be crushed flat, when Tant realized in a rush of clarity that there was space below the wag. The bottom was almost a yard off the ground! He started to laugh in relief, when the machine sharply turned and the last two wheels went straight for his head, missing his face by an inch but rolling over his left arm, mashing it flat, every bone pulverized from the colossal weight. Shrieking at the pain, Tant tried to pull away and the bottom of the wag slammed against his head, sending him into blackness.

Seconds later, the sprawled body of Tant appeared behind the transport, with a small cut on his forehead and his entire right arm bloody pulp. Tears streaming from his aching eyes, Ben rushed over and shot Tant in the heart with a crossbow quarrel, making himself the new leader.

"TRIPLE STUPE BASTARDS," Ryan Cawdor muttered, easing his foot off the gas of the LAV-25 armored personnel carrier. "Guess they never saw an APC before and didn't know what it could do."

"Well, they sure know now," J. B. Dix said, tilting back his fedora as he watched the tiny outpost vanish into the distance behind them through an aft blaster port. When satisfied the danger was over, J.B. removed his finger from the trigger of his Uzi submachine gun and slung the deadly weapon over a shoulder. Lying on the deck between his boots was a bulging satchel of explosives, with a Smith & Wesson M-4000 scattergun tucked between the straps. Even in the tight confines of the APC, the Armorer never let his weapons get far away from a ready hand.

Ryan nodded in agreement as he steered the wag around a fallen tree and some large potholes. The driver's seat of the predark machine was designed for soldiers from that time period, large men loaded with lots of equipment. Ryan was barely comfortable in the chair, and his wild mane of black hair brushed against the control panel set in the ceiling directly above the Plexiglas ob port used to see outside. The man's face was seamed by a long scar, courtesy of his brother Harvey, and a crude leather patch covered his left eye. A SIG-Sauer blaster, with a built-in baffle sound suppressor, was tucked into the leather holster at his right hip, the curved handle of a panga knife jutting from its customary sheath, within easy access. Hanging nearby from hooks set into the rough metal walls were a bolt-action longblaster and a sleek AK-47 machine gun.

Sitting against the aft doors, Jak Lauren merely grunted in reply as he continued to strop a knife on a whetstone with steady strokes. The pale teenager was dressed in camou-colored military fatigues and a battered vest decorated with feathers and bits of mirror and metal sewn into the seams and collar. But that was a trick; razor blades were sewn inside the collar and any enemy grabbing him soon discovered that the hard way when they lost fingers. The youth was a true albino. His skin was dead white, and ruby-red eyes peered from a cascade of snowy hair. A massive Colt Python .357 jutted from his belt, and at least a dozen leaf-bladed throwing knives were hidden on his person.

"Fools die," Jak stated coldly, tucking away the leaf-bladed throwing knife and, like magic, another appeared in his hand. "What else new?"

"I saw wags on the side of the road," Dean Cawdor said, a Browning Hi-Power blaster held casually as he watched the horizon for any signs of pursuit. "Think they might try and come after us?"

"Those wrecks? Even if the wags worked, they'll be busy squabbling over who's in charge now that we killed their leader," J.B. stated, adjusting his wire-rimmed glasses to a more comfortable position.

"Good," Dean said, clicking the safety on his blaster with a flick of his thumb. The boy tucked the blaster into his belt. Although only eleven years old, going on twelve, Dean already carried himself with the deadly assurance of a seasoned warrior and seemed to look more like his father with every passing day.

"I just thank Gaia they thought a wooden beam would stop us," Krysty Wroth said gruffly. "Could have been a lot worse."

The shapely redhead squatted comfortably on the steps leading to the overhead turret, checking the loads in her Smith & Wesson .38. Krysty had lost the blaster in that hellish garage at Front Royal when she'd gotten caught by Overton's sec men. But J.B. had found the blaster under a bench when he'd done some work on the LAV, the weapon discarded there, apparently, by one of the blue shirts. The neat .38 handled better than the powerful .357, and she was happy to have it once again in hand.

Krysty was a beautiful woman, her complexion flawless, her abundance of fiery hair gently moving as if stirred by secret winds only she could feel.

"Those coldhearts could have smashed a hornet's nest

against the side of the LAV," she continued. "And then we would have been in real trouble."

"Hornets?" Jak asked, pausing in his work.

A tall man with silver-gray hair was resting against the ammo locker and raised his head at the conversation, arching an eyebrow. "Indeed, madam, I do understand," Doc Tanner rumbled in a deep stentorian bass. "Once the nest hit us, the hornets would target our wag as an enemy and come swarming in through every blaster port and vent. Their painful stings would soon drive us outside where the others could easily slay us in the confusion."

Wearing a frilly shirt and an outlandish frock coat, the old man would have been a strange sight even in his own time period, and his resplendent crop of hair made Doc appear much older than he really was. A slim ebony swordstick was laid casually across his lap, and a massive double-barreled blaster jutted from the cavalry gun belt around his waist. The Civil War museum piece seeming incongruous with the rest of his dapper attire.

Krysty gestured with an open palm. "Old trick," she said. "My mother used it often against the big muties."

The old man pulled a few inches of shiny steel blade from within the ebony stick, then slammed the sword back into its sheath. "Deuced clever, I must admit."

Ryan glanced over his shoulder at Krysty. "Hornets," he said after a while. "Glad you're on our side, lover. That would work even better on folks in an open cart, or on horseback."

"Pretty good," Jak agreed, tucking away his whetstone.

Biting off a piece of beef jerky, Dr. Mildred Wyeth chewed and swallowed the mouthful before speaking. A stocky black woman with bright, intelligent eyes, her lightweight denim jacket was unbuttoned, showing a heavy flannel shirt and a gun belt supporting a sleek target pistol, the ammo loops on the side of the belt filled with oily brass cartridges. A rare predark field-surgery kit holding medical supplies lay protectively between her boots, the canvas lovingly patched here and there.

"For some reason, that reminds me of a war story I once heard," the physician said. "Way back before sky-dark, some nation, I forget which, sent a battalion of their best tanks into northern Africa to establish a supply base for their troops. They expected little resistance from the locals as the farmers had almost no technology. They carried stone knives and went hunting with blowguns. It was supposed to be a slaughter, and it was. But for the other side."

Both hands steady on the steering levers, Ryan barked one of his rare laughs. "So the tanks got destroyed, eh? Good for the Africans."

"How?" Dean asked curiously, resting both elbows on his knees and leaning forward. Mildred and Doc came from before skydark and knew all sorts of things. Some of the information was useful for staying alive, but some was just fun to hear about—wild stories about things like airplanes and supermarkets.

Wrapping the remaining piece of jerky in a clean handkerchief, Mildred tucked the dried meat into a pocket for later. For once, they had plenty of supplies. Front Royal had given them all the food, fuel and ammo they could carry for this trip. Their mission was too important to chance failure over a can of beans or a handful of bullets. But as her Baptist minister father drilled into her as child, waste not, want not. Life in the radioactive hell of Deathlands was bitterly harsh, and every morsel of food saved could mean another day of life.

"How did they stop the invasion of armored tanks? Simple, really," she answered. "The locals would run away from the tanks, carefully luring them near the edge of a high cliff. Then when the tank was in the right position, hunters hidden in the bushes would use blowguns to shoot a poisoned dart into the tiny slots in the armor that the drivers used to see through. Blind and paralyzed, the soldiers couldn't change course, and the massive machines would roll off the cliff and smash to pieces when they hit the bottom."

"A veritable David-versus-Goliath story," Doc rumbled in wry amusement. "Good for the hunters."

Dean stole a glance at his father. "So the fancier the tech, the easier it is to smash," the boy concluded.

"Usually," Ryan answered, busy driving. "But not always, son."

"Everything has a weak point, but sometimes Goliath still wins," J.B. added, pulling a fat cigar from the breast pocket of his jacket and placing it in the corner of his mouth. "Sad but true."

"Ahem," Mildred said, leaning forward in her seat until almost touching noses with the man. "It smells quite bad enough in here with seven sweaty people packed like sardines. We don't need you adding to the pollution by smoking a hundred-year-old cigar."

"This is a brand-new one," J.B. retorted, pulling the stogie free and gesturing. "Hand rolled on the thighs of expert virgins exclusively for the baron of Front Royal himself!"

Everybody in the APC burst into laughter.

"My dear John Barrymore," Doc chuckled. "Expert virgins?"

"Nice work if you can get it," Krysty said, smiling.

As the military transport easily rolled over a low hill, Ryan merely snorted as he shifted gears.

"Didn't mean it that way," J.B. said with a frown.

"Horseshit," Jak scoffed.

Quizzically, J.B. took a sniff. "Seems to be mostly tobacco," he said slowly. "But yeah, I think there's a little horse in here, too."

"Also makes your breath taste awful," Mildred added softly.

J.B. winked at the physician and tucked the cigar away. "Don't want that, do we?"

Blushing slightly, Mildred started to add something, but was cut off when the wag jounced over some rough ground and the companions were nearly thrown from their seats. Desperately, the friends grabbed for anything welded solidly to the frame of the APC. The interior of the LAV-25 had been badly damaged by fire when its prior owners died, and the seat belts were only ashen smudges on the bare metal skeletons of the wall seats. Layers of blankets cushioned the seat struts enough for them to sit on for long periods, but every serious pothole threatened to throw them to the floor.

"Need rope," Jak muttered, releasing his grip on the belt of linked 25 mm rounds going into the electric cannon in the turret. "Make belts."

"Good idea," Dean said, massaging a bruised elbow. "But we already used it all tying our extra supplies to the outside."

"Hold on to your ass harder," J.B. suggested with a grin.

Extracting herself from a jumble of fallen supplies, Krysty ducked around the ammo belt feeding the machine gun and walked to the front of the wag. "Have

we lost the road?'' she asked, resting a slim hand on the
back of the chair in an effort to stay upright.

"Ten miles ago,'' Ryan answered brusquely, concentrating on the task of driving. A strange rustling noise
came from the outside as the LAV plowed through some
bushes. "We're crossing a field at present, heading
straight for a blast crater. J.B., give me a rad count!''

Quickly, the man checked the predark device pinned
to his collar. "No rads,'' he reported. "Must have been
a clean bomb.''

"Clean?'' Doc asked in surprise.

Reclaiming her seat, Mildred answered, "The isotopes
used have a short half-life. There would be no residual
radiation remaining after only a few years.''

"Clean,'' Jak snorted. "Right.''

Dean pressed his face to a defensive blaster port and
saw only a rippled expanse of glass stretching in every
direction. "Must have been a big nuke.''

"No such thing as a small nuclear blast,'' Ryan stated.

Curiously, the boy studied the unearthly landscape
surrounding the APC and tried to imagine what the area
was like before everything was vaporized in a micro-
second flash. Had there been a thriving city here, or a
military complex? Or was this a lost strike, a bomb that
missed its target and destroyed only woods and fields?
There was no way to ever know. Nothing remained but
the solid slab of slightly bluish glass, the soil fused crys-
talline from the extreme heat of the hellish detonation.
Distorted objects were almost visible within the trans-
lucent material, broken buildings forever trapped in the
middle of toppling over, and some charred human figures who would spend eternity desperately trying to
swim to the surface of the solidified pool.

The boy turned away from the blaster port, lost in

thought. None of the other companions spoke, the sterile
vista outside affecting even these hardened warriors.
Hours passed with a low hum filling the wag from the
tires under the vehicle as the APC raced across the wide
expanse of the cracked glass lake. Only the soft crackle
of static from the radio marred the near silence. The
electronic device had been salvaged from the ruins of
another APC, and since it was tuned to the command
channel of the blue shirts—the invading force at Front
Royal—Ryan brought the radio along just in case. But
with the heavy blanket of decaying isotopes in the plan-
etary atmosphere, even the most powerful radio trans-
mitters had a range of only a mile. Nearly useless, but
it took up little space.

Shifting gears, Ryan guided the APC up a sharp incline and off the fused soil onto dead earth, not even
weeds growing from the gray, sterilized soil. Slowly,
over the miles, streaks of dark earth reached into the
dead zone, and soon tufts of grass dotted the land. Trun-
dling through a shallow river, the LAV broached some
gentle rolling hills, and soon the black ribbon of an ancient road was visible in spots through the dense covering of weeds.

"Get hard, people!" Ryan ordered, downshifting so
their speed was more manageable. "We're past the crater, so Shiloh must be close."

With trained ease, the companions prepared their
weapons, sliding off safeties and making sure spare
ammo was available. Jak climbed into the turret of the
APC and checked the action of the 25 mm cannon, while
Doc took the gunner's spot and readied the 7.62 mm
ultrafast chain gun.

"Gaia, I hate crossing nuke craters," Krysty muttered,

unwrapping some tape from the handle of a gren and placing the live charge in the pocket of her shaggy coat.

"Bad vibrations from all the death?" Mildred asked, closing the cylinder of her Czech ZKR Olympic target pistol. The physician knew that Krysty could sometimes perceive things beyond the usual five senses of other people. Her early warnings of unseen danger had saved their lives more than once.

"Just the opposite," Krysty said. "I can't feel anything in those cursed areas. Absolutely and completely nothing."

"Sort of like going blind," Mildred suggested.

Krysty nodded and gave a shiver. "Very much so, yes."

Glancing at a map taped to the wall, Ryan followed the ancient road to a lush forest of trees. Turning eastward, he started a long sweep around the obstruction until reaching a wide field. He braked to a halt, but didn't turn off the engines, and for a few minutes, the companions studied the area carefully with weapons in hand. A few hundred yards ahead of them, the ground seemed to stop abruptly, and beyond was the limitless vista of the open sea. The sound of distant waves breaking on a rocky shore could be faintly heard over the rumble of the engines.

"Clear," Jak said from the turret.

"Clear," Doc agreed.

Waiting another minute, Ryan finally turned off the engines and silence filled the transport. Rising from the chair, the one-eyed warrior took his Steyer longblaster from the wall and worked the bolt, chambering a round for immediate use. "Jak, stay where you are and cover us in case of trouble. When we move out, I'll be on point. Dean, stay with Mildred, Krysty, then Doc. J.B., take rear guard.''

Leaning the rifle against a stack of crates, Ryan worked the slide on his SIG-Sauer 9 mm pistol and holstered the deadly blaster. "Stay sharp," he ordered, reclaiming his rifle. "This is just a recce, not a stand-up fight like at the caves. Keep a two-yard spread, and no noise. Overton's blue shirts could be close, and we want to take them by surprise."

"Ready?" J.B. asked, jerking back the bolt of his Uzi.

"Go," Ryan said.

J.B. unlocked the aft double doors and kicked them open. The armored slabs swung aside on squealing hinges, and a wealth of fresh air poured into the vehicle. Hopping to the ground, J.B. gratefully stretched his legs as he listened to the sounds of life. Crickets were chirping, and a bird sang softly. Good—their presence meant there were no big predators.

The rest of the companions watched from the blaster ports, the barrels of their weapons sticking out of the APC like porcupine quills. Satisfied there was no immediate danger, J.B. slung the Uzi over a shoulder and pulled the minisextant from under his shirt. Centering the mirror on the dim sun, he cut the horizon in two, adjusting the focus with tiny movements until satisfied.

"This is Shiloh, North Carolina," he stated, tucking the device away.

"Good." Ryan stepped to the ground and the men moved away to clear the way for the rest of the companions. The last person exiting, Dean closed the double doors and heard Jak bolt them from the inside.

Sweeping across the field in a standard search pattern, the companions found nothing of interest, which annoyed and disappointed them at the same time.

"Any signs of military traffic?" Ryan asked, feeling the tension of expected battle flow from his body. "Campfires, spent shells in the grass, a used latrine?"

"No signs of anything," J.B. answered, tugging his fedora down tight as protection from the wind.

Going to the edge of the field, Mildred found herself looking down at the ruins of a predark city partially covered with sand dunes. The beaches were festooned with driftwood and seaweed, and the ragged stumps of concrete pillions—the decaying remains of a once mighty seaport—jutted from the waves like the broken teeth of a sunken corpse. A telephone pole without wires rose from a sand dune, its crossbars filled with bird nests. Off by itself, a rusty stop sign waggled in the gusting wind.

Overhead, the purple sky was slashed with streaks of fiery orange, black clouds racing by as if moved by private hurricanes. Sheet lightning flashed, and distant thunder rumbled in natural majesty above the rattling stop sign.

The other companions joined Krysty at the edge of the cliff, and scowled at the ruins below.

"Son of a bitch. You sure this is the right place?" Ryan demanded gruffly.

Behind the companions, the main engine of the predark wag ticked softly as the metal slowly cooled. Then the top hatch of their armored vehicle squealed open on stubborn hinges, and Jak rose into view. Even with the armor and weapons of the Bradley APC surrounding him, Jak was clearly uneasy amid this desolation.

The youth said nothing, but his expression was one of intense scorn.

"This isn't their base," Krysty stated, lowering her blaster. "This isn't the home ville of anybody."

"Obviously, madam," Doc announced lugubriously, easing down the hammer of his gigantic LeMat pistol. "Nobody resides at this location but ghosts, and mayhap a few sand crabs. It is a simple village returned to its primordial state, with nary a humble cottage remaining to be balanced by a river's brim."

"Walt Whitman?" Mildred asked, squinting, thumbs hooked into her gun belt.

"No. Me," the man said, smiling broadly. "Just me this time."

Removing his hat, J.B. grimaced as he smoothed the brim. "Crap," he announced. "There's not a blaster or a war wag in sight, and the blues were lousy with pre-dark military supplies. Seemed like Overton had more weapons than Wizard Island and the Anthill combined!"

Dean scratched his head. "Mebbe this is the wrong Shiloh," the boy suggested. "We knew it wasn't the one in Virginia because that town got nuked in skydark."

"Could be the Civil War battleground we once visited in The Smokies," Mildred offered. "There's even a redoubt nearby, the one with all the tunnels. That could be where they're getting the weapons and wags from."

"Makes sense," Ryan said, nosily sucking on a hollow tooth. "But Tennessee is a mighty long way from Front Royal. If their home base is there, why choose a ville in Virginia as their capital city?"

"A diversion," J.B. stated, as if it were obvious. "Or mebbe Overton lied."

Mildred fiercely shook her head. "No way. He was in too much pain to be inventive. The home base of the people who attacked Front Royal is someplace named Shiloh. That we can count on as a fact."

The salty breeze from the Lantic felt good on his skin

as Ryan stepped closer to the cliff for a better view. He heard a stick snap under his boots. Only the noise sounded more metallic than wooden.

"Everybody freeze," he ordered softly.

The companions went motionless, straining to detect any possible dangers. The field was empty, and nothing could be heard but the waves on the beach below.

"Now listen to me very carefully. Back away from the cliff and only step in the exact same spots you did getting here," Ryan continued in a deceptively calm voice. His heart was pounding in his chest, and suddenly his palms were damp with sweat.

"What's wrong?" Dean asked, worried. His father looked so strange, every muscle was straining, yet he was poised as if in the middle of walking.

Not daring to even turn his head, Ryan spoke to the ocean. "I just stepped on a land mine."

Chapter Two

Dropping the Uzi, J.B. lay flat on his belly and crawled closer to the motionless man. Gently parting the autumn grass, he saw a low swell in the soil under Ryan's boot.

"Dark night, you're right!" J.B. whispered. "Now stay calm, and don't move. If it hasn't gone off yet, it's not a TD or fire-string."

"Explain that to me later." Ryan felt the ground give slightly under his weight. "Hurry. The cliff is giving way."

Sliding his knife from its sheath, J.B. started quickly trimming away the grass and soon had a clear view of the mechanism. It was a fat disk with handles and a low cylinder rising from the middle topped with a simple pressure switch.

"Everybody get behind the LAV," J.B. ordered. "It's a Bouncing Betty."

Watching where they stepped, the others retreated to a safe distance and climbed back into the LAV.

"Hope the hull will stop a Betty," Krysty said, as she flipped up the driver's hatch and stood on the seat to see outside.

Doc climbed into the turret and did the same with the auxiliary hatch. Dean wiggled up there with him and squinted into the distance at the men on the cliff.

"What's a Betty?" the boy asked nervously.

Bent over, watching through a blaster port, Mildred

said, "The worst type of land mine," she replied. "If any of the damn things can be called good. This type will blow off your father's leg with the first explosion, then a secondary charge will heave the mine a yard into the air and a third charge will spray out a ring of steel bearings. Cut a dozen men in two at fifty yards. It's designed not to kill, but to maim."

"Gotta be Overton," the boy growled, his hand going white on the rim of the hatch. "Who else has predark weapons like that?"

Krysty glanced at the turret. "Agreed. We walked straight into a trap. This was the perfect location to recce the ruins of Shiloh, and they knew it. Those blue shirts of his must have gambled we would go check the place and planted some mines here just in case."

"Bastards!" Jak spit.

"Clever bastards," Mildred corrected, licking dry lips.

Minutes passed with only the steady ocean wind blowing over the field, and J.B. cursing as he worked on the mine.

"Well?" Ryan asked, his heart pounding in his chest. The Deathlands warrior had faced death a hundred times, but this was unclean somehow, cowardly. They sometimes used booby traps, but they were always designed to kill enemies, not mutilate. Was this revenge for what he had done to Overton? No, that made no sense. It was impossible for them to know who would step on the mine. Just the luck of the draw it was him, nothing more.

"Don't rush me," J.B. whispered, probing the mechanism with homemade tools—a coiled spring from a pen and a piece of stiff wire from a coat hanger.

Sweat trickling down his face, Ryan thought of how he sometimes teased J.B. about the oddball bits of junk the Armorer gathered in their journeys. He would never do that again.

Wiping off his face with the back of a hand, J.B. grunted something to himself and finally stood alongside the trapped man.

"Well, old buddy, I've got good news and bad news," J.B. said while drawing his scattergun and working the pump action, ejecting live shells until it was empty. "I can get you free, and the primary charge won't go off."

Ryan knew what that meant. "But the other two will."

The man nodded as he slid in fresh shells, simple buckshot instead of the usual flesh-shredding alloy fléchettes. "So when you move, hit the ground to get under the spray."

"And the scattergun is going to buy us some yardage." It wasn't a question.

J.B. lay on his belly and aimed the S&W M-4000 at Ryan's partially raised combat boot. "Best idea I got. You ready?"

An insane laugh bubbled up from inside and Ryan couldn't stop himself from chuckling. "I have a choice?"

"Nope."

"Then I'm ready. Now." Moving like lightning, Ryan dived to the left.

He was still airborne when the ground burst apart with a soft thump and the deadly mine leaped skyward. Instantly, J.B. triggered the scattergun, the blast slamming the land mine far over the edge of the cliff. Half a heartbeat later, the device violently detonated, and a hissing sound filled the air from the passage of the bearings. The half ring of trees along the clearing shook madly, leaves and branches tumbling to the ground in a cascade of destruction, along with the occasional bird and squirrel. Bloody feathers and bits fur were all that remained of the minced bodies.

The reverberations of the blast echoed for a few moments, then silence returned—dead silence without a bird singing or a cricket chirping.

"Thanks," Ryan said as he rose from the ground.

"Easy as pie," J.B. said, standing and dusting off his clothes. The Armorer kicked a clump of earth with his boot and watched it disappear over the edge of the cliff. "However, if that had been a PMR-2, or a Valamora…" He left the thought unfinished.

Ryan grunted in acknowledgment. "Let's go."

With extreme care, the two men retraced their steps to the APC, watching the ground closely, placing the toe of each boot into the heel mark of the footprint they made walking to the cliff. As they neared the wag, Krysty stuck her head out of the top hatch and whistled sharply. The men jerked their heads upward, and watched as she raised an open hand with the fingers splayed, then closed it into a fist. She then tapped her wrist twice with one finger.

"Company coming," J.B. whispered, working the bolt on his Uzi as quietly as he could.

Ryan nodded, leveling his longblaster. "And fast. We better chance running the last yards. Go!"

Sprinting forward, the men raced around the LAV. In the open doorway, Mildred and Doc waited with weapons poised and stepped out of the way as the two men scrambled inside just as they all heard the soft noise of a gasoline engine from the trees.

"There were voices on the radio," Krysty announced from the driver's seat as Ryan closed the aft doors and J.B. slammed home the locking bolt. "Somebody must have heard the land mine go off and sent out sec men on a recce."

"Kill the engines and play dead," Ryan directed, sliding the barrel of his Steyr out a blaster port. "Let's see who it is before we do anything. Jak, man the cannon. Dean, the chain gun."

Everybody moved quickly, and the rumblings of the diesel engines died away just as a Hummer packed with armed men rolled into view through the bushes. All of them were wearing blue shirts and carrying AK-47 assault rifles. At the sight of the APC sitting in the field, the driver slammed on the brakes, nearly losing several of the sec men.

"Hey, Sarge, is that one of our wags?" a blue shirt asked, puzzled.

"Shit, no! It's a bunch of ours put back together!" answered the driver in horror.

"Ryan," a burly sec man cursed. Ammo belts for a machine gun were draped across his chest like bandoliers, and he was cradling a massive M-60 machine rifle. "It must be that bastard Ryan."

"Cawdor? Black dust, let's get the fuck out of here before he returns!"

"Yeah, sure," the driver said, lifting a rocket launcher into view from the empty front seat. "Let's blow it to hell first."

As the sec man leveled the rocket launcher, a sharp crack came from the APC and he toppled over with most of his head gone, blood everywhere. The LAW hit the dirt and rolled away into the weeds.

The big sergeant pushed the dead man from the Hummer and, loudly grinding gears, he slammed the Hummer into reverse. The blue shirts behind him wildly fired their assault rifles, the 7.62 mm rounds ricocheting harmlessly off the hull of the APC.

"Alive?" Jak asked, jerking back the arming bolt on the belt-fed cannon.

"Fuck them," Ryan snarled, firing his longblaster out the aft blaster port again.

Jak ripped loose with a string of shells just as the Hummer charged backward out of the clearing, the barrage of rounds tearing apart the spot where it had just been.

"Can't let them get away!" J.B. growled, burping the Uzi. "We could have an army after us next time!"

"Hold on!" Krysty cried, and the LAV rolled after the fleeing Hummer in full reverse.

Once past the bushes, the woman jammed on the brakes and jerked the steering levers hard. The heavy APC wheeled around in a sharp turn and paused. There was some dust hanging in the air from the passage of the Hummer, but no sign of the vehicle itself.

"Where are they?" Krysty asked, squinting through the tiny ob port in the armored hull. The overgrown roadway stretched to the south and north, directly ahead of the copse of trees.

Ryan and the others pressed their faces to the ob ports and blaster ports. The billowing dust obscured the fields and trees in every direction.

"Three o'clock!" Mildred shouted. "They just went around that bend in the road."

Krysty pressed the gas pedal to the floor. The big Detroit engines purred for a moment, building power, then awoke with a roar. Their eight wheels spun crazily in the loose dirt, then the five-ton wag leaped after the enemy.

Grabbing stanchions, Ryan climbed forward to a po-

sition near Krysty. He braced one hand against the low
ceiling, while the other gripped the back of her chair for
support. He swayed with every bounce, but remained
standing. Ryan watched the speedometer steadily climb
to fifty-five, then inch toward sixty mph, nearly the top
speed for the predark wag. He also saw the fuel gauge
drop just as fast. They were burning fuel at an unprec-
edented rate. There had been no chance to fill the tanks
before the chase, and soon the LAV would run out of
juice, becoming a perfect target for the rockets of the
blue shirts.

For the hundredth time, the man wondered where the
blues were getting their predark weapons.

In triumph, J.B. cried out, "There they are again!"

The Hummer barreled along at its top speed, often
going airborne for a moment as it hit fallen logs and
other hidden objects. With twice the number of tires, the
massive LAV plowed over such minor obstructions with
only minor jarring. On the flat surfaces, the Hummer
started to pull away, but when the road got rough again,
the LAV caught up quickly.

Jak fired single rounds from the 25 mm cannon at the
zigzagging Hummer. He was tempted to go full-auto, but
the linked belt of shells was already half consumed and
there was no spare. He wasn't going to waste the precious ammo on a fast-moving target unless absolutely
necessary.

Crouched in the small space for the gunner, Dean
drilled a spray of rounds toward the fleeing blues, sparks
off the Hummer registering several hits. The enemy fired
back with AK-47 machine guns, a hail of rounds pep-
pering the armored hull of the APC with no effect. Then
the big M-60 spoke, chugging out a slow stream of
7.62 mm rounds. Random dents appeared in sections of

the weakened hull, and the Plexiglas shield in a ob port shattered into pieces.

"Those are armor-piercing rounds!" Ryan cursed, glancing about the interior of the wag to asses the damage. There were no new spots of sunlight to indicate a penetration. "Anybody hurt?"

Hugging her med kit, Mildred looked over the crew. "No blood showing," she reported in relief.

"Not yet, anyway," J.B. growled, slapping a fresh clip into his Uzi. "But we better chill these bastards quick!"

Hesitating to use the deafening LeMat inside the wag, Doc grabbed a spare AK-47 and started shooting through the starboard blaster port, spent brass spitting from the ejector in short golden bursts. But after only a dozen rounds, the weapon stopped with the bolt thrown back, showing the clip was empty.

Raking the Hummer with sporadic bursts, Dean concentrated the whining chain gun on the sec man with the M-60. Sparks flew off the armored body of the military transport, but nothing more. The 7.62 mm rounds were unable to achieve penetration.

"Aim for the tires!" Mildred suggested, placing her shots with care. Clutching his chest, the big man in the Hummer cried out and dropped the M-60 over the side.

"Already did," the boy replied hotly. "Must be puncture proof like our own."

Rummaging in the pile of supplies, Doc was unable to locate any more ammo clips for the Kalashnikov, so he dropped the useless blaster and drew the LeMat, waiting for a suitable target to present itself.

Just then, the Hummer deliberately slowed, and a lone man jumped out, carrying a short plastic tube. As the

APC bore down on the man, he extended the tube to a full yard in length and pointed it toward them.

"That's a LAW!" Krysty shouted in warning, starting to fishtail the wag to make them harder to hit.

"Hold us steady!" Ryan spit, thrusting his longblaster out the smashed ob port and firing a fast five times at the stationary target.

The sec man staggered from the multiple impacts and toppled over. Promptly, there was a bright flash on the ground and something streaked across the road to disappear in the distance.

As the APC thumped over the body, Ryan quickly reloaded his rifle. That rocket would have blown the APC apart, but the blues couldn't use the antitank while still riding in the Hummer because of the back-blast. Launching a LAW rocket spewed a fifteen-foot-long cone of flame out the back end. The back-blast would have fried every one of them alive. Leaving the wag had been a gutsy move that nearly succeeded. Their adversaries had guts, and that alone made them truly dangerous.

In a deafening explosion, Doc fired the LeMat. The buffeting concussion slapped the companions, but the spare gas can strapped to the side of the Hummer erupted into a fireball. Screaming in pain, the blues beat at their burning clothing with jackets, and Krysty plowed straight into the pool of fire, coming out the other side in a heartbeat. The blues weakly began shooting again. They were toasted, but still alive, and the Hummer wasn't seriously damaged.

One of the blues threw a lump at the APC, and the war wag shook as something exploded under the prow.

"Chem gren," J.B. stated, tilting his head. "We better

hope they don't have any thermite. That would melt our hull like candle wax!''

"Payback," Jak growled, switching the selector switch on the cannon to its top position. A stuttering stream of shells chugged from the muzzle, the barrage of 25 mm rounds tearing up the surface of the road as he tracked the fleeing vehicle.

Stoically, the sec men maintained fire with the Kalashnikovs as their blackened wag darted off the road and into a field of wild corn. The tall stalks swallowed the vehicle whole.

Inside the wag, the floor was coated with hot brass shells that poured from the turret. Her hair a wild corona, Krysty shifted levers, and the LAV executed a sharp turn, two of the wheels leaving the ground as it angled after the fleeing blues into the abandoned farmland. Straight ahead was a solid wall of sundried corn stalks. There was no sign of the Hummer or its crew. Behind them, the fire on the road was starting to spread to the dry plants.

"Where are they?" Krysty demanded as the APC plowed through the wild corn, crushing the brittle stalks beneath its tires. It sounded like a million winter leaves rustling in a strong wind.

Ryan dropped the spent clip from his SIG-Sauer and slammed in a fresh one. "Circle to the right. We must have passed them."

"Look for the smashed stalks of their trail!" Mildred added.

J.B. started for the rear of the wag. "Everybody keep a watch for any loops! They might try to swing around and get behind us!"

Unexpectedly, the shortwave radio lashed on top of their bedrolls began to crackle with a transmission, the words barely discernible above the background noise. There were just a few hastily barked commands, then hissing silence again.

Stepping close, Doc turned up the volume to the maximum. The normal static boomed in the confines of the wag, and after a few moments he lowered the volume to its normal level.

"They're trying to call somebody for help," he announced. "Most disconcerting."

"Can we tell which way? Triangulate on the signal?" Mildred asked hopefully.

Still watching their wake, J.B. shook his head. "Not without special equipment. Dish antenna and such."

"Damn."

"They had to be close," Ryan said thoughtfully, shifting his stance against the shaking of the floor. "Krysty, go left!"

The woman obeyed and the signal faded.

"Go back!"

She sent the APC as ordered and cried out in delight as they found the path of flattened plants. Hitting the gas pedal, Krysty steered the massive transport straight along the slim trail, the unbroken stalks on either side spraying into the air from the passage of their much wider vehicle.

As they followed a serpentine curve through the corn, the Hummer came into view once more. Struggling with the hot breech of the chain gun, Dean fed in a new ammo belt. At his father's command, he raked the Hummer. A blue shirt loading his blaster cried out and dropped the weapon, almost falling from the Hummer. The others hauled the corpse back inside, and used the dead man as a shield, firing from behind his bloody form. Then a bulky satchel came flying over the Hummer from the front seat and landed squarely before the LAV.

"Shit!" Krysty shouted, and yanked on the steering levers, sending the LAV into the unbroken stalks to their left.

The world seemed to shatter from the titanic force of the detonation, blinding light flooding in through every port, and the war wag shook as it was slapped by the gigantic concussion. Ropes holding the supplies snapped and the piles of boxes toppled over, burying J.B. and knocking Jak out of the turret. He hit the floor sprawling and went limp.

The crackling radio clearly gave a report to somebody about a satchel charge of C-4 being used, results unknown.

"I'll give you unknown," Krysty growled, shifting into high gear and making the massive machine go faster.

The dry cornstalks shattered as the APC streaked across the field, the big engines screaming. The muscles stood out on Krysty's arms as she worked the levers, forcing the multiton wag into a tight arc, swinging back the way they had just come. A few seconds passed, and she spied a dark blotch moving amid the cornstalks directly ahead of them.

"Go for it," Ryan commanded, and braced for the impact.

Grimly, Krysty held the course. At the last moment, the driver saw them suddenly looming close and screamed in horror. Then the Hummer disappeared from sight below the prow of the LAV. The companions lost their footing as the nose of the war wag went high, aiming toward the sky. Underneath the floor was a terrible crunching noise, mixed with high-pitched shrieking. The APC tilted at an angle, almost flipping over, then leveled out and was back in the corn again, riding on even ground.

Braking to a halt, Krysty returned to the crash site and stopped a short distance from the flattened wreck. Stepping from the rear of the APC, the companions approached the destroyed Hummer, warily walking over the crushed cornstalks to avoid the pieces of broken machinery and twitching meat.

Gore-splattered limbs jutted from the smashed chassis, red blood and gasoline dripping from a dozen spots. An eye lay on the ground near the splintery stock of a Kalashnikov. Shards of glass from the windshield were sprinkled across the cornstalks like diamond dust. Circling around the site, Ryan found a sec man dangling out of the crumpled metal, still struggling to get free in spite of the fact his body was shredded below the waist.

"Help me..." he panted, blood welling from his mouth at the words and dribbling down his chin.

"I'll end the pain," Ryan said, going closer, a hand on his blaster. "Just tell me where your home base is. Who is your leader?" There were more questions he wanted to ask. A lot more. But those were the most important—where and who.

"H-help me..."

"Where is your home base!" the warrior demanded.

Drooling blood, the man blindly reached out a trembling hand with only two remaining fingers.

"He can't hear you," J.B. said, resting his Uzi on a shoulder.

Ryan turned. "Mildred?"

The physician shook her head.

"Fair enough." Drawing his blaster, Ryan put a 9 mm round into the dying soldier. The man jerked at the impact and went still.

"Let's go," Ryan said, holstering the piece. "There's nothing here to salvage."

Doc sniffed the air. "And we had best hurry, my dear Ryan. I think the cornfield is on fire."

"Yeah," Dean said from the turret, squinting into the distance. "And it's coming this way fast."

Chapter Three

Moving quickly past the remnants of the Hummer, the companions climbed into the APC and took seats. Settling in, Doc began the lengthy process of reloading his LeMat, while Mildred checked on the unconscious Jak. The teen was lying on a bedroll, a wet compress on his bruised forehead. He had received a small concussion from a falling ammo box, but otherwise seemed undamaged.

"Let's go," Ryan said, slamming home the bolt. "This corn is burning fast as a fuse."

Starting the engines took a few tries, but Krysty finally got the diesels to turn over. A slight shudder was detectable in the floor as she struggled to slide the stick shift into neutral.

As the wag rumbled forward, a nasty grinding noise came from the engine. It became steadily louder.

"Fireblast, we do have damage!" Ryan cursed. "Must have been that damn satchel charge. No chance to fix it now. Keep going!"

Fluttering his eyelids, Jak tried to speak and began to cough.

Dampening a cloth with water from a canteen, Mildred turned to the youth and saw gray tendrils of smoke rising from the nearby vents. Dropping the canteen, she tried to slide the vent covers closed, but they were firmly jammed in place. Muttering curses her minister father wouldn't have approved, the physician grabbed some more rags from the pile and started stuffing the openings closed. Dean rushed to assist and, working at opposite ends of the craft, they got the larger holes sealed. That helped, but not much. Wisps still seeped into the vehicle around the doors and hatches.

"Get moving!" Mildred barked, splashing more water on the rags to keep them wet. "We have to get out of this or risk suffocation!"

"I'm worried about that," Ryan answered, placing a palm on the hull. The metal was still cool to the touch. "It's the external fuel cans. Those flames get too close and we ignite like a bomb."

"Drop them," J.B. stated, snatching another duffel bag from the loose items on the floor. Yanking open the top, he began tossing in food packs and spare ammo in case they were forced to abandon the LAV to run for their lives. He might be mistaken, but the engines sounded bad, and seemed to be getting worse by the second.

Ryan forced his attention away from the struggling engines. "Can't lose the fuel. We're going to need every drop to reach the next Shiloh. We're low as it is. Worst comes, we can always cut the cans loose."

"Might have to!" Krysty shouted. As she peered out the broken ob port, smoke stung her eyes and made them water. "The fire is keeping us from the road, and I can't see a thing through this bastard corn. Gone wild, this stuff could stretch for miles. Which direction do we go, north or south?"

Restraining a cough, Ryan gestured. "Doc, you're the tallest. Get into that turret and guide us!"

"With the greatest pleasure." As the old man holstered his blaster and clambered into the turret, J.B. passed up his Navy telescope. Forcing back the top hatch, Doc tied a handkerchief to his mouth as protection from the thickening smoke, then extended the antique instrument to its full length.

"Forest to the right, ocean to the left," he loudly announced, studying the golden field. "The corn goes for another mile and then seems to abruptly stop. There might be a dip in the ground!"

"Or another cliff," Krysty added, working the clutch and throttle trying to smooth out the engine vibrations.

Bending at the knees, Doc stooped back inside and dogged the hatch shut. "Indeed, madam." He coughed to clear his throat. "Our choices are exceedingly poor."

"The fire is closer," Dean said from the aft doors, a note of tension in his voice. "I can see flames over the top of the cornstalks."

In spurts, the LAV struggled to roll through the ancient farmland, the dry plants bending slowly out of their way, then rising intact again as the APC crept along.

Studying the motion of the billowing smoke, Ryan made his decision. "The wind is from the sea, going toward the cliff. Head for the trees."

Her prehensile hair coiled protectively against her scalp, Krysty stomped on the gas pedal. "Do my best," she muttered, mentally sending a prayer to Gaia to aid them once more this day.

Behind them, thick plumes of black smoke masked the horizon, wild tongues of orange flame rising to fill the sky with hellish illumination as the rapidly growing inferno raged completely out of control.

ON THE OTHER SIDE of a distant mountain range, a small child stumbled through a lush field of green grass. It had been early morning since her mother left to gather wood for their campfire, and now it was late afternoon. Susie was trying not to cry, but she was hungry and dared not eat the dead squirrel before the greenish meat was cooked. That was how her daddy had died so many months ago. She missed him so much, and often awoke crying from bad dreams, seeing him thrash about foaming at the mouth until her mommy cut his throat. Susie never wanted to eat meat after that, but it was the only food they had. She had tried grass, but it tasted nasty and too much made her bad sick.

"Mommy?" she called out softly, hugging a bundle of rags. Her dolly had once had a head, but it was long ago. "Mommy, where are you?"

Only the whispery winds in the trees answered.

Following a bear path through the woods, the tearful child watched the prickly bushes for signs of muties that might attack, clutching her doll for protection. She was supposed to run away from strangers and animals, but if something was hurting her mommy, Susie would kill it dead with the sharp knife hidden inside her dolly. Oh, yes, she would. Daddy had showed her how.

A strange sound caught her attention, and she headed in that direction. Pushing her way through some vines, the girl cried out in delight at finding a bush still heavy with summer berries. Odd that the bear hadn't eaten them, but this would mean more meat for her mommy to eat! That should make her so happy. Greedily, Susie stuffed her face with the mushy blueberries, rivulets of purple juice flowing down her chin, until she thought her belly might burst. It felt so good not be hungry again, if only for a little while.

Taking one last handful, the child curiously walked

through the trees munching steadily. The weird noise came again, louder this time, and there were faint voices—men talking and shouting.

Susie started to run and shout for her mother, but stopped. People were dangerous, even the right ones without extra arms and such. Sometimes they tried to eat you, or worse, her mother had warned. Susie carefully obeyed the warning, even though she wasn't sure what could be worse than getting eaten by a nasty mutie.

More voices came through the forest, and the crack of a whip. That sound she knew from when they stayed at a ville and the sec men beat a man to death for stealing a blaster from the baron. It was a very bad thing to do because blasters were only for sec men, or barons. Her mommy wouldn't let her watch the beating, but Susie heard the whips, and it seemed to take forever for the poor thief to die. Her daddy said it was a good thing he got chilled. Thieves were worse than muties because muties didn't know any better.

Wiping her hands clean on her ragged dress, Susie followed the faint voices through the foliage until coming to the top of a steep hill. Filling the valley below was a wonderful ville, unlike anything she had ever seen before. There were houses made of brick, and many, many people, some in chains and others herding them forward with whips. More thieves? A squat building near a river had six big chimneys with black smoke pouring into the purple sky. Thick rope stretched from the building to a machine, then spread out across the ville like a spiderweb. A tremendous bowl sat in the middle of the ville, the huge white machine towering over the tall chimneys and casting the land underneath into dark shadows.

More people were digging into the side of a rocky hill, chained thieves dragging stone blocks over to a wall they were building around the whole area. A wall of stone. Susie was in awe. She had never seen such a thing before. It was wonderful! Certainly no mutie or mean old coldheart could get through that. Well, except for sting-wings, and they were little.

"Hold it right there, kid!" an adult voice growled.

Still holding her doll, Susie turned and looked up at the two big men standing in the weeds. They were wearing clean blue shirts and carrying longblasters. The tall man had a bushy beard, and the other was short and fat.

"Hello, sec men," she said, giving a curtsy. Her mommy said to always be polite to sec men, or they would tell the baron on you. "I'm looking for my mommy. Have you seen her?"

"Oh, crap. This must be that bitch's kid," the tall man growled irritably. "I was hoping she would run away and get lost or something."

"Well, she didn't," his companion snapped, doing something to his weapon. "And you know what that means."

Frightened, Susie stayed still as the adults argued. When the sec men were done, mebbe they could help her. She thought about offering them some berries, but only had a few and wanted to save them for her mommy.

The tall man scratched at his beard. "Come on, Sarge. She's too small to work in the mines."

"And we can't let her go. No exceptions, or it's our necks. That's what the boss said." The short man aimed his longblaster at her. She hugged her doll tight, feeling very scared for some reason. Susie wanted to run, but knew they could catch her easy.

"Aw, she's just a kid!" He sounded very angry for some reason.

"Not any more."

The blaster fired once, the sharp report seeming to echo through the forest and into the valley where the giant machine stood poised and nearly ready to be activated.

WIPING AT THE DIRTY windshield with his hand, Stephen stared at the blockhouse ahead of the caravan and frowned in displeasure. In a squeal of metal on metal, he ground the rickety old van to a halt. In slow procession, the two trucks behind the rusty wag also stopped, the drivers fumbling with the unfamiliar brakes and gearshifts.

Chewing a lip, Stephen rested his arms on top of the steering wheel. Straight ahead was a fork in the road, the left branch going to some nameless pesthole ville, the right heading directly toward Front Royal. Strategically positioned between the branches was a stout blockhouse made of whole logs cemented together into a formidable structure. Blaster slots were notched into the thick walls, the only door fronted by a half circle of sandbags a full yard high. A dozen sec men armed with blasters stood behind the sandbags watching him sitting in the lead wag, but that wasn't what made Stephen so apprehensive. It was their clothes. They were wearing the wrong clothes.

Setting the parking brake with a yank, Stephen stared at the leader of the sec men as he came closer. The rest of the troopers stayed where they were, their longblasters held casually, but with their fingers on the triggers. They weren't expecting any trouble, just ready for it. From previous trips, Stephen knew there were more sec men hidden in the trees to give additional support should the need arise. This fork was a major approach to the ville and was always well-defended.

It was the shirts that bothered him. The material was brown, not the blue of Overton's private army. What had happened in Front Royal during his absence?

As the sergeant stopped well away from the van, Stephen rolled down the window and managed to smile, politely keeping both of his hands in plain sight. He had a revolver at his hip, and a shotgun was clipped to the ceiling. But the slightest move toward either of those weapons would probably be the last thing he ever did.

"Hey," the sec man said in greeting.

Stephen nodded. "Good morning, sir. How much?"

Hooking thumbs into his gun belt, the sergeant snorted a laugh. "That's all done with. No more tolls on this road by order of Baron Cawdor."

Something was wrong here; Stephen knew it and took a chance. "Cawdor?" he asked, trying to sound puzzled. "I thought the baron here was named Overton."

A sneer replaced the smile. "He's dead. Got chilled by his own troops. Nathan Cawdor is the rightful baron here."

Dead? So the invasion failed. Sweat broke out over Stephen's body as he smiled to the news. "Great! I heard Overton was a real son of a bitch."

"Pretty bad," the sec man agreed, looking at the line of trucks. "All three of these wags belong to you?"

"Yeah, we caravan through the hills together. Safer that way, you know, muties and coldhearts."

The smile returned, but not with much warmth. "I hear you. Much trouble in the passes?"

"No. A few stickies, nothing more. We travel at night when it's too cold for anybody to try jacking us."

"Pretty smart." The smile stayed, but the eyes became hard. "What's the cargo?"

Stephen started to say wire, but stopped himself. For some reason Overton had wanted insulated cable from predark buildings and lots of it. Who knew why? Mebbe he wanted to electrify all of Front Royal. Yeah, right. Few villes were able to sustain a constant supply of electricity. Most folks considered it a myth. And there was no chance that Nathan would want the cable for the same purpose as Overton. But what else could copper wiring be used for? An answer was needed immediately, and Stephen surprised himself by dredging up a vague memory of a phrase he heard somewhere.

"Refined metal," he lied smoothly. "For making jacketed bullets." The sec man looked properly impressed. "Plus, a few passengers."

"Muties?"

"Norms, I assure you."

Narrowing his eyes, the sergeant seemed skeptical. "How many?"

"Ten."

"Any skilled workers, carpenters, masons?"

"Hell, I have no idea," Stephen answered honestly. "You'd have to ask them."

"Mebbe I will. Any jolt or weed?"

"I don't traffic in drugs," Stephen snapped, then hastily added, "sir."

The sec man chuckled. "Saved yourself a hanging here, friend. You must have been here before."

The words were so matter-of-fact, Stephen almost admitted the truth. Only a lifelong habit of lying stopped him. So the sec men were looking for folks who dealt with Overton, eh? That news could be worth something to a smart man.

"Nope," he replied amiably. "The last owner sold me his wags for some predark medicine I found in a ruin. He had the bleeding cough and was dying."

A minute passed, with the sergeant studying the expression on Stephen's face.

"It was a fair trade," Stephen added hastily, as if cutting off an expected argument. "He lived."

The sec man made no reply.

Stephen knew this was another test to rattle his nerves, so he tried to appear frightened, which was easy, and slightly confused. Innocent folks always seemed to be confused.

"Nothing else?" the man asked. The guards at the blockhouse were watching the exchange, their blasters pointing toward the caravan. From a truck behind him, Stephen heard one of the other drivers nervously cough, the noise unnaturally loud in the tense silence.

"Okay, okay, I'm also hauling shine," Stephen admitted, ever so slowly lifting a clay jug into view. There was a cross of tape on the side patching a small crack. "Good stuff, mighty smooth."

"Nothing wrong with hauling shine," the sergeant said tersely, a hand going to the checkered grip of the blaster on his hip. "If it's clean. An outlander sold some to us once that killed two of my men and made another go blind. Took us a week to find him again, then it took him a week to die."

Wordlessly, Stephen uncorked the jug and took a long pull. The home-brew whiskey burned his gullet like flaming battery acid, but he managed not to gag.

"Have a sip," he said hoarsely, offering the jug. "Good for what ails you."

Grinning, the sergeant started to reach for the container, then glanced at the blockhouse. "Thanks anyway, but it's not allowed," he said sternly, lowering his hand. "The baron forbids drinking on duty."

"A wise policy," Stephen agreed, placing aside the jug. "Smart man."

"That he is." The sergeant turned toward the cabin and tugged on an earlobe, then dusted off his shoulder. The guards relaxed and slung their blasters. A few started smoking hand-rolled cigs.

"Okay, here are the rules," the sergeant said, speaking in an odd singsong way as if quoting from memory. "There ain't no jolt or slaves in Front Royal. Anybody says different is lying. Stealing gets you whipped, rape gets you hanged. Stay on the road. There are land mines in the fields. Watch out for cougars, we've had some killings at the farms. You spot anybody wearing a blue shirt, avoid them like a mutie with the plague. Report finding a blue, and you get a reward. Understand?"

"Sure. A blue shirt?"

"That's what I said." The soldier waved the van onward. "Welcome to Front Royal."

Starting the engine, Stephen touched two fingers to his forehead, and the sergeant actually snapped a formal salute in return. Once the road took the blockhouse out of sight, Stephen braked to a halt and climbed from the van. As he stiffly walked over to the first truck, the driver stuck his head out the window. The glass was long gone, replaced by a sheet of tar paper to help cut the wind.

"What now, fatty?" the muscular man snarled. Dressed in badly cured animal skins, he reeked of rotting flesh enough to mask the sour stink of his unwashed body. In the front seat alongside him was a skinny woman snoring loudly, a chicken bone from dinner sticking out of her slack mouth.

"Taking a leak," Stephen said, strolling into the forest. "Be right back."

The moment he was hidden by the bushes, Stephen bent over and violently retched, the shine burning much worse coming out than it had going in. When he was finished, Stephen wiped off his mouth with some leaves and weakly stumbled to the van. Starting the engine with fumbling hands, he continued driving toward the ville.

Okay, Overton was dead; now he would work for Nathan Cawdor. Fine. Barons were all the same, murdering coldhearts who lived on blood. Only their names changed. And if Nathan was a good man, well, then, he could always travel north to BullRun ville and work for the mad bitch in charge up there. She kept a mutie assassin to chill her enemies. That was more reasonable. But either way, he would stay in business, finding things for the monsters who ruled the world. Life would go on without interruption.

Stephen was a survivor.

THE SOUND OF HAMMERING filled the streets and houses of Front Royal, along with the steady sawing of wood.

Watching the work across the ville, Baron Nathan Cawdor stood on the third floor of the destroyed keep, the shattered brick walls rising only to his knees. At the base of the keep, workers picked through the rubble, salvaging individual bricks and cleaning them off to add to the growing pile.

A few blocks away, scaffolding rose around the ville castle like loving hands, holding the weakened walls in place until the sloping supports could be trusted to hold the awesome weight of the new granite blocks.

Day and night, the construction continued, repairing the tremendous damage done by the invaders. The bod-

ies were gone from the streets, the damaged cobblestones in the main courtyard replaced with fresh ones.
The new horse stable was only a wooden skeleton, the
horses temporarily housed in the great hall of Castle
Cawdor.

Nathan shivered slightly from a cold wind. His clothes
were patched but spotlessly clean, the boots shiny with
polish. Oiled blasters rode at each hip, and a monstrously
huge .44-caliber Desert Eagle pistol rested in a position
of honor in a shoulder holster. The weapon had been
pried from the cold gray hand of Overton as he lay
sprawled in the mud.

"Afternoon, my husband," a lovely woman said, ad-
vancing with a cape folded over an arm. Her long hair
was tied back off her plain face, and a knit scarf was
wound about her throat, accenting her pale skin. She
wore a long coat over a loose gown of royal brown, and
heavy pants peeked out from below the pleated skirt. An
Ingram M-10 submachine gun had been slung over her
shoulder for easy access.

Lady Tabitha Cawdor walked toward her husband and
offered him the garment. "It's too cold for you to be
standing here without a coat."

"Do our sec men have coats?" Nathan replied wearily, watching the armed guards walk the palisades of
the walled ville. Many had tied blankets around their
bodies with lengths of rope as protection from the wind.
Others wore less and shivered. "Do the workers below,
do the old?"

Gently, Tabitha brushed a hand against the baron's
scarred cheek. Her fingernails were stubby and cracked,
her hand covered with scabs, the wounds still healing
from her many days of torture. "No, my love, they do
not."

"Then while I stay here in public sight, neither do I," Nathan answered. "If I can't make them warm, I can at least share the weather and make them feel less miserable."

She glanced at the sky and drew her coat closed tighter. "Any sign of snow?"

"Thankfully, no. Every day gets us closer to repairing the wall and drawbridge. Once we're behind stone again, I can turn our attention to fixing the homes and other buildings. How's the laundry coming?"

Tabitha almost smiled. Laundry, such a nice way of referring to stripping the dead of their torn clothing. "The sewing is nearly done on the shirts," she reported. "Next we dye the blue cloth brown, or rather purple, as quickly as we can. In a few days, everybody will have an extra shirt to wear. Then we start on the boots and pants. Come the full moon, even the old will be warm."

"Good. And the food supply?"

"Adequate. With the hunters bringing in more meat daily, we should survive until spring." She offered the coat again. "Please?"

"I can't."

Tabitha gestured at herself. "Yet I can?"

"You just gave birth," he said tolerantly. "They understand."

Pushing a wheelbarrow full of bricks, a man wearing rags for boots paused to catch his breath in the street below and waved at the couple standing high above the ville. Nathan stood taller and nodded in reply. Flexing his hands to restore circulation, the worker returned to his task and pushed the bricks toward the construction crew at the barbican of the front gate.

"Is the baby healthy?" Nathan asked in sudden concern, taking his wife by the arm. "Is that why you're really here?"

"Alexander is fine. Sleeping with his wet nurse, and a dozen sec men," Tabitha added pointedly, patting his cold hand. She was too thin and sickly to breast-feed the infant. However, many woman in the ville had lost newborns in the terrible war, and it had been no problem to find one willing to suckle the next baron.

"The guards are necessary. Overton tried using you to seize the ville," Nathan growled, the tendons in his neck tightening from barely controlled rage. "Our son would make an even better key."

"Your uncle's bastard son is dead," she reminded him, shivering in spite of the warmth of her coat.

"Besides," a new voice stated, "I'm here now."

The Cawdors turned at the pronouncement and watched as Clemont Brigitine Turpin stepped into view from the exposed stone stairwell. The grizzled soldier was dressed in heavy leather clothing, with an Enfield longblaster slung across his wide back. Two bandoliers of ammo crisscrossed his chest, the handle of a knife jutted from his boot and a hatchet was slung at his side where a handblaster should have been.

"My dear Lieutenant Turpin," Tabitha said, smiling.

His broad features dusky with a growing beard, the big man scowled. "Clem," he replied in a friendly manner. "Just Clem, my lady. I ain't no royalty. Just a grunt."

"Chief of my sec men," Nathan corrected sternly, noting the other man's serious expression. Few things bothered Clem, and most of those got aced immediately. The big backwoodsman wasn't a believer in either forgiveness or patience.

Just then a squad of sec men climbed out of the hole

in the floor where the stairs ended and moved quickly across the bare expanse of concrete. Longblasters at the ready, the guards circled the Cawdors, keeping close together. Every man carried an AK-47 salvaged from the war, a bulging pouch of precious ammo clips slung over his side.

"What's the matter?" Nathan demanded. "Have more blues been found in the woods?"

"Hell, no," Clem drawled, his thick accent slurring the words. "Patrol finds them, they chill them. Don't need to bring that detail to you. But there's a new problem, yeah. Our spy from BullRun ville says their baron believes you plan on invading them with the new troops that arrived last month."

Softly, the mountain wind ruffled their clothing, finding bare skin through every tiny lace hole and opening.

"But Overton's troops are dead."

"She don't know that."

"And she wouldn't believe us if we told her." Nathan glanced at the handful of people working on the front gate. "We will have to move fast if they're planning on attacking first. The ville can't withstand a charge by blind rabbits at the moment. Not until that damn drawbridge is repaired!"

"We can stop them," Clem stated confidently.

Nathan frowned. "Unless she's not sending her army, but just one man. One thing, actually."

Clem furrowed his brow. "Y'all mean an assassin?"

"A mutie by the name of Sullivan." Nathan drew the Desert Eagle and dropped the clip to examine the load. "Shit-fire, I had heard the thing was dead years ago. I once saw him rip the throat out of a griz bear on a bet. Didn't even work up a sweat."

"Are you serious?" Tabitha asked, sounding frightened.

"Totally. He's a monster, and damn hard to kill. Many have tried and failed. Sullivan drank their blood and mutilated the corpse for laughs."

Without speaking, Tabitha tucked her hands up the sleeves of her coat, and they heard the soft metallic clack of a blaster's hammer being cocked.

"I'll be in the nursery until further notice," she announced, and strode toward the stairs.

"Stay with her!" Clem ordered, pointing, and half of the attending sec men started after the woman. The rest clustered tighter around the baron.

"Sullivan," Nathan muttered, checking the ammo in his snub-nosed .38 revolver. "This could be worse than Overton."

"Mebbe you should stay out of sight till I find this asswipe," Clem suggested, sliding the Enfield off his shoulder and working the bolt. "Direct the rebuilding from inside the castle, or mebbe the barracks?"

"I won't hide," Nathan answered brusquely, holstering the blaster. "Besides, Sullivan is an expert at disguises. He can even mimic another person's voice so that in the darkness you think it's them. Damnedest thing. I heard that was how he chilled the last baron of BullRun castle."

"I could interrogate everybody new," Clem suggested. An assassin was something novel to the hunter. Barroom brawls were more his kind of fight.

Walking to the edge of the roof, Nathan gazed upon the hustling ville. "Not necessary. Sullivan can use gloves and cosmetics to hid his green skin, and wigs to cover his bald head, but there's one thing he can't alter. His height. Take troops, ten-on-ten formation. The second group stays away from the first to give cover fire. Then go through the ville and strip naked anybody you find over six feet tall. Men and women.''

The remaining sec men murmured in apprehension.

''We'll also double-check any crips,'' Clem added. ''Pretending you don't have legs would be a good way to hide height.''

Nathan nodded. ''Consider anybody sitting a potential enemy, and be ready to act.''

''Oh, we'll capture him, Baron,'' a sec man stated confidently, brandishing his blaster. ''Have no fear of that!''

''Capture? Don't even try,'' Nathan retorted, turning away from the ville. ''When you find a bald man with greenish skin, chill him on sight. Which means a head shot, one in each eye. Then set the body on fire.''

Then Nathan added softly, almost as if speaking to himself, ''Hopefully, that will be enough.''

Chapter Four

Shuddering and clanking, the APC crept along the smooth shore of the North Carolina river basin. The soft sand rose high, almost to the rims of the seven tires. The eighth hung in tatters off the rim, flopping about uselessly as the wag forged onward with ever decreasing speed.

With the tip of his knife, Ryan removed the damp rag from an ob port and looked outside. On the horizon, black clouds filled the sky, and orange flames licked upward from the raging inferno of the cornfield.

"Far enough?" Krysty coughed. The interior of the wag was misty with smoke and reeked of pungent human sweat.

"Yeah," he decided. "We're a good mile clear of the cornfield. Stop here and let's see how much of a wag we still have."

"Sure," Krysty grunted, fighting the clutch to shift into park. The gear refused to cooperate, so she tried neutral and managed to kill the engines. The cacophony from underneath the metal floor receded and finally stopped.

Climbing into the turret, Doc threw open the top hatch, and cool fresh air flooded into the APC. "Ah, ambrosia of the gods," he said, inhaling deeply.

Fanning herself, Mildred sported a smile. "That's redundant."

"Yet still true, madam. *Pro veritas Libertas!*"

Rising from his seat, J.B. pulled at the sticky clothes clinging to his body. "I'm going to see what the damage is," he said, getting a tool kit from a storage locker under the seat.

"I'll cover you," Ryan stated, removing a canteen from the wall. "Krysty, prime the chain gun in case we get visitors. Doc, Dean, start transferring the gas from the external cans to the fuel tank. Mildred, Jak, you two stay right there. That was a hell of a knock you took."

"N-never better," the teenager whispered weakly from the floor, moving his arm to expose the bloody bandage on his head. His normally pale skin was flushed pink, his shirt damp with sweat. Mildred had given the teen two aspirin for the pain, and checked the focus of his vision. She said it had to do with concussions and brain damage.

"Glad to hear it," J.B. said, undogging the aft doors. "'Cause you look half-dead."

"F-fuck you."

As J.B. exited the wag with Doc and Dean right behind, Ryan exchanged a look with the physician.

Mildred nodded, waving him on. "Go fix this thing."

Stepping over the youth, Ryan took an AK-47 from a stack and checked the blaster. There was a full clip in the breech, and he had a good dozen loose rounds in his pants pocket. Climbing out, Ryan walked around the wag checking for any signs of external damage.

The armor plating was dirty and scratched with blurry streaks from where soft-lead bullets ricocheted off the hull. Blood was splattered everywhere from the blue shirts they had crushed. While Dean stood guard with his Browning in hand, Doc was busy untying the fuel cans from the charred netting. On the ground, a pair of legs jutted from underneath the vehicle and J.B. could be heard muttering curses to the sound of metal hitting metal.

Resting the stock of the AK-47 on a hip, Ryan knelt in the sand. "How's it look?" he asked.

"Found a busted axle," J.B. replied, "and we're definitely losing oil and hydraulic fluid. Dark night, this thing is a mess!"

"What are the chances it'll carry us to the next Shiloh?"

"Considering what was done to this wag, it's a wonder the thing got us here."

"Fireblast." Ryan glanced around. They were trapped with a dead wag in the middle of nowhere. Not good. "Can you fix it?"

"Don't know, but I'll try. Only need four wheels to stay mobile."

"Good thing we have eight."

"Seven, but that should be enough."

"Need anything?" Ryan had great belief in the talents of the Armorer. The man was a master gunsmith, an expert at booby traps and could fix anything made of steel that rolled or floated.

"Some light would be great."

From a box strapped to the hull, Ryan retrieved an oil lantern. The reservoir was half-full, more than enough. Igniting the wick with a butane lighter, he trimmed the flame to something manageable and passed the lantern under the APC.

"Thanks."

"No prob."

"My dear Ryan, would you suppose it safe enough for us to chance a campfire?" Doc asked, passing a fuel can to Dean. "I fear we shall be here through the night, and nobody could possibly notice our small column of smoke amid that Dantean conflagration.''

"Nights get cold. Be nice to have hot food,'' the boy added, hugging the container with both arms. Setting the bottom of the can on his belt buckle to help with the weight, Dean waddled around the wag with his precious cargo.

Ryan nodded. "Keep it small.''

An explosion sounded from the east, and Ryan spun about, his weapon ready. A fireball rose skyward from the blanket of black clouds masking the wildfire. Then the Deathlands warrior felt his heart race as a small mushroom cloud formed above the cornfield, the sea winds dissolving the eerie sight almost as soon as it formed.

Backing closer to the wag, Ryan listened to the crackle of static on the radio, waiting to hear voices, but minutes passed in silence. It had to have been some ammo cooking off from the heat. The way that Hummer was bouncing around, the blues could have dropped any number of weapon or grens.

"Gaia's demise,'' Krysty said unexpectedly from the turret.

Ryan stared up at her. She seemed strangely tense and nervous. "What was that you said?''

"Gaia's demise,'' she repeated. "The end of the world.''

"Just rising smoke, lover,'' he said. "Any hot explosion will make a mushroom cloud. Nothing special.''

Staring at the distant fields of fire, Krysty made no reply, her hands poised on the rapid-fire cannon, long hair billowing in the sea breeze.

"Lend me a hand,'' Mildred called, climbing from the APC with an arm load of boxes.

Shouldering his longblaster, Ryan took the top crate and found it full of pots and pans. "The fire is just for warmth," he said gruffly. "We shouldn't stay here longer than necessary."

"I'm not making dinner," Mildred replied, placing the box on the ground and removing some glass jars. "Going to brew some coffee. Help us stay sharp. Been a long day, and it's not over yet."

"Sounds good," he said, relenting, feeling his stomach respond to the possibility of eating. Damn, he was a lot hungrier than he wanted to admit.

"Mebbe we can break open a few of the MRE packs," he added. "Hunting would be pointless. The fire will have scared away any game for miles."

Mildred lifted a silvery foil envelope into view. "Way ahead of you."

Taking a seat on a rock, Ryan balanced the AK-47 on his lap and watched as she ripped open a package and spread out its contents, carefully inspecting the smaller envelope of beef stew, another of coffee, sugar, a log of processed cheese, crackers, salt, pepper, chewing gum. The MRE food packs were Meals Ready to Eat, military rations from long before skydark. The Mylar foil was chem proof and airtight. If the packs were stored carefully, the condensed food would last forever. But the tiniest pinhole could turn the chow into deadly poison. They occasionally found a few MRE packs or self-heats in the redoubts, and sometimes they were edible, but more often they weren't. These came from Overton, and the foil was in perfect condition, almost brand-new.

"Behold, madam," Doc announced, dropping a load of gnarled gray sticks on the ground. "Driftwood a-plenty. Is this enough, or shall you require more?"

"That's enough," Mildred announced, starting to

whittle on a piece of driftwood with her belt knife. She piled the shavings together and carefully lit them with a single match. The flickering flame almost died, then brightened and spread across the dry wood.

"There we go," she said, adding small sticks to the growing fire. "Just need some water for the pot."

"I'll go get some," Dean offered, setting down the last fuel container. "The wag is topped off."

"Fine. Get it from the basin," Mildred directed him, opening a second envelope and pouring the contents into an iron pot. "The water here is fresh, fed by the river, not salt."

"Be right back," the boy said. Grinning, he grabbed a bucket and dashed around the APC.

Thrusting his stick into the hard packed sand, Doc squatted on his heels. "Ah, the vigor of youth." He chuckled. "Pity it's wasted on the young."

As Mildred fed the fire, Ryan watched the growing shadows, maintaining a constant vigil. The moonlight on the water gave a clear field of fire in case somebody approached by boat, or swam toward shore. There was no smell of salt here. This water fed from several inland rivers and flowed to the sea in a sort of natural harbor. The light from the fire had nearly disappeared to the east, the shoreline was empty for more than a mile to the south and dense forest was to the north. It wasn't the best of spots for a camp, but good enough for one night. Nobody could get close without being detected.

Carrying a brimming bucket, Dean returned to find Doc breaking sticks of driftwood over his knee and adding them a piece at a time to the crackling campfire. Mildred was already stirring a pot of stew, a row of tin mess kits laid out with salt and forks. With his back to the APC, his father stood guard, the AK-47 balanced in his hands.

"Over here," Ryan called.

The boy complied, and his father checked the water with a rad counter. There was only the usual background reading. "Clean enough," he decided. "Better filter it anyway."

"Okay." Carefully, Dean poured the fluid through a clean piece of cloth and filled a large coffeepot. Placing it next to the fire, Mildred added a handful of crystals and soon the smell of beef stew and coffee spread across the site, the campfire throwing shadows on the aide of the APC as night slowly claimed the smoky Carolina sky.

"Hey, is that coffee I smell?" J.B. called out, wiggling the toe of a combat boot.

"Sure is," Ryan answered. "Want some?"

"Pretty soon," he replied to the tune of metallic pounding. "Is Krysty inside?"

"Yeah."

"Ask her to try the main engine."

"I heard," she replied from above. Climbing down from the turret, the redhead took the driver's seat, turned the ignition and pumped the gas pedal as the engine struggled to catch.

"Nothing," she shouted out the side blaster port. Only a slice of the road was visible through the tiny slit, showing the legs of the Armorer underneath the APC and Ryan standing near an open toolbox.

There was some more clanging. "Again!"

With little hope, Krysty turned the key and was astonished when the big Detroit power plant roared into life, gray smoke puffing from the louvered exhaust ports.

"Damn, I'm good," J.B. said from under the wag.

Turning off the engine, Krysty waited a few moments, then turned it on again. She did this several times.

"We have an engine again," Krysty announced. "Runs smooth as silk."

"Good work," Ryan told J.B., giving the man a hand as he crawled out into view.

Standing, J.B. placed the lantern aside. "No, not good news. 'Cause engine is all we have." He was inspecting a shiny ring of metal.

"What's that?" Ryan asked curiously.

"A bearing cone."

Ryan moved closer. "Never saw one before."

"Folks aren't supposed to. These are sealed units and don't come off, or apart."

"From the Hummer?" Mildred asked.

"No, it's ours and I found two more on the ground. That was the grinding noise. The bearings are busted." J.B. placed some tools in the kit and closed the box. "We took shrapnel damage from that satchel charge. The minor engine is leaking coolant from a bad crack in the block. I used some parts from the main engine to patch the second, so we have lights and heat. But as for going anywhere, the wag might as well be sunk in concrete. The transmission assembly is in pieces. Don't know how we got this far."

The man began wiping his greasy hands with a rag soaked in fuel. When most of the black was rubbed off, he walked to the campfire and poured a cup of coffee. "This wag has definitely taken the last train west."

"You sure?" Mildred asked.

J.B. sipped the coffee, holding the tin cup in both hands to savor the warmth. "Oh, yeah."

"Triple red, people!" Ryan commanded, standing and working the bolt on his AK-47. "The blues would be fools not to sweep this area on a recce first chance they get. They catch us standing here chatting, and it's the long sleep.''

The tired expressions of the companions vanished in a heartbeat, and they drew weapons.

"Dean, prep a LAW rocket," Ryan added brusquely.

The boy nodded and raced toward the APC.

Her boots ringing on the metal floor, Krysty walked through the APC and sat in the doorway. Behind her, Jak lay snoring peacefully amid the piles of supplies.

"Okay, so we walk out of here," Krysty said. "The question is where. Do we continue on to Shiloh, or the closest redoubt?"

"Front Royal," Dean suggested, climbing into the wag. "We can get another wag there."

"Doubtful," his father replied.

"Besides, my young friend, traveling anywhere on foot means we have to leave most of the supplies behind," Doc stated. "A most dangerous proposition. Too many weapons will slow us and get us chilled just as fast as not enough."

"Maybe we could rig a litter," Mildred suggested.

"We're not leaving anything behind," Ryan announced. Kneeling by the dying red embers of the campfire, he poured a cup of coffee and drained it in a few gulps.

"And we're not walking, either," he stated. "J.B., let me see the map."

Digging in his bag, the Armorer unearthed the folded plastic sheet and passed it over. Carefully spreading the map on the ground near the remains of the fire, Ryan flicked a butane lighter and read by the tiny flame. Aside from blasters, he considered butane lighters the greatest invention of the predark world. A hundred years later and the things still worked.

"Look at this," he said, jabbing a finger at the map. "We can travel by water. North Carolina is damn near split in half with this river basin. We'll build a raft and row inland. Get us halfway to the next Shiloh, and only about sixty miles south of the redoubt in Kentucky. We can get more supplies and ammo there. Not much, but some."

"And then what?" Krysty asked.

He scratched an ear. "Don't know. We can try and buy a wag, or some horses, from a local ville. Got more than enough spare blasters. And even if we don't find anything, the basin will still carry us a week of walking in two days."

"Upstream," the redhead stated.

"Flat water," J.B. corrected. "Easy stuff. No rapids or white water falls."

"A raft," Doc said hesitantly, rubbing his chin. "Dubious, sir. Most dubious."

Brushing back her beaded hair, Mildred looked up from the map. "We can do it. We've built them before."

"Indeed, we have, madam. But a raft large enough to hold all of the supplies? It would require two, maybe three, really big ones. Chopping down that many trees will take us a week. Maybe more."

Suddenly, the chain gun roared into life, shattering the night. The companions dived for cover, digging into the beach, their weapons sweeping for targets, as a stuttering stream of 7.62 mm rounds sliced across the landscape and started tearing apart a tree. Bark flew off the trunk, splinters went everywhere, then there was a crack and the oak dropped heavily to the ground. The chain gun stopped, followed by ringing silence.

The top hatch swung open, and Dean rose into view. "We don't need axes," the boy stated confidently. "We can shoot down all the logs we want."

As he rose from the damp ground, Ryan's first reaction was fury, until he realized the cold common sense of the matter. "Good work, son. But next time, trim the top first, then cut out the bottom."

"Sure, Dad!"

"But the noise!" Mildred complained. "No, wait. Skip that. We need to get the cutting done now, before scouts arrive."

"Exactly. And it makes no difference if we use all the ammo. Can't haul the chain gun or the cannon along. Both are too heavy."

Tilting back his fedora, J.B. gave a twisted grin. "That 25 mm cannon will level the forest in a few minutes. We'll have enough logs for an armada of rafts."

"Even better," Ryan said. "Doc, we have enough rope?"

"Certainly, and sufficient canvas for tents."

The tents would cover the supplies on the raft and keep them dry, and would hide exactly what the companions were hauling from observers. Many folks would eagerly risk death for the chance of getting their hands on a working blaster.

"Sounds good," Ryan decided. "Dean, cut more trees. Keep going till I say stop. Doc, you're on sentry duty with me. Here!"

Doc caught the AK-47 and checked the longblaster, while Ryan chambered a round into his Steyr SSG-70. "Krysty, stand ready with a LAW. Shoot on sight. Mildred, make lots more coffee and stew."

"I'll dig a shallow pit to hide the flames."

"And I'll start removing the tires from the LAV," J.B. said, pouring a fresh cup of coffee while it was still warm. "Attached to the bottom of a raft, they'll triple our buoyancy. Which means that much more ammo and food comes along for the ride."

"Excellent."

"One good thing about this," Krysty said, walking closer out of the darkness with the rocket launcher resting on a shoulder.

"What's that?" Ryan asked. As far as he was concerned, they were standing on the gallows just waiting for the noose.

"At least we won't be encountering any land mines."

"Hopefully. Okay, let's move with a purpose, people!" Ryan ordered. "It's a race against the clock now."

Chapter Five

Falling...forever falling... Down through infinity he plummeted, the burning stars swirling around and around, comets lancing out to pierce his naked flesh with white-hot heat. Red blood erupted from the ghastly wounds, then froze solid from the horrible cold. Desperately, he tried to draw a breath and scream from the terrible pain, but there was no air, only the incredible cold and endless falling. Hurtling at unimaginable speeds, faster and faster into a void beyond comprehension.

A meteor raced by, twisted faces trapped in its fiery tail. The faces looked deep into his eyes, and he couldn't turn away. Shame filled his tormented soul as more faces were presented in a hellish pageant. A litany of crimes. Some wept for clemency, others raged in bestial fury, while a few simply stared with the utter emptiness of acceptance. Fire engulfed him, and he entered the faces, shattering the skull bones and plunging into the morass of living brain tissue like a surgeon's scalpel.

Now he was swimming in blood, rising bubbles filled with nightmarish scenes. Animals stood before him on display, and opened their own chests to spill their beating organs on steel tables under harsh lights. And none of them had hearts, only clocks, bloody clocks ticking softly inside their dying bodies. He ordered them to go away, then pleaded with hot tears flowing down his cheeks, to no avail. The animals died in droves, only to be replaced with men in chains, their knowing eyes damning him for the monster he was.

Wailing, he clawed at his face to stop the visions, fingernails gouging into his eyes. But his hands were ghostly things, phantasms of ethereal flesh, and there was nothing he could do to stop or even slow the grotesque litany. The clothing of the men melted away, their hairy bodies becoming the supple flesh of beautiful women. Long flowing hair, full breasts, only the best. An endless parade of naked woman whipped and humbled, chained supine on the terrible table as the silver knives removed their skin and flesh. Eyes staring, clocks for hearts! Impossible beings gruffly laughed behind him and placed cold hands on his own bare flesh. Revulsion filled him like acid, and he tried to vomit, but could only convulse, muscles writhing, limbs flailing.

Then a special face filled his vision, expanding to fill the ocean of blood until the mouth was a door that opened on a dead man hanging by his own belt in a filthy underground cell. Not my fault! The silent words echoed in his head as the beating of his heart changed into the ticking of a clock, the noise building into a deafening crescendo until shattering the universe into a million shards of tinkling glass that fell away in a molten rain.

There a flash of light, and he was falling through a blue sky with white clouds. Mountains appeared, oceans, forests! A hurricane wind buffeted his form with savage fury, as the world expanded, rushing ever closer. Suddenly, his lungs filled with air and at last he could scream, a raw wail of anguish and absolute terror that lasted forever.

With pillow softness, he slammed into the ground and

lay there breathing in the sweet earth slightly damp from a summer rain, tufts of grass tickling his face. Alive, he was alive!

Painfully standing, Silas found himself in a field of green grass under a blue sky dotted with white clouds overhead. But those colors were wrong. The sky was purple, slashed with orange fire. Wasn't it? A low rock wall cut across a field, and a copse of trees stood guard to the west, stout protection against the coming storm. The nuke storm. Skydark, doomsday. Not his fault!

A town of old buildings was in the distance, a church tower bell ringing the time as a beautiful woman in a flowing dress floated toward him, her hair flowing in the wind. She was carrying a bouquet of flowers that died, withered and blossomed again in an endless cycle of death and rebirth. Not his fault!

"Why, there you are!" The woman laughed. "But I should introduce myself, my name is Tanner, Emily Tanner."

Snarling in glee, Silas reached behind his back and drew a small automatic. "Excellent," he cackled. Jacking the slide and leveling the weapon at her face, he pulled the trigger. The gun violently exploded, a fireball engulfing his hand as the weapon detonated blowing off his fingers.

Emily neither flinched nor frowned as Silas screamed from the pain, staring at the white bones protruding from the ruin of his arm, warm red blood pumping out of the shattered limb.

"My husband is Dr. Theophilus Tanner," she continued, twirling the flowers like a lace umbrella on her shoulder. "Do you know my husband, by any chance?"

"Not my fault!" Silas shrieked, dropping to his knees and trying to staunch the flow of blood from the arm with his free hand. But the flesh was too slippery, and he couldn't get a grip on the tattered rags of meat.

In the distance, a steam locomotive puffed along iron rails, gliding past the black doors of a redoubt, and nearby a child raced across the field, guiding a kite in the sky, the cloth tail dancing merrily. A small dog yipped and barked alongside the child, and Silas vaguely recognized the boy as himself. How could that be? Then a dark shape stepped between them, blotting out the golden sun.

"Hello, fool," Doc snarled, slowly drawing a blade from the ebony shaft of his walking stick. The needle-sharp tip glistened in the bright sunlight, and it flashed forward.

Silas could only gasp as the steel slashed across his face, opening the flesh to the bone, his cheek peeling away and rivers of blood gushing forth. He tried to beg for mercy, but no words would come and the blade slashed across his throat, filling his lungs with choking blood. It slashed again, between his naked legs, his penis dropping to the soil. A black wave of ants boiled out of the soil, covering the twitching member and consuming the tender pink flesh.

Emily laughed gaily and threw flower petals as Doc began to dissect the scientist, his heart falling onto the ground, the gears and pendulums still connected by the major arteries, beating away to force the blood from his countless wounds.

Suddenly, the sky turned purple, and sheet lighting thundered as Doc peeled off more skin from Silas's naked form, his beating organs splayed on the grass like offerings to some pagan god. The pain was beyond imagination, and the blood was everywhere, now inches deep across the entire field. Then Doc dropped the sword and drew a huge pistol. Silas begged for death, for release from the incredible agony. But Doc pointed the weapon away from Silas and fired, the muzzle-flash igniting the blood into a lake of flame. Tongues of fire filled his mouth and the open cavity of his chest. It crawled up his rectum and inside his belly until it bulged. The bugs swarmed over him, through the crackling flames, endless, eating his flesh, and Silas drew in a lungful of fire and insects as he was consumed alive...

BOLTING UPRIGHT in bed, Silas Jamaisvous screamed at the darkness, his hands clawing at empty air.

With a bang, the door to his bedroom slammed open and armed sec men wearing clean blue shirts rushed in, the muzzles of their AK-47 blasters searching for intruders.

"What is it, sir?" a corporal demanded, his face tense with worry. "Are you hurt? Were you attacked?"

Silas tried to speak, but his throat was too dry and sore to do much more than squeak.

"Nobody in the closet," a blue shirt said, closing the door.

"Window locked tight," another sec man reported, jiggling the steel lattice that covered the huge window overlooking the Great Project. The tiny dots of torches moved in the blackness on the distant ground, the cool fire of orange moonlight bathing the huge satellite dish that dominated the ville by its sheer size.

"Out of the way, fools," a major commanded, brushing through the sec men. Going to a humming refrigerator, the officer grabbed a frosty bottle of mineral water and crossed the room to thrust it into the elderly man's hands. Silas greedily drank the icy water, savoring every drop as the horrible delusions of his nightly dream faded.

"Thank you, Sheffield," he whispered, placing the empty bottle on his sweaty blankets.

Major William Sheffield merely nodded, and returned to the refrigerator for another bottle. The airtight cap was loose, these bottles refilled from a nearby stream, but it was still mineral water. Only weeks ago, the stream had been polluted with acid rain and tox chems to the point it was gelatinous. Now the stream flowed pure and clean again, thanks to the Great Project.

"Same dream, sir?" Sheffield asked softly, guiding the bottle to the man's pale lips.

Silas nodded as he drank again, strength and sanity returning with every beat of his heart.

"The same," he acknowledged as a tremor shook his body and the old wound in his thigh ached deeply. "It has been the same nightmare every night since I tried to force a chron jump! Was I insane? The jump haunts me, chases me through my dreams every night. No escape. There is no escape. How did Tanner survive a chron jump sane? What makes him so special? Was it the redoubt itself? Did the computers malfunction?"

Sheffield gestured. "Everybody out!" he thundered. "Stat!" Stiffly saluting, the guards shuffled into the corridor and closed the door.

"I don't think it's wise to be discussing such things in front of the troops, sir," the major said, drawing a chair closer. He took the seat and glanced about. "The fewer people who know the existence of the redoubts, the better."

"Yes. You are quite correct," Silas agreed, mopping the sweat off his face with the edge of his blankets. The bed was moist beneath him, and there was the unmistakable ammonia stink of urine mixed with the sweat. Damn it, the dream was killing him. He awoke feeling weaker at every dawn, another slice of his sanity gone forever.

Back at El Morro in San Juan, the scientist had believed he held the key to controlled jumps through the redoubts, and had attempted to go backward through time to slay Tanner—at least he thought that was why he wanted to go back. He assumed there had been good reasons for the gamble, but they were gone, along with most of his memory. At first, Silas thought he had jumped back to the late 1800s of Vermont. But it became clear rather quickly that he had become mired in a jump nightmare. One that would leave him for a few months, and then return in shocking clarity. First no more than once a month, then once a week, now three or four times a week. Soon it would be every night, and after that who knew? Perhaps it would start claiming him during the day, and his brilliant mind would be gone forever, trapped in an endless fantasy of his own creation. From somewhere deep in his childhood the words ''as ye sow, so shall ye reap'' came unbidden to his mind. Silas shook off the religious nonsense. The dream was merely a forced feedback loop from the electromagnetic field of the mat-trans chambers, probably augmented by his proximity to the high-voltage transformers of the dish. Yes, of course, that was the answer. Once the Great Project was finished and the Kite was operational, he could leave Tennessee and be free from the dream forever.

''If I don't go mad first,'' he muttered, plucking nervously at his bushy eyebrows.

''Sir?'' Sheffield asked.

''Nothing important, Major.'' Silas wanted to leave the bed and wash, but that would have to wait until the sec chief departed. A wave of shame tightened his chest, and he forced it away by sheer force of will.

"Has there been any word on Tanner and the others?" Silas asked harshly.

Sheffield scowled. "Nothing for over a week, sir. They left Front Royal in a repaired LAV-25 and disappeared. But we have sec men watching every driveable road from the north, south and east, with land mines and traps on all major bridges. Ryan will never reach Tennessee alive."

Rubbing his sore leg, Dr. Silas Jamaisvous stared at the eager young officer sitting rigidly on the small chair. The man was so strong and proud. His blue uniform was spotless, his blasters glistening with oil, boots polished like a mirror.

"That's what Overton said once," Silas stated coldly.

"But I'm not playing politics with Cawdor," Sheffield said, standing. "Believe me, as long as they keep to the roads, I'll present you with their heads on a silver plate in only a matter of days, mebbe less!"

"Perhaps. But isn't the Bradley Light Armored Vehicle, Piranha class, Model 25, amphibious? Isn't the transport also designed to be used as a boat?"

The sec man was confused. "Is it, sir?"

"That is unknown to me," Silas scowled. "I think we had better find out very quickly."

Chapter Six

A sting-wing darted from the rushes along the basin.

Standing on the shore, the gentle waves lapping around his combat boots, Ryan saw the movement out of the corner of his eye. He drew his SIG-Sauer and fired. The silenced 9 mm blaster coughed, and the winged mutie exploded in midair, bloody feathers tumbling down onto the beach. There was a disturbance under the sand, and blue-shelled crabs rose into view like ghosts from a grave. They climbed over the tiny corpse, tearing the mutie apart with their sharp pincers and stuffing their mouths full. One large azure crab had a dozen tiny copies on its back and passed morsels of the sting-wing over its quivering antennae to the clicking brood.

A gray dawn was beginning to break in the fiery sky, and Ryan stood guard over the others as they finished conveying the last of the fresh water and ammo onto the bobbing rafts. Stout ropes moored the crude craft to the stump of a dead tree, a gentle current tugging them away from the shore.

There had been enough logs from the felled trees to build a dozen rafts, but the companions decided on just two. Lashed together with ropes and chains, the first was small, only ten feet squared, three of the inflated tires from the LAV bolted to the belly of the craft. A small pile of ammo, food and other supplies lay in the middle of the raft. A sheet of canvas covered the goods, and multiple ropes secured the cargo. A tiller made from a door off an ammo locker was at one end, tight between two upright stanchions. J.B. was dubious of the arrangement, but Ryan had assured the man it would work fine.

The second raft was much bigger, thirty feet squared, with four piles of supplies set between the tires bolted underwater at each corner. This kept the center clear, helped to balance the craft and gave the companions something to crouch behind in case of a fight. Another door served as a tiller. The bobbing craft were attached to each other with stout metal chains, which would keep them together through riptides or fog. But in case of emergency, they could cut the larger raft loose to block pursuit, and shoot the ammo boxes on board to eliminate their pursuers.

The end of the logs were ragged and full of splinters, and the companions had done nothing to change that. The wild array of jagged kindling made a very good defense against unwanted passengers—man or mutie—climbing on board.

Ryan studied the rafts with a critical gaze. Tree trunks with the bark still on, old rope, rusty chains and a handful of nails. They didn't look like much, but hopefully they would last long enough to get them to Tennessee.

Whistling a sea chantey, Doc was on the larger craft, testing the ropes holding down the canvas-covered piles. Jak stood on the other with his back to the shore, taking care of business.

"Well, that's it for the supplies," Krysty said, wading to shore from the front raft. She stomped the red river mud off her boots, sending the crabs scurrying away, dragging their breakfast along with them.

"All the fuel's on board?" Ryan asked.

"Yes." Krysty shook her head, her hair spreading out

a corona of fiery glory to rival the coming dawn. "Food, blankets, all six of the rocket launchers. I'm surprised how much the rafts could hold."

"Just hope it's enough," Ryan said grimly, then glanced at the nearby APC. "Better wake Dean and Mildred, and get going. We can each catch some more sleep once we're far from here."

"I'll get them, lover," she said, and walked off.

"Lend me a hand, Ryan?" J.B. grunted, dragging a lumpy duffel bag toward the water.

"What is it?" Ryan asked, grabbing the rope and helping to lift the bag off the ground.

"Battery from the APC," J.B. replied as they waded into the cold water and splashed toward the nearer raft. "I'm going to wire a headlight to the thing so we can see at night. Scare a lot of folks and save us a pile of killing."

With the morning breeze ruffling his silvery mane of long hair, Doc watched the two men approach from the second raft, his .44 LeMat held tight, the hammer cocked back and ready.

"The halogen bulb will explode," Ryan stated. "Won't be able to take that much direct current."

"I used different thickness of wires to cut the voltage so the headlight wouldn't blow. I can make it work. Shit!" J.B. shifted his balance, nearly going under as his boot slipped on a smooth rock. "Close call."

Ryan changed their direction away from the cargo raft. "Then we put this on the lead raft, so we can see where we're going."

"Sounds good."

Zipping his pants closed, Jak turned and gave the men a hand hauling the heavy bag over the ring of splinters.

"Good for fishing," the teenager commented, lacing

the bag to the ropes covering the canvas mound. "Fish see light at night, come close, spear all we want."

"We never made any spears," J.B. said, heading for the cargo raft.

Jak jerked a thumb. "Doc has. Long ones."

"You made spears?" Ryan called out, climbing on board. He was dripping wet from the waist down, the water trickling down between the log deck and back into the basin. "Good thinking."

"These are not spears, my dear Ryan, but poles for punting," Doc replied, trimming small branches off a sapling with his pocketknife.

"Barge poles," J.B. translated as the older man gave him a boost on board. A thick piece of canvas draped over the splinters gave easy access to the deck of the homemade craft. "We can use them to push the raft along, in case we get stuck on a sandbar."

"Exactly." Tilting the pole, Doc visually inspected the shaft, rotating it this way and that. "A bit off plumb but nothing serious." He tossed it onto the deck.

"Punting," Ryan said as he changed into dry clothes and socks. He laid the wet garments on top of the canvas mound to let the sun dry them.

Trimming another sapling, Doc shrugged. "It is an Old English word, and I disremember its origin. Sorry."

Sliding on his boots, Ryan saw that Dean was walking backward along the shore, unraveling a greasy length of knotted rags from a slopping bucket. The other end of the line went through the top hatch of the LAV and down inside. Backpacks perched on their heads, Mildred and Krysty were already wading across the basin, heading for different rafts. Once the boy played out the length to the end, he lit the end with a butane lighter. The shredded blankets began to burn fiercely, giving off huge volumes of greenish smoke, the fire crawling up the length very slowly.

Dean waited a moment to make sure the fire had caught, then waded into the river. As soon as he was in the water, the crabs came out of hiding and began to finish the last few scraps of the dead sting-wing, rooting in the sand for every tiny gobbet of flesh.

"Hate to lose the wag," Krysty commented as she changed her pants.

"No choice. It's deadweight," Ryan stated. "And with any luck, if some blues find the wag, they'll think we all died the explosion."

"Can't hurt."

When Dean was on board, Ryan looked around the beach and ordered a last check of the supplies. It would take the grease fuse hours to reach the APC, but time was still against them. The blues could arrive at any moment, and if they left something important behind there would be no easy way to get it back.

"We have canned food, MRE packs, seven ammo boxes, a case of grens, bedrolls, blankets," Doc called out from the cargo raft. "Extra rope—"

"All of the rope," J.B. interrupted.

"Fuel, fresh water, pots and pans."

"Med kit," Mildred added, patting the bag at her side.

"Same," Jak announced, squatting by the mound, looking under the canvas. "Ready go."

The sun broke the horizon at that moment, flooding the world with its dim light. "All right, then," Ryan decided. "Cast off!"

At the helm, Krysty snapped the mooring line like a whip, and the knot around the tree stump came undone. Urged on by the gentle currents, the rafts began to leisurely float away from the Carolina shoreline.

Using the poles, the companions guided the rafts into the deep water where the saplings couldn't touch bottom. Drifting freely, Doc and Jak worked the tillers, steering them farther out until land was no longer in sight.

Behind them, a faint trail of smoke was discernible, rising above the horizon from the smoldering remains of the cornfield.

Shifting his weight from boot to boot, Dean tried to gain his balance on the moving raft. "I thought having the tires under the logs would make these things steady," he said, swallowing hard.

"It does," J.B. replied, spooning cold soup from a U.S. Army tin can. "Dark night, you should been with us a few years back when we took a raft trip down the Hudson in Newyork. Now, that was a rough ride."

Slightly green, the boy nodded assent and sat on the deck, waiting for his stomach to catch up with them from the beach.

Hours passed. The companions took turns at the helm and catching up on the sleep lost during the frenzied building of the raft during the night. The gentle current was getting stronger, urging them on a more southerly course, but they angled the rudder against the easy pull and maintained a steady course to the north and Tennessee.

"I make our speed at three knots," J.B. announced, studying the sun overhead. "Not bad."

"Wind is with us," Ryan said, testing the breeze with a damp finger. "That helps."

A bug buzzed near the raft, and a fish leaped from the basin and back into the water. The insect disappeared.

"I'll catch us dinner," Dean said, and unscrewed the handle of his bowie knife, withdrawing line and hooks.

"You'll need bait," Krysty commented, and reached

inside a box to retrieve a wad of grease-soaked paper. "Try some of the fatback. It's getting old, and we can't risk eating it anymore."

"Fish love bacon," Jak added, whittling on a sliver of wood from the end of a log. "Rancid, the best."

Cutting off a tiny cube, Dean baited a hook and cast it overboard, raising and lowering the line to suggest life in the bait.

"How odd," Mildred said, kneeling on the raft and almost sticking her face into the water. "Those are barracuda. Saltwater fish."

"Must be muties," J.B. stated, as if that settled the matter.

She stood. "Could be. But they seem to be dying."

"Should they not?" Doc asked, amused.

The physician waved that aside. "That isn't the point. How did ocean fish get this far into a freshwater basin?"

"Mebbe caught by the tide or something."

"Perhaps," she relented. "I only hope that—"

The raft shook hard as it struck something underwater. J.B. shifted the helm, and Ryan did the same.

"Sandbar?" Krysty asked, looking overboard, one hand gripping the ropes tight. "No, look!"

Just below the surface of the water was the wreck of a sailing ship. The hull was smashed inward near the bow, schools of fish darting about the rigging and cabin.

"*Obsession,*" Krysty read off the submerged ship. "Nice name."

As they passed by, Doc reached out with his ebony stick and tapped the propellers. The blades turned without hindrance and spun merrily.

"The engine is gone," Ryan said, frowning. "She's been looted."

Jak grabbed a barge pole and thrust it downward, meeting no resistance. "Clear water," he announced.

"Must be floating freely."

Mildred frowned. "Lord, I hope so."

More and more wreckage filled the waters beneath them until it seemed as if they were sailing over a submerged junkyard of smashed, rotting, vessels.

"Ten o'clock," Ryan warned, pointing at the horizon, one arm on the helm.

A smudge on the horizon grew steadily in size until they could see that the dark mass was a pile of wreckage, rising from the water like an island. An oil tanker lay among a pile of destroyers, gunboats, battleships, aircraft carriers, boats and seagoing vessels of every kind, all jammed together.

"Tumble down?" Jak asked.

Blinking from the windblown spray on his face, Ryan agreed. When skydark raped the world, debris from the nuked cities rained across the continent. The Manhattan blast threw cars and buses across the greater tristate area, the vehicles blown off bridges and shotgunning out of tunnels to fly for a hundred miles from the concussion of the nukes. Houses had been found on mountaintops, toilet seats in the middle of a desert and once Ryan found an intact bridge spanning a grassy field in the middle of nowhere. Anything close to an atomic blast was vaporized, but the objects farther away were melted and sprayed outward, then smashed apart and sent flying, and after that, merely airborne.

"The debris must have been drawn here by the current," Ryan guessed. "Then one ship got caught on a sandbar or mebbe it got entangled with another sunken ship. A second was caught, and so on until there was an island."

"Or maybe it was an oil rig," Mildred said. "But I honestly don't recall if there was any deep-sea drilling going on offshore of North Carolina."

"Want to stop by and see if it's inhabited?" J.B. asked, adjusting his glasses. "Might have some wags we could trade for, salvage."

Ryan frowned. "Pointless to try. Even if we found a wag, how the hell would we get it to the shore? Best keep traveling."

"Besides," Krysty added, placing a hand on her blaster and loosening it in the holster, "after that bastard Poseidon, I don't trust sailors much."

"Amen to that," Mildred added grimly.

RISING FROM HIS CHAIR, the old man shuffled across the bridge of the predark battleship in bare feet, his single garment of stitched canvas highly decorated with embroidery patterns and service medals from a hundred nations.

Slanted windows fronted three sides of the room, affording a panoramic view of the river basin. On a clear day, green haze could be seen from the distant shore, but everywhere else the blue waters of the basin ruled supreme.

The bridge was a half circle of electronic equipment as dead as the previous owners of the vessel. Radar screens were dark and lifeless, radios silent as the deep waters themselves. Near the stairwell, a stove made from an oil drum radiated heat. On top of the stove was a sterling-silver punch bowl full of simmering fish stew, the tiny heads bobbing about staring at nothing amid the long strands of kelp and diced turtle eggs.

Crumbling some dried mold into the stew, the commodore used a spoon carved from a lifeboat to take a taste, then added a bit more. The stores in the holds of the ships that comprised the island were finally running low after so many decades, but that didn't matter anymore, as all of his people would soon be dead.

The thought saddened him, and the whitehair walked to the southern window to gaze out upon the featureless vista of his watery domain. The commodore sighed. The crew of the Navy had lived here since skydark. Sometimes they sent expeditions to the shores for food or tools, but the crew always came back. There didn't seem to be any other living beings in the world. They found ruins, but no people. Just twisted, shambling mockeries of people, mindless creatures who wantonly killed with their clawed hands and howled at the sight of fire. Sometimes a hellhound was found, but thankfully those were rare. And very deadly.

Now the Navy men were alone. The last humans in the world. A plague had swept through the island ville ten winters ago, killing half the population and every woman. Even the babes. For over ten long years, the surviving men had lived in the towering pile of metal. He knew some of his crew found relief doing things the Manifest didn't approve. But if it kept them quiet, so be it. In life, some poor bastard was always the barrelboy.

A smudge of smoke on the western horizon caught his attention, and the whitehair walked to the telescope to train the instrument in that direction. The focus was poor, one lens replaced by a lens from a pair of eyeglasses, but he managed to achieve a kind of clarity. The smoke wasn't the plume of a seagoing vessel heading their way. There was just some sort of fire on the mainland. But under the magnification of the scope, he noticed something moving on the water, moving against the current. How could that be?

At first, he couldn't believe his eyes, thinking madness had finally claimed his mind. But the longer he watched, the more convinced he became that this real. Not a delusion brought on by loneliness and advanced age.

"Women!" the commodore cackled as he adjusted the focus of his telescope. Two tiny rafts were coming this way, and two of the occupants were clearly women, a redhead and a black woman. "Those are women!"

The commodore trembled slightly as the memory of his last woman filled his entire body, the softness of her skin, the weight of a breast in the palm of his hand, the feel of a nipple as it hardened with desire, the scent of her moist passion, the delicious heat as he slid inside.

Then he noticed their position. By the blood of the captain, the rafts were hundreds of yards past the island and dangerously close to the currents!

Quickly shuffling across the tilted floor of the battleship, the old man tugged repeatedly on a tasseled cord and a bell rang loudly, the peels echoing slightly as they reverberated down the metal hallway of the military ship.

"General quarters!" the whitehair shouted over the bell. "We have company a port beam!"

"Company?" said a big man appearing at the bottom of the angled ladder. Bare chested, he was covered with homemade tattoos, and a machete hung at his right hip. "Who left the island without permission, sir?"

"Nobody, bosun! It's new folks! Fellow survivors!"

Trying to hide a smile, the man looked skeptically at the whitehair. "Been having a nip of the brew again, have we, sir?"

"It's true, you ass!" the commodore yelled. "Outlanders are here, and two are women. Live women!"

The bosun recoiled. "It's a lie."

"No, mate, it's true! See for yourself!"

Bounding up the stairs, he rushed to the telescope and soon found the pair of rafts to the west of the island. "By the coast gods," he cursed. "It's a bunch of people, and some are women, and they're near the damn currents! They'll be swept away and killed!"

The commodore stomped a foot. "I know, you fool! Send the last working longboat, use every drop of juice! But get those women. We must have them alive!"

"Women," the bosun repeated, rubbing a sweaty hand on his thigh. "Aye, we'll get them, sir, and chill anybody who dares to try to stop us!"

WATCHING AS THE JUNKYARD island receded into the distance, the companions started to relax when the side of a huge oil tanker split apart as colossal doors spread wide. Filling the interior was a full-size dockyard. Oil lanterns hung in clusters, boxes and crates were stacked before warehouses and swarms of men worked with winches and cranes. Then from the shadows, two sleek speedboats darted into view, skipping across the waves at incredible velocities.

"Triple red!" Ryan shouted, keeping a grip on the helm and drawing his hand blaster. With a thumb, he flicked off the safety.

Prepared for possible trouble, the companions leveled their weapons and dropped into firing positions, tracking the incoming ships.

Dean dropped the clip in his Browning Hi-Power to check the load, then slammed it back in again, jacking the slide. "They might be friendly," he ventured hopefully.

"Not at that speed," J.B. admonished. "Friends don't come charging full speed at total strangers."

A bearded man on board one of the rushing vessels called out through a megaphone, but the words were distorted from the sheer distance.

"Something about heave to," Krysty said, brushing the tangles of hair away from her ears. "But I couldn't get the rest over the noise of those engines."

Ryan grunted at the pronouncement. He knew her hearing was a lot sharper than most people's.

"Fuck them," Jak spit, easing back the hammer on his .357 magnum Colt. "Lies, anyhow."

Withdrawing the Navy telescope from his pouch, J.B. extended the device to its full length. "Hard to see with all the bouncing," he complained, using a hand to cushion the telescope end rather than press the hard metal directly on his face. Only a fool did such a thing. It was a good way to lose the eye completely.

"Well?" Ryan demanded impatiently.

"They're heavily armed," J.B. announced, compacting the scope to the size of a soup can, "and carrying nets."

"Alive," Mildred growled, drawing her ZKR blaster. "We know what that means."

Suddenly, the two speedboats began to separate, arcing in different directions around the near stationary rafts. Taking a stance on the rolling deck, the physician braced her blaster at the wrist and drew in a slow breath. The foremost speedboat was still far away when she fired three times. The pilot slumped at the wheel, and the craft veered off sharply heading out to sea.

"Take the tiller!" Ryan ordered.

Holstering his piece, Jak switched with the big man, and Ryan unlimbered the Steyr. Working the bolt to chamber a round, he wrapped the strap about his forearm to help steady the aim and tracked the coming speedboat through the scope for a single heartbeat, then fired.

The cowling flipped off the outboard motor, and the engine caught fire. The boat slowed dramatically, and the men on board threw buckets of water on the burning machinery. Then J.B. opened up with the Uzi. Black dots peppered the hull, a windshield cracked, two men dropped and another tumbled overboard, his face gone.

Sporadic gunfire came from the junkyard island as the rafts continued floating away, the current that had carried them there building in strength. Then another vessel appeared from within the tanker, a huge powerful boat covered with predark weapons—machine guns and torpedo tubes.

"Damn, it's a PT boat from World War II!" Mildred shouted. "That can easily catch us and blow these rafts out of the water!"

"Unfortunately, they do not want us dead," Doc said grimly, cocking the hammer on his LeMat. "However, we do not reciprocate the sentiment." Doc fired twice, the booming revolver sounding as if it exploded rather than merely discharged, a lance of flame more than a foot long vomiting from its pitted muzzle. The first .44 miniball missed, but the second round impacted directly on the hull, making only a small dent.

"By the Three Kennedys!" he cursed, waving the weapon to disperse the smoke. "That floating tank is armored better than the *Merrimac*!"

Holding his blaster in both hands, Dean emptied a clip at the massive boat. If the boy hit the vessel it wasn't discernible. He reloaded and tried again.

"They're not even going to waste ammo shooting," J.B. drawled, slapping a fresh clip into the Uzi and triggering short controlled bursts. Instead of the men, he was aiming for the torpedo tubes, hoping for an explosion. "They'll just ram us, and bust these rafts into kindling!"

"Then rescue the female survivors," Mildred said, stuffing her jacket pockets with grens for close combat.

"Rape, you mean." Thumbing fresh rounds into her Smith & Wesson pistol, Krysty could see the men on board, laughing and jeering in unbridled lust. The sight made her blood run cold. After being almost raped twice in her lifetime, she would rather chill herself than let them have her as a prisoner, a helpless plaything to be abused for their sexual torture. Or even worse, a breeder to bear children as fast as possible until she died on a birthing bed whelping another slave for them to ravage.

Grabbing the AK-47, Krysty flipped the selector switch to full-auto and emptied the last clip at the rapidly approaching warship. The fusillade of rounds ricocheted off the hull with no effect.

Swaying to the motion of the building waves, Ryan swept the enemy boat with rounds from the Steyr, but the copper-jacketed 7.62 mm rounds of the longblaster were useless against the military armor of the hulking PT boat.

"Fireblast!" he stormed, dropping the spent weapon. "Small arms are useless against that behemoth. Mind the backwash. I'm going to use a LAW!"

Grabbing a fat tube from under the canvas mound, Ryan yanked the weapon to its full length. The sights popped up on top, and a large red button was exposed.

"Clear?" Ryan demanded, zeroing the aft port. The water was getting rough, waves chopping at the raft.

"Clear!" Krysty shouted.

Heading straight toward the rafts, the PT boat loomed before them as Ryan pressed the launch button. A volcanic cone of exhaust stretched for several yards from the rear of the tube, and a rustling firebird launched from the tube and streaked toward the PT boat.

The rocket hit the vessel amidships, punching through the hull and detonating. Torn to pieces, the deck lifted off the gunwale as the boat was blown apart, men and machinery spewing outward in a geyser of destruction.

As the current quickly took the rafts away from the sinking wreckage, Ryan tossed the spent tube overboard and grabbed another. Warily, he waited for another speedboat to appear, but no more vessels ventured from the junkyard ville.

"I don't like this," Krysty said suspiciously. "They gave up too quickly."

Holstering his blaster, Dean suggested, "Mebbe they don't have any more boats."

"I saw a dozen more at the dock," J.B. replied, feeling uneasy. "A few had to be in working condition."

"There's something wrong here," Ryan agreed, collapsing the launcher. "Damned if I know what, though."

"We shot the shit out of them," Mildred stated forcibly. "They're just scared of folks with guns."

"Could be," Ryan said reluctantly. "Then again, they charged straight into our blasters and didn't shoot back when they wanted prisoners. That doesn't sound cowardly."

"No," she agreed. "No, it doesn't."

Unexpectedly, the rafts lurched in a rush of acceleration that nearly knocked the companions off their feet.

"Now, what was that?" Krysty demanded. "A riptide?"

"Hey," Jak said, throwing his weight against the tiller. There was no response. "Going south. Can't stop."

"Same here," Doc shouted, struggling with the helm. "The current is too strong."

Choppy waves broke over the front of the first raft, covering the companions with misty spray.

"Does that taste salty?" Krysty asked, touching her lips.

In sudden understanding, Mildred dipped a hand into the rough water and licked a finger. That was brine, sure enough.

"Sweet Jesus, this is why they stopped chasing us!" Mildred shouted. "We're caught in an underwater river!"

Once, long ago, the physician had seen a television program on such events. A severe earthquake would occasionally lower a large section of land, and the sea would rush along an existing riverbed, pushing the fresh water out of its way as it plowed inland. Nukes or some natural disaster had to have rearranged the Carolinas, and now they were trapped in a reverse river, probably heading for a blast crater.

"This is taking us to a blast crater!" she shouted over the raging waters. "A really huge mucking big one!"

"We could jump," Dean offered hesitantly, with no real enthusiasm for the plan.

"Caught in the flow," Ryan grunted, straining at the helm. The aluminum door was shaking wildly in his grasp, but seemed to be helping a little. No rocks hit yet. "Jump and we'd be dragged into the whirlpool."

"The what?"

"Two rivers going in opposite directions—of course there's a whirlpool." J.B. yanked off his glasses and placed them securely in a shirt pocket.

"There it is!" Krysty cried out, pointing.

An islet of land was faintly visible ahead of them, the blue water from the river rushing toward the east, and the darker sea waters racing toward the west. At the apex of the islet was a large depression of white water. Mist rose from the location, and a low steady roar could be heard, then felt in the trembling logs of the raft.

"Hot pipe, no wonder they stopped chasing us!" Dean panted, stuffing MRE packs into his pockets.

After lashing a rope around about her waist, Krysty joined Ryan at the helm, fighting for control of the craft. "Easy. Don't fight it!" Ryan shouted. "Trim into the flow. We need speed!"

"Fast, then sharp!" J.B. called out from the cargo raft, with Doc beside him at the tiller.

"Together!" Ryan shouted, stealing a glance at the chains mooring the crafts in tandem. "Must be together, or we go in!"

"Follow your lead!"

Hair plastered to her head, Krysty yelled, "We going to shoot past the rim?"

"Unless you got a better idea!"

The entire world seemed to be vibrating. Spray soaked them in a matter of seconds, the thickening mist blocking any view of what was coming. A low moan came from the vortex, the noise raising and lowering.

Suddenly, the mists parted and there it was again. The river dropped away to their left, the swirling cone of water extending out of sight. Every loose item on the raft tumbled away as the craft tilted dangerously to the right. Pots, pans and the last LAW rocket flew off and the supplies bulged under the canvas sheet, straining to break loose.

Speech was impossible, so Ryan shouted orders into Krysty's ear. She nodded and drew her revolver, praying to Gaia that the others would understand. Krysty fired three shots into the air, then two shots, then one.

In unison, both teams strained at the helms, forcing

the doors to angle away from the whirlpool. Instantly, they began to swing that way. But the hinges were tearing free from the log, and the shaking doors slashed flesh like a butcher's knife. Blood flowed from their hands as the companions fought for their lives against the savage fury of nature.

The rafts broke free of the whirlpool, sent flying yards high by their momentum to violently splash down in the briny waters on the other side of the islet. The logs writhed, and a dozen ropes snapped, but the chains held and the rafts didn't break apart.

Everybody took the moment of peace to catch their breath, and flex tired hands. Behind them, the vortex swirled and moaned, but the ocean waters were now working with them to shove the rafts away from the deadly whirlpool.

Drenched, J.B. grabbed Mildred by the collar and soundly kissed her. She returned the favor.

Doc merely beamed like an idiot. "By gad, we made it! Huzzah!"

"Not yet," Ryan shouted, his ears ringing slightly from the pounding surf. "White water ahead!"

Rising from the rushing waters were dozens of rocks and boulders, the river crashing against them in foamy waves that shot twenty feet into the sky.

In shock, Dean realized they were going downhill, the river waters increasing to incredible speeds. The crashing waves hid the rocks from sight, and the mounting currents buffeted the rafts helplessly from side to side. He wanted to shout advice, or a suggestion, but not a damn thing came to mind.

"We're heading for shore!" Ryan bellowed, tightening his grip on the battered door from the APC. Through the waves, he could see green trees to their right. The islet had to have been the tip of a delta. Dry land was only yards away.

Then the front raft bounced off a rock, and the timbers cracked from the impact, the chains straining to hold the tiny craft together. Another boulder appeared, and Jak shoved with a pole as Ryan and Krysty leaned into the tiller. At the last moment, the craft swung away from the granite outcropping with the second raft sluggishly lagging along in its wake. But not fast enough.

A green wall of moss-covered granite loomed into sight, and the cargo raft smacked the rock a glancing blow, the logs yawning wide below their boots as the ropes were tested to the breaking point. Once more the chains saved the raft from total destruction.

The sky was full of falling water, boulders everywhere. Then a low thunder could be heard, a rumble that grew in force of volume until there was nothing else in the world.

A terrible suspicion grew in Ryan, and he again tried for the shore, but it was too little, too late. The companions didn't have time to curse or scream as the homemade rafts sailed over the edge of the gigantic waterfall and tumbled downward into the misty abyss.

Chapter Seven

Storm clouds hide the stars overhead, thunder rumbling softly in the distance as the blue shirt rattled the lock on the storage hut. Satisfied it was secure, the sec man walked around the corner, heading for the next point on his nightly sweep of the complex. The chore was an easy job, the forced workers at the ville were starved to near death and beaten constantly. Any worker who showed any sign of rebellion or pride was executed immediately. Some were gut shot to slowly bled to death, while others were staked out and fed to the muties hiding in the hills. The lucky ones were set on fire, or simply buried alive. Dr. Jamaisvous demanded that the construction schedules always be met, and he wouldn't tolerate any excuse for failure. No sec man would dare to risk receiving the type of punishment they dished out on a daily basis.

Whistling a tune, the sec man turned a corner and recoiled from a sharp pain. Breathless, he stared at the wooden handle jutting from his chest and felt the strength flow from his limbs. With fading eyesight, he realized a grinning slave in rags was holding the shaft of the pickax.

"Victory or death," the slave whispered as the guard toppled over into a pool of blood.

More slaves scurried into view and carried the warm corpse into the slave quarters, while dirt was kicked over the spilled life fluid. A crowd of starving people blocked the doorway, but they instantly parted before the murderers and closed after they passed, hiding any possible sight of what was happening.

The back room of the slave quarters was the lav, merely some holes sawed into the floor above a reeking pit. In a dark corner, they stripped the sec man naked. His boots went one way, pants another, holster, blaster and ammo elsewhere.

"Is that enough?" a woman grunted excitedly, fondling the wheelgun as if it were a living pet. A jagged scar covered half of her face, the eye dead white. "Do we have enough?"

"Yes," a bald man replied coldly. "This gives us twelve rounds for every blaster."

"A full charge and a reload," another gushed. "Black dust, I never thought we would ever get that much."

The bald man cocked back the hammer on the wheelgun. "Get the torches. When you hear the first shots, start the fires."

"Victory or death," the conspirators whispered in unison.

"Death to Jamaisvous," the leader growled. "Now, go!"

THE CAPTAIN of the guards was in a kiosk sipping a warm beer when a strangled cry came from the darkness. Dropping his boots to the floor, the sec man stood and drew his blaster. Listening carefully, he edged to the doorway and pushed open the door with fingertips. Nothing was in sight.

"Damn sting-wing again," he muttered.

Instantly, there was a flash of silver and the captain was driven back into the kiosk by a slave holding a stick with a jagged sliver of glass tied to the end. With his throat slashed, it was impossible for the sec man to breathe. Blood filled his mouth and trickled onto his shirt. With fumbling hands, he tried to fire his blaster, but another slave was upon him, slashing with another piece of glass. Pain lanced his hand, and he saw the grinning man holding the bloody blaster, his own twitching finger still on the trigger.

The guard spit at the slaves, and they stabbed him in the eyes, breaking their glass knives. Screaming, he fell to his knees. More glass was produced, and the killers slashed at his belly until his intestines slithered onto the gory floor as months of abuse were paid back with interest in a few hellish seconds. Finally, the corpse dropped lifeless upon the steaming entrails.

''Victory or death,'' the slaves whispered to one another, and began rummaging through the room for more ammo, or anything else that might be used as a weapon.

PAUSING IN HIS PATROL of the grounds beneath the dish, a corporal fought back a yawn and strained to hear what had made the strange noise. It was a sort of moan, mixed with a slapping sound. Was some sec man having sex with a slave while on duty? He'd have the man's balls cut off for dereliction of duty.

The noises came again, and he followed them to a spot beneath the dish. The night here was as black as pitch, a circle of night within night, and the corporal proceeded at a careful pace.

A toolshed sat near the concrete base that supported the dish. Bending close to a window, he heard the noises more clearly and grinned. A slave's rags were draped over the window to hide what was going on inside, but through the rips in the cloth he could see three naked women stroking one another, caressing and kissing, hands cupping breasts and stroking between open thighs. Unable to tear his eyes away from the delicious sight, he pressed closer to the window as a large-breasted slave lay down upon a worktable asking to be taken. An older woman with streaks of silver in her red hair climbed on her face and began rocking back and forth. Then the younger blonde buried her face between the woman's thighs. Their moans and cries of pleasure grew louder as their sex play became more passionate and inventive.

Rubbing the front of his clothing, the corporal glanced around to make sure nobody else was near, then holstered his blaster and slid a hand into his pants for some relief himself.

Instantly, the shadows rose behind him and a woman grunted with exertion as she drove two long spikes into each of his ears. Convulsing, the corporal gurgled incoherently. The slave waited until he was still, then scratched on the window. A few seconds later, the three women stepped from the hut, wearing blue shirts and boots, and carrying blasters.

"Here," said the fourth slave, passing over a set of keys.

"Victory or death," the older woman whispered in reply, and they separated quickly, leaving the corpse on the cold ground.

WEARILY WALKING from his bathroom, Silas Jamaisvous turned off the lights and poured himself a stiff drink from a crystal decanter. The amber color of the predark liquor was that of new honey, the smell ambrosia. He only hoped it would mix with the drugs and give him a night of dreamless sleep for once.

Opening a small vial, he added a measured dose of morphine, then doubled the amount. Even with the drug, he still wasn't sleeping well. The dream, always the terrible dream.

Draining the glass in a few swallows, Silas sat on his bed and kicked off his velvet slippers. The room was nicely warm, the heavy curtains blocking any noise of the troops on patrol outside. It had been a long and fruitful day of work. The master computer system for the Kite seemed to be working fine today, but the real test would come tomorrow when they tested the focusing mechanism. Having the ultimate weapon meant nothing unless it could be used with surgical skill. Clubs were for cavemen, and he was a scientist.

Snuggling under the covers, Silas fought against the drug coursing through his veins, formulas and mathematical equations filling his mind. But finally, he relaxed and let hated sleep claim him once again. Almost immediately, sweat formed on his brow, and his eyelids began to flutter.

Groaning and mumbling in the delirium, the man couldn't hear the cover come off the air-conditioning vent in the wall. It was maneuvered inside the shaft, and a figure slowly emerged from the wall, lowering himself to the floor, the bare feet making not a sound. The invader waited until his vision became adjusted to the dark, then drew a length of rope from around his waist. Holding an end in each hand, he crept toward the snoring man.

Standing above the sleeper, the slave watched the rise and fall of the madman's chest, savoring this moment of revenge. Then he bent over to slide the garrote around the unprotected throat of the man who had tortured to death so many people in the name of his holy science.

"Victory or death," he said through clenched teeth. "And it's death for you, whitecoat!"

A muffled cough sounded and the room flashed with light. The slave stumbled backward, bleeding from the chest. He hit the wall and dropped the garrote, drawing a blaster. Again the cough sounded, the muzzle-flash of the silenced weapon strobing the darkness as the soft-nosed rounds punched the slave to the ground with sledgehammer force.

Brilliant lights flooded the room, and Major William Sheffield walked over to the dying slave, the unfired blaster still in the unfortunate wretch's hands.

Coolly, Sheffield shot the skinny man once in each eye, cracking open the skull. A trickle of brains flowed down the wall and onto the floor.

"Secure the room," the major ordered, and a platoon of sec men poured in from the hallway to swarm around Silas, forming a living wall of protection.

A sec man exited the closet with a silenced pistol, an electronic device of some kind strapped to his face.

"It was amazing," the guard said, sliding off the visor. "I could actually see in the dark. Everything was colored green, but I could truly see."

"Yes, you did well," Sheffield said, swinging his weapon at the guard. "Pity you let the slave get so close to the commander."

"Sir?" the guard asked, frightened.

Sheffield shot the man in the heart, the .45 caliber round from the U.S. Army Colt automatic driving him into the closet.

Crossing the room, he shot the man again to make sure of the job, then strode over to the mumbling scientist.

"Dr. Jamaisvous?" he said loudly, shaking the man. There was no response. Impatiently, he slapped the old man hard. Nothing, but more mumbling.

"Okay, we handle this ourselves," Sheffield stated to the troops. "Sound the call, but do it quietly. We know the slaves have been planning something for a while. I thought it was a mass escape, but it looks like they might plan on killing us first."

Cradling an AK-47 longblaster, a corporal wearing a bulletproof vest snorted. "Bad choice, sir. They might have had a chance in hell of running away."

INSIDE THE MAIN OFFICE for the power plant, the chief engineer for the complex stopped eating a sandwich when he heard an odd banging noise. Grabbing some gloves, he quickly stepped onto the main floor of the plant to see if there was something wrong with the cranky steam generators again. The damn things were always overheating, losing pressure or blowing a valve.

Clearly highlighted in the red glow of the main furnace, the engineer gasped at the sight of three sec men lying on the ground, slaves beating them with coal shovels. Then one slave turned the edge of the shovel on a cringing guard and decapitated the man on the spot, the head rolling away, leaving a crimson trail.

"Motherfuckers!" the engineer shouted, and grabbed his blaster, but a shovel from behind smashed his arm. His dropped weapon skittered away under a lathe.

Clutching the broken arm, the engineer tried to make it back to the office, but halfway there he saw slaves standing in the doorway, the men and women armed with the AK-47 blasters from the arms locker.

"As if you scum know how to operate a blaster," he said with a sneer, backing away. But fear filled his belly, and bitter vomit rose in his throat.

In reply, the slaves clicked off the safeties and worked the bolts, chambering rounds.

"No, stop. I can help you!" he pleaded, tears running down his chubby cheeks. "I know what's going on here. I can protect you from the Kite!"

"Liar," a slave snarled, and fired once, hitting him in the left knee.

The pain was excruciating, and the engineer dropped to the floor, clutching the ghastly wound, a shard of white bone visible in the flesh. "No, please! Let me live! I beg you!"

"As you let the children live?" another spit. "And the women after you used them?"

"Please…"

"Yes, we should let him live," a tall woman said unexpectedly. "Let him stay alive all the way to the furnace!"

The slaves crowded around the engineer and bodily hauled him away. Though weak from blood loss, the terrified engineer fought like a wild animal, kicking and biting, until beaten partially senseless by the wooden stocks of the blasters.

Weeping uncontrollably, the engineer was shoved into the second furnace and the grille slammed shut. There came the telltale whoosing sound of building pressure, and he screamed for salvation. Then the searing flames engulfed the man, and he keened hideously. Unconcerned, the slaves walked away, leaving him to enjoy his last few moments alone with his precious machines.

SILENTLY MOUTHING CURSES, a sec man toppled off the roof of the power plant, his face dark purple, a length of knotted rope wound around his constricted throat.

Screaming, a sec man stumbled out of the officers' lav, his pants dragging around his ankles and blood pouring from his ass, the feather shaft of an arrow protruding from between his plump cheeks.

The door to the dining hall was thrown open and slaves poured out, carrying weapons and ammo belts. Inside, a dozen sec man lay sprawled on the linen-covered tables, black tongues sticking out of their foaming mouths, the beer mugs dripping a bluish liquid on the freshly scrubbed floor.

Shouting orders, armed sec men piled out of the barracks, and the night came alive with blasterfire as they were cut down in the street by hidden snipers.

Suddenly, sirens blared and lights clicked on, filling the complex with blinding illumination. But the tactic failed miserably. Instead of startling the slaves and making them run away in fear, it gave them heart. They used the visibility to shoot down additional sec men, then seized their longblasters to kill more of the blue shirts.

"Victory or death!" a woman yelled, waving a bloody longblaster. The rally cry was repeated by a hundred people in rags, brandishing weapons of every possible description.

IN A THUNDEROUS crash, the side of the main warehouse broke apart and an Abrams M-1 tank rolled out of the building, crushing under its massive armored treads several Hummers that had been commandeered by slaves.

Oddly, nobody fired a weapon at the tank, and the commander began to laugh as the gunner tracked the machine guns of the military juggernaut after the slaves scattering throughout the complex.

As the Abrams rumbled past the barracks, a glass window shattered and a slave leaped upon the machine, clinging to the thick barrel of the 120 mm cannon like a monkey. More laughter sounded from within the

Abrams, and then a series of metallic clanks announced the main gun was being loaded. Light poured from the barrel, and the slave released the handle of the gren in his hand and threw it down the barrel. The men inside cursed in shock. Releasing the cannon, the slave fell to the soil and tried to run, but the military tank loomed above him like a wall of death. He darted to the left, the right, but not fast enough. The treads caught his leg, and he was pulled underneath the massive machine shrieking and wailing until his head was mashed flat.

Then the gren detonated, flame shooting from the cannon and out every port and hatch. Steam rising from its vents, the Abrams stood motionless in the street, the smell of death pouring from the broken vehicle.

With the destruction of the Army tank, the fighting became pandemic in the ville. Shots rang out constantly, screams coming from every building. The fighting went hand-to-hand at the armory, as each side struggled to reclaim the precious cache of ammo. Triumphantly, the sec men gained control of the building, ruthlessly shooting the slaves crawling in through the broken windows and shimmying out the fireplace flue.

Then a horn sounded a single clear note, and the slaves raced away from the structure. Weapons at the ready, the sec men stuffed grens into their pockets and waited for the next assault when the floor below erupted in a strident blast. The entire building lifted into the air, the tunnels below the foundation clearly visible for a split second before the tons of masonry plummeted earthward in a grisly rain.

That was the turning point of the battle. Now the slaves openly challenged the sec men, blaster for blaster, man for man, and the blues were decimated every time they tried to make a stand. Soon the sec men were ducking for cover, then retreating to strategic locations, and finally running for their lives before the relentless advance of the ragged horde.

"RETREAT TO THE BUNKER!" cried the sec chief, launching a flare into the nighttime sky. The incandescent charge soared upward and detonated in a pyrotechnic display visible from everywhere in the complex.

A shot hit him in the chest, the blow to his vest only making him grunt. Then a tracer round took him in the throat, and the man toppled off the roof of the Hummer, launching a second flare with his last ounce of strength. The charge went wild, rocketing down a street, glancing off the side of a building and streaking into the night to explode among the trees. Few saw the heroic act, even fewer the second flare. But the first signal had been spotted, and the wounded blue shirts obeyed the desperate command, fleeing toward the concrete block located in an open field.

The bunker was a stout concrete building, its original purpose lost forever in time. But the windows were sealed with iron plate, the walls reinforced with multiple layers of bricks, the domed roof smooth concrete over riveted sheets of cold iron.

"Hurry!" a corporal shouted, standing in the doorway, one hand on the portal, the other gripping the jamb. Sec men stood behind him, firing their blasters in controlled bursts at the bloodthirsty throng racing across the field. Dozens of sec men poured into the building, plunging deeper into the structure to make room for their brethren guards so close on their heels.

Carrying a flamethrower, a sec chief appeared from within the bunker. "That's everybody. Close the door."

"We have a man out there!" the door guard dared to respond.

The sec chief squinted into the chaos. A single sec men was running toward the bunker only a few yards ahead of the slave army. Arms pumping, legs flashing, the blue shirt raced pell-mell across the field, leading the way for the howling killers, a herald announcing the holocaust.

"Fuck him! This is a direct order. Close the door, Corporal."

Confused, the sec man jerked his head at the running blue shirt so close to the bunker, and the slaves so close behind. With a grave expression, he began to push the heavy door closed, the opening narrowing by the heartbeat.

"Wait," the runner wheezed. "Please, wait!"

The armored door closed with a boom, the heavy locks sliding noisily across the array of iron bands.

Stumbling to a halt, the sec man stood in the middle of the field staring dumbfounded at the bunker. "Damn you," he panted. "Damn you all to hell."

A longblaster shot took the man in the shoulder, spinning him, blood spraying from the impact. Now facing the triumphant slaves, the blue shirt made no effort to run or draw the weapon at his hip. There seemed to be no point to the act. Howling in victory, the slaves swarmed over the standing man, and he disappeared within the mob.

Reaching the bunker, the slaves fired their blasters at the door and walls, the 7.62 mm rounds chipping the bricks but nothing more.

"Find some explosives!" shouted a big woman, a pistol in one hand and a bloody piece of scalp in the other. "Let's blast our way in!"

A scrawny man stood before the door as if defying it with his mere presence. "I say we break it down and catch the bastards alive!" he shouted. "Then we crucify the lot of them! Who's with me?"

The slaves cheered their approval. A bracing girder used for supporting the dish was found, and ten of the largest slaves grabbed hold and charged at the iron door. The end of the steel girder flattened as it hit, and the door shook dangerously on its hinges.

"Again!" screamed the leader, and the girder slammed against the iron portal, making it rattle loosely.

"It's coming free!" a woman shouted. "We're almost in!"

A tiny slot opened in the door and several blasters fired. Two slaves toppled over with ghastly head wounds. But more rushed boldly to take their place, and one man shoved an AK-47 into the port and emptied the clip, twisting the barrel about in a circle, trying to chill everybody on the other side. Screams of pain told of some degree of success.

The girder crashed against the door once more, and suddenly clear moonlight washed over the battlefield.

Startled, the slaves paused in the attack, some of them plainly frightened. Above the complex, the ever present storm clouds were thinning away to nothingness and twinkling stars could be seen overhead, the fat moon a silvery orb to rule the sky.

"Beautiful," a woman cried.

A man recoiled in fear. "Ain't natural. No clouds in the sky? Ain't natural, I tell ya!"

The leader of the slaves started to reply when he heard a low-key humming and realized there was a surge of power going through the high-tension lines feeding the dish, the accumulators audibly charging. His heart pounding, the slave had no idea what to do. Was this an attack? Were the blues electrifying the door?

Just then a man screamed, clawing wildly at his face. Then another did the same, and another. Caterwauling people fell off the roofs of buildings, untriggered rifles exploded, loose ammo crackling like popcorn and Hummers burst into fireballs.

A FEW MINUTES LATER, the battered door to the bunker was forced open by scc men who immediately retreated, covering their mouths and noses and trying not to gag. The portal was closed posthaste, the edges sealed with rags and anything that could be shoved into the jamb to keep out the horrible stink.

The blue shirts knew they would have to wait a few hours for the stench to dissipate. But there was no rush. The rebellion was over. Everything within a mile of the bunker was now stone dead.

INSIDE THE MAIN LAB of the complex, Silas Jamaisvous stood at a control panel, an empty syringe of adrenaline sticking out of his arm.

Woozy, he pulled down the switch operating the bus bar disconnecting the main relay assembly from the power grid.

"It worked," he whispered in delight. "It really worked!"

"Yes, it did," Sheffield said from the corner of the lab. "And we really need to talk about that."

Chapter Eight

Ryan awoke, still hearing the thunder of the waterfall.

"Son of a mutie bitch," he muttered. "We survived after all."

Struggling to his hands and knees, the man realized half of his face was cold and the other side painfully hot. He been lying facedown in the mud with the sun baking his blind side.

Painfully sitting upright, Ryan felt like the loser in an ax fight. He remembered going over the waterfall and not much after that. Sluggishly, the one-eyed man felt for his SIG-Sauer. He was amazed to find it still there. Trembling fingers jacked the slide, and he holstered the useless blaster. It was coated with mud. Firing a round now might make the weapon explode.

Drawing the curved panga, he stood and surveyed the landscape. They were in a shining sea of smooth water, tiny tufts of brown grass dotting the surface, and farther out was the occasional dead tree draped with moss and green with mold. The smell of salt was strong. The water was about a foot deep, the ground underneath the soft muck of decaying plants. It was a swamp formed from the runoff of the ocean river. To the east rose a high cliff, a waterfall cascading from the top, filling the air with a fine mist and a beautiful rainbow.

The Deathlands warrior frowned. Cliffs behind, swamp ahead, not much choice of direction to take.

Wiping the salt mud off his face, Ryan counted off the rest of the companions and was relieved to find everybody present. They were lying limply about, but no limbs jutted at odd angles, and no pools of blood were visible. Krysty lay near him, with one cowboy boot missing, her fur coat looking like it had drowned itself. A few yards away, Mildred was draped over a piece of the raft. The unconscious physician still gripped her med kit.

The smaller raft was intact. One of the logs was broken in two, but the canvas still retained the supplies within. But the cargo raft was destroyed, boxes and timbers strewed everywhere for hundreds of yards.

Nobody dead, one raft still whole. With this little damage, Ryan realized it couldn't have been a proper waterfall with a straight drop. It had to have been merely a steep incline, and they were flushed onto this muddy field like so much shit. Vaguely, Ryan had disjointed memories of swimming, fighting to reach the surface, people shouting. After that, it was blank. One raft lost. Could have been worse, a lot worse.

"Krysty?" he asked, sloshing closer to the woman.

"I'm alive, lover," she replied, struggling into a crouch. "Just barely, but still pulling air."

Finding the other boot, Ryan gave it to her, then helped the woman to stand. "It's a miracle we survived," he stated.

"Thank Gaia." Krysty coughed and tried to wipe the clinging muck off her sodden clothes.

Resembling a corpse escaping the grave, Mildred arose from the watery mud. "Anybody hurt?" the physician asked wearily, feeling her own arms and chest for broken bones.

"We're okay," Ryan replied. "Battered, but no serious damage."

"Good." Mildred hawked and spit to clear her mouth. "Looks like we're in a runoff swamp," she said. "Better than a rad pit, I suppose."

Quickly, Ryan checked his lapel and saw no readings from the miniature Geiger counter. "Clean," he reported, then actually smiled as he noted the disheveled appearance of his friends, dark mud covering them like camou armor. "Well, sort of anyway," he added.

Favoring his right leg, Doc struggled to stand, the black-powder charges from the LeMat dribbling out of the holster and down his leg like black blood.

"How inconvenient," he rumbled in annoyance, then addressed the others. "By any chance, does anybody see my stick?"

"Over here," Dean cried, and splashed across the water. By a rotting tree, he plunged his hands into the silt and pulled the ebony swordstick free.

"I saw the light flashing off the silver," he said, returning the weapon.

"Thank you, lad. Good show." Doc twisted the lion's-head handle and pulled out the sword for inspection. The steel was foggy with condensation, but otherwise undamaged.

Dean shrugged. "No prob."

His limp fedora perched on a stick to dry, J.B. was sitting on the undamaged raft, holding his glasses by the stems and rinsing them in the seawater.

Knife in hand, Jak stood nearby, staring hard at the desolate land stretching before them. It resembled his home of Louisiana.

"Clean blasters!" the pale teenager barked as an order.

Sliding the patch to the front of his face, Ryan looked about and saw nothing of possible menace. "Explain," he commanded.

Jak frowned. "Swamps alive. Lots life, snakes, rats. Not here, but could be."

Heeding the sage advice, the companions moved to the raft and got busy. Sparingly using the clean water from the canteens, they cleaned their weapons and made sure each was in working order. Then with guards posted, they attempted to clean themselves. Dean found a depression in the land two feet deep, and they washed as thoroughly as possible in the makeshift tub.

"What's wrong with the soap?" J.B. asked, trying to work up a lather in his hands.

"This is salt water," Mildred said, pouring another skimmed cup of swamp water over her hair. More silt rinsed out of her beaded plaits. "It takes a special kind of soap to foam in brine."

"Swell," he grumbled.

After the ablutions, somewhat cleaner and pounds lighter, the companions sat on the raft eating cold MRE rations. The warm water rose to their knees, and they closely watched the surface for undulating ripples that meant the presence of snakes. Swamps were the worst kind of terrain to cross. Mud weighed you down, great holes could open beneath you at any stop, the air was thick and difficult to breathe, plus most of the animals were poisonous.

Chewing a ration bar, Dean glanced at the waterfall. "Looks like we walk from here."

"Where is here?" Krysty asked, her hair flexing and waxing around her as if drying itself in the pale gray sunlight.

"I checked earlier," J.B. replied around a mouthful

of peanut butter and graham crackers. He took a pull of water to clear his throat. "We're still in North Carolina. About twenty miles from the Tennessee border."

"That's good news," Ryan said, wiping the inside of a metallic foil bag with a finger to get the last of the military cheese. The stuff was gray, but he knew that was the normal color of cheese. Carrot juice was normally added to make it more appetizing, but he guessed the MRE packs were designed to be cheap, as well as last forever.

Placing aside an empty envelope of corned-beef hash, Mildred rinsed her spoon clean and tucked it into a pocket. "Well, if it's any comfort, there's no way the blues will never find us out here." She gestured at the empty expanse.

Removing her coat, Krysty hung the garment over a dead tree. It had felt as if she were carrying another person on her shoulders. "Hate to leave the supplies," she said, stretching. "But I suppose there's no way to haul them along.

"We can make backpacks," Ryan said, standing. Wading around the stationary raft, he peeled away the canvas sheet and took stock of the jumbled boxes. "Bare essentials. Only food and ammo. We each get one gren, J.B. gets the rest of the explosives, Mildred any medical supplies. Leave the rest."

"Dry socks," Jak added sternly. "Live in swamp, dry socks save feet."

"He's right," Mildred said, respectfully appraising the teenager. "This place is a breeding ground for fungus. We'll change our socks every time we break for food, and I'll spare some sulfur to try and keep out infections."

"Swamps," Doc muttered, fluffing the muddy frills of his shirt. "Sweet nature's toilet."

Everybody laughed, but it was Mildred's comment that struck a resonating cord within Ryan, and once again he debated the wisdom of their goal. Should they be heading for the town of Shiloh, or the site of the infamous Civil War battle? The historic Shiloh was only a few miles away from a redoubt. Shiloh ville won the debate because it was closer.

"Might as well get moving," J.B. said, wiping off his palms with a moist towelette included in the MRE pack. "Miles to go before we sleep and all that, eh, Doc?"

"Without a doubt, my friend."

As the companions rose, the raft moved unexpectedly, floating to the surface of the dirty water.

"Dark night," the man whispered in surprise. "Salt water is more buoyant than fresh."

"Is this deep enough?" Krysty asked, lifting a boot and inspecting the water-mark level.

Mildred pushed at the logs with a hand, and they moved. "Seems so, yeah."

"There's no current," Dean said, crossing his arms. "Are we going to drag it behind?"

Splashing closer, Ryan was already at the rear of the craft, lifting the mooring lines from the mulch and testing their strength. "Half of us will push," he stated, "the rest can drag."

ROWS UPON ROWS of cots filled the makeshift hospital of Front Royal, temporarily located inside the long dining hall of Cawdor Castle. The great table had been moved to the end of the hall and converted into a surgical bed, leather straps draped over the bloodstained surface to hold down the sec men who needed limbs removed or other major surgery. The ville's supply of predark ether had been used up the first day, and now the healer poured shine down the throats of his patients until they fell unconscious.

Thankfully, the screams of agony hadn't been heard in days. The seriously hurt were out of their misery, dead and buried, either from the wounds they received in battle, or from the meatball surgery trying to save them. The rest of the brown shirts and civilians lay on the simple cots, waiting for medical attention to their bullet wounds and stumps. The air reeked of feces, whiskey and blood, and the painful moaning never stopped, day or night.

Several of the local gaudy sluts moved among the patients emptying bedpans into a wheelbarrow they pushed along. In this time of emergency, everybody in the ville worked. On the other side of the long hall, a pair of children carried a steaming wooden bucket of freshly brewed tea from the kitchen. Carefully, they filled the cup next to each cot. If the cup was full, they dumped it on the floor and filled it with fresh. Made from old willow bark, Healer Mildred had said the brew would help some of the wounded with their pain. Amazingly, it did with some, but others not at all.

Kneeling alongside a sec man who had been crushed by falling rocks during the war, the new healer adjusted the folded blanket under his head. "There, is that better?" Sullivan asked softly.

"No," the sec man moaned. "Neck still hurts…"

Irritably, Sullivan grabbed the trooper by the throat and savagely twisted. There was a snap, and the patient went limp.

"See?" the mutie whispered in amusement. "I said that I could end your pain."

There was no reply.

Moving to the next patient, Sullivan found the man soundly asleep. Good. They should all fall asleep, then die. There were plenty of troops in the world to replace them, so why did Baron Cawdor worry about a few damaged people. It just made no sense. But then Sullivan's job wasn't to be logical or reasonable, just to murder the baron and leave. Nothing more. Of course, the baron was surrounded by a squad of trigger-happy sec men, so the chilling would take some special planning.

Awake, and carving a pipe from a corncob, the next patient merely had two broken legs that were setting nicely. Sullivan set the bones himself, and made the cast from leather belts and kindling. Pretending to be a healer was his easiest disguise. It was impossible to torture people for years and not to learn something about how to keep them alive. Being zealous in the questioning was a beginner's mistake. Cut off a man's hand, and he would bleed to death in minutes. Ah, but bind the arm with twine to retard the circulation, then cut off the hand, and your patient could live for days. Any damn fool could stab to death a man chained to the wall, but it took an artist to teasingly peel off every inch of skin and still keep the prisoner alive and sane.

The door to the kitchen eased open, and a woman rushed into the dining room. Adjusting the moist bandage on a burned face, Sullivan noted her arrival with interest. Few of the locals seemed to be in any hurry these days. It was as if the war had drained them of not only their strength, but also their very will to live.

The newcomer was plump and full breasted, highly attractive for her species. She looked over the hospital with obvious distaste, nose wrinkling at the pungent stink. Sullivan didn't like the smell, either. But it was either suffer the stink, or open the windows and have the patients freeze to death at night. Personally, he preferred the latter. Extremes of temperature meant little to his kind.

With a start, she saw him looming over a patient and hurried over, holding her skirts in a fist to keep the cloth from touching the dead and dying.

"Sullivan," she whispered, coming close. "They know! Run for the hills."

Placing aside the sharpened piece of reed he was using to drain a pus-filled wound, Sullivan slowly turned his head. Her eyes were lovely, and as cold and hard as his own.

"May I beg pardon?" he asked politely. "My name is Daniel Lissman and—"

"They know who you are, and why you are here!" she whispered urgently, coming closer. "They call me Terry and I work in the gaudy house. Last night I heard a couple of the troopers talking. They're going to claim the baron's wife, Tabitha, is feeling poorly, fell off a horse or something, and when you go into that room, you ain't coming out!"

"Indeed," Sullivan murmured, stuffing his hands into his pockets and thumbing back the hammers on the two snub-nosed revolvers. "And why do you call me, what was the name…Sylvester?"

Glancing over a shoulder, Terry spoke fast. "Cut the shit. I also fucked Overton's men when they were here, and aside from Ryan, you were the only thing they feared. Big guy, no hair, likes to do the dead."

"Really now!"

She sidled closer, the thick smell of stale perfume and

sweat radiating from her body. "I saw you last night at the graveyard, so don't tell me different."

Calmly, Sullivan debated the possibilities. This could be a trap by the baron to trick him into revealing himself. Or it could be the truth, a whore looking to connect to somebody more powerful for a better life.

Slowly standing to his full height, the mutie looked down at the big woman and spread his arms in a friendly manner.

"This is an interesting tale," Sullivan said, resting a hand on her shoulder. She trembled at the contact, as he increased the pressure until she thought the bones would break.

"We should discuss it in private," he added, lifting the woman a few inches off the floor and carrying her away.

Terry tried to speak, but the pain was too great.

Moving quickly, Sullivan headed for the door to the basement. Once out of sight, he could question this Terry thoroughly and learn the truth.

"Wait, Healer!" a man shouted.

Only a yard from the door, Sullivan stopped and turned, hugging Terry close to him as if they were close friends.

Maneuvering through the maze of cots, a brown shirt was rushing toward them. He was armed, but the blaster was holstered. Sullivan relaxed a little and smiled, his mind racing with new possibilities. Unexpectedly, Terry slid her arm about his waist and shook her torso to make her ample breasts jiggle. She was playing his lover. How very interesting.

"How can I help you, Lieutenant?" the mutie asked politely.

The man gulped some air. "Lady Cawdor has fallen off her horse in the stables. She can't breathe! Come quickly!"

"Oh, no!" Sullivan cried out, releasing his prisoner. Terry stayed next to him, breathing hard. He could feel the heat of her breasts through his clothing and was repulsed. "Elevate her legs at once and loosen her clothing. I'll get some instruments and be right there!"

The sec man paused for a moment, unsure of what to do.

"Go!" Terry barked. "Every second you waste could mean her life, fool!"

With a grim expression, the sec man nodded and dashed away.

"See?" Terry stated, rubbing her bruised ribs.

"You were correct," he said. "What is the price of this assistance?"

Terry leaned forward, her face shiny with avarice. "Take me with you," she demanded, almost pleading. "I'm nothing here but a slut. Somewhere else, with your help, I could marry well, become a lady. Mebbe the wife of a baron!"

It was a fair price. He thought about the offer.

"Too much," Sullivan decided, and slapped her across the face, the bones audibly cracking. Her skull partially crushed, Terry slumped to the floor, burbling blood through the ruin of her mouth. Not caring if anybody else was watching, Sullivan then kicked the woman, caving in her chest. She tumbled across the floor, arms and legs flailing like a rag doll's.

Moving to a cabinet, he ripped open a duffel bag, the old canvas patched many times with different-colored cloth until it was almost a camou pattern. Reaching inside, he started withdrawing glass bottles filled with an oily liquid, greasy rags tied about the necks.

Lighting the rags, he threw the Molotov cocktails across the room in every direction. Flames engulfed the cots, and the patients started to scream, beating at the sticky fire covering their bodies with bandaged hands. Sec men rushed in and gasped in horror. Sullivan used the diversion to ruthlessly mow them down and steal a longblaster.

Stuffing the last two bottles into his jacket pockets, the mutie stepped outside and hosed the street, shooting anybody in sight. The screaming from inside the castle continued as he darted across the courtyard, spraying controlled bursts from the Kalashnikov at the rooftops and windows. No horses or wags were in sight, so he ran for the barbican, hoping to cross the drawbridge and reach the safety of the woods. Once he was among the trees, it would take an army of guards to find him again.

A brick-lined tunnel went through the barbican of the outer wall, and several men stood in a cluster near a smoking oil drum, the ragged holes in the sides of the metal allowing the heat of the fire inside to radiate outward. Without pause, Sullivan gunned them down, dropping his blaster when it clicked empty and grabbing another weapon from one of the dead men.

A swarm of brown shirts charged from the shadows, and Sullivan kicked one in the throat. One fired a pistol, the round scoring a bloody furrow along Sullivan's cheek. The mutie shot the norm in the groin, and shoved the wooden stock of the longblaster backward, crushing the chest of another. Then a wounded brown shirt lurched from the pile of corpses and tackled him around the legs. Furious, Sullivan kicked the man aside, and another grabbed his arm. The mutie buried his teeth into the norm's throat and ripped out a chunk of flesh. He was released instantly.

Sprinting from the tunnel, Sullivan scanned the other side of the drawbridge for an ambush, saw nothing and charged for the distant woods. Freedom was only a hundred yards of open field away. A flurry of motion in the air caught his attention, and Sullivan spun, firing upward. Unharmed by the bullets, the heavy fishing nets dropped across the bridge, pinning him in place. Dropping the blaster, the mutie grabbed the line and ripped a hole. But before he could wriggle through, more netting fell from the palisades overlooking the bridge, and then a third net, a forth and a fifth. Trapped under the layers, Sullivan crouched, fumbling for a weapon when a stunning blow drove him to the wooden planks. Dazed, the mutie drew his pocket pistols and got off two rounds, when the blasters were pounded from his grasp by a horde of sec men wielding clubs.

Roaring in wild fury, Sullivan managed to stand under the combination of nets and men, struggling to reach the edge of the drawbridge and the moat below. Already the gills in his throat were opening for oxygen. Sullivan could breathe underwater, but the pitiful humans would drown.

The brown shirts struck him from every direction, but he forged onward and reached the cobblestones edging the bridge. Searing pain lanced through his shoulder, and he saw the barbed point of an arrow sticking out of his shirt. Mentally forcing away the pain, he lurched forward again and another arrow slammed into his boot, pinning his foot to the planks.

Reaching through the netting, Sullivan grabbed a knife from a brown shirt and tried slashing his way loose, when another wave of humans swarmed over him.

Pain filling his universe, he fell to the planks, never losing consciousness as he was trussed with ropes, then bound with chains.

Cradling a broken arm, a sec man spit in Sullivan's face, and another aimed a handcannon. A sergeant slapped the blaster away.

"He's trapped now, so don't chill the bastard," the brown shirt growled. "We're gonna haul his ass to the docks and hang him before the whole ville. Baron Cawdor himself is gonna tie the rope around its stinking neck!"

Cheering in victory, the joyous brown shirts lifted their captive off the bridge and hauled him back inside the ville. Masked by the nets, the mutie managed to hide a smile and calmly waited to meet the man he had been sent to kill.

Chapter Nine

Mindless miles of flat swampland stretched before the companions. In hard labor the slow hours passed, noon coming and going as they trod the sticky mud. The raft floated through the salty water, only occasionally catching on sandbars and submerged tree trunks. Rumbling storm clouds offered scant protection from the sun, and soon the swamp was steaming from the heat, sweat pouring off their bodies. Everybody stripped down as far as they dared, the bare necessities being boots and gun belts, although J.B. clung to his fedora and Mildred her med kit. Fat mosquitoes buzzed about them constantly, stealing sips of their blood until Ryan opened the fuel can and splashed some about as cologne. After that, they were left alone with the flies and the itching bites.

The barge poles hadn't been found, and none of the local trees were of any use, so Doc was on the point position, testing the unseen ground ahead of them with his swordstick. A rope was tied around his waist as a precaution, and twice he dropped into sink holes and had to be dragged back to the surface.

"I have had fun before," Doc muttered, stabbing the water and taking another step forward, "and this is not it."

"Could be worse," Mildred grunted, both hands holding tight to the rope over her shoulder. The physician had removed her damp pants and tied her shirttails in a knot between her breasts so she could take off her sports bra. Support wasn't an issue here; the temperature was. Winter in Virginia, summer in Carolina, how had any people survived when skydark destroyed the weather patterns of the world this much?

"Worse? Hades only has nine levels, madam," Doc reminded her, a half smile growing in spite of himself. He stabbed more water and found the ground acceptable. "And this would be five, or six?"

"No more than four, surely."

Holding tightly on to the wet rope over his shoulder, Ryan leaned into the task of hauling the raft. Privately, he appreciated the banter. It helped relive the boredom of the endless walking.

Just then, something bawled across the swampland, the noise echoing into the distance to be answered by another of the same.

"Gator," Jak stated, dropping the rope and drawing his Colt Python. "Stay sharp. They fast."

Checking the draw on the SIG-Sauer, Ryan heard the harsh breathing of some of the companions and decided he was pushing them too hard.

"Ten-minute break," he announced. "One sip of water each. If you've got to use a bush, go in pairs."

"Rather have some more gasoline," Krysty said angrily, slapping at a fly that landed on her bare arm. Her respect and love for life didn't quite extend to the creatures that feasted on her blood. She kept her pants on, as none of her underwear was dry enough to wear, and removed her thick shirt. The bra she had found in the California redoubt was thin lace and kept her cool enough, even if the underwire did itch a bit.

"I'll get it," Dean offered. Releasing the rope, he

disappeared under the hot canvas to reappear with the fuel can.

"Pretty low," he stated, unscrewing the cap.

Krysty cupped her hands, and the boy poured her a small splash.

J.B. stepped out of the muck onto the raft and pulled out his telescope. Extending the tube to its maximum length, he swept the horizon ahead of them.

"Could be land to the northwest," he said, adjusting the focus. "Yeah, that's green trees, pines and oak, which means dry land. Salt water would kill those."

"Distance," Ryan asked, removing the bandanna around his forehead and wringing it dry.

J.B. tucked the scope into his munitions bag. "Five miles, mebbe less."

"Excellent." Doc exhaled, spitting on his chapped hands and rubbing them together. "Under a spreading chestnut tree, the Deathlands warrior stands...."

"Stop misquoting, Longfellow," Mildred snorted, spreading some grease on her lips from a small tin box. The bearings were still in the tires under the raft, the old grease a soothing balm for the thirsty people.

Doc arched a silvery eyebrow. "Laughter is the best medicine, madam."

"Tell that to a person with rad poisoning."

"Cynic."

"Old coot."

With a warning shout, Krysty fired her blaster, the S&W .38 booming in the eerie stillness of the Carolina swamp. The others spun about, weapons searching for danger.

"Sorry," she apologized, mopping the sweat off her brow. "Thought I saw something move in the water."

Fanning himself with the hat, J.B. squinted. "Just a log."

"No, it isn't," Ryan said, wading around the raft. Drawing his panga, he stabbed the log and lifted it out of the muck. There were eyes and teeth. He twisted the blade, and the body dropped back into the swamp and sank from sight.

"A mutie snake," he stated, sheathing the blade. "Bastard bushmaster. Poisonous. Nice shooting."

"Thanks."

J.B. sneezed loudly.

The companions turned fast, their weapons level.

"We have company," the Armorer said, sliding the Uzi off his shoulder.

A humanoid being stood thirty feet away from them. It was dressed in tight clothing with most of its hairless body exposed. Tools hung off a net vest, and a sleek metal helmet covered its head, three red eyes staring out from the dark interior. The warrior was holding a long bamboo spear, tipped with a mirror-bright steel blade. Minutes passed in silence.

"Greetings," Ryan said in an even tone. The SIG-Sauer was in his hand, but not pointing at the mutie.

The swamp dweller tilted its head and clicked loudly. Surprisingly, Jak tried French. *"Parlez vous français?"*

The being craned its head forward on a long neck and clicked some more, then pointed its spear to the south, then the north.

"No farther," Krysty translated, her hair waving nervously about. "He's claiming the rest of the swamp."

Surreptitiously, Dean moved his hand to the grip of his blaster. Instantly, the mutie leveled his spear, two hands gripping the shaft as if braced against a recoil.

"It's a distance weapon of some kind," J.B. said, working the bolt on his Uzi.

"Everybody relax and put the blasters away," Ryan ordered, stepping between the mutie and the others. "Trader always used to say that it was easier to make deals than bullets. He hasn't attacked yet, and we all know he had the element of surprise."

"We are headed for the land," Ryan said slowly, in case the creature could understand. This swamp was close to Georgia, and they once found a race of underwater muties there called Dwellers. They had trouble speaking, but easily understood human speech.

"Doesn't look anything like a Dweller," Mildred noted.

The creature clicked at Ryan and dropped its spear into the water. Finally understanding, Ryan slid the Steyr off his shoulder and hung it back on upside down, then drew his blaster and dropped it on the deck of the raft. Empty-handed, the two stood face-to-face, then the creature clicked again and stepped aside.

"Thanks," Ryan said honestly. "Much appreciated."

The mutie clicked once loudly, then sank below the water, hardly making a splash or a ripple.

"Fascinating," Doc said, and walking forward he probed the swamp with his stick. The ebony shaft hit mud until he reached the spot where the mutie had been standing. There was no detectable ground there. Deciding to test the depth, he found it was beyond the limit of his stick and arm combined.

"This is the end of the swamp," Doc stated, wiping off his stick on a damp handkerchief. "We've reached deep water. Mayhap a lake, or even the original river of this area before the nukes reshaped the landscape."

Swatting at flies, Ryan studied the raft. "I think we

lost enough supplies that it'll float with all of us on board."

"Only one way to find out," J.B. said with a grin, dropping his rope.

Pushing the raft ahead of them, the companions trod water until no longer able to touch bottom. Carefully, they climbed onto the craft and saw that the salty water washed over the logs, but they stayed afloat.

"Some of us could swim alongside," Dean suggested, precariously balanced on the very edge of the raft.

Harshly, Ryan vetoed that idea. "Everybody stays on board. There could be anything swimming around down below."

"Bullets can't go very far through water," J.B. commented. "Nothing can, really."

"So we move fast," Ryan stated. "J.B., use your shotgun. I'll use the Steyr."

The Armorer stared at the water with scorn. "I guess we have to."

Going to opposite sides of the raft, the men flipped their longblasters over and started using the wooden stocks as oars, steadily stroking in unison. The others kept watch as the men slowly paddled away from the swamp and into the hidden sea. Despite the crudeness of the oars, they soon built up a good speed, and the dot of greenery expanded to a wide strip. Soon they could discern a faint smell of living plants.

"Land," Krysty said, sighing. "I'll cook dinner if somebody else gets the wood."

"A deal, dear lady," Doc said. "Chopping wood will be a delight after dragging the *Cornucopia* through mud for ten miles."

"But, once we get to dry land," Dean said, "this raft will be useless. Too bad there isn't some way to keep the cargo with us. I like having enough to eat and spare ammo.''

"Too true, lad,'' Doc rumbled.

"Got three wheels,'' Jak suggested, thumping the bottom of the raft.

Paddling in easy strokes, J.B. chewed the inside of his cheek, "Yeah, mebbe. If there's enough wood, we could make a cart and roll the stuff along. But we'd be traveling slower than shit in winter.''

"Better dump the excess, and only take what we can carry,'' Ryan decided, muscles rippling in his powerful arms as he pulled the blaster through the water. Thankfully, the Steyr had a plastic stock, but J.B. was doing irreparable harm to the tiger wood of his scattergun. "If we travel too slowly, the blue shirts will find us, rather than the other way around, and they have too many advantages as it is.''

Resting his back against the canvas mound, Doc barked a bitter laugh. "Too much ammunition. I daresay this is a problem we have never faced before.''

"Hush,'' Mildred said urgently, staring into the murky depths. "I saw a disturbance underwater.''

"Snake?'' Jak asked, drawing his blaster.

"Could be.''

Ryan and J.B. continued paddling, but watched the surface of the water carefully for any unusual movements.

Suddenly, a hundred of the beings resembling the humanoid they had encountered earlier silently rose from the water, completely surrounding the raft and its startled occupants. Each was armed with a long spear and what seemed to be a needle-thin knife made out of intricately carved bone.

"It's a trap!'' J.B. shouted, hefting the shotgun and

pumping a round into the chamber. But before he could act, the strange beings turned their backs on the humans, forming a line around the raft, their bamboo spears leveled as if for battle.

"What the—? They're here to protect us," the Armorer said in realization, lowering the scattergun.

"We do have permission to be here," Ryan noted, placing the Steyr on his lap.

"Protect us from what?" Mildred demanded suspiciously. Few folks these days knew the word *honor*, and even fewer obeyed its simple rules.

"Look there!" Krysty pointed. Something large was moving through the lake, coming straight toward the raft, the water foaming white in its wake.

The mutie from the swamp rose into view as smoothly as if it were riding an elevator. Excited, the creature waved its arms and gestured at the land, clicking so fast the noise was like a stick dragged across a picket fence.

"Thanks again," Ryan said with unaccustomed feeling. "Okay, move with a purpose, people! We've got to get to land if there's going to be trouble!"

Ryan and J.B. put their backs into stroking, and the rest of the companions started paddling with their bare hands.

"Mebbe we should stay and help," Dean suggested, bent at his task.

"Too vulnerable out here," his father barked. "On land, we can offer them assistance. But out here, we're only a liability, making them protect two things."

The boy nodded in understanding and redoubled his efforts.

With excruciating slowness, they gradually pulled away from the line of clicking beings when the raft violently shook as if it struck a rock. For a heartbeat, the companions thought that's all it was, just a rock. Then the tiny craft heaved upward, going higher and higher to finally flip over and spill them overboard.

Desperately holding his breath, Ryan grabbed the sinking Steyr before it got out of reach and started for the surface. Stroking with one arm, he got a brief glimpse of a dark shape moving among them at incredible speed. Whatever their attacker was, it wasn't one of their guardians or a rock. A submarine?

Reaching the surface, Ryan caught his breath and saw that the raft was destroyed. The logs were smashed and floating away freely, the thick chains snapped apart, the precious supplies sinking to the depths below.

"Gator!" Jak shouted, splashing around, a knife in his hand.

Kicking to stay afloat, Ryan looked at the dry land so terribly far away. "Back to the swamp!" he shouted, and started swimming in that direction.

With every kick, every stroke, the man waited to feel the crushing bite of the alligator seizing a limb. But he reached the muddy banks alive and struggled into the knee-deep water. The others were only seconds behind, and the companions moved away from the invisible border and checked their weapons.

"Everybody here?" Ryan demanded, working the bolt on the Steyr.

"Looks like," J.B. announced, cleaning the droplets off his glasses. "Dark night, was that a gator? The bastard thing must have been over thirty feet long!"

"Seen bigger," Jak commented, shaking the excess moisture out of his Colt Python.

"How did you chill it?" Mildred asked, pouring the water from her med kit to lessen its weight.

"Didn't. Aced whole ville."

"Oh, hell," Doc said, scowling at his LeMat, the fresh charge of black powder dribbling out. "Lost my swordstick, too. Can somebody loan me a blaster?"

Steyr in hand, Ryan tossed over the SIG-Sauer. Doc made the catch and expertly dropped the clip to check the ammo, then slammed it back into the butt of the pistol and jacketed the slide to chamber a round. Doc might prefer an old-fashioned revolver, but he knew how to work a modern blaster perfectly well.

"What's going to stop it?" Dean asked, checking his pockets for spare clips. He found only two; the rest had gone to the bottom.

"Grens will," J.B. stated, passing out the military spheres from his munitions bag. "Don't get crazy. That's it for explosives. One each. The rest went down with the raft."

"This is enough," Krysty said, unwrapping the electrical tape from the handle. The ball was green with a black stripe, high explosive with steel shrapnel, exactly what they needed. Too bad they had only these few charges.

Out on the watery expanse, noises and splashing were coming from under the turbulent surface. Red blood spread outward from the aquatic combat, obscuring whatever was happening.

"I don't think our friends are winning," Ryan growled.

Then a large shape rose into view. A dozen spears were sticking out of its hoary hide, but the triumphant beast had a limp warrior dangling from its huge jaws. Tossing the body aside, the gator rolled over, showing its pale belly to the sky, then dived out of sight.

Tucking the gren into a pants pocket, Krysty furrowed her brow in thought. "An animal that size can't live in this swamp," she decided. "There's not enough food. The mutie must come from somewhere else to feed on these guys when it's hungry enough. It's probably the terror of their world."

"Starving mean dangerous," Jak noted grimly.

"Well, they tried to protect us, so we return the favor," Ryan stated, making sure the panga was still in its sheath. "Besides, if they lose, it'll come after us next, and without the raft there's no way we'd last long enough in the water to ever reach land alive."

"Gator follow dry land," Jak agreed.

"Any weak points?" Mildred asked pointedly.

"Eyes, belly. Ears best, but hid."

In a rush of water, the bawling gator lifted into view again with the chief clinging to its back by a bone knife, wildly stabbing at the beast with a spear.

"Light it up!" Ryan shouted, and started firing.

The companions aimed for the head, away from the chief, but their small-caliber rounds bounced off the thick hide. Only the .357 magnum slugs from Jak's Colt Python punched holes in the gator. Then the chief came free from the mutie creature and went flying. Riding the Uzi into a tight group, J.B. sprayed half a clip of 9 mm Parabellum rounds, hoping for a lucky strike. Undamaged, the beast was gone beneath the choppy waves.

"By the Three Kennedys!" Doc shouted in frustration, and began the laborious process of cleaning and reloading the .44 LeMat. As a precaution against rain, he always keep a few charges of ball and powder inside plastic film containers. It wasn't much, but until he got fresh supplies of black powder, it was all he had for the handcannon.

Dean reloaded the Browning Hi-Power and splashed

away from the fight. "I know what to do. Jak, come with me!"

Snapping shut his Colt, the pale teenager stared at the running boy, puzzled, then smiled and took off after him.

"Hurry!" Ryan shouted, removing the spent clip from the interior of the Steyr and dropping in a fresh one.

There was some splashing nearby, and a score of the humanoids rose from the lake and shuffled onto the swamp. Some were bleeding from cuts, a few helped others walk and none looked in fighting shape. The chief stood directing the others, and Ryan could now see the being wasn't a human mutie, but more like an insect. A beautiful rainbow chitin was exposed through the slashes, and small quivering antennae were visible under the helmet, which Ryan now thought of as a crown, as only the chief had one. The smooth tan hide covering the bug was actually clothes, laced tight and with pockets. Some sort of fish hide, and not the human skin it resembled from a distance.

"It's camou," Krysty stated, "to hide their natural bright colors."

"They look like water beetles," Mildred added thoughtfully. "Only without the wings."

Ryan went to the chief and pointed toward the lake, then lifted his hand. "One?" he asked, raising a finger.

The beetle warrior gave a single click.

"Okay, there's only one of the fuckers. If it was more, we'd be running. But we can chill one gator."

"How?" J.B. asked, thumbing rounds into a spent clip.

"The mouth," Krysty replied stoically, snapping the cylinder of her weapon closed. "We let it get close, then blow it apart from the inside."

Holstering her ZKR, Mildred held out a hand. "Shotgun," she said to the Armorer, and he passed over the weapon.

A beetle stuttered loudly and threw its spear into the lake as the gator charged from the water, the shaft jutting from its head. The beast shook off the spear and plowed through the beetles, snapping one in its powerful jaws and crushing the insect. The warriors jumped on it, stabbing wildly, but the spear points could do no more damage than the 9 mm rounds of the blasters. Flipping on its back, the gator crushed a beetle and lashed its tail at another, removing the head.

"Son of a bitch!" Mildred roared, and fired the shotgun. The spray of buckshot hit the speckled hide, doing scant damage. Cursing furiously, the woman worked the pump and ejected the rest of the buckshot cartridges, then shoved in new ones from the loops on the strap.

Pulling the pin, Krysty threw the gren, and it landed in the gator's open mouth. But the beast hawked the obstruction loose and the sphere rolled into the lake and detonated, throwing water to the sky.

Startled, the beetles backed away from the blast, and the gator lashed out its tail randomly. Closing in for a kill, Mildred dived out of the way just in time, losing her grip on the scattergun. It vanished beneath the swampy brine.

The range was too close to try a gren again, so the humans pounded the beast with their weapons, dodging out of the way when it came close. The chief led the beetles back to the fight, and started launching the barbed points of their spear like crossbow bolts from the shafts. But nothing seemed to do anything more than annoy or distract the thirty-foot reptile.

Taking a stance, Doc leveled the LeMat and pulled the trigger. The percussion cap gave a bang, but the charge didn't ignite. A misfire. For the first time ever, Ryan heard the old man use a word the scholar normally pretended didn't even exist.

As if sensing a weak member in the pack, the gator charged at the gray-haired man, its stubby legs propelling it just as fast on the mud as in the water. Doc stood his ground and waited. Holding the blaster with both hands, he triggered the weapon at point-blank range. The LeMat threw flame and thunder, and the gator recoiled, hissing in pain as black blood flowed from a puckered wound in its torso. It tried circling Doc, and the man fired again, a miss. Then a piece of the mutie's scalp was blown away, exposing its bare white skull. Doc fired again and was rewarded with a dry click. Empty.

Rolling over, the gator lashed at Doc with its deadly tail. With the grace of a fencer, Doc swayed out of the way and pulled the SIG-Sauer, shooting a fast dozen times at the beast. But the 9 mm slugs glanced harmlessly off the dense hide of the giant mutie.

While the humans reloaded, the beetles rallied and launched another salvo of spearheads. By now the mutie was mad with blood lust and pain. Bawling in rage, it snapped its terrible jaws and lashed its tail, the entire lower half of its muscular body swaying from the pendulum force of the killing limb.

Aiming from the hip, Ryan fired the Steyr at a rock under the beast, and scored a ricochet into its belly, thin blood pumping from the wound. The beast turned its furious attention on him alone. Ryan braced for a charge, when there came the report of a big-bore handgun and he saw the hide of the beast spray out dark blood. Instantly, the creature shook itself as if trying to dislodge something on its skin.

Walking through the swamp, flies buzzing everywhere, Jak came on as steady as a machine, firing his .357 magnum pistol again and again, every round smacking into the mutie gator. With each impact, the gator went mad as if jabbed with white-hot pokers. Its breathing became labored, white foam dribbled from its jaws and weakly the beast charged the pale teenager.

As Jak reloaded, Mildred stepped between them and fired the wet, filthy scattergun, the fléchette round blowing off the gator's front leg. Now the animal screamed and hastily turned, hobbling for the deep waters of the lake.

Ryan and the chief both shouted as the humans and beetles converged on the killer. As the creature was no longer able to dodge, the small-caliber rounds found its eyes. Blind, it spun in a circle, lashing out with its tail and catching a beetle across the torso. But the warrior was merely knocked aside and not pulverized. The beast was weakening fast. Mildred fired again, opening its chest, and the beetles filled the wound with their spears, one penetrating more than a yard. Dark blood poured from its mouth as the dying mutie crawled relentlessly for the safety of the water. Then Ryan stepped in front of the beast and fired directly into a gaping eye socket. The gator jerked as if hitting a wall and dropped flat in the shallow swamp, a pool of blood spreading wide until it seemed to cover the entire surface of the Carolina swampland.

"That was one tough son of a bitch," J.B. stated, jerking the bolt on the Uzi to clear a jam. "What the hell was on those bullets, the snake?"

"Bushmaster," Dean said proudly, holding up the

bloody snake head for the others to see, the white fangs glistening in the afternoon light, the hollow tips moist and still dripping. "I thought of the poison, but only Jak's blaster could carry a dose."

"But my LeMat is more powerful," Doc said.

"You fire miniballs, solid slugs," Ryan explained. "The magnum was loaded with hollowpoints. Perfect for the job."

"Just a drop of venom in each," Dean boasted, "and a dab of mud to keep it there."

Doc smiled. "Good call there, young Dean. And exemplary shooting, Jak."

"Shit," Jak said, dropping the spent shells from his blaster and rinsing the weapon in the dirty water. "Big target. How miss?"

"I'm just glad it's chilled," Krysty stated wearily. She looked around for a place to sit, and saw nothing.

Mildred straightened from examining the still form. "It's snuffed," she reported. "No doubt of that."

Shuffling forward, the chief offered his spear to Jak. The teenager grunted in thanks, and Dean offered the bushmaster in return. It was accepted reverently, then the chief called out a series of long clicks. The surviving warriors waved their gory spears overhead and swarmed over the gator hacking it to pieces. Whether for food, or just to make sure it was really dead, none of the companions knew or cared.

"Now what?" Dean asked, rinsing his hands in the brine.

Ryan slung the longblaster over a shoulder and looked at the distant speck of green. "We start swimming."

Chapter Ten

Reaching the shoals of the island, the companions climbed wearily over the exposed tangles of tree roots and finally reached dry land. Going inland, they found pine trees growing thick along the shoreline, the ground covered with needles. Drained, the friends dropped to the soft carpeting and fell asleep almost immediately. Ryan found himself to be the last one awake, and dragged over a rock to sit on as he took first guard duty.

Hours later, Krysty awoke and relieved him at the post. Choosing a spot, Ryan lay down and finally allowed himself to succumb to exhaustion. This had been a long and hectic day.

RYAN AWOKE to the smell of coffee and roasting meat. Sitting upright, he pushed aside the blanket covering him and stared at the boxes and crates dotting the campsite.

A fire was crackling in a pit, and the carpet of needles had been cleared away from any possible flying embers. J.B. was stirring something in a pan that sizzled, and the coffeepot bubbled softly, emitting the most tantalizing aroma. On guard duty, Mildred was sitting with her back to a pine tree, blaster in hand. There was no sign of the others.

"We got our supplies back," J.B. said in greeting, using a knife to flip over some meat in the pan. "The beetles retrieved most of the stuff from the bottom of the lake. They even found Doc's swordstick and my hat."

"Damn nice of them. How bad is it?" Ryan asked, pouring himself a cup of coffee. The smell alone invigorated the man. He understood how predark folks could get hooked on the brew.

Using a sock to protect his hand, J.B. took the iron pan off the fire and slid a steak onto a tin plate from an Army mess kit. "Good and bad," he remarked, passing over the food. "The ammo is fine. The boxes are airtight, and the brass was only underwater a short while. No problem there. We got back four more grens and two Claymore mines. We found a fresh-water spring inland a couple of hundred paces from here. Have to boil it first to be sure, but it reads clean."

"And," Ryan prompted, cutting into the meat. It was tough but edible. He guessed it was some of the gator from yesterday.

"Everything else is gone, including the last rocket launcher. We barely have enough food for another day. A lot of the MRE packs got opened when the raft was torn apart, and more floated away. I think the beetles stole some, but probably because they were pretty. Not for the food. They have enough meat to feed a whole ville for a month. The can of fuel is gone, as well as all of the medical supplies, bedrolls, rope and the tent canvas. That is our only pan. So if you want hot food with the steak, you have to wait till it's washed."

"This'll do," Ryan answered with a full mouth. Hunger was the best sauce.

"On the other hand," J.B. added, gesturing with his head, "that huge roll of leather over there is the gator. They skinned the huge bastard and gave us the hide."

"Guess it's a reward for helping them." Ryan

grinned, wiping his mouth on his hand. "Make nice boots."

"Weighs a ton."

"So I would guess, but we can't leave it. That would insult the chief." Ryan laid the plate aside. "Just stuff it in the big duffel bag with some salt to keep the smell down. When we're a couple of miles from here, we'll throw it away."

"Speaking of awful smells," Mildred said, tossing a bar of soap on the ground at his boots, "you'll find the spring a hundred feet to the north."

Ryan tucked the bar into a shirt pocket. Breakfast had disguised the odors for a while, but now the stink of the swamp muck, mixed with dried gator blood and sweat, was returning strong. "Anybody else there?"

"Everybody washed earlier. It's all yours."

Taking his weapons, Ryan moved through the pine trees, easily finding the spring. Clear water bubbled from the ground, forming a still pool, and Ryan checked the area. The water was crystal clear, and nothing could get within ten feet of him without being seen first. Stripping, the one-eyed man washed his clothes to get out the stink of the swamp, then hung them over some bushes to dry in the sunlight. Next, he grabbed a handful of pine needles and rubbed them vigorously into his combat boots to remove the sour smell of sweat and sulfur.

Making sure his blasters were within easy reach, Ryan submerged his tired body in the pool and scrubbed himself clean using the tiny bar of soap from an MRE pack and some more pine needles. He was surprised at the amount of grime that came out of his hair, and on impulse decide to shave using his knife. When finished, Ryan felt enormously refreshed and lay on the bank of the spring to let the warm breezes dry him off.

There was a rustle in the bushes, and he drew the blaster with lightning speed as Krysty walked into view.

"Hi, lover," she said, smiling. "Nice view."

Immediately, Ryan felt himself stirring under her frank gaze. "You missed breakfast," he said, clicking the safety back on.

She sat and kicked off her boots. "Had mine earlier. Doc and I have been on recce. Dean spotted some smoke drifting over the trees, and we followed it to a ville about five miles away. Good walls. No rads. Seems okay."

His interest shifted to their mission. "Any chance of getting a wag there?"

Krysty stroked his cheek, tracing a fingertip along the jagged scar. The man wore his life on his body, the network of healed wounds telling more than anything else could. He was a stone-cold killer when necessary, and yet would share food with strangers—when there was extra. No starry-eyed dreamer who lived on wishes, he was the ultimate pragmatist, and yet many times during their travels they helped save villes he might never see again. Ryan only wanted to live in peace, but constantly shook the world until its teeth rattled. Krysty considered him the only real man she had ever known.

"Ask me that again later," the redhead whispered, slowly unbuttoning her shirt.

THE SUN WAS HIGH when the companions left the pine island and headed for the mainland. They were carrying all of the remaining supplies, along with the gift from the beetle warriors. A narrow land bridge crossed the inlet, and soon they were walking through fields of scrub grass. Broken stone walls sectioned the landscape, showing that the area used to be farms at one time. Mountains rose in the far distance, the rocky crags seeming to support the ominous dark clouds filling the sky.

A beaten path wound through the grassy fields and windswept arroyos. Soon the companions reached a flattened dirt road leading toward the high stockade of a ville. The outer wall was made of logs and stones, rising to twice a man's height, the top bristly with sharp sticks and a few strands of rusty barbed wire.

Sec men armed with homemade blasters stood guard at the open gateway, the man and woman watching the companions closely as they approached. The guards were tense about the open display of blasters, but they said nothing as Ryan and the others walked into the ville.

"They must get a lot of outlanders," Krysty surmised.

Ryan frowned. "Or the guards are fools."

Inside the walls, they found a bustling community built from the remains of a predark city. The houses and buildings were arranged in orderly rows, the streets clean hard-packed dirt. A gallows stood by itself, though no rope dangled from the killing bar. People walked about carrying baskets and buckets. The aroma of frying fish was in the air, along with the smell of horses.

"Whoever built this place knew what they were doing," Mildred said in admiration. "See how far apart the lavs are from the public water well? No cholera here."

"Good defenses," Ryan agreed, gesturing to tall towers made from felled trees. Sec men stood guard holding crossbows, with strange curved axes hanging from thongs at their hips.

"Throwing axes," Jak noted while straightening his collar, being very careful of the razor blades hidden within the fabric. "Mighty hard learn, kill good."

Doing a recce, the companions entered the ville commons and watched a potter spinning bowls from red clay, a horde of children staring in fascination at the process. A fat woman was selling beer from a tub, while a white-hair tailor mended the shirt still on a burly man and a barber cut hair.

"Civilization," Mildred said, sighing. "Such as it is."

"Better than that junkyard ville," Dean stated.

"True enough."

Ryan worked the slide on his SIG-Sauer, ejecting a live round. The brass spun in the air and he caught the bullet, returning it to the clip.

"Now they know we're armed and have ammo," he said, holstering the piece, "that should hold down the chilling."

The crack of a whip made Doc stop in the street, a hand going to his swordstick. "Mother of God," he muttered.

Near a kindergarten jungle gym, now a coop full of cackling chickens, a line of people tossed shafts of grain on a millstone. The great slab of granite rotated along on top of another, grinding the wheat into flour. Four thick poles embedded in the top stone were being pushed along by a dozen people in chains, their backs bent to the arduous task. An overseer watched their progress and touched up their speed with the flick of his bullwhip.

"Slaves," Doc said, starting forward.

Ryan stopped him with a grip of iron. "We don't have the time or the firepower," he said harshly. "First we take care of ourselves, then we'll see what can be done about the slaves. Forget it for now."

Radiating fury, Doc glared at Ryan, a vein in his forehead pulsating steadily. He knew the one-eyed man had never been a slave of another. A captive, yes. Forced to work and kill for some baron's amusement, yes. But never a slave, and so he couldn't really know the emotions welling within him. Slowly, the old man relaxed his stance. "Yes, you are correct," Doc rumbled. "It is not a matter to be taken care of today."

Ryan nodded and continued walking.

Leaving the marketplace in their wake, the companions reached a strip mall from predark days. The display windows were long gone, replaced with wooden boards, but it was still a mall. The supermarket was now a tavern, the bank a gaudy house. Some local toughs lounged outside, chatting to a young woman with an old face. Upon seeing Ryan walking their way, the men took their leave.

"Hey, miss!" J.B. called to the woman. "Over here!"

Dressed in the loose, revealing clothes of her trade, the blonde ambled toward them and opened her blouse, exposing small but pert breasts.

"Whatcha want, stud?" she asked coyly. "I'll do ya right here for some of that brass I saw you flashing. Or we can go to my tent if you're shy. I'm Dancing Feather, the hottest slut here, no matter what that bitch at the Red Bear tavern says."

"That's not what we want," Ryan said, withdrawing a single 9 mm round and bouncing it in his palm. "Tell us about this place. Who's in charge?"

The whore beamed a smile and closed her blouse, stealing a quick jealous glance at Krysty and Mildred.

"Old man Polk is the baron here," she said, sidling closer and reaching out for the bullet. "He's okay. Finds us enough to eat each winter, don't allow no rape in public. But ya better hop when he says frog, or you'll serve the wheel. Any sec man can load that in his blaster and fire it."

So that's where the slaves at the grinding stone came

from—local criminals slow to obey. Ryan withdrew his hand. "More."

Placing hands on hips, she glared in hostility, then burst into laughter. "Okay, fair dealing. This is Flat Rock ville, and unless you're a stupe, that's obvious." She jerked her head toward a squarish boulder in the middle of the ville located near an empty flagpole and a World War II howitzer in remarkably good condition.

"Get a lot of strangers?" Krysty asked.

"I sure do!" Feather grinned, wiggling her hips suggestively, then ceasing the act since it was getting her nowhere. "Yeah, sometimes outlanders arrive, but not very many these days of the mutie in the water. Big nasty thing, lots of teeth and—"

"Not interested," Ryan interrupted. "Is there a stable where can we buy horses?"

"Buy a horse?" Feather gasped. "You that rich?"

Ryan said nothing.

She shrugged. It wasn't her business. "Go down the street, past the burned-down church. Then follow your nose."

Ryan tossed her the bullet. "Thanks."

Tucking the round someplace safe, the slut watched them walk away. The bullet would buy her a week of sleeping under a roof and all the stale bread she could eat. And just for talking. Outlanders were idiots. Then she reconsidered that. Mebbe they really did have enough jack to buy horses. They certainly gave up a brass easy enough.

Heading across the town, the companions passed numerous folks in the street, many of them carrying long poles tipped with curved blades or heavy nets laced with dull copper wiring.

"Gator hunters," J.B. guessed.

Shifting the duffel bag on his shoulder, Jak snorted. "Too late."

Beyond a hole in the ground filled with rubble and stained glass, Ryan found their goal. The stable was a former gas station, the horses corralled in the service bays, water troughs where the fuel pumps used to be located. The office was now living quarters, ratty furniture resting on bricks instead of legs. Iron grates covered the window, and curtains made from shag carpet had been hung to afford some level of privacy.

Ryan knocked on a metal sign bearing the logo of a winged horse. "Customers!" he called out. "Anybody home?"

Out of a back room walked a man with a protruding belly, his clothes covered with food stains, a throwing ax in his hand.

"Oh, just outlanders." He grimaced. "No jobs here. Got a stable boy for the mucking. Try the farms north of here."

"We're here to buy," Ryan said, lifting a fistful of rounds from his pocket. The action also showed the SIG-Sauer resting on his hip. The demeanor of the stable owner changed on the spot.

"Well, well! Why didn't you say so?" he gushed, tossing aside the ax and rushing over to push up the garage doors. They rose with a squeal of tortured metal, and he stepped inside. "Want a horse, do you? Fat Tom got the best in the world."

"Highly doubtful," Mildred commented, wrinkling her nose at the smell of used hay and fish-oil lanterns.

A scrawny stable boy sat in the corner, polishing a saddle with spit and a wad of congealed grease. Mounds of dirty hay covered the stained concrete, and split rails sectioned the repair shop into a double row of small stalls. Horses of various colors stood in each, nibbling hay, and watching the humans with fearful expressions. Obviously, they were beaten into submission and not won over with kindness. Ryan immediately classified the stable owner as a coward. There was no other reason to beat animals who delighted in working for humans. Men with horses had conquered most of the old world, because they enjoyed being together.

"Not bad," J.B. said diplomatically, thinking he wouldn't want to store shit here. "How many do you have?"

"Ten," Tom said proudly, picking his ear. "But one's a swayback we'll be eating this winter, and two are colts not strong enough to carry a baby."

Walking among the animals, Ryan studied them carefully. Good legs and withers. No sign of split hooves or mange. Their coats were rough, with burrs caught in the tails. The horses needed a serious currying, but otherwise were in good health.

"We'll take them," Ryan decided.

"Which two? Or did you want three, mebbe?"

Her cascade of fiery hair gently waving, Krysty held out a hand and stroked one of the nervous beasts. The animal instantly calmed and nuzzled her palm affectionately. "We're buying all seven."

Fat Tom roared in laughter, his belly bouncing. "Not even Baron Polk has that much jack! I need some for working the fields. You gonna feed my family this winter? Thought not."

"Trade you," J.B. said, dropping the duffel bag to the ground.

The stable owner stroked his greasy chin. "Your redhead doesn't look like she has the coughing sickness. Of course, I'd want to inspect her cunny first before taking a ride, but if she's any good, I'd trade you two horses for an hour with her.''

"That's fifty-nine minutes longer than you would be breathing," Krysty said, low and cold, her blaster partially drawn.

The man cackled and slapped a knee. "Good un! She's a fireblast, that one. Redheads, God love 'em.''

"Try again," Ryan stated in a voice of granite.

"Well, I'll trade four horses for that fancy scattergun, four eyes.''

"In your dreams." J.B. frowned.

Fat Tom shrugged. "Just talking. No offense meant.''

Sensing the bargaining was getting serious, Ryan lowered his backpack to the floor and withdrew an oily blanket. Unwrapping the bundle, he hauled into view a AK-47 without a stock.

"Nuke me," the man whispered, reaching for the weapon and drawing his hands away before touching it. "That a rapid fire?''

"Eight hundred rounds a minute.''

He snorted. "Ain't that much ammo in the whole world!''

Ryan didn't contradict the man. "We have two clips, one with ten live rounds, the other empty. Plus, fifty spent rounds you can reload. The stock is gone, but you can whittle a new one.''

"Ten rounds for a rapid fire. That's one trigger click. No deal." Then he added, "Besides, got a blaster. Made it myself.''

Ryan had spotted the weapon hanging on the wall when they first entered. It was made of corroded iron pipes bound together with rusty barbed wire and leather straps. He doubted if the shotgun would work more than once without blowing apart. Suddenly, he knew the local was lying for some reason, and shifted his position to keep a watch on the garage doors.

J.B. dropped the heavy duffel bag. "Well, you haven't got one of these."

Squinting suspiciously, Fat Tom watched as J.B. opened the drawstrings and lifted out the roll of hide.

"Aw, I don't need a coat," Tom sniffed. "Never gets bad cold down here."

With a flip, J.B. unrolled the skin, sending it across the floor of the stable almost reaching the door. "It's not a jacket, you fat fool," he stated. "This is the hide of the gator from the swamp. That's a hundred pairs of boots, plus gun belts and some jackets."

"No, it can't be." Tom touched the wide expanse of hoary skin in disbelief. "You chilled Frankenstein."

"Just a gator," Jak corrected.

"A dead gator." Licking his lips, the stable owner looked at the companions. "Well now, that is a lot of strong leather. Yeah, sure, I'll trade you seven horses for ole Frank."

"Plus tack," Krysty added, the chestnut mare licking her palm. She had already decided on which horse she would ride.

"Of course, of course," he muttered, fingering the hide. Even marked with scars, burns and bullet holes, the durable skin was still beautiful, and flexible. He could probably make bulletproof vests from the stuff and sell them to barons for a fortune. Ammo, food and sluts till he died.

"Anything you want," the man said, beaming. "Saddles and reins. Blankets, too. I wouldn't want to cheat you on the trade. Fair deal Tom, that's me. Ask anybody above the soil."

With instincts honed in a hundred trades, Ryan knew

that was too much, too fast. The hide had to be worth a hell of a lot more than they thought possible. "Eight," he corrected, testing the limits of the deal. "Plus tack, plus feed."

"But there's only seven of you!"

"And we'll need one to haul supplies."

"Oh, use the boy," Tom countered hotly. "He's young and strong, why burden a horse? They're expensive."

The stable boy was cowering, and new shadows appeared on the wall from people standing in the doorway.

"Incoming," Ryan said with a smile.

Tom scratched his head. "What's that mean, huh?"

"I know," J.B. answered, pulling the Uzi in front of him.

Doc crossed his arms and rested a hand on the LeMat. "Could be friendlies," he hedged.

There came the click-clack of a blaster, and Ryan spun, shooting from the hip just as the man with the shotgun fired. A sprinkling of buckshot took Ryan in the shoulder as he dived for cover. Fat Tom started pleading as the stocky man in the doorway fired again, blowing the plump man off the floor.

"Three, two, one," Ryan said, standing.

In unison, the companions unleashed a volley of lead. Torn to pieces, the attacker fell into the trough, the scattergun breaking in two as it hit the ground. A line of holes in the trough began to leak water. Then a flurry of arrows hissed into the stable, thudding into the split rails, posts and walls.

"There's more," Krysty announced, snapping off shots. Nearby, Fat Tom lay dead on the floor, his guts splattered over the wall and dribbling onto his shocked face.

Crouched behind a bale of hay, J.B. shoved the Uzi over the top and fired a short spray. A man cried out, but it sounded fake.

"It's the assholes from the tavern," Ryan said, clearing a jam.

"Bitch Feather," Jak snarled.

"No, this is my fault," Ryan stated harshly. "I wasn't paying attention for once. Not a blaster in sight here, and we come waltzing in with an arsenal. Of course somebody is going to try and chill us."

An ax flew between the horses and slammed into the floor, biting inches into the wood, missing Doc's hand by a hair. He withdrew quickly.

"They will try," Doc corrected, watching the doorway that led to the living quarters. A figure darted into view, and he snapped off a shot from the LeMat, catching the man in the throat. Clutching his shredded flesh, the man stumbled and fell, quietly bleeding to death in the doorway.

The horses were whinnying in fear, making it hard to hear movements outside. "You there, boy," Krysty demanded, crawling on her belly. "Where's the back door?"

"Ain't got one," the boy whimpered, huddled in the corner. "Just the front."

"Ladder to the hayloft?"

"The what?"

"Where you store the hay!"

The boy gestured at the floor.

In understanding, Krysty cursed the slovenly stable owner. There was no way out, and they were trapped in a tinderbox. "Sure hope they don't want to burn us out!" she muttered.

"That would chill the horses," J.B. said, firing at the

ground and hitting a booted foot. The owner screamed, fell into view and was chilled. "They can't get us, and we can't leave. It's a standoff."

"So what do we do?" Dean asked, sliding a fresh clip into his gun. Surrendering their blasters wasn't an option. They would only get chilled afterward as the coldhearts laughed at their stupidity.

"Change rules," Jak said, holding his breath as he fired his .357 magnum pistol. A rope overhead snapped, and the first door to the garage rolled to the ground in a loud crash. The teenager tried the same trick again, but the second door only slid halfway before getting stuck. The third didn't move an inch.

"Use the horses," Ryan said, wriggling between the rails of a stall. The nervous animal reared at his presence, but Ryan soothed the horse with soft words. When it was calm, he laid a sack of feed across its back, then draped over a blanket, cinching it tight with some reins.

Moving quickly, the others did the same. Then whooping and firing their blasters, they chased the beasts out of the stable. The horses stampeded for freedom, charging into the street past the waiting gang of coldhearts.

"Fuck!" cried one, nearly trampled in the rush. "See those lumps? They're on the damn horses!"

"Could be a diversion," said another, notching a steel arrow into his crossbow. The deadly weapon was carved from solid oak, the steel bow salvaged from a predark car chassis. His crossbow could drill a three-pound bolt through a man at two hundred paces. Silent, and reusable, it was his preferred weapon. He only wanted the blasters for what they would buy—women, more arrows and jolt. Lots of jolt.

Charging inside, the coldhearts found the stable empty. "If they're not on the horse, or in here—" a man started to say.

A sharp whistle made them spin, and the companions cut loose from the living quarters, the barrage of rounds tearing the attackers apart, limbs flailing from the multiple impacts of hot lead.

When the smoke cleared, Ryan took the point and entered the stable, checking the bodies to make sure none were only pretending to be dead. Without remorse, he dispatched a pair who seemed remarkably undamaged. After gathering their backpacks, the companions walked from the stable and found a squad of sec men racing their way.

"Here come the Marines," Mildred quipped, shifting the med kit over her shoulder to a more comfortable position. She knew Ryan was wounded, but there was little blood, and now wasn't a good time for repairs.

"What the fuck is going on here?" the sec man in the front demanded, a loaded crossbow in steady hands. His head was shaved, except for a thick lock hanging from the back, and his clothes were old but clean. A quiver of arrows was draped over his shoulder, and zip gun was tucked loosely into a holster designed for a much larger pistol.

"Who are you?" Ryan demanded, the stock of his longblaster resting on a hip.

The man scowled. "I am Corporal Anson, sec chief for Baron Polk, and I ask the questions here, outlander. Now for the second and last time, what happened?"

"Dueling is forbidden, you know," another sec man added.

"Does this look like a duel?" Dean retorted.

The second man shrugged. "Could be."

Ignoring the fool, Ryan addressed the corporal. "We

just arrived today and came here to buy horses, when a gang tried to back-shoot us. They aced Fat Tom, and we aced them. No duel, just a straight theft.''

"Ratter, you alive?" Anson called into the stables.

A pile of hay shifted, and the stable boy crawled into view. "I didn't see nothing," the youth said standing meekly. "I was working hard."

"Hell boy, that's what you always say," the sec man grumbled.

"Can I go?" Ratter pleaded.

Anson swatted at the boy. "Git!"

Ratter dodged the blow and scampered out of sight around the stables.

Taking his time, the corporal studied the companions. "Well, your story sounds legit, but I think we'd best go talk with the baron. He doesn't like killing in his ville."

"Unless he authorizes it," Ryan said.

"Is it different where you come from?" Anson asked bluntly.

"No," Ryan admitted, slinging the blaster over his undamaged shoulder. "Lead the way. Mebbe we can talk some business with the boss."

The corporal eased off the string on his crossbow. "It has been known to happen. That is, if he decides not to hang you."

"Fair enough."

"Looking to become a sec man by any chance, there's lot of openings."

"Not likely," Ryan answered, then tried a shot in the dark. "We have info on Frankenstein."

"You do?" Anson asked, excited. "What kind of information?"

Satisfied his hunch was correct, Ryan smiled and said no more.

AFTER THE PEOPLE had gone, Feather snuck into the stable and found Ratter looting the kitchen of food. Tiptoeing close, she hit the boy over the head with a stone, and he dropped to the floor. Unsure of his condition, Feather hit him a few more times until the blood ran freely from his mouth and nose.

Tossing the stone away, Feather grabbed the bag and finished the job he started, then left quickly.

As she pelted down the streets, the gaudy slut chortled in her newfound wealth: a bag of food, weapons, clothes and a bullet. The old doomie in town had been right—this was her lucky day! Pity about what the mutie had foretold about the outlanders. The black-haired cyclops seemed nice. Too bad he was going to die.

Chapter Eleven

"He will lie," said the female mutie, leaning on the table, "but believe every word."

Lunch long done with, Baron Jackson Polk looked up from the crumbling book on chemistry he was struggling to read and stared at the doomie. "What was that?" the man asked.

Althea said nothing for a moment, listening to the silence of the throne room. The predark auditorium was shaped like a seashell, with a raised dais at the apex of the truncated cone. Radiating outward across the room were hundreds of seats, and the softest whisper on stage would carry to the farthest reaches. Simply amazing. Many of the farmers and fishermen thought it was magic, and secretly worshiped the wizard baron. Knowing a good thing when he heard it, Polk did nothing to change their opinion, and having a doomie for a lover only helped his mystique of being more than just a man.

Her solid white eyes seeing nothing, the beautiful mutie came closer and took his hand. "The black man with one eye," Althea whispered, "he will lie, but believe every word. He has come to kill, has already killed and must kill more. His destiny is in blood and fire."

"An assassin?" Polk asked, probing for details.

"Yes and no. He hasn't come for you, doesn't know you, cares not for you. He seeks the sky killer who threatens the world."

"Sky killer. A plane?"

The woman wobbled on her feet, and the baron snapped his fingers. A servant appeared to slide a chair into place before she fell. Polk waited until Althea caught her breath. When he'd first found the mutie woman ten years ago, he took her to his bed because she was blind. His disfigurements were such that he couldn't stand to have another person see him without the robes of state. Then Polk learned of her gift and realized what a treasure the doomie was. Twice in his reign as baron, Althea had foretold of attacks by coldhearts, giving them enough time to prepare a deadly welcome for the raiders, and once she warned him of a close friend who plotted to chill him and become baron. Sadly, that also come true. Althea was always correct.

But now the baron wondered if her gift of seeing the shadows of the future had driven her over the edge into madness. Believe a liar—what was the point in that? Besides which, she always reminded him that the future wasn't set in stone. Sometimes when they were alone in his chambers, Althea spoke of karma, a person's destiny, but also of yarma, a person beating karma through courage and wisdom.

"Some water, my dear?" Polk suggested, pushing the carafe forward. There was no response. "Wine, then?"

"I need sleep," Althea whispered, and walked from the throne room holding her temples.

The moment she was gone, a sec man entered the throne room and shouted, "My lord, several of the fishing captains request an audience."

"Let them enter," Polk commanded, rolling his chair to the edge of the dais.

When the sailors arrived, they took seats in the first row and were forced to crane their necks to look at the baron. Polk could smell the salt and tar on them even from his elevated vantage point.

He glowered down at them. "Well?"

Twisting a cloth cap in craggy hands, a big man in rough-hewn clothes stood, "I'm Dwight Lane, captain of the *Dixie Rebel.* Baron Polk, the big swamp mutie aced another five of my men yesterday when it ripped apart my nets and stole a full day's catch of fish. My lord, our crews are starving, and each has lost kin to the mutie."

"Some of us have lost more than that," Polk stated forcibly, his anger readily present.

"Of course, sir," Lane said, smiling uncomfortably. "Now, what we would like, with your permission, is to organize the crews of our five ships, and the whole ville, into a single hunting party to track down and kill the thing!"

"Useless," the baron stated. "Without blasters, nobody stands a chance against the behemoth. Plus, there are the bugs to worry about. A hunting party that size could easily be thought of as an invasion force, and while we're hunting the beast, they're burning our homes."

"But something must be done!" Lane shouted.

Another captain stood, a grizzled sea dog with weathered skin like canvas. "I was born here, my lord, but I'll be leaving on the next high tide. Living be hard enough without working every other day to feed that hell demon!"

"Give us the secret of the black powder!" another shouted.

"We'll make blasters and hunt it down ourselves."

"Then turn against me," Polk stated.

"To kill ole Frank!"

"Don't bother," Ryan called, walking down the center aisle. "We already chilled the gator."

Murmurs ran through the crowd of people, some frightened, others disbelieving, as the ville sec men led the way for the heavily armed outlanders. The strangers were carrying more blasters than anyone had ever seen before.

Drawing a flintlock pistol from under his blanket, Polk used both hands to cock back the striking hammer. Their leader was a big man with hair black as midnight, and a patch covered one eye. But Althea spoke of a black man with one eye. This fellow was close, but clearly not the killer she spoke about.

"Who are you?" Polk demanded.

"Outlanders from the north, my lord," Anson announced. "They had some trouble with Fat Tom, a horse merchant who tried to steal their weapons."

"And they chilled him first," Polk deduced. "The man was a coward and a thief. Good riddance."

"What was that you said about ole Frank being dead?" Lane asked. "Is it true?"

"Lies," another sailor said scornfully. "They're not from here, why should they care?"

"We don't," Ryan replied. "It attacked, so we chilled it. Nothing more."

"Big words," Polk said slowly. "Prove it. Bring the body in here."

Ryan met the man's gaze. "How much is the reward?" A public statement was what the one-eyed man wanted, something the baron couldn't pretend had never been agreed upon. A man's word was often only as good as the number of people who heard it.

The baron rolled to the very edge of the stage, the front wheels of his chair hanging off the edge. "Everybody from the Dead Swamp to the ravine knows I posted a bounty on the mutie. What is it you want? Blasters? I'll pay you blasters.''

''Got them, and better than you have,'' Ryan said in frank honesty. ''But we could use some horses.''

''One each,'' Polk stated. ''My very best, with full tack.''

''We also need to carry supplies.''

Polk grew grim. ''Enough haggling. Ten of my top animals and all the ammo and food you can carry without breaking your bones. Just prove to me it's dead!''

The man threw off the blanket, and his pant legs were flat with nothing inside. ''He took my legs and my son on the same day. If you knew my hatred of the beast, you'd shit with fear. Now, if you truly took care of Frankenstein, I'll pay your price. But if this is a trick, you won't leave this room alive.'' Somehow, only those last words echoed throughout the auditorium.

Sliding the duffel bag off his shoulder, J.B. tossed it onto the floor. ''There, all the proof you should need.''

Impatiently, Baron Polk snapped his fingers, and servants rushed to gathered the bag. Opening it under his supervision, they removed the leathery roll and spread it across the stage.

It was thirty feet long, eight wide, the colors matched and there was the scar from his own pistol! The baron couldn't believe it. This was the hide of the monster, every bullet hole and ridge layer of rough hide forever burned into his memory from that awful day.

''How?'' he weakly whispered.

''We joined forces with the beetle warriors,'' Ryan said. ''They helped a lot. Mean fighters.''

Lane sneered. ''The clicks? Bah, man, nobody has seen them in years. They're breathing dirt.''

"We fought side by side with their chief yesterday afternoon," Ryan stated. "Nice folks, once you get to know them."

Polk waved the trifle of the beetles aside. He didn't care if they laid claim to the Dead Swamp and Salt Lake. They were of no conceivable use to him.

"So it's finally over, the beast is dead. Truly dead." Polk sat up straight in his chair. "Name your price."

"Exactly what we agreed upon. Ten horses and supplies, blankets, food enough for a week. A tent if you have any."

"We don't."

"Then some canvas will do, and we'll make a tent."

"And explosives," J.B. added.

"Are you insane? "

"We had a deal," Ryan reminded harshly.

"And I will honor that," Polk retorted. "But not at the expense of my people. Horses, tack, food, blankets and such, all you can carry. Shine and women, all you want. But not one live round and no explosives of any kind. I won't have you strip this ville defenseless. Understood?"

"Black powder," Doc added. "One pound."

The man chewed his cheek for a while in thought. "Who says we got any?"

Doc glared. "I heard the earlier conversation as we entered, and I have seen your cannon, sir. It is a fully functioning weapon."

"That it is," Polk said with pride. "Half a pound, no more.

"Done?"

"Done," Ryan said.

Polk turned his attention to the others in the throne room. "Captain Lane, I believe we now have nothing further to discuss. So I shall expect the quota of fish delivered to my ville to be doubled by the next moon. Anything less will be considered theft from me and dealt with harshly.''

"Of course, Baron," the man managed to say without stuttering.

As the fishermen took their leave, Polk turned to a waiting steward. "Get a carpenter and nail this on the wall behind my throne," he directed him. "Let everybody see that ole Frank is dead."

"At once, Baron," the liveried man said with a bow.

"Now, as for you outlanders," Polk said genially. "Please stay for dinner. I wish to hear the details of the matter."

Apprehensive, Ryan glanced at his friends. They seemed uneasy, too, but he couldn't think of a polite way to refuse.

"Certainly, Baron," he said. "Our pleasure. But we do need to leave first thing in the morning."

"Why the rush? Stay awhile. I have a great need for people with your talents."

"Sorry, but we have to find some friends," Ryan said evenly.

Polk nodded. "And chill them. Yes, I can see it in your faces. Fair enough. You did your part, and I will do mine."

THE COMPANIONS CHECKED the horses and supplies as they were delivered to the courtyard of the ville, and everything was in fine shape. Dinner proved to be sixteen different things done to fish, and a roasted opossum. The companions ate the food, but Jak was in heaven. He stuffed himself with four portions and had to loosen his belt when they finally left the table for cigars and brandy. Around midnight, Polk took his leave, and the companions were left to their own devices. Doc, Jak and Dean excused themselves, while the rest took advantage of the baron's liquor cabinet. The brandy was merely winter wine, but strong flavored with plenty of kick.

"Too bad Clem decided to stay at Front Royal," Mildred said, sipping her drink. "We could have used him fighting that damn mutie. The man is a hell of a shot."

"He wasn't so hot," J.B. muttered. "Just an unwashed mountain man. Completely useless."

Ryan and Krysty remained neutral to the conversation, sensing a personal matter going on.

Wiggling closer, Mildred pressed a warm hip against the man. "I know that Clem liked me," she said, "but there's my medical condition to consider."

Glasses in hand, J.B. stared at her in total confusion.

Mildred took his hand. "I have a very small heart, and there's only room for one man there."

Speechless, J.B. squeezed her hand with all of his strength. If it hurt, she said nothing. Releasing her, J.B. rose and strode out of the room. Mildred sighed and sipped at her drink again.

"Damn men and their idiot pride," Krysty said, sloshing her drink as she gestured. "You better go have your way with him right now."

"That was my plan," Mildred said with a smile, placing aside her unfinished brandy. "See you in the morning."

"Remember how shy I was when we first met?" Ryan said with a grin as the woman strode from the room.

Krysty stared at the man over the rim of her glass. "You damn near forced me on the spot. I barely was able to seduce you in time."

Reaching out a hand, Ryan gently stroked her living

hair, and the woman trembled under his touch. "Mebbe we should go to bed ourselves."

She hiccuped. "My plan exactly."

WALKING ALONE through the quiet street, Doc paused in the darkness just outside the circle of light from a crackling campfire.

"Hey, there," he called to the group, "mind if I join you?"

Dropping the chicken leg he had been gnawing, the overseer stood up with a hand on his bullwhip. The big man had his weight equally balanced on both feet, and Doc knew immediately this was a trained killer. He had expected no less.

"Whatcha want?" the overseer growled dangerously.

"To get warm." Doc grinned. "Maybe talk some business."

"Yeah?"

"Of course."

As Doc approached, the slaves whispered among themselves.

"Shut up," said the boss, not even glancing in their direction, and the slaves went immediately dead quiet.

Stepping into the light, the big man saw Doc was clearly armed with a blaster, but that only made them equal. In the right hands, a bullwhip could cut a man like an ax. All it required was the room to swing.

"What kind of business we talking here, whitehair?" the overseer asked, grinning. "Mebbe ya need something warm to pass the night? They ain't pretty, but they'll do what they're told, by thunder. Long as you don't chill them, you can do whatever you wish. You want a man or a woman?"

Disgusted, Doc went for his blaster. The plan had

been to chat with the man, get his confidence, lure him into a false sense of security, then strike. But the odious callousness of the overseer was beyond his limits of endurance.

The blaster came out of the holster and the bullwhip cracked, the weapon slapped from his grasp.

"So this is jacking, eh?" the overseer snarled, the leather spinning about his body. "Nobody steals my animals!"

The whip lashed out, and Doc stabbed upward with his stick, the knotted leather wrapped around the ebony shaft. The overseer cursed and pulled hard to free his weapon. Doc resisted for a moment, then released the stick and it went flying toward the man. Caught by surprise, the slave master dropped the whip to dodge out of the way.

Still holding the handle, Doc lunged forward with the bare blade of his sword and stabbed it deeper into the man's belly, then twisted the blade to enlarge the hole. Blood gushed from the wound, and the overseer sighed as he fell to his knees and toppled to the ground.

Retrieving the ebony cane, Doc wiped the blade clean on the dead man before sheathing the sword. After locating his LeMat, the scholar rummaged through the fellow's clothing, unearthing a ring of keys and a tiny .22-caliber homemade blaster. Mildred called such things zip guns, but he had no idea why.

"Here," he said softly, tossing the keys to the first prisoner. "The guards at the gate are drunk on brandy I bought for them, but move fast. I do not know when the shift changes. The swamp mutie is dead, so lay a fake trail to the east, then double back and scatter into the forest."

Doc pressed the zip gun into the hand of a woman prisoner. "Know how to use this?"

She nodded and pulled back the rubber band to see if there was a cartridge inside the thin pipe.

"Here is a knife each," Doc said, dropping a bundle on the ground. "And some bread. It was the best I could do."

"Bless you," she whispered, hugging the weapon.

"Why?" a man asked gruffly, working the locks on his ankles. There was a click, and he stood free from the chains. Red rings circled his ankles from the constant rubbing of the iron cuff, scars that would never go away, inside or out.

"Did you like being a slave?" Doc shot back.

"No," the man spit.

"Neither did I. Good luck." Doc turned and walked into the shadows.

THERE WAS A KNOCK on the bedroom door.

Grabbing his longblaster, Ryan rolled naked out of bed, and Krysty leveled her own revolver at the door.

"Yeah?" Ryan asked, pretending to yawn.

"Me," a familiar voice said.

Sensing trouble, Ryan padded across the room and unbolted the door, letting Mildred slip through.

"What's the matter? Is the baron planning on robbing us?" Krysty asked, stepping into pants.

"Worse. The old coot freed the slaves," she said quickly.

His chest glistening with sweat, Ryan inhaled deeply. "I expected as much. Do the sec men know what happened?"

"Not yet, but they will soon."

Ryan laid the blaster on the warm bed and started to get dressed. "Wake the others and get the horses."

"Already done. They're downstairs packing food."

"Let's go."

Hurrying downstairs, the companions mounted their horses and rode casually to the front gate. The guards were snoring on the ground, and they passed through without hindrance.

Once outside the walls, they pressed the horses into a full gallop.

"Which way are the slaves heading?" Ryan demanded.

"The freed prisoners," Doc said, stressing the words, "are dispersing into the forest."

"That's east," Dean said, tightening the reins on his mare. "Good, because we're going north."

"West," his father corrected.

"But the closest Shiloh is in Tennessee," J.B. said, holding on to his fedora.

Just then, barking hounds sounded from the ville and a bell began to clang.

"I'll explain later," Ryan said, urging his mount to greater speed. Privately, the one-eyed man wanted to be furious at Doc for causing this unnecessary trouble, but he couldn't find a good reason. They had been planning on leaving in the morning anyway, and to be honest, Ryan had briefly considered freeing the slaves himself. He supposed there were just some things a man had to do no matter what the consequences.

Chapter Twelve

Dawn was breaking on the horizon, the indigo clouds of night lightening into the purple and orange of a new day. Sleepy people rose from their cots and beds, stumbling out of their cottages and huts, shuffling across the dirt to start another long day in the bitter fields. The rains had come late this year, and the soil was yielding poor crops. Many of the plants grew twisted and wrong, the grain inedible or deadly poison. Game was scarce, and few cans of predark food were found these days, so farming was the only hope of surviving another year.

Suddenly, the roar of a powerful machine broke the morning stillness as an open-topped wag full of armed sec men drove into the middle of the ramshackle ville. The machine was closely followed by a line of trucks draped in canvas. Armored and bristling with weapons, the war wags stopped with a squeal of brakes in the middle of the gawking crowd, the population backing away from the fearful machine. Some of the smaller children started to cry, clutching their mothers, while burly men with callused hands stepped forward brandishing sickles and axes.

"What are you doing here?" a towering giant demanded, squinting in hostility. "Go away!"

In the vehicle, a clean-shaved lieutenant in a crisp blue shirt stood and raised a small cone to his mouth. "Greetings and salutations, my fellow Americans." His loud voice boomed across the motley collection of huts. "I bring you great news from the baron of the United States!"

Instantly, a few men on the outskirts of the crowd dropped whatever they were doing and raced into the field. But black shapes plowed through the summer weeds to cut them off, and the men found a dozen more Hummers encircling the little ville.

"Return and obey!" a loud voice ordered.

Most of the escapees turned and skulked back to the crowd. But two bolted past the war machines, nimbly racing for the forest. The deadly whine of autofire sounded, brass shells arcing into the air like a golden rainbow. The stuttering line of tracer rounds reached out to sweep across the escapees, and the dead men tumbled to the ground, torn to pieces from the heavy-caliber bullets.

"As I said," repeated the sec man in the first Hummer, "greetings and salutations. We have come to offer you a once-in-a-lifetime chance to help feed your families and assist in rebuilding our wounded nation into the glory it once was! America reborn from the ashes! And only you can help!"

Murmurs came from the crowd. Some glanced at the fields, and the ring of wags turned on their headlights.

"Don't live in no America!" an old man shouted. "This be Tennessee!"

The lieutenant scowled at the man until he lowered his head. "As I was saying," the blue shirt continued, "you will receive the fabulous honor of being allowed to work for the glorious Great Project and help us rebuild America! It is a noble cause, one you will tell your grandchildren about with pride. Yes, you very people can become soldier-workers whose strong backs and brave hearts will gloriously fulfill our nation's ultimate destiny!"

There were more murmurs from the farmers, and the sec man began to wonder if any of them knew half the words he was using from the speech given to him. He decided it was time to cut to the bone of the matter.

The officer tossed the paper aside. The major was an ass; he knew how to do this. "All right, listen up you, brain-dead hillbilly scum!" he snarled. "We're here to gather everybody in the ville capable of doing a day's work. No pregnant women, crips or babies. But everyone else is coming with us!" He paused a moment to let that sink in.

"We asked this service of Shiloh ville down the road. The leaders of that ville foolishly refused us." The sec man paused again. "We begged them to reconsider, but they refused to help America and forced us to punish them severely."

The lieutenant took a breath and lowered his voice. "Shiloh will no longer worry about how to bring in their crops or hunt for food." The whisper changed to a shout. "Or anything! Have you seen what remains of their ville? Well, have you?"

Sobs came in reply, and he knew they had seen. This was why Dr. Jamaisvous waited a day before sending them to the next ville, to let the word spread and the fear build.

"As workers for the New American Army, you'll receive three meals a day, clean housing, and after one season you'll be sent home with a blaster and a pocketful of ammo. We have done this before and will do so again."

Faint hope brightened in their faces, and he smiled benignly at the crowd. God, what a lie, the officer thought, but kept a straight face. "That's the deal. Work and reap rewards. Or defy us, and force us to again bring down terrible destruction."

As if on cue, the overcast atmosphere rumbled and miraculously cleared, the heavily polluted clouds thinning until an azure sky was visible. Sunlight flooded the ville. Some of the people stared in wonder; others gasped in fear at the unnatural sight.

"Yes! The sky is ours to command. Watch!"

Another rumble, and the clouds rolled in to obscure the sun. As they touched, sheet lightning flashed and continued raging for more than a minute.

"Get in the bastard wags," the lieutenant ordered, supremely confident.

Beaten, the people of the ville walked toward the waiting line of vehicles. Sec men armed with long-blasters separated them, the men going in one truck, the women into another. A young woman saw the leering faces of the blue shirts and realized her horrible fate. With an anguished cry, she pulled out a knife from under her skirt and slit her own throat. Bright blood gushed from the wound, and she fell limply to the ground. At the sight, the farmers tensed, fear overlapping into anger, rage fueling courage. Heads started to rise in defiance, and hands became fists.

In unison, the sec men fired their weapons into the air, and the heavy autofires on the wags added their awesome barks to the deafening cacophony. Hot shells rained over the farmers, making them wince and hide behind raised hands. Stunned, shaken, their hesitant resolve broke, and once more they started to climb into the wags. Iron shackles lay on the floor and they chained themselves without instructions, knowing it would be the last free act of their short lives but having no other choice.

As the wags started rolling away, the babies wailed as the whitehairs held them tight. Nobody left in the ville believed that they would ever see any the departing villagers again. Not alive, anyway.

HOOVES POUNDING the misty ground, the companions rode hell-bent for leather through the early Carolina morning. The Flat Rock sec man had chased them for miles through the night, but Baron Polk had dealt fair and given the companions his best mounts. They easily outdistanced the older nags. However, soon after losing the sec men, they began to hear the long howl of hunting dogs. Hounds were a lot faster than horses on a short pull, and the companions were forced to slow and try to stealthily evade the relentless dogs.

"It's been a couple of hours since we heard them," J.B. said, glancing over his shoulder. "I think we finally lost them."

"Can't hear anything," Krysty said, closing her eyes to listen hard. The breeze rustled the leaves on the trees and a small animal was being eaten alive by something that purred, but nothing else. No barking dogs, no shouting riders. "I think we lost them."

"Said so," Jak stated. "Double back over creek, sprinkle black powder. Works good."

"My black powder," Doc complained, uncomfortably rolling to the gait of his animal. At least he still had enough for a few reloads, which was better than nothing.

Reaching a creek, the companions reined in their mounts and let the wheezing animals drink for a while, before forcing them onward.

"But they were still thirsty," Dean said, stroking the

sweaty neck of his pinto mare. She nickered in response, her long ears twitching happily.

Rocking at the hips to the gentle stride of his stallion, Ryan answered, "Never let a horse drink its fill. Slows them down too much. They get enough to stay healthy, no more."

"Should feed them soon," Krysty added, leaning forward as her mare daintily stepped over a pile of bricks. "We left in such a rush, we forgot to bring along feed."

Tightening her thighs, and holding on to the pommel of her saddle with both hands, Mildred leaned sideways and studied the grass rising from the low mist. "Plenty of grass around," she said, swinging back upright. "It shouldn't hurt them too much to live on just summer grass for a while."

"Okay, short break," Ryan said, reining his stallion to a stop. "No fire, cold food only. Stay alert. We leave in five minutes."

Guiding the horses to a nice section of grass, the companions tethered the reins to bushes and tugged hard to make sure they were secure. Shaking themselves to adjust to the lack of weight on their backs, the horses relaxed and began chomping at the tender blades, munching contentedly.

Opening his saddlebag, Dean took out an MRE envelope and ripped it open. Most of the food packets he dumped back inside the bag, but he kept the one marked Creamed Beef. Ripping off a corner, he sucked the food down and stuffed the empty foil back in the saddlebag. Loose trash on the trail would lead the dogs to them like bees to honey.

"Hey, Dad, can horses eat apples?" Dean asked, wiping off his mouth with a pocket rag. "There are some trees over there."

"Sure can," Ryan said around a mouthful of dried fish. Swallowing, the man looked over the area and nodded in approval. "Go gather a bunch. Doc, stay with him as cover."

Pulling up his pants, Doc stepped into view from behind a bush. "Certainly, my dear Ryan," he said, splashing some water from a canteen onto his hands and washing quickly. "Hmm, we shall need something to carry the succulent fruit. John Barrymore, may we borrow your hat, please?"

Arching both eyebrows, J.B. lowered the self-heat he was eating from and turned slowly, but the man and boy were yards away and moving fast.

"Old coot," the Armorer growled, smiling.

Reaching the trees, Doc stood guard while Dean knelt on the ground, and, folding up the front of his shirt, started gathering apples. A plump one rolled away, and he made a successful catch.

"None from there, dear boy," Doc said, the LeMat held ready. "Too many bruised apples can give a horse cramps."

"Okay," he replied, then stood and emptied the fallen fruit from his shirt. Tucking the garment into his pants, Dean grabbed hold of some low branches and scampered up the trunk as if it were a ladder.

"Ah, youth," Doc said with a sigh, and removed a wedge of cheese from the pocket of his frock coat. It was hard and crunchy on the edges, but still edible. There was movement in the bushes. Doc dropped the cheese and aimed the LeMat, thumbing back the trigger. Then he spotted the squirrel nibbling an apple and withheld firing. The miniball from his weapon would leave nothing of the squirrel to cook for dinner. It was the one drawback of big-bore blasters. Game had to be at least as large as a fox, or it was a waste of ammo. Retrieving the cheese from the ground, Doc wiped it clean, cut away a suspicious area and continued to eat.

"You know, horses are like wags, aren't they?" Dean spoke from the foliage. "Got to constantly watch this and feed them that."

"True words, lad. But I would love to meet the wag that could make more wags," Doc said, taking another bite. "I daresay humanity lost something important when we stopped riding."

Returning to the others, Dean passed out the apples, keeping a couple of the best for his mount.

"Here, girl," he said, offering the fruit. The pinto lifted its head and sniffed the offering, then took the whole apple in its mouth and started crunching.

"Careful fingers," Jak warned, feeding the fruit to his mount. The horse was a young dappled stallion, lean muscles rippling under its coat. "Can't see good. Take finger accidentally."

"I know," Dean replied, stroking his horses neck. "I watched Dad before doing mine."

"Smart move," Mildred acknowledged, coming over and inspecting the mare. "Damn, I thought she was limping. That's a bad cut on the fetlock. You better clean that with witch hazel before it gets infected."

"Me?"

Mildred went to her mount and came back with some bandages and a plastic bottle. "A rider tends his own horse," she explained, giving him the bottle and cloth rags. "They trust you more that way."

Speaking soft words, the boy tended the animal. It shook at the sting of the witch hazel, stomping its hooves, but he got the cut thoroughly cleaned and wrapped tightly.

"Gaia, they found us," Krysty said, standing and dropping the partially peeled apple from her grasp.

Seconds later, howls sounded from the east.

"Mount up," Ryan commanded, rushing to his stallion.

He checked the belly cinch, then climbed into the saddle. Shaking the reins free from the bush, he started off at a brisk canter. The rest did the same, then kicked their horses into a full gallop.

"Thank God spurs haven't been rediscovered," Mildred said, holding the pommel and bending low over her animal. "Come on, girl, faster!"

At top speed, the companions crossed a field, jumping over a low hedge and starting a flight of robins.

"Fuck!" Jak cursed, glancing over a shoulder. "Give away position!"

Angling away from the soaring birds, Ryan led the companions over some irregular terrain to where a broken expanse of a paved road peeked out from the grass.

After a hundred yards, Doc reached into his saddlebag and found his last container of black powder. Slowing to the rear of the pack, the old man leaned low in the saddle and shook it out, the wind spreading the powder into a fine spray. Stuffing the empty powder horn into a pocket of his frock coat, Doc slumped in the saddle, concentrating on staying mounted.

The sloping land flew beneath the pounding hooves of the horses, the baying of the hounds rising and falling as the dogs found the companions' trail, lost it and found it once again.

Ryan heard the low moan of winds whistling in a ravine. Moving to the south, the warrior saw that the land was cracked wide alongside the weedy field. Slowing his mount, he trotted close to the edge. The division was shallow, only a sheer drop of one hundred feet, but there was a bridge only a few hundred yards behind them. The structure was a box trestle, dripping with ivy and hanging moss. Older than predark, it looked solid and that was a gamble he was willing to take.

"No way we can jump this," Krysty said, fighting to retain control of her mount. The horse was trying to walk in a circle to get away from the chasm. She pulled on the reins to keep the animal under control. "Whoa, girl. Good girl. Easy does it."

"Why should we jump?" Dean asked, confused. "There's a bridge."

"My point exactly." She smiled. "Once we're on the other side, nobody can follow us. Especially the dogs."

"Follow me!" Ryan shouted. Kicking his mount into a gallop again, he backtracked to the bridge and rode across to the other side.

"We were headed north," J.B. said, stopping near his friend. "Going to try for an ambush?"

"Better," Ryan replied, sliding off the horse and heading toward one of the pack animals. Digging in the bags, Ryan found a hurricane lantern filled with oil reeking of fish.

"Good dry timbers," J.B. announced, running his hand along the supporting beams.

"Trap?" Jak asked, holding the reins in one hand, his Colt Python drawn to give cover. Far below, a riverbed was visible, but there was no sign of any water. Just bare gray stones and smooth black pebbles lying across the red clay bottom of the riverbed.

Removing the flue, Ryan tipped over the lantern, spilling out the rancid oil. "No time for traps or bombs. Those dogs are too damn close."

"And the sec men right behind them," Mildred added tersely.

Removing the wick from the lamp, Ryan lit it with his butane lighter. The rag caught at once, and he dropped it on the planks. Smoky flames spread across the planks and over the sides, following the path of the flowing oil.

The howling was closer.

"Let's go," Ryan grunted, climbing back into the saddle. "Just in case one of the dogs makes it across before the bridge collapses."

Kicking their mounts into a gallop again, the companions rode away from the burning bridge, knowing they were safe from pursuit for the moment—but also knowing that there was no way back into North Carolina. The plan to head into Tennessee was abandoned as they rode deeper into the wild country of Georgia.

STANDING IN THE throne room of the castle, Nathan Cawdor bowed his head in contemplation. He didn't believe in torture. It served no purpose except personal revenge. Information was always more easily bought, or stolen, than extracted.

But as he looked down upon Sullivan lying wrapped in his cocoon of netting and chains, Nathan felt a fury build within. His mother had referred to it as the bloodfire, a sort of madness for violence that ruled the Cawdor bloodline.

"I have no wish to kill you," Nathan said. "Or rather, I had no wish. To the best of my knowledge, you had harmed nobody within the walls of this ville. Plus, you saved many lives in the hospital sewing wounds and removing crushed limbs so gangrene wouldn't rot my men."

The room was packed with sec men and civilians. Justice wasn't served in the dark. Only tyrants ruled from the shadows because daylight made them wither and die.

Hands clasped behind his back, Nathan walked around the supine prisoner. "No, my plan was to find you and send you back to BullRun ville alive and unharmed."

The mutie sneered at the man, not believing a word of the pretty speech. Barons would always say golden promises before the crowd, then feast on flesh in private. Soon they would be alone, and Sullivan would discover his real sentence.

In a flash of anger, Nathan kicked the bound man. "You idiot! I had no wish to kill you. But after seeing what you did to the patients, nukestorm, you set wounded men on fire merely to hide your escape with their death screams!"

"Hang him!" a woman shouted from the crowd. "Peel off his skin and feed it to the dogs!"

Patiently, Nathan allowed the interruption as the woman was the wife of a now dead sec man. "Yes, Sullivan, I would be justified in torturing you to the point of death, then leaving you alone in the dungeon for a year to heal and grow strong, then start the torture again, and continue on until I was too old to wield the pliers or hot irons. So my sons would take over, and their sons and theirs, and it would still not be enough! There can never be enough revenge for what you did!"

Nathan turned away from the man and walked to his throne. Sitting down heavily, he sighed. "There is no choice but the ultimate punishment."

Sullivan tried not smile. This was why he had done the act, to infuriate them beyond reason. Nathan always killed common thieves with firing squads, and hanged rapists and other such scum. Only once did he burn a man alive, a traitor who turned against the ville and allowed coldhearts past the walls. But Sullivan couldn't be burned alive. His skin was resistant to flames, and once his ropes were weakened he would break loose, kill the startled baron with a single blow and escape over the wall in the confusion. The fool was playing right into his hands.

Nathan drew a blaster and weighed the weapon in his palm, deliberating justice the way a butcher did meat. Was this enough, or too much?

Standing along side the throne, Lady Tabitha took his free hand in both of hers. "You have no choice, dear."

"I know," Nathan said, holstering the weapon. "This coldheart mutie deserves the very worst punishment we have. Once, I burned a man alive at the stake for treason, and you all still remember that smell. It haunts me at night and clings to my clothes. No amount of washing or soap will ever remove the memory. And that day I made a solemn vow to never repeat that again for any reason."

The crowd held its breath, anxiously waiting.

"Captain of the guards!" Nathan called out formally. Clem stepped forward and saluted. "Yes, my lord?"

"Bury him alive."

Icy panic filled the mutie as he realized this was a death sentence with no escape. "No!" Sullivan screamed, and he stood, ripping the nets apart with bare fingers. He shook back and forth, trying to escape from the chains, but they weren't cold iron forged in some Deathlands smithy, but predark steel. The metal didn't even strain at his awesome strength. Gasping for air, terror a fist in his belly, the mutie started to weep as his bones broke in the blind madness of trying to escape.

There was a gunshot, and Sullivan fell to the floor, blood pooling around him, spreading outward in pumping waves. He tried again to rise, a chain snapping loose in his death throes. There was another shot, and Sullivan collapsed, his body exhaling its last breath and going still.

Ceremoniously, Nathan slid the clip from the execution blaster and laid them down separately on a silver tray. "And so it ends today," he said sternly. "Anybody buried alive would soon go insane and live out their last few hours in a delirium of escape and freedom fantasies. The very worst thing I could do was threaten him with the act. Sullivan punished himself, and I ended the matter."

"What about Baron Markham of BullRun ville?" Clem drawled, watching the corpse for any signs of returning life. "Y'all know she sent the mutie here."

Leaning back in his throne, Nathan nodded agreement. "Because she believed we were attacking her, and she was too weak fighting off some samurai baron from Washington Hole to withstand an attack by us."

"I would be happy to make a stand against her, my lord," a bearded lieutenant said, kneeling. "My life for yours!"

"Thank you, Jarod, but that won't be necessary," Nathan acknowledged graciously. The baron turned to address another man. "Clem, would you go to them as an ambassador and talk the truth? We aren't enemies. Tell them of Overton and enlist their aid. His plan was to divide the baronies so we couldn't work together. If that was his greatest fear, then that's exactly what we should do. And quickly."

The chief of the sec men scratched his neck. "She may not believe me, but I'll sure as shit try."

"Thank you."

"What about those Casanova assholes?"

"I'll deal with them later," Nathan said in a low, dangerous voice.

Clem smiled. "Gotcha. You're a pretty good baron."

Startled at first, Nathan smiled back at the man. "And I'm pleased to also call you a friend."

"Beg pardon, my lord," a sec man asked politely. "What about the…ah, Sullivan?"

Stepping in front of her husband, Tabitha scowled at the dead mutie. "As he lived, so shall he die," she said in controlled anger. "Burn the body."

IT TOOK A FULL CORD of wood to finally consume the mutie, his flesh oddly resistant to the conflagration. But at least he was reduced to ashes, the residue thrown into the river to be washed away.

Chapter Thirteen

Five large men walked their horses to the edge of the ravine and stared at the ruined bridge.

"Escaped," the biggest man hissed. "They have escaped again. This is intolerable!" An M-60 machine gun was resting on his shoulder as if the massive weapon were a simple longblaster, the linked belt of ammo dangling to his knees. A hairy pouch slung over his other shoulder bulged with a spare belt. The handles of knives jutted from each boot, and a revolver rode in a holster at the small of his back. Covered by his loose shirt, it was almost undetectable.

"Mebbe we should give up," said one of the others, kicking some charred wood over the edge. It tumbled out of sight. He tugged at his good-luck necklace, which was made of human ears. "I mean, we've been after these people since Thunder Pass!"

"Stop your complaining," a bald man snapped, his head covered with colorful tattoos. He carried a machete in a shoulder holster, and dried human scalps dangled from his belt as ornaments. "In the morning, we'll find a way across once we have some daylight."

"How's the food?" a thin man asked. Clothes seemed to hang off his skeletal frame, yet he ate more than any two of them. A sawed-off shotgun rode at his hip, extra rounds lining his tan-colored belt. The ornate buckle was carved from white bone.

"We're down to only a few pounds of meat," a hairy man said. Carrying a bolt-action longblaster, he was bare chested in spite of the evening chill, bandoliers of ammo crisscrossing his herculean torso. "But we have those fresh supplies we caught escaping from the ville."

On the back of a pack horse, the bound captive squirmed and kicked from within a rolled blanket. A bamboo tube fed enough air for the gaudy slut to breathe, and the blanket hid her from the casual sight of strangers.

"Gut and cook her," said Scarface, displaying pointed teeth. Starting at his forehead, a long jagged slash traversed his features, going into his shirt and out of sight. "We'll think better with a full stomach."

TWO DAYS LATER, the companions were camped on the top of a hill overlooking the ruins of a predark metropolis. Silvery with reflected moonlight, dark monoliths rose from the jumble of fallen structures and windblown debris. A great amphitheater, or sports arena, stood by itself at the far end. No lights shone from the hundreds of windows, and no smoke rose through the many holes in the roofs. There was no smell of machinery, and no sounds marred the stillness of the evening.

"It's dead," Krysty stated knowingly, as she added more sticks to the campfire. As a precaution, the companions had dug a hole for the fire so the flames wouldn't be discernible to anybody below, but their precautions seemed unwarranted.

"There's nothing on the map," J.B. said, sounding annoyed, squinting to read by the flickering light. "My best guess would have been that this area was nothing but peach orchards."

Ryan rubbed his unshaved chin. "Strange," he admitted. "Very strange."

A few yards away, the horses whinnied in the darkness from hunger. Yesterday, the companions had passed a field full of rye. But after inspecting the grain, Mildred refused to let them feed any to the horses. It was contaminated with an ersatz mold she said could be fatal.

Unfortunately, they were entering desert, and grass was getting scarce. With no other choice, the companions went through their supplies, feeding the horses everything they could—the rest of the apples, bread, granola bars, crackers, dried vegetables and peanut butter. Combined with the tiny sugar packets from the MRE coffee packs and what green grass they could find, the mixture had sustained the animals until now.

"We've got to find them something to eat, or the horses will start to weaken," Ryan said, chewing on another piece of smoked fish. "Then they'll rebel, and we'll have to chill them."

"Shoot the horses?" Dean asked askance, looking up from his work. The Browning Hi-Power was lying on a clean piece of cloth completely disassembled. The boy was cleaning each piece thoroughly before rebuilding the blaster.

"No," his father replied coldly. "We'll ride them till they die. Get every mile out of them we can. I'd prefer to find food and keep them for the rest of our journey."

"Me, too!"

"Maybe we should check out the ruins," Mildred ventured, sipping her tin cup of cold turkey bouillon. "Dried cereals on the supermarket shelves, cans of corn, envelopes of oatmeal, could be lots of food down there.

"The big one looks like a Hyatt," she continued.

"Good hotel. I always stayed at them for medical conferences."

Ryan sucked a hollow tooth. "Don't recall ever looting a hotel before. But come to think of it, they would have lots of usable items. Tons of canned goods for the kitchen, good knives, too. Soap and shampoo, TP, radio and blasters in the sec office."

"Should be lots of clothing. I could use a new belt."

"Socks," Jak said.

"There could be nothing. Rats usually get everything not in a can, and rust gets that," Ryan countered, putting aside the gnawed fish. Whatever Flat Rock did to preserve the stuff almost made the things inedible. His teeth ached from chewing on the smoked trout. "I think we stand a better chance finding food on the road. We'll leave the roads and start cutting cross-country."

"Well, there's a redoubt to the south of here," J.B. said, reading the map. The firelight glistened off his glasses, casting tiny rainbows across his face. "But it's over 150 miles away."

He turned the map over. "Now, just sixty miles to the north is the town of Shiloh, of which we know nothing. But to the northwest is Shiloh battlefield. There's a redoubt there, and it's only a hundred miles away."

"Two birds, one stone," Krysty said sagely. "I vote for simplicity."

"Ville near redoubt had horses," Jak reminded them. He stood and stretched his arms, working a kink from his neck. It had been a long time since he did this much riding, and surprisingly, it was his back that was sore, not his ass.

"That ville also had lots of folks who wanted us chilled," J.B. reminded the teenager.

Jak drew his blaster and checked the load in the cylinder. "Don't care. You decide. I relieve Doc horses." As silent as a jungle panther, the pale teenager slipped into the darkness and was gone.

"Anything useful in the Shiloh redoubt?" Dean asked, assembling his weapon without looking. Springs tucked into place neatly, and the carriage entered the oiled frame without hindrance.

Watching the work with approval, Ryan shook his head. "The base was stripped bare. Although, there are miles upon miles of tunnels under the redoubt, and we never did more than a fast recce into those. Could be anything stored down there."

Finished, the boy eased the clip into place and jacked the slide. "Mebbe that's where Overton was getting his blasters from, the Shiloh redoubt."

"Could be," Ryan said thoughtfully. "It just could damn well be the spot."

The talk went on far into the night, and soon the decision was made. They would bypass all of the towns named Shiloh on their list and head straight for the Civil War battlefield of Shiloh Church.

THE CAMPFIRE WAS dwindling to red embers, the unburned ends of logs glowing in the darkness. Soft snoring came from the still figures under the blankets around the fire pit, along with the occasional mumbled word.

Blaster resting on his lap, J.B. sat sipping cold coffee and listening to the night. The insects and birds told more of what was happening in the area than vision could. An owl hooted its eternal question, something with wings soared overhead and a line of ants marched over his combat boot seeking the crumbs from their dinner.

The thin grass rustled as a dry breeze blew over the campsite. Then there was another rustle, but the breeze had ceased.

With instincts honed in a hundred battles, J.B. stood and threw a bundle of branches onto the embers. The oil-soaked wood burst into flames, filling the area with bright light that revealed a dozen figures near the horses, fumbling with the reins.

"Thieves!" J.B. bellowed, firing single shots from the Uzi, unwilling to go full-auto and possibly kill the horses. One murky figure cried out, grabbing a shoulder. Another doubled over, clutching his stomach, and toppled to the ground.

The companions clawed for their weapons and rolled away from the campfire as the invaders seemed to stab themselves in the faces with tiny sticks. Dodging left and right, J.B. fired twice more, then something gentle hit his chest. He glanced down and saw a tiny barbed quill jutting from a button.

"Blowpipes!" he cried, plucking the deadly barb from his clothing, trying not to touch the glistening end. It had to be poison of some kind.

A thundering roar illuminated the night as Doc triggered the LeMat. Three more of the shapeless figures holding blowpipes cried out in pain and fell aside, throwing their arms wide. A roar shook the darkness as Mildred fired the S&W shotgun, then the gunshots overlapped one another as the companions unleashed a hellstorm of lead and copper at the intruders. Many of the figures dropped to the ground, but the ones behind them leaped on the horses and galloped away, vanishing into the night.

"They got the horses!" Krysty cried, kneeling in the cold soil, two hands supporting her S&W .38. She strained to catch a glimpse of the thieves, but even her vision couldn't find a target in the blackness.

"More wood!" Dean shouted, and dropped a load onto the campfire.

The circle of light expanded, and something went motionless in the tall weeds nearby. Springing forward, Mildred grappled with a man who broke free from her clutches and started running. Jak threw a knife and the figure stumbled, then Ryan tackled the intruder, driving him to the ground.

Wrestling in the thrashing weeds, the man escaped again and Jak slashed for the neck. The blade missed the target, but scored a deep furrow across a leaf-covered shoulder. Pivoting, the intruder snarled wordlessly, lashing out with hands full of vines. The thorns raked Jak's face, just missing his eyes. The teenager thrust a knife into the man's belly as Ryan clubbed the thief over the head with the SIG-Sauer. With a crunch of bones, the man fell to the ground.

"Over here!" Krysty shouted, an oil lantern held high.

In the yellowish light of the fish-oil lantern, the humanoid on the ground gasped for breath.

"Mutie," Jak growled, wiping his blade on the dirt. He usually cleaned the knives on the clothes of the dead, but this time that wouldn't work, as the horse thief was naked. Sort of. The humanoid creature was covered with vines, but he wasn't wearing them; the plants were part of him, the roots buried deep into his skin. His clothing was merely leaves of different colors mimicking cloth.

The mutie spasmed once, then went still. The leaves limply drooped, the vines turning brown.

"Symbionts," Mildred said, inspecting the still form. In death, it simply looked like a man partially covered with ivy. Then she noticed the thorns on the hands. Experimentally, she closed a limp hand into a fist, and barbed thorns extended from the knuckles. Releasing the hybrid, she stood. "Plants and man intermixed. They can't live without each other."

"Bastard good disguise," Ryan grunted in annoyance. His shirt was slashed, but the skin underneath only lightly scratched, with no bleeding. "Triple-blasted stuff probably alters to any style, so they can pretend to be part of your group in the darkness."

"Certainly easy enough to tell in the light," Doc agreed. "But by then it is probably too late for most norms."

"We killed six," J.B. announced, the Uzi held steady. "But there were at least twenty more from the tracks. It actually looked like some acted as shields, dying so the rest could get the horses."

"Gaia," Krysty muttered. "They sure wanted the animals badly."

Breathlessly, Dean burst through the weeds. "They took everything," he panted, "horses, tack, reins, all of it. Nothing's left."

"Fireblast," Ryan said, removing the half clip from the SIG-Sauer and slamming in a full magazine. "I don't care if it's a bastard army of the things out there. We're going after those horses. Without them, we're on foot. J.B., gather what supplies we have and divide them into six packs. Mildred, bank the fire so it'll last through the night. Nice and big. Understand?"

"Make them think we're still here. Gotcha."

"Jak, you're our best tracker. Find their trail and don't

lose it! We'll follow soon, so leave a trail for us.''

The pale teenager nodded and blended into the weeds.

REACHING THE BOTTOM of the hill, the companions easily found the tracks of the horses and followed them to a large pile of rubble. Ryan whistled once, and Jak stepped out of the shadows under a rock slab.

"Went into ruins," Jak said. "Couldn't follow. Rads.''

"Thought so," Ryan muttered. Piles of rubble rose over their heads, the monolithic buildings soaring even higher. He checked the rad counter on his lapel. The readings were nominal.

"The area is clear," he announced. "Let's go."

Staying low, the companions moved through the weeds and over the predark wreckage, following the faint trail of the green muties. A hoofprint in the soft sand, a broken weed, a tiny pool still rippling, a crushed leaf bending back into shape, a drop of blood on a rock. Jak moved almost without pause, the nebulous marks a wide highway for the Cajun hunter. Ryan and Krysty stayed with him most of the way, but sometimes they were forced to wait until he resurfaced a dozen yards away, waving them onward.

Under the colored moonlight, the companions crept past a tall office building that rose like a knife thrust from the mounds of broken masonry. The front door was covered completely, but third-floor windows were missing where the rubble was piled high, and they knew others had been inside. Whether greenies or norms, it was impossible to tell.

Walking out of the crumbling suburbs, Ryan and the others found Jak crouched, studying a broken parking lot of macadam. Ahead, the downtown monoliths stood silent and foreboding. Nothing stirred the scrawny weeds; not a breath of air moved over the desert city.

"There." Jak finally pointed, then headed to the left.

A long squat building stood amid an array of houses crushed flat, a sprinkling of sand dusting the ruins. The metal frame of a garage sagged nearby, the beams consumed with rust and age. The building itself was made of brick, granite slabs set as lintels around the doors and windows. The roof was sharply sloped with no skylights or ventilation grilles offering a possible entrance. A bare flagpole leaned away from the building, large stone eagles flanking either side of the recessed doorway. Words were carved into the granite lintel, partially dissolved by acid rains.

"National Guard armory," Ryan whispered. "Is that the spot?"

"They there," Jak said, nodding, peeking between the fins of a corroded car radiator. "Nasty."

"Yeah, this isn't some library or bank converted into a fortress," J.B. countered. "It's a military fort, built to store weapons and troops."

"Blasters and ammo by the ton," Dean said eagerly, then frowned. "No, those must be long gone."

Kneeling on the shell of a transmission, Krysty agreed. "Can't chance a rush. That door is a death trap," she added softly, scrutinizing the building. "One man with a rapid fire could hold off a score of invaders."

"Not sure if the greenies have blasters, but we're not going to use the door anyway," Ryan stated. "I know another way inside."

"The fort was designed to hold off rioting mobs," Mildred said, shifting her hold on the med kit. "How are we going to get in?"

"Mobs are stupe," Ryan replied, his Steyr cradled in

his arms. "Only people are clever. Stay close. No noise, five-yard spread."

Slow and silent, they moved around the building with weapons at the ready. In the backyard, the sand was winning over the weeds, the sideways chassis of a large truck gradually returning to the earth from which it was once mined. Empty oil drums used to store fuel were scattered about amid broken pallets, miscellaneous metal parts of unknown origin and stacks of rotting tires.

The rear of the armory was a solid wall of brick and granite, the slit windows covered with bars and located some fifty feet off the ground near the gutter of the sloped roof.

On the loading dock, massive steel doors stood in a row, blocking any possible entrance that way, and off to the side, a short set of stairs led to a smaller door of riveted steel.

In a two-on-two combat formation with Ryan on the point, the companions proceeded along the cracked concrete to the loading dock as if moving through a minefield. As he reached the top, a dark shape on the floor smelled familiar, and Ryan touched the soft material. Warm horse shit. Jak had been right. This was the place.

"How did you know?" asked Krysty, pressing her mouth to his ear.

"Front door too small for horses," Ryan whispered tersely. "Greenies had to get the horses inside somehow."

At the loading doors, Ryan raised a hand palm outward and the others froze. Inspecting the tracks, he found grease on one and tentatively identified it as animal fat.

The glass in the view slot of the door was gone, replaced with wood paneling. Drawing the SIG-Sauer, he aimed the barrel at the wood and gave a horse whinny. Something moved inside and he emptied the clip, the soft coughs of the silenced blaster counterpointed with snapping noises as the slugs plowed through the paneling. Immediately, the companions pushed up the door and found two greenies lying on the floor, their vines already withering.

Lowering the door, Doc and Dean dragged the bodies into a corner while J.B. stood guard with the Uzi. Straight ahead was an empty area with faint stripes painted on the terrazzo floor, the warehouse for the armory. Across the room was a door marked Washroom, and a hallway. Keeping to the walls, the companions crossed the storage room in groups, each covering the other in case of traps or snipers. But no one had witnessed their intrusion.

Holstering the SIG-Sauer, Ryan removed the longblaster from his shoulder and gently worked the bolt, the click-clack sounding unnaturally loud in the gloomy stillness. When no one challenged them, Ryan held up two separated fingers, then pointed to the left and the right. Understanding the signals, the companions split into two groups to avoid offering a group target.

The quiet of the armory was unnerving. The thick walls kept out the soft desert breeze, and not even the drip of water marred the near perfect silence. Gaping doorways lined the corridor, opening onto dusty offices, a looted storage closet and private bedrooms for officers.

The end of the hallway was a branching intersection with more doors. Two proved to be locked, and by the cobwebs on the hinges it was safe to say neither had been used in years. However, a set of double doors ,had clean hinges, dripping with fat. Easing their way through, the companions realized this was the barracks for the troops. The rows of bunks were coated with dust and cobwebs, but a clear path led through the barracks to a group of figures sitting in a circle, nosily eating.

Moonlight streamed through the right side windows, illuminating the bizarre scene. A horse lay in the middle of the muties, its hide peeled back to allow them easy access to the pale meat and organs. The leafy muties were removing morsels with their bare hands and stuffing the food into their mouths, gobbling and slavering in joyous repast.

Doc made a gagging noise and leveled the LeMat.

"Chill them!" Ryan shouted, triggering the Steyr, the 7.62 mm round blowing the head off a feasting greenie.

Dumbfounded, the muties could only stare in shock as the humans steadily advanced, firing their weapons. Mouths smeared with blood, the greenies fell to the floor, riddled with bullets, but two of them managed to grab blowpipes and stand before receiving fatal head wounds.

Moving among the dead, J.B. checked the corpses just to make sure, and Ryan turned away, holstering his blaster. "Okay, let's find the rest of the horses."

Quickly, the companions went through the armory, opening every door, exploring every room. But they found only decay and refuse, gnawed bones and junk. Within a quarter hour, they regrouped in the barracks.

"Hey, over here!" Dean called from the armory. "Found them!"

The companions converged on the corridor to find Dean standing near an open doorway. The hinges had been ripped from the jamb, the door itself resting against the wall. A strong smell of blood and feces emanated from inside. The boy's face revealed barely controlled anger.

Lighting more candles, the companions proceeded carefully inside the room. In the flickering glow, they saw the rest of the horses lying on the floor, muffled cries coming their bound mouths.

"The monsters!" Mildred said, furious. "The greenies cut the leg tendons so the horses couldn't run away."

"Damn," Jak said grimly. "No fix that."

Krysty drew her blaster. "Nobody can fix that kind of wound. These horses are cripples. They'll never walk again."

"Stinking bastards," J.B. spit, leveling his Uzi. The Armorer fired single shots, putting the crippled animals out of their misery.

"Done," he said finally, slamming a fresh magazine home. "Let's get the hell out of here."

"Gladly, sir," Doc rumbled, wiping some splashed blood off his cheek.

Holding a candle high, Ryan inspected some shelves. Aside from empty shoe boxes and wire coat hangers, there was nothing. "Damn. Find any of our packs anywhere while you were searching?" he asked.

Making sure the horses were dead, Mildred stood. "Not a thing. Just garbage and cobwebs."

"Great. No horses, no food, only the ammo in our pockets," Krysty growled. "Mebbe we should just head for the nearest redoubt and jump out of here. We're not going to take the blues with what we have."

"Mebbe," Ryan said, walking toward the door. In the corridor, he turned, a new expression on his face. "Jak, in the parking lot you took a while to decide coming here. Why?"

"Odd tracks," the teenager replied. "Horses here, greenies elsewhere. We want horses. Came here."

"But they obviously took the saddles and backpacks someplace else."

He shrugged. "Looks like."

"Which means there are possibly a lot more of them," Doc stated, then gestured grandly at the armory. "This degenerate abattoir is merely their kitchen, for lack of a better word."

"We find their nest, we find our packs," Dean concluded. "The ruins aren't very big. It'll only take us a few hours to recce."

"Agreed," Ryan said, working the bolt on his longblaster. "Let's go get those supplies back."

Chapter Fourteen

Hidden in the shadows, a greenie watched the norms below from behind the sheet of mirrored glass in the tall building. He made fists, and the knuckle-thorns slid in and out as he debated attacking them now or waiting until they met the master and were helpless.

The choice was clear, and the symbiote left the room to gather more of his leafy brethren. Soon, oh, so very soon, the feasting would begin.

RETURNING OUTSIDE, Jak found the trail in the parking lot and started toward the ruins with the companions close behind. The moon was descending toward a bank of clouds, signaling the end of night. Soon, Ryan and the others would be visible.

The square foundations of homes and stores lined the streets in an orderly procession, most of the holes filled with debris, sand and weeds. Rubble was everywhere underfoot, along with bits of rusting machinery and a dusting of sand. In another hundred years, the desert would claim the predark city, eventually swallowing the monoliths under windblown drifts. Already the windows facing windward were frosted white from the constant bombardment of the hard particles.

Intent on the trail, Jak darted past a manhole missing its cover. Ryan knew that the lid had been probably taken for the iron. Manhole covers made good armor for war wags, or folks could melt them down for horseshoes, or even nails. As a child, Ryan remembered finding a lot more of the smaller items from similar predark ruins. But now the buildings were getting picked clean, and people were turning to making things once more. Doc considered that a step toward rebuilding civilization, but Ryan wasn't sure. The first things most folks made were blasters and gallows.

Stopping at an intersection, Jak went down on a knee to study the ground closely, his fingers hovering above the pavement. A bug was crushed at one point, and a stone overturned, its wet side now facing the nighttime sky.

"Trouble?" Ryan asked, cradling the longblaster in his arms. He could tell somebody had passed by very recently, but not how many, or where they were headed. Jak's expertise was tracking.

"No prob," the teenager replied, starting to move about in an ever expanding spiral. Frowning, he finally stood.

"Two groups," Jak stated, pointing toward particular buildings. "One there, other there."

"Hotel and the sports arena. Any difference in the depths?" Ryan asked. "The muties carrying the supplies should leave a deeper print."

"None. Mebbe share all."

"Or thrown it away," Mildred suggested. A plait of her hair was blown into her mouth, and she spit it out. "We better move fast, or we'll be feasting on horse steak for the next week."

"Okay, we split into teams. Krysty, Jak and I will check the arena. You folks hit the hotel.

"Good or bad," Ryan continued, "we rendezvous at

the insurance company here in thirty minutes. If the other team hasn't arrived, go find them.''

''Thirty and counting,'' J.B. said, looking at his wrist chron. ''Check.''

Without further comment, Ryan and the others headed toward the arena.

Unfolding the wire stock of his Uzi, J.B. took the point for his group and started toward the hotel. The main building was a mirrored-glass cylinder, and it was impossible to see if there were any lights or movements in the upper stories. On street level, two low wings stood on either side.

''Swimming pool and restaurant,'' Mildred said, stepping over a bent driveshaft that was brown with rust, ''if this hotel follows the usual style.''

''No tracks,'' Dean said, looking at the street, ''that I can see.''

''Nor I,'' Doc added, sliding the selector on his blaster from the .63-caliber smooth bore, to the .44-caliber revolver. Against the resilient greenies, the buckshot charge would do scant damage. But the solid-lead miniballs would, and could, remove heads with the precision of a cannon.

The windows lining the east wing were gone, windblown sand filling the pool nearly to the top. Swinging around the hotel, they found the restaurant to be in a similar condition—broken and deserted. A lizard darted from the shadows and disappeared into the soft sand as if it were water. Not a trace remained of its passage.

''We go in,'' J.B. said, straightening his fedora and pulling on his fingerless gloves tighter. ''Remember, go for head shots, just like stickies.'' Nobody replied, but they raised the sights of their blasters higher.

Under a crumbling overhang, a rusted sign squeaked

as it swung back and forth from the gentle wind. Mildred stopped it with her hand, then laid it down flat. Now that they could hear, there was only the soft moan of the desert wind, and the patter of sand hitting glass.

Proceeding in silence, they found the lobby of the hotel dark and smelling of mildew. The front counter sagged in the middle, and a shoe-shine stand was alive with busy termites. The floor was bare concrete, pronged strips at the bottom of the walls showing the floor had once been carpeted.

"Damn, we could track them easy on carpeting," J.B. said, lighting a candle. The tiny flame illuminated only a few yards, but it was better than nothing.

"There's an interesting fact I learned on my junkets," the physician said, holding her own candle high to inspect the ceiling. The tiles were in place, with no indications of bullet holes or accumulated residue from other candles or torches. "In my day, nobody wanted to stay on the thirteenth floor of a skyscraper. Supposed to be bad luck. So the hotel people used the thirteenth floor for themselves as offices and storage. Often, the elevators don't even list it as existing, but we could get there by taking the service stairs. Service elevator, too. But without power, those are dead."

"Twenty stories," J.B. mused, looking behind the counter. Piles of key cards lay on the floor, along with a smashed register. "Thirteen would be a good spot for an ambush. Whether invaders started searching at the bottom, or at the top, once they were higher than thirteen, the greenies could come boiling out and trap their prey."

"So we start there," Doc said grimly. "Lead on, my friend."

Going past a line of pay phones and washrooms, J.B.

pushed opened a swing door with the barrel of his Uzi. Stacks of chairs lined their left, wooden easels and plastic signboards to the right.

"No cobwebs," Dean said, scuffing the floor.

Mildred reached out and lifted a green leaf off the sharp end of an easel. "I'd say we found them."

The service elevator was straight ahead, steam tables and room-service carts in neat rows along a wall with faded lines painted on the floor.

"Tidy folks," J.B. commented, the Uzi sweeping for targets.

Mildred nodded. "Hyatt was the best."

At a door marked Service Stairs, J.B. and Dean stood guard, while Mildred turned the handle and eased it open. Almost instantly, a hairy fat spider darted around the edge and dashed onto her hand. Disgusted, the physician shook it off. The insect landed on the floor, and Doc crushed it under his boot.

"Filthy things," he muttered. "Always did hate them. Especially since our past close encounter."

As expected, the stairwell was pitch-dark, but under the candles they could dimly see the stairs were marked with the prints of countless bare feet. Assuming combat formation, the companions started up the concrete stairs, watching for traps.

Oddly, their footsteps didn't echo, and, reaching the fourth floor, they discovered why—the stairwell ended abruptly. Nothing was above them but the empty interior of the gutted hotel, each level painstakingly removed to make the building hollow.

Astonished, the companions stepped onto on the carpeted floor, looking upward at seventeen stories of banked windows and a very distant skylight. Vines and creepers covered the interior; hammocks hung like nest-ing pods along the sides. The middle was clear all the way to the roof, the ragged ends of steel beams and rough concrete slabs marring the vertical checkerboard of mirrored glass.

"Those hammocks are arranged so the greenies can catch sunlight while sleeping," Mildred guessed. "They climb the vines to get to their beds."

"We can't follow up there," Dean stated, listening to the building creak faintly as it swayed in the wind. "We get halfway and snip! Down we go."

"By Gadfrey, this is a mighty fine defense," Doc said in annoyance. "Positively Horacic in its simplicity."

"But where the hell are they?" J.B. demanded, studying the floor underfoot. The carpeting was clean, no spots from dropped food or drink. "There's hammocks here for a hundred, mebbe more, and we've only chilled twenty or so."

"Could be room for new families," Mildred said, wrinkling her nose at the sharp smell of the vines. It was similar to ivy, but resembled hemp. Clearly another mutation. "But more likely, the rest are chilled. "

"Hey, that's why they risked death to get our horses," Dean realized, a flash of anger coming, then going just as quickly. "They were starving to death."

"Not much to eat in the desert," she agreed as a spider ran by, boldly going over the toe of her boot.

"Sure as hell hope they're chilled," the Armorer said gruffly. A vine brushed against his neck, and he swatted it away. "Otherwise, there's only two options. They're either terrified of our blasters and have run away in hiding—"

"Or else," Doc finished with a grimace, "the greenies are preparing a major ambush, and this whole city is one huge trap."

As THE MISTS faded from the mat-trans unit, Dr. Silas Jamaisvous appeared, standing on a hexagonal platform of tiny lights twinkling from inside the hidden machinery. Next to him was a forklift, its prongs filled with foam boxes sealed with yellow-and-black-striped warning tape.

The man waited a few moments for indications of jump sickness to hit, and was relieved when none occurred. Sometimes he was driven to the floor in retching agony, but those bouts were occurring less frequently these days. It was as if his constant nightmares of the chron jump were somehow making him immune to the smaller miseries of disintegration and instantaneous travel.

Climbing into the seat of the forklift, Silas started the electric motor and carefully drove the machine off the portable gateway and onto the bare concrete floor. Stacks and crates of every description filled the Quonset hut, long rifle boxes, drums of fuel, foot lockers, backpacks, everything his growing army needed. Even the hut had come through the gateway, painstakingly carried one piece at a time until Silas was finally able to have his troops take down the canvas tent around the gateway and surround the unit with the more secure domain of the hut.

Silas knew many of the secrets of the mat-trans system, and aside from controlling the jump destination, the man also knew where a lot of military equipment was stored, tons of matériels and supplies that hadn't been touched since he personally ordered Special Forces troops to place it there a hundred-odd years ago. Richard Overton had marveled at the AK-47 assault rifles and radios. But those were toys compared to the weapon Silas was working on now, a weapon that would burn the pollution from the Deathlands forever and give him absolute mastery of the world. It would mean an end to war! After the necessary bloodshed of retribution, of course. But then, nothing was free.

Parking near the door, Silas rose and placed a hand on a glowing pad on the wall. There was a hum, and the door disengaged, cycling open onto a small enclosure. Directly across the neatly mown grass was the laboratory, to the right the barracks, to the left a brand-new wall of concertina wire, topped with crackling electric prods.

"Guards!" he called, stepping onto the neatly raked soil.

Several armed sec men in crisp blue shirts ran over immediately. "Sir!" a young corporal saluted.

Silas returned the salute, trying not to appear dismayed at the age of the trooper. Most of the replacement sec men were young, hastily recruited from distant villes after the slaughter of so many veterans by the rebelling slaves. The barbed wire was only one of many steps taken to make sure such a disaster was never allowed to happen again. He blamed himself for the slaughter. He had been too lenient last time. No more.

"Drive the forklift outside the enclosure and have some workers haul these components up the main ladder to the dish for assembly," Silas commanded, walking stiffly and trying to hide his limp. "And make sure that nobody is to enter the warehouse for the next twenty minutes. No, make that an hour. Just to be safe."

"Safe, Dr. Jamaisvous?" the sec man asked, nervously glancing at the thick door of veined steel.

The predark scientist scowled. "Your ape brain could never possibly understand the reasons why. Just do as you are ordered."

"Yes, sir!" With exaggerated care, the sec man piloted the machine along a walkway and through the gate in the electric fence.

Chained slaves were waiting there, and each took a box from the stack and started shuffling toward the gigantic dish.

A teenager took a foam box and started for the ladder at the base of the bunker. His steps were hesitant, and almost immediately he tripped and dropped the container. The foam broke apart on the flagstones, and the computer module inside tumbled into view and shattered on the ground, pieces spraying for yards.

"Masters, I am sorry," the slave said, going to his knees and hastily sweeping the bits into a pile with bare hands. "Forgive me!"

"Clumsy idiot!" an overseer cursed, and lashed the teen with a knotted bullwhip. The sweat-stained shirt split across the back, and blood welled from a deep slash. The slave cried out, and the laughing sec man coiled the whip for another strike.

"Hold!" Silas roared.

The overseer froze, confusion on his features. "Sir?"

Silas stared at the bleeding youth. The strapping young farmer was too tired to haul a small box a hundred feet. "Bleeding to death isn't going to help this worker get more done today, is it?"

"I'll make him work," the overseer boasted, and the line of chained slaves cowered.

Hands clasped, Silas stared coldly at the fool. "Indeed. You are relieved of worker supervision and assigned to the wall," he said, his voice rising in power. "We have no need of fools here. Go!"

Stunned, the overseer stumbled away, unable to comprehend what he had done wrong.

Looking about, Silas choose a sec man and pointed. "You there, Corporal!"

"Yes, Doctor?" the older man asked, saluting briskly.

"Congratulations. You are now an overseer. Feed these workers and give them a ten-minute rest every two hours. Finishing a job is much more important than *trying* to finish the job. Understand?"

The sec man saluted. "Yes, Doctor. Hail the New America!"

Sighing in frustration, Silas walked to the lab and locked the door by throwing a dead bolt. Luxuriating in the air-conditioning for a moment, he limped to a computer console and continued the diagnostics on the new software. Building the dish was only the first step in controlling the Kite. They also needed precise calculations to focus the power station. Even the slightest mistake could result in nothing happening to the target, or his own sec men dying in droves.

The intercom buzzed.

"What?" Silas snapped, pressing a button. "I told you I was never to be interrupted in the lab!"

"Glorious news, sir!" A voice crackled through the speaker. "Ryan has been captured!"

A minute passed before Silas could speak. "What was that again?" he asked in disbelief.

"One of our patrols caught them in some ruins east of here. The major has them in the main courtyard. Do you wish to talk with the prisoners, or should we chill them, sir?"

"Do nothing!" Silas ordered, sliding a rainbow colored CD-ROM from the mainframe computer and tucking it into a shirt pocket. "No, summon more guards in case they try to escape. I will be there at once!"

Turning off the intercom, Silas hastily hobbled from

the lab and headed down a hallway for the exit. Could it be true that after so long a time, he was finally going to chill Tanner? Maybe that would stop the nightmares. His heart beat faster with hope. Yes, it had to! Free, he would be free from that cursed man once and forever!

Rushing from the building, Silas found a dozen sec men around a LAV-25 that was parked in the courtyard. Sheffield stood nearby with an unreadable expression.

"What's wrong?" Silas asked.

"Judge for yourself, sir," the major replied, crossing his arms.

An iron cage was attached to the rear of the APC with heavy chains, and it had obviously been dragged behind the transport through mud and fields. Horribly jammed inside was a group of wounded men, arms and legs sticking out of the bars of the impossibly tight confines.

More chains had been attached to a cross made of wooden beams. A man was chained and tied to the beams, his arms outstretched. He was covered with dirt, sweat cutting paths through the caked road dust. Dressed in combat fatigues and military-style boots, he had long black hair, was tall, heavily muscled, and a terrible scar bisected his face. But the prisoner had two eyes, and his teeth were filed to sharp points.

A smoking cigar dangling from his mouth, a grinning sergeant stood nearby the prisoners, his AK-47 leveled and ready as if expecting trouble.

"Are you in charge of this patrol?" Silas asked in a deceptively calm voice.

"Yes, sir, Dr. Jamaisvous!" the sec man stated proudly. "Gave us quite a fight, but we brought Ryan in alive and kicking."

"Dullard! Poltroon!" Silas raged, hobbling closer. "This isn't Cawdor! Can't you see he has two eyes!"

His smile fading quickly, the sergeant puffed nervously on the cigar. This wasn't going as planned. "Well, we sort of figured he took the eye from a dead man and shoved it in as a disguise. But we found him with those five others—one's a blonde, another a redhead and they had plenty of blasters."

"And he admitted to being Cawdor?" Sheffield asked in a monotone.

The sergeant scratched his head and looked at the other sec men, watching from the hatches of the LAV. "Well, no. Not exactly, sir. But we figured out who they were pretty fast. Who else could they be?"

"Anybody, you ass!" Silas lowered his bushy eyebrows until they touched. "Mercies, coldhearts, ville sec men, anybody at all. Ryan travels with six other people, not five!" he reminded harshly. "Two of them women, not men. Can't you tell the difference, or haven't you read the posted description? As per standing orders!"

"I…" The sergeant swallowed hard, losing his cigar. "My apologies, sir. None of us can read."

Conflicting emotions raged within Silas, and he glared at the sweating sec man for several minutes without talking. Finally, he spoke.

"You will have to do better next trip, Sergeant," Silas said sternly, the threat of severe discipline clear in the tone.

"Yes, sir. Thank you, sir!" The man almost fawned in his gratitude. "We'll leave today and find them fast!"

"See to it," the old man stated with a glare. "As for your prisoners, it's no great loss. We can always use more workers. Put them in chains and send the whole group to the wall. There's a constant need for fresh bodies in the stone quarry."

"Yes, sir! At once!"

Silas dismissed the matter with a wave. "You may go."

As the LAV drove away, dragging the prisoners behind, the rest of the guards returned to their duties, and Silas headed for the laboratory. Holding a palm to the wall plate, Sheffield opened the door for the man and entered after him, closing it tight behind them, making sure the lock was engaged.

"How utterly disappointing," Silas remarked, leaning heavily on his cane as they walked.

"Fucking idiots, is more like it," Sheffield growled. "Now that we're alone, how do you wish the sergeant punished for the failure?"

"For being illiterate? No. We're short on men as it is. More the fool I for not remembering when it is that I now live."

When, not *where,* Sheffield noted privately. The whitecoat often said such things, and he was starting to believe the idea. It certainly explained where the military blasters came from. His palm print opened doors everywhere across the complex, except for the warehouse. Whatever was inside, the old man hoarded it like a virgin did her cunny. Which only made Sheffield want it that much more.

Pausing at a control board, Silas checked the voltage on some dials, then turned to the officer. "Major, do you know the alphabet or how many continents there are? How many planets? What a gerund is? The name of the moon, or any of the laws of thermodynamics?"

The sec man scowled. "The moon has a name?"

"Since the 1965 International Conference of Astronomers. Its official name is Luna, and the sun is Sol."

"Interesting," he admitted. "But that doesn't put bullets in a blaster. Just a pretty song, nothing more. I'm a

practical man, sir. Taught myself to read labels so I
could steal food and not chems. I learned to chill a man
with just a knife in nine different ways, or skin him alive
to make him talk. I know how to cook dynamite, avoid
rad pits, raid a ville and fix wags. Do these other things
matter in the real world?''

"The real world," Silas repeated with a sigh. "No, I
suppose they don't. As a scientist, I must concede the
logic of your argument."

Unexpectedly, Silas laid a hand on the man's shoulder. "However, if you are to be my successor, they soon
will. We shall start your lessons with the most important
one of all."

"The warehouse?" the major asked eagerly, naked
avarice shining on his face.

Smiling, Silas hobbled for the doorway. "That and
much, much more. Come with me."

APPROACHING THE SPORTS ARENA, Ryan called for a
halt. The building stood five stories tall, the outer wall
ringed with clusters of lights. Some small windows, or
vents, were noticeable, but no doors.

"Jak, stay here as anchor," Ryan said cautiously. He
had a feeling they were being watched. "Krysty and I
will sweep around the building on a recce."

"No prob," Jak said, putting his back to the concrete
wall of the arena so he could see in every direction.
Weeds and desolation filled his vision. Predark ruins
were nothing but unburied cemeteries to him.

Patrolling along the side, the man and woman soon
found the front entrance, metal rings in the concrete
showing where a line of turnstiles had to have once been.
An iron grate was pulled off to the side, and Krysty

tugged on the barrier to see if it could move. Rust had welded it into a solid mass.

"Nobody's used this for a while," she commented.

Ryan merely nodded, unable to shake the feeling of being scrutinized.

The interior Plexiglas doors were wide open, debris keeping them from closing.

"Could be a trap," Krysty said, easing back the hammer of her revolver.

"Could be anything," Ryan countered, then added, "What's that smell?

Her hair flexing, Krysty sniffed. "Flowers?"

Moving deeper into the structure, they found the front hallway completely filled with flowering plants of a thousand different colors, the air rich with their sweet perfume.

"Don't see anything moving," Krysty said, watching for traitorous intent among the leaves.

"Perfect place for the greenies to go camou," Ryan noted. The hallway resembled a jungle with blossoms clustering thick on the walls, yet the floor was bare, as if inviting visitors.

"How can they grow without sunlight?" he asked.

"Mebbe some of it is still outside," Krysty guessed. "These could be just the roots."

"Roots seek nourishment," Ryan noted grimly.

A short flight of wide stairs went up a level, the steps and railings festooned with hanging leaves that offered no resistance to being pushed aside. Bracing himself, Ryan experimentally tore off a leaf. It came loose in a normal manner, and nothing else happened. They both relaxed.

The perfume smell thickened as the hallway opened onto a sports field, the ground covered with wags of every kind—cars, trucks, wooden wagons, bicycles, motorcycles, Jeeps, vans and even a few Hummers. Strewed among the vehicles were countless backpacks, suitcases, duffel bags, swords and blasters of every description.

"Thank Gaia!" Krysty cried out. "There's our stuff!"

"What the hell is going on here?" Ryan demanded softly as they approached the backpacks and saddlebags. "The greenies rob travelers and just toss the stuff here to rot? That doesn't make any sense."

"Not to rot, as offerings," Krysty said, pointing with her blaster. "I think this is their temple."

Standing majestically amid the piles of tributes was a huge flower, its stalk thicker than a tree trunk. Rainbows marked in hypnotic swirl patterns spread skyward from the plant. Oddly, there seemed to be no pistil or stamen, and Krysty wondered how the plant reproduced without pollination.

There was a funny tickling in his throat, and Ryan coughed on the thick smell of the plant. However, it was remarkably pleasant, and he felt his heart beating faster, a familiar tingle starting in his groin. Fireblast, this was no place to think about sex, Ryan chastised himself. Concentrate on the job, man!

Feeling woozy, Ryan tried to speak, but Krysty turned toward him, her eyes moist with emotion, her face flushed red. The fiery heat of lust welled within him, and Ryan crushed the redhead in his arms. Her lips so soft and warm beneath his own, their tongues intertwined in a long soulful embrace.

Something shouted a warning in his mind, but it was already too late.

As he murmured tender words, his hands roamed across her yielding body, savoring the womanly curve of her firm buttocks as her hips thrust against him in a delicious manner. Hands removed her coat—his or hers, he had no idea—as somebody undid his gun belt and pants. Krysty knelt before Ryan and took him full into her mouth, her fingers stroking and caressing. He grabbed her hair and thrust himself harder toward her, striving to get deeper into the sucking wetness. Her nails raked across his muscular thighs, the pain shattering the wild delirium for a split second.

That was when he noticed the bones on the ground, skeletons and clothing covering the dirt, which was filled with tiny roots. It was a carpet of death. Icy adrenaline flooded his body as the realization came that they were in a terrible trap. This plant wasn't ambulatory like some mutie foliage. Instead, it lured in victims with a sweet perfume and drugged them into a sexual fervor until they had to mate. Probably doing so on and on until they eventually died of starvation, still trying to blindly copulate. Their rotting bodies would feed the roots in the ground, and the death flower would blossom in hellish beauty.

"No," Ryan whispered, trying to push Krysty away. "Trap…we gotta…go…."

She pulled away from him, her face distorted in animal need. "Take me," Krysty commanded, starting to remove her clothes.

The blood was pounding louder than cannons in Ryan's ears, and he heroically struggled to fight the drunkenness of unfettered desire by thinking of dead friends and torture. He knew that once started, there would be no stopping until they collapsed from exhaustion, and in that weakened state, they would never again be able to resist until death claimed them both. It was now or never, and the Deathlands warrior forced himself to act.

"Wake up!" he cried, slapping her across the face as hard as he could. "We're being drugged. Horses for them, humans for their god!"

In frustration, Krysty shoved Ryan backward and he fell to the ground. Dropping her pants, the redhead sat astride him, tearing at his shirt, uncaring of the long furrows her nails dug into his chest. As she started to blindly hump against him, the electric velvet of entering the woman almost shattered his last resolve of sanity.

Using his last ounce of strength, Ryan threw her off. She rolled aside onto her hands and knees, rubbing her buttocks against his bare stomach.

"Now!" she yelled at him, spreading her legs. "Inside me! Now!"

Ryan grabbed her, and with a guttural cry he climbed on top and inside. The sensation was maddening, and Ryan bit his own tongue to stop the sweet perfume from claiming him. Pain was the answer. Only pain stopped the siren call of the plant's perfume. Then his memory flared, recalling Krysty's special muscles, and how she used them as no norm woman could to pleasure a man. Ecstasy worth dying for, pleasure beyond understanding. Die inside her, yes, yes! That was worth any price!

Ryan rammed his cock all the way inside her to bring him as close as possible to her, then slapped the barrel of the SIG-Sauer across the base of her skull. Krysty gave a gasp and slumped over unconscious.

A fresh wave of perfume flooded the arena as the flower spread wide its glorious petals. It was fighting for its next meal.

Raw fury boiled inside Ryan at the concept, and he focused his rage in order to survive.

"Die!" he roared, firing his blaster at the plant. Holes were punched in the lush petals, and vines snipped, greenish sap oozing from the small openings.

Standing on shaky legs, the mostly nude man grabbed his gun belt and reloaded, his whole world reduced to the ammo clip and the gun.

Grabbing Krysty by the hair, knowing that to pull on the living tendrils was agony to her, Ryan dragged the woman along behind him across the feasting bower, sheer willpower placing one foot ahead of the other. Whenever his will seemed to lag, Ryan fired the blaster close to his face, the sting of the muzzle-flash shocking him back to reality for a few precious moments.

Once past the doors, the perfume seemed to thin, but the desire still raged within the man. The steps wavered under his sight, but he plowed ahead, unstoppable in his determination to live. Sweat pouring off his body, Ryan staggered through the hallway of flowers, raging at the world, screaming curse words, doing anything he could think of to keep his anger fully fueled. Another yard was crossed, and still another.

Suddenly, reaching outside, Ryan stumbled to the concrete and kept moving forward on his knees, dragging Krysty behind, firing his blaster. A cool breeze blew over him, every breath taking away the rutting madness from his mind and body. Overcome, he slumped to the sidewalk and lost consciousness.

Minutes later, greenies rose from the weeds in the rubble and started dragging the exhausted man and woman back inside the temple of their living god.

Chapter Fifteen

Storm clouds filled the atmosphere above the planet Earth, and sheet lightning flashed constantly while hurricanes and tidal waves savaged the continents. And sterile deserts slowly spread across the world like a plague of dry rot.

The burned-out hulks of numerous satellites circled the tortured planet, some bristling with antennae, others smooth armored spheres of unknown purpose or design. Stationary above the former state of Tennessee floated a great black satellite, a slim ferruled cylinder with enormous shiny wings outstretched. Raw sunlight fell upon the millions of tiny glass squares composing the wings, and smooth pulses of electricity fed down the central supports and into the cylinder. There, computers hummed as accumulators stored the power, then from the bottom of the cylinder a concave dish extended into view and began beaming invisible rays at the ruined world below.

The beams spread outward in a cone formation as they bathed the polluted air, making the storm clouds dissipate until there was only a clear azure sky.

The rays descended until reaching an area in the desert where strands of bare wire had been strung in yard-wide squares across miles of dead land. The cone washed over the wire, and now tiny waves of electricity flowed into a series of transformers that unleashed the harnessed power in a network of high-tension lines toward a crumbling city on the horizon.

The ruins seemed to stretch for miles, tilting skyscrapers threatening to topple over, fires burning in gutted houses, rats feasting on bloated corpses strewed along the streets. Blast craters dotted the ground, their fused-glass bottoms glowing with deadly rads. A layer of frost covered the city like a death shroud, and what few bridges remained were eaten by blisters of red rust, just barely hanging over polluted rivers full of dead fish and decomposing ship hulls.

As the cables reached the decimated metropolis, slowly lights flicked to life inside the buildings, and the picture began to change. Window cracks sealed, and roofs straightened into proper alignment. The frost melted away, and the weeds withered and died. The hordes of rats ran shrieking into the sewers as the graffiti flowed off the sides of the strong buildings, and grass began to grow in yards and trees began to blossom. The roads smoothed as the potholes were filled, painted lines racing into existence along the clean macadam. The bridges became level, the rust falling away like autumn leaves, exposing the shiny steel underneath. A car rolled around a corner, then another and another until traffic flowed through the bustling city streets as in the days before the nukestorm.

But the restoration didn't stop there. A tumble-down shack rose again as a brick school, the field full of graves transformed into a ballpark and a playground. The junkyards and bomb craters became fields of golden wheat that reached into the distance. Factories disgorged machinery and clothing into softly humming electric trucks. Machines rolled out of warehouses and thrust electric prods into the rivers. Soon the water boiled and began to run clear again, all the way to the blue ocean. The prods were withdrawn, and fish jumped from the waters, rejoicing in their newborn life.

Outside the city, hordes of slavering muties touched the electrified fencing and withered into ash. Stalking the perimeter was a black dog with writhing tentacles sprouting from its shoulders, accompanied by a puma-like beast with a scorpion tail and insect mandibles. The beasts moved like well-oiled machines, but they, too, bumped the fence and vanished like flash paper in a candle's flame.

First one, then a dozen people appeared on the sidewalks, smiling and not carrying blasters. Soon they become a hundred, a thousand. Far away, farmers rose from the wastelands, the electric fences repelling the muties, as tractors plowed the land, planting more crops. Then the skies gently rumbled, and a soft clear rain fell on the world. Children rushed outside to play in the falling water as forest turned green and the world began to gradually turn into a blue-white sphere from the view in space.

Then the television screen turned blue.

"And that is our weapon?" Major Sheffield asked, sitting back in the chair, reeling from the amazing deluge of bizarre sights and sounds.

"Yes and no," Silas said, turning off the television and VCR.

"Unlimited electricity is merely one aspect of the Kite. The device is actually simplicity itself, as you saw. Solar cells in a high Earth orbit turn direct sunlight into electricity, which is gathered in transformers and broadcast to Earth as low-frequency microwaves."

"Like the microwave oven you showed me?" the sec man asked in horror.

"Different frequency, but the same principle. However, these beams cannot harm a fly, and are easily harnessed by those squares of wiring, which can be placed above croplands or cattle-grazing fields. Doing no harm to the cattle or crops, I might add. And then you have electricity, free, clean power. Gigawatts upon gigawatts."

Silas hobbled over to the television and got the tape out of the VCR. He slid the cassette into a box and stored it in a drawer along with his other videotapes. "A single Kite was designed to supply enough energy to run predark New York City and most of its suburbs. However, nowadays that's enough for all of the North American continent."

"Incredible!" Sheffield exhaled, chaotic thoughts swirling in his mind. "And this machine exists?"

"You have already seen it used against the slaves," Silas stated, reclaiming his hardwood chair. His bad leg was stiffening, and it was becoming difficult to rise from soft chairs without assistance. A simply intolerable condition. "Unfortunately, its military applications were also its doom. There is absolutely no way to stop such a microwave satellite from being converted into a deadly weapon of war. Simply change the focus, and you have a microwave beamer capable..." He smiled. "Well, you know what it can do."

The grotesque vista of what had been found after opening the doors to the bunker that night was a sight the officer would never forget. "And you created this, sir?"

"Good Lord, no," Silas snapped, annoyed for some reason. "It was invented by a fellow American, Paul Glaser of Boston, back in 1970, but the United Nations would never allow the power stations to be built. Partially because of business and politics, but mostly because whoever got one in space first, could stop everybody else from building the second power station. Thus, only one was ever built, and that was done secretly. The Pentagon had planned for the coming war by building a Kite, the mat-trans network…and other things.''

Sheffield waited eagerly, but Silas didn't oblige with more information. The sec man wasn't ready to learn of the redoubts. He was already clearly reeling from the video. The silly thing was just a promotional tape made to try to sway politicians. Silas easily changed a few of the scenes to make the material more relevant. Nothing could explain the function and promise of a working Kite better then simply seeing the device in action.

The officer rose and went to the barred window of the lab, staring at the dark skies. "Why, with this satellite we could cook the rad pits clean, or bury them under molten rock! Burn the rads and chems from the atmosphere!''

''Correct.'' Silas smiled. ''That is, once we achieve complete control. At present, we have only a focus for a few minutes a day.''

''Why is that?'' the major asked.

Sensing danger, Silas grew cold. ''Technical problems,'' he demurred. ''But those will soon be solved. All I need is more time to finish creating software to master the Kite. Its security systems are quite good, but can be beaten. Already I am up to five minutes a day before being booted off-line by the onboard systems.''

The major turned from the window. ''Five minutes of the Kite could stop an army!''

''If I do not miss.''

The sec man studied the whitecoat. The man stood straight, but his shoulders were hunched, dark circles around his eyes. He was exhausted, possibly dying. "The nightmares are coming every night, aren't they?" he guessed.

"Yes," Silas whispered, his face sagging. "It is becoming more difficult to concentrate each passing day."

"Well, I could send out more patrols," the sec man ventured, leaning forward in his chair. "Cover the fields, as well as the roads and bridges. Try to find Ryan and others and chill them as quickly as possible."

"Yes, do so. His death should end the nightmares and let me sleep again." His voice broke in a sob. "Sleep!"

"But that would seriously weaken the defenses of the complex," Sheffield continued. "It might be best to recall all of our troops and concentrate our strength here. We can mine the roads and lay more traps. This project is too important to be derailed by some mutie-loving outlanders."

"Which is why I am telling you this, as insurance against their possible arrival. If I should die—" Silas paused uncomfortably, his cheek twitching uncontrollably for a moment "—or become insane, then you shall assume the mantle of authority and bring America back from these days of barbarism. Deathlands is ruled by the strongest, not the wisest. Stupidity reins, muties and cannibals roam in packs, healers tortured as sport to amuse drunk barons. The madness must be brought to an end at any price. America will be reborn!"

"Victory or death," Sheffield said sarcastically.

Silas grunted. "Precisely. And today we shall start to clean house. To remove some potentially dangerous trash."

"Sir?" the sec man asked nervously.

Wincing as he stood, Silas walked to a wall map, favoring his leg. When Tanner stabbed him with that trick sword, he had to have severed a nerve. The wound was healed, the muscles strong, yet Silas still limped like the old man he appeared to be. Just another debt to be paid.

"Overton was sent to seize control of Front Royal, to turn it against the other villes in the area in a civil war. When they were weak, we would move in and forge the three largest into one huge city, the capital of New America. My America!"

"But Overton failed," the major stated, "because of Ryan and the others."

"Yes," Silas hissed, thumping his cane onto the floor. "So I am going to remove those three villes in case they decide to join forces against us. Look at this."

The sec chief walked closer as Silas drew some free-hand curves on the map with a black marker. "BullRun is the farthest east, thus the easiest to target. Next is Casanova and finally Front Royal. I can only use the Kite once every twenty-four hours, so it will take three days before Front Royal will be reduced to ashes.

"And I need targets to fire at." Silas lovingly stroked the map, smearing the lines. "Each time will give me greater control of the Kite, each use allowing me more access to its computers. In three days, I will crack the final codes and have total command over the orbiting power station."

"And what does the dish have to do with this?" the major asked curiously.

"That is what I need to punch a radio signal through the static and interference of the overhead storms and reach the Kite. How soon will the repairs be completed?"

"Two days, three at the most."

Silas smiled. "Ah, then in four days, we become the new rulers of America, and the great cleansing of humanity can finally begin. Thousands of the impure will die. No more muties! Isn't that glorious?''

"Oh, yes," the major agreed, feeling the two hearts in his chest pound with anger. "What a wonderful day that will be for our people."

AS THE GREENIES DRAGGED the humans back toward the arena, two loud reports split the night and the muties tumbled to the sidewalk with most of their heads removed. Holstering the blaster, Jak hurried around the curved building and inspected the sprawled man and woman.

"Ryan," the teenager said softly, shaking him by the shoulder. "What happened?"

The warrior struggled into consciousness. "Wags," Ryan hoarsely whispered. "Dozens of wags..."

"Inside arena?" Jak asked eagerly.

"Don't go! Plant fumes..." Ryan collapsed.

Standing, Jak glanced the entrance to the arena and sniffed. He didn't smell anything but some flowers. What fumes? From the condition of Ryan's and Krysty's clothes it looked as if they were caught in the middle of hot sex, but while on a recce in hostile land? That didn't make sense.

Adjusting what clothing they were still wearing to cover as much as possible, Jak again looked at the arena and made a decision. Raising the Colt Python, he loudly fired twice, then three times and once more. He quickly reloaded and waited for the rest of his friends.

Minutes later, a long whistle cut the air. Cocking back the hammer of his .357 magnum pistol, Jak replied with two short whistles and the rest of the companions came charging into view.

"We were going to the insurance company and heard

the shots," J.B. said, easing the tension on the trigger of the Uzi. Then he spotted the nearly naked couple. "What the hell happened here?"

"Ryan hauled out," the teenager said, glaring at the dark hallway of the building. "Muties tried drag back in."

"Indeed," Doc rumbled, removing his frock coat and draped it over Krysty. "And what happened to their clothes?"

"Don't know," Jak answered, scratching his head. "Said wags inside. Also plant fumes."

"Fumes?" Mildred carefully walked closer to the doorway and sniffed. Instantly, she felt her heart beat fast and a sudden rush of warmth between her legs. The physician backed away quickly and gulped in the clean desert air.

"There's something odd with the atmosphere, sure enough," she stated, staring hard at J.B. for a moment before forcing her mind back to reality. What was wrong with her? All she could think about was sex! Was that the problem?

Taking a lungful of air, Mildred walked into the entrance and waited. Nothing happened and she felt no different. Exhaling, the physician allowed herself a small sip of air, and her hips ached as her tingling breasts brushed against the soft fabric of her bra. Hastily, she rushed outside, gasping for breath.

"What's wrong, Millie?" J.B. said, holding her by the arms.

"S-some sort of drug," she replied, shaking. "Makes you crazy for sex. Probably once you go in, you never come out again."

"So the wags are bait," Dean decided.

"A logical deduction," Doc mused, leaning on his stick. "How utterly vulgar."

"Utterly lethal," Mildred corrected. "The question is, how do we check inside? What we need are gas masks."

"I know something just as good," J.B. said, slinging his blaster. "Got any shine?"

The teenager produced a bottle with less than half an inch of brown fluid. "What for?"

"Protection," the Armorer said, taking the bottle and splashing some of the homemade whiskey on a handkerchief.

Breathing through the reeking cloth, he approached the sports arena. The alcohol fumes were giving him a slight headache, but aside from that he felt normal. Holding his breath while he anointed the cloth again, J.B. walked around the dead muties and ventured farther, past the stairs, to finally reach the playing field.

In the dim moonlight, the scene explained itself. Bodies lay everywhere, and a huge blossoming flower sat in the middle of a hundred rusting wags. Their own backpacks were lying clearly in sight at the base of the huge plant. An offering to the god of the greenies, or bait for them? On a hunch, he fired a few rounds from the Uzi at the huge blossom. The stalk shook from the passage of the bullets, but there was no other effect. Realizing the shine was exhausted, J.B. retreated even faster than he entered.

"The bastard thing must feed off the bodies as they rot away," he finished explaining to the others.

"What if you were alone?" Dean asked.

It was a good question. "Probably just do yourself to death," J.B. said, passing the boy his stuttergun. "However, there's enough wags in there for an army, some of them in good condition. I'm going to steal us some wheels to replace the horses."

"Not enough," Jak stated, inspecting the bottle.

"Here," Mildred said, passing over the bottle of witch hazel from her med kit. "Use it sparingly. That's all we have."

J.B. removed the cap and took a sniff. "Whew! Even better than the shine. This'll work fine."

"Not go alone. I come," Jak said, digging a rag from his jacket. It was stained with oil from cleaning his blaster, but still serviceable. "Get backpacks first?"

"I'm going to chill that big flower first," J.B. corrected, shoving two more shells into the feed of his shotgun. "That seems to be the source of the drug."

"How are you doing to ace the weed?" Dean asked, shouldering the Uzi. "Bullets didn't work."

The Armorer frowned. "I know, and setting it on fire might only make the perfume deadly. We need some way to neutralize that bastard thing, kill it root and branch."

"Maybe there is some herbicide in one of the stores," Mildred hesitantly suggested, glancing at the ruins. "No, these are office buildings and such. Not a hardware store or greenhouse in sight."

"Explosives?" Jak asked.

J.B. frowned. "If we had a lot, sure."

"How about car batteries?" Doc suggested.

"Yeah, not bad," J.B. said, considering the idea. "Good call. I think that should work fine. Jak with me. Doc, Dean, you two are on guard duty. Mildred, see what you can do with Ryan and Krysty. Don't start a fire. We aren't going be here that long."

Holding the witch-hazel-soaked masks, the men stealthily entered the sports arena. The bones of a hundred corpses littered the floor, bits of clothing and boots visible amid the greenery. Backpacks and duffel bags were prominent lumps, and the barrels of discarded weapons were everywhere. The men walked hurriedly among the wags, inspecting them for damage and rust. Too many of the vehicles were civilian cars with bald tires, the bodies stripped of bumpers, seats and chrome to save weight and increase gas mileage. Few had hoods, and none had batteries.

Spotting a van in decent condition, J.B. used a knife blade to flip the grille lock, lift the hood and check inside. The battery was gone like the rest, a corroded mess eaten away by its own internal acids.

"Here," Jak announced, lugging a battery into view. The lead terminals on top were covered with flaky white material, but the casing seemed intact.

Removing the plastic caps with one hand, J.B. kept his mouth covered as he walked the heavy battery to the plant and awkwardly poured out the concentrated sulfuric acid onto the base of the stalk. Instantly, the plant seemed to lose color and the aroma in the air took on a sour smell.

Splashing on more witch hazel, Jak brought over another battery and did the same thing to the flower. Now the leaves began to wilt, the blossom closing its petals protectively. Dropping the dead battery, Jak flexed his hand and a knife slid into his palm. Slashing at the fibrous petals, he hacked open a hole, and J.B. poured the contents of another old battery directly inside. Now visibly wilting, the flower withered and began to turn brown.

Closely watching the roots they were standing on, the men nervously waited a few minutes to make sure the acid had worked. Acid rain in the Deathlands could strip the flesh off a man's bones it was so strong. But out here on the East Coast, the rain wasn't that strong, and was coming with less frequency. That was why Virginia and Georgia had living green trees, and not just endless sterile sand.

Experimentally, J.B. lowered his cloth and inhaled. "Dark night, what a smell!" He coughed, waving a hand at the air. "It's like burning tires mixed with shit and rotten eggs."

"Feel okay?" Jak mumbled behind his wad of cloth.

"I feel like vomiting!" the man replied, holding his nose shut and gasping for air through his mouth. "Shit! I can taste it!"

Hesitantly, Jak lowered his mask and risked a sniff. "Smelled worse," he said, while pocketing the damp rag. "Not by much, though."

"Come on, let's find a wag we can use."

RYAN AWOKE to the sound of an engine. Groggily, the man grabbed for his blaster and tried to sit up. "Not taking me anywhere!" he snarled, fumbling at the gun belt.

"Hey!" a familiar voice shouted.

Dizzy, Ryan tried to focus his vision and realized he was fully dressed and sitting on the sidewalk resting against the facade of the arena. Mildred was beside him, her fingers on his wrist checking his pulse. Doc and Dean stood a few yards away with blasters held at the ready, obviously on guard duty.

"What happened?" he asked around a mouthful of hairy cotton. His head was throbbing, and every muscle was sore.

Mildred released his wrist and offered a canteen,

which was gratefully accepted. "Jak chilled some greenies trying to drag you and Krysty back inside the arena."

"Fucking plant!" Ryan snarled, forcing himself to stand. "Don't go inside! The perfume is a drug!"

She nodded and took back the canteen. "Yeah, we figured that out pretty quick. Put some witch hazel on rags, and J.B. and Jak aced the flower and got us a wag."

Grunting in reply, Ryan drew the SIG-Sauer and checked the clip. It was empty, and he seemed to have no more loaded magazines. Fireblast, how many rounds had he fired to get them out of the building? Loose rounds were sewn into his jacket, a few more in the pocket, and Ryan started thumbing bullets into an exhausted clip.

"Glad to hear it's chilled," he stated grimly. "Where's Krysty? How is she?"

"Fine, lover," the woman answered from the darkness. She was sitting nearby on a piece of rubble, massaging her temples. The woman's wild abundance of red hair was hanging limp. He had never seen her so tired before. "Just don't expect much loving soon. Feel like I just lost my cherry during a fistfight."

"Had to," Ryan stated, slamming in the slip and jacking the slide, but clicking on the safety.

She hushed him with a finger on the lips. "I know. You saved us both," Krysty said. "Thank you. I have a nukestorm of a headache, but that's better than the alternative."

Revving engines sounded again, and a Hummer rolled from the building, easily passing through the wide entrance. At the steering wheel, J.B. bounced the wag down the front steps and parked on the sidewalk. Jak stood in the rear, his hands gripping an M-60 machine gun that rested on the gimbal of a short steel post, a long belt of ammo hanging from the breech.

"Replacement for the horses," J.B. said with pride, turning off the engine. "It's in great shape with a full tank of juice. We got our backpacks again, plus a ton of ammo, six Kalashnikovs, the 7.62 mm machine gun, half a case of grens and two LAWs. No food, but we're armed for war."

"Better," Jak said, resting an arm on the M-60. "We know location."

Ryan came closer. "You found a map."

A nod. "Couple of blue shirts are staring at the dirt inside. They must have stopped here on a recce, just like us."

"Indeed," Doc stated. "So where are they located?"

"Tennessee." J.B. grinned widely, holding out a folded piece of plastic. "Big red circle around Shiloh battlefield."

"Excellent!"

"Idiots," Krysty snorted.

Accepting the map, Ryan studied it closely. "So they're right next to the redoubt. About a hundred miles away."

"Less than a day in a Hummer," Dean added, climbing into the rear of the vehicle and finding his backpack. Undoing the straps, he stuffed his pockets with spare rounds for his blaster, and stuffed a chunk of smoked fish whole into his mouth, chewing contentedly.

"It would be a day's journey if we travel straight there," Ryan agreed, rubbing his cheek. Then the man hawked and spit to clear his throat. There was still a faint taste of the perfume in his mouth. Damn stuff was like glue. "But we're not going to travel directly to their base. The blues are smart. There might be more land mines and traps on the roads. How's the fuel?''

"Tanks are full of condensed fuel. That'll last us over a thousand miles. Plus, we have a can of regular juice.''

"Even better. So we take two days, mebbe three at the most.'' Ryan spread the map on the hood of the Hummer and the others gathered around. "We'll do an end run and head straight for this valley west of Shiloh. If they're expecting us, they'll be watching the north, east and south, but why waste sec men guarding their backs?''

"Sounds good,'' J.B. said, starting the engine. "Climb aboard and let's smoke this ville.''

"I just hope Overton didn't have a real army,'' Mildred said, taking a seat in the rear. "You know, thousands of men, tanks, planes. Sounds crazy, but he did have brand-new AK-47s, unlimited ammo, Hummers, radios. Who knows what else?''

Spotting his Steyr on the floor, Ryan took the passenger seat next to the driver. "We'll recce them from a distance, soft and low,'' he said, checking over the blaster. He had no recollection of losing it inside the arena, which only showed how far gone he had been. Hit his woman and dropped his weapon. Fireblast, he had to have been totally out of his mind.

"You sure that flower is aced?'' Ryan asked grimly, settling the longblaster into the crook of his arm.

"It's triple chilled,'' J.B. stated confidently. "Shriveled like bacon in a pan.''

"Has there been any problems with the greenies?'' Krysty asked. "I wonder why they haven't attacked yet.''

"Killed god,'' Jak said, patting the vented barrel of the long M-60 blaster. "Scare most folks.''

"Wished I could have seen it," Dean stated, loading another clip and tucking it away in his jacket.

"Too dangerous," Mildred countered, setting her med kit on the floor between her boots. "You're too young. The perfume might have driven you permanently insane."

Then she hid a smile and added, "And Doc is too damn old."

"Indeed, madam," Doc rumbled in his deep stentorian voice. "Perhaps you are unaware that some men are milk, while others are whiskey. Some sour and turn bitter with age, while the years make others stronger."

"What a load of crap," she snorted, grinning in spite of herself. "Crazy old coot."

"Ah, but that is my story and I am sticking to it."

Starting the Hummer, J.B. checked the gauges one last time, and looked longingly at the dark video monitor set in the control hump between the front seats. If the radio worked, the onboard computer probably did, also. But without a CD-ROM to boot the system, it was useless.

Turning on the headlights, J.B. pulled away from the arena, and headed the wag westward out of the ruins. The potholes were bad, but he managed to avoid most of them. The few he hit were taken easily by the Hummer with only minor shaking of the passengers. He once rode in a jeep, the military wag used before the Hummer was created and wondered how anybody got to the fight without losing teeth.

The headlights illuminated something in the road ahead of them, and J.B. turned to go around. But the obstruction continued onward until reaching a gaping hole in the ground where a strip mall once stood. Having no choice, J.B. angled away from the area and took off due south. But again they found debris blocked their way. The piles of rubble had been connected with chunks of concrete, effectively sealing the area between the hotel and the insurance building.

"This looks fresh," Krysty warned, her hair blowing in the wind.

"Head north for the desert!" Ryan commanded. "We know that way is clear."

The Hummer raced across the predark city, past the arena and the armory, only to find more rubble stacked over ten feet high, rusty iron rods sticking out of the broken concrete like pungi sticks.

"The little bastards have sealed us in!" J.B. cursed, accelerating along the line of rubble. The crude wall was unbroken, extending from building to building, the only breeches the foundation holes where stores had burned to the ground.

"Try ramming through!" Dean suggested, trying to watch every direction at once. The attack would come soon. No point to trapping a prey unless you planned on doing some chilling.

"Can't! This is a Hummer, not an APC!"

"Try anyway!"

"Triple red! Here they come!" Ryan snapped, working the bolt on the Steyr and firing smoothly. In the darkness, a greenie cried out and fell to the ground.

But dozens more darted from the ruins, scrambling over one another in their haste to reach the rolling transport. J.B. swerved wildly, but more were ahead of them. Flooring the accelerator, the Armorer headed straight toward the pack, screaming a battle cry. Suddenly, the M-60 began to chatter and the greenies fell away, missing arms and faces. But as the Hummer plowed into the mob, they parted and dived for the sides of the wag, holding on with one hand while thrusting with knives, hoping for a lucky strike. The companions thrust blasters into leafy faces and blew them off in ruthless slaughter.

Some of the muties dived under the vehicle, and it thumped over them, their bones cracking audibly. J.B. veered to the left, then the right, losing the howling pack, and raced across the open area between the monoliths. But as they gained some distance, a steady hissing could be heard, along with a metallic tinking.

"They got a tire!" Ryan yelled. "Stop the wag and get that bastard knife to dig it out. These military tires are self-sealing once the hole is clear."

Brakes squealed in protest as J.B. slowed the Hummer and jumped to the ground. Just as quickly, the companions formed a firing line between the wag and the oncoming greenies. The night was strangely still, not even insects chirping to break the quiet.

"Shoot on sight," Ryan shouted, facing away from the others to cover their rear. "Our blasters have a lot more range than those blowpipes. Don't let them get close!"

There was movement in the darkness, and the companions opened up with their weapons, the muzzle-flashes illuminating the night for yards. Greenies were running toward them with inhuman speed.

"Behind us!" Ryan shouted, firing.

Jak started to hammer the ruins with the M-60, the heavy weapon laying down a hellstorm of copper-jacketed lead. In the far distance, a glass window shattered and something screamed briefly, then went silent. Howls sounded from behind them again, and as they turned, the noise stopped, then started once more.

"Ignore the noises," Krysty said, dropping a speed loader into her revolver. "Only shoot when you see them. That's an old trick to rattle us and make us waste ammo.''

"And we contemptuously thought they were unintelligent muties,'' Doc stated, holding the LeMat in a combat grip to steady his aim. Only six more shots and he was out. "More the fools we.''

Swearing softly, Jak struggled with the bolt to clear a jam, the live cartridge hitting the ground with a musical ting-a-ling. "They not dumb.''

"Got it!'' J.B. cried, standing triumphant, the broken blade of a knife shining between the teeth of his pliers. "Bastard thing was wedged in tight. Almost as if they knew exactly where it should go.''

"Get in, use the Uzi,'' Ryan ordered, sliding across the Hummer. Taking the wheel, the man shoved the transmission into gear and started forward slowly, allowing the companions to climb into the wag.

"Everybody in?'' Ryan shouted as he gunned the engines.

"Clear!'' Dean replied, shoving a fresh clip into the handle of his Browning semiautomatic pistol.

A greenie stuck its head into view from a manhole and spit. Doc cried out, dropping his blaster to the floor of the wag. Swinging the M-60 about on its gimbal, Jak peppered the manhole with 7.62 mm rounds, but the mutie was gone.

Krysty lobbed a gren at the hole. The sphere bounced twice and went right into the opening.

Ryan hit the gas, and the Hummer raced away as flames erupted from the ground, resembling the muzzle-flash of a cannon.

"Knife!'' Mildred ordered, and Dean passed her a blade. The physician sliced apart the sleeve of Doc's frock coat, exposing his upper arm. There was a purplish bruise there, the flesh already tinged with yellow around a tiny barbed dart. Plucking the dart free, Mildred cast it away and cut a crisscross pattern into the flesh. Laboring to breathe, Doc made no response, sweat appearing on his pale face. Sucking at the wound, Mildred's mouth burned as his blood came out. She spit it outside the wag and repeated the process until it no longer hurt her to extract blood from the wound.

"That'll do," Mildred decided, looking at the spot with her flashlight. "I got the poison out fast enough."

"Thanks," Doc mumbled, color already returning to his features.

"Don't thank me yet," the physician warned, opening her med kit and pouring the last few drops of witch hazel on a bandage. "This will hurt even worse. It'll keep you alive, though."

"I stand ready, madam," he said through gritted teeth.

Mildred laid the damp cloth on the wound, and Doc sharply inhaled at the contact. She quickly tied it off with a field dressing as he continued to breathe rapidly.

"Don't use that arm to shoot," Mildred ordered, wiping the blood off her hands. "The recoil of that monster handcannon will open the wound and make you start to bleed. This is only a pressure bandage. Once we're clear, I'll stitch it closed properly."

Clumsily, Doc lifted the LeMat with his left hand and rested it on the side of the Hummer. "I am no Sissiphant, madam," he stated.

She nodded in understanding. "You're welcome, you old coot." Just then, a swarm of greenies charged from the darkness into the headlights once more. Ryan wheeled away from them as Jak gave the muties another taste of the M-60. Then J.B. added the ripping killpower of the Uzi, and a handful of the attackers fell over dead.

This time, the greenies didn't get close and they raced away, leaving them behind.

"Can't keep this up forever," Ryan stated, shifting gears. "Eventually, they'll get our range and do us all like Doc."

"You have a plan. I can hear it your voice," Krysty said, using fingernails to yank two spent cartridges from the cylinder of her blaster. She slid in live rounds and eased the S&W closed. "Whatever the hell it is, you have my vote to try."

"Me, too," Dean added, carefully removing a dart from the headrest of the seat in front of him. He tossed it away, then spit on his fingers and rubbed them clean on his pants.

Stomping on the gas pedal, Ryan turned the Hummer and headed directly toward a group of greenies they'd encountered earlier. The muties greeted them with a wave of barbed darts that hit the windshield and bounced off.

Angling for the low point in the barrier, the Hummer started to climb sideways up the mass of debris, the tires spinning wildly as rocks crumbled away under their weight.

"Shift right!" Ryan bellowed, twisting the steering wheel.

The companions dived to the right side of the wag, their weight holding it steady as the transport jounced and bumped over the timbers and automobile parts. Then the rubble shifted, and the Hummer slid out of control. There was a strident crash of wood, and the predark wag reared on its aft wheels, threatening to flip over. Ryan hit the brakes, then the gas, regaining control of the machine, and the Hummer madly rolled back onto the street.

Waiting below, the greenies charged, and the companions fired in a volley at the mass attack. Doc leveled his LeMat pistol and fired twice through the chaos. A greenie loading a blowpipe jerked backward, slamming into a greenie behind. They both fell, blood gushing from huge wounds.

As the Hummer pulled away, its engine roaring in high gear, a dozen of the muties lay sprawled on the cracked macadam, dead or merely pretending. There was no way of knowing.

"Now we can leave!" Ryan shouted, fighting the wheel. The wag streaked across the ruins. "It was a diversion to get them going in the wrong direction. We're busting out of here right now!"

As they zigzagged past the potholes and manholes, the insurance building rose before the companions, its mirrored windows darkly reflecting the tiny racing vehicle.

"Blow us a hole!" Ryan commanded, heading straight for the tinted-glass doors.

The 7.62 mm blaster ripped into life, spraying the facade of the insurance building. Cracks appeared in the revolving doors, nothing more. But the large ground-floor windows shattered into a million pieces. Shifting gears, Ryan plowed through the jagged opening and into the building. Cresting the sill, the wag landed on top of a mahogany desk, smashing it under their tonnage. Fighting for control, Ryan rammed into a room divider, and for a brief instant, he saw a skeleton in a pin-striped rags holding a cup slumped before a dark computer screen. Then everything went flying as the Hummer plowed across the office, leaving a trail of total destruction.

A headlight winked out as Ryan headed straight for a

short hallway. The fit was so tight that sparks sprayed out from the armored chassis scraping along the marble facade, then the wag smashed aside a set of double doors and reached the cafeteria. Tables squealed as they were forcibly shoved out of the way, plates, newspapers and chairs flying everywhere.

The M-60 blaster spoke again, clearing away the windows, sand pouring into the room. But the angle was too steep, and the Hummer couldn't gain enough purchase in the shifting sands.

"Fireblast, we need a shim!" Ryan shouted, braking to a halt amid the destruction. "J.B., Dean, get that soda machine!"

The two jumped from the Hummer and raced to the huge soda dispenser. Rocking it back and forth, they got it moving and started slowly waddling it toward the pile of sand pouring in though the broken window.

"Incoming!" Jak shouted, firing the M-60 into the hallway. A greenie was torn apart and dropped to the carpeting.

Krysty pulled the pin on a gren and threw it hard at the marble wall. The sphere hit and rebounded out of sight. A few moments later, a thunderous explosion shook the room and smoke poured down the hallway. Jak wasted rounds shooting into the smoke just in case. Muties crawled into view, blood gushing from the hideous stumps of missing limbs. But they still tried to reach the wag even as they died.

"This is not a fight, but a jihad!" Doc cried in realization. "A holy war of revenge! They will never stop until we're dead."

A greenie dropped from the ceiling panels, landing amid the companions. Krysty blew off its head, and Dean slit its throat as it fell from the wag.

Suddenly there was a crash as the soda machine toppled over in place. "Get in!" Ryan shouted, but the others were already aboard.

Gunning the engines, Ryan headed for the machine, knowing it could never support the awesome weight of the Hummer for more than a few seconds. But those moments should be everything he needed. The hood of the war wag lifted as the wheels rolled on top of the soda machine, metal started to crunch. Ryan hit the gas and shifted gears. The wag started to lose some height. Greenies ran screaming into the room, and Dean threw a gren. The LeMat boomed. A dart hit the inside of the windshield, then with a lurch, the studded tires caught on the sill and the Hummer climbed up and out the window, rolling into the night.

As they sped away from the ruins, Dean saw the interior of the insurance building come alive with flames, black silhouettes of the muties dashing about screaming in pain and rage.

"Goodbye, Georgia," Mildred growled, slumping in her seat. "We have three days to rest before reaching Shiloh."

"Plenty of time," Ryan said, loosening his grip on the steering wheel. "The only point on our side is that we're not racing against the clock."

"Thank Gaia for that," Krysty said with a smile.

Chapter Sixteen

The awful stench was the first thing that Clem noticed. He sniffed again and tried to figure out what it was. Wood smoke, definitely, mixed with the tang of a blacksmith shop and other things he couldn't recognize.

"Muties?" asked the young corporal riding point alongside him.

"Don't think so," Clem drawled, chucking the reins. "But I don't like it. Blasters out, and watch yourselves."

The squad of brown shirts needed no further prompting and drew their longblasters. In an effort to impress Baron Markham of BullRun ville with the seriousness of the matter, Nathan Cawdor had given the ambassadors the best AK-47s they had and plenty of ammo. Where words might fail, anybody too stupid to listen to troopers armed with rapid fires and talking peace was just too damn dumb to let live.

Cantering over one of the many low hillocks so prominent in northern Virginia, the men stopped in their tracks, the horses whinnying in fear. Lying before them was desolation like nothing they had ever seen. Stretching for perhaps a full mile were the ruins of the ville, cottages and huts crumbling even as they watched. The castle itself was mostly gone, a glowing pool of lava exactly where the predark fort should be standing. Only a few of the outer buildings still existed. Bricks fell from the side of building and hit the ground, bursting into their component ash, the powdery cement blowing away as dry dust. Only the windows seemed to be undamaged, the glass remarkably clear and sparkling clean as if brand-new.

There was a depression in the ground with the remains of fish at the bottom, as if it were once a pond. Even the soil itself was blackened as if charred by a terrible fire. Yet countless trees still stood, the bark peeling off the gray trunks, brittle leaves carpeting the ville even though it was only early autumn. A field of brown crops stretched to the north, every breeze snapping the stalks and clearing whole areas. The smoking corpses of people lay everywhere, their clothing flaking into ash, their crispy skins split apart to expose coooked flesh and black bones. Exploded blasters lay near the hands, the stocks twisted and partially slagged.

Sprinkled across the horrible landscape were stingwings and birds alike, wings outstretched as if still in flight. Skinny rats scampered among the assorted destruction searching for food, but none was touching the many corpses so readily evident.

"What the hell happened here?" Clem asked softly, pushing back his bearskin hat. He might have to wear the uncomfortable uniform of Front Royal while in the ville, but on the road, the mountain man quickly returned to his more familiar garb.

"Not much left," a sec man whispered, the overwhelming feeling of death filling the air.

"Nothing left," Clem corrected him. At those loud words, the artesian well in the middle of the ville broke apart, the wooden beams bursting into ash and the stones plummeting out of sight into the ground. Minutes passed, but there was no sound of a splash from the blocks striking water.

Frowning, Clem withdraw a plug of tobacco and bit off a chaw. He had seen a hundred different kinds of chilling, but nothing resembling this. The hooves of his stallion were already thick with the dust of the land.

A sergeant checked the bulky rad counter they had found hidden in Overton's room at Cawdor Castle. He worked a few dials and tapped the meter. The needle swung about but didn't enter the red area. "Reading clean," he announced. "No rads."

"Didn't think it was a nuke." Clem chewed thoughtfully. "And it sure as shit wasn't acid rain."

A soft breeze from the mountains moved over the annihilated fields, the plants crumbling into dust and blowing away. Then a section of the castle broke part, the bricks and mortar separating as the masonry tumbled to the ground.

"Well, lightning didn't do it, either," a private stated firmly. "I seen lightning hit, and it don't do this."

Sliding off his horse, a lieutenant knelt on the road and reached out to take a handful of the black soil. He carefully inspected it before daring to take a sniff.

"No smell of fuel or black powder," he said, standing and tossing the piece of dead earth away. "Hell, ain't no chem burn I know. Not napalm, thermite or even willy peter."

Shifting in his saddle, Clem translated the term in his head. "Willy peter" was slang for white phosphorus. J.B. had told him about the predark chem. It burned ten times hotter than a Molotov cocktail, but was controllable, unlike thermite. Once you ignited that stuff, all a man could do was run away fast, or fry like a chicken on a spit.

Thunder rumbled, and the man glanced upward to see fiery streaks of orange slashing across the purplish sky, a billowing array of dark storm clouds ravaged by the endless hurricanes of the upper atmosphere. Nothing unusual there.

Glancing down, he noticed the line in the soil where the strange effect stopped and the green grass started once more. The boundary was sharp, as if a line had been drawn with a sharp knife and a string. What weapon could do that?

"Dead," a sec man whispered, making the sign of the cross. "All dead."

"Whatever it was happened fast, too," Clem added, jerking his chin. Off to the side lay the still body of a horse, half of the mare within the circle of destruction, the rest on cool green grass.

The lieutenant went into the woods and returned with a long green stick. Placing the tip against the black soil, the sec man pressed downward, and it easily sank all the way down until his hand almost touched the surface. Withdrawing the stick, he examined the length of the sapling.

"No resistance," he rumbled, coughing to the taste of the bitter ashes. "Whatever did this penetrated mighty deep into the earth."

"There's lava over there," a young sec man said hesitantly. Impulsively, he reached for his blaster, then released the weapon. There was nothing here to shoot. Whatever battle had been fought was long over. "Mebbe it was a volcano? I heard of them from my ma. Mebbe the ville just got cooked with steam."

Spitting out a long stream of brown juice, Clem frowned deeply. "Let me tell ya, kid, no steam nor lava did that," he stated as a fact.

"Don't like this," the lieutenant muttered, cracking his knuckles and stepping onto the strange soil. He sank to his knees and quickly stepped back onto the road. A rat scurried by, and he resisted the temptation to shoot it out of sheer annoyance.

"Mebbe Overton..." the corporal started.

Clem snorted and glanced around at the hellish vista. "Can't be. If his coldhearts could do this, why not just show us and declare himself baron? Who would be crazy enough to try and fight this with blasters and knives?"

"More likely it's removing potential enemies," the sergeant said gruffly, fighting to keep his horse calm. The animal was very unhappy and wanted to leave the moment they had arrived. He didn't blame it a bit. "Chill before getting chilled."

Nobody spoke for a few minutes, thinking seriously about that possibility.

"Might be," Clem agreed, pausing to spit again. "That is, if this be a weapon and not some bizarre natural effect of the Deathlands. We be mighty close to the Washington Hole. All sorts of crazy stuff happens there."

"Hey, look at this," the lieutenant said, holding up a small gray object. "It's an intact bullet."

Leaning over in the saddle, a sec man glanced around closely. "Say, there's lots of them. Over there, and there!"

"Weirdest thing," the lieutenant said, frowning. "It's not damaged in the slightest."

"Oh, nuke me!" Clem exclaimed in sudden understanding, and he hawked out the whole chaw. "They must of been shooting at the sky, and the slug fell without hitting nothing!"

"The sky," a sec man whispered. "You mean, a plane?"

"Or a bomb?" another asked in a hoarse whisper.

"Fucked if I know!" Clem wheeled his horse about. "Everybody, back to Front Royal! We got to warn Baron Cawdor before this thing strikes again!"

"Wait, sir!" the lieutenant shouted, waving.

"What for?" Clem demanded hotly, the reins tight in his hands.

The sec man took the reins of his own mount and handed them to a surprised Clem. "It took us two days to get here with full supplies. If you drop everything except your blaster, and take my horse as a spare, you can get there in one day."

Clem tied the reins to the pommel of his saddle. "Smart thinking. See ya back the Front Royal!" With a war whoop, the chief of the sec men kicked his horse into a full gallop. Yards away, his saddlebags dropped to the road, then his water bag, the bedroll and then he was gone from sight over a hillock.

"One day," the lieutenant said. "I just hope it's enough time to evac the ville."

"To do what?" a sec man asked. "Run away?"

"And what else can we do against a plane dropping bombs?" the sergeant retorted.

The rest of the brown shirts didn't reply as the lieutenant climbed on the largest horse behind a private and they started riding southward to their homes. Hopefully, the ville would still be there when they arrived.

SMOKING A CIGAR in the morning light, the blue shirt watched the road winding down the side of the steep hill through his binocs and fought back a yawn. It was another two days until his relief came, and he could go back to the complex for hot meals and slave girls. Sniper duty was boring. Anybody he saw was fleeing the Tennessee River valley, and he wasn't allowed to loot any food or have a woman. The survivors might meet Ryan coming along on the road and give away his location.

The mined bridge over the river was clear as always. Horses and people could cross safely, but Major Sheffield said that if a big wag like an APC or a Hummer tried to go across, the whole thing would blow sky-high. He'd liked to see that. It would help relieve the boredom.

To the south rose the foothills of the big mountains. They were little things, only a couple hundred feet high, hardly worth calling a hill. More of a mound, really. A dirt road wound down the steeply sloped side, zigzagging along to finally go over the top near the peak. Personally, the sec man didn't think any wag could travel over the rocky terrain without busting an axle, or worse. It was for walking, or horses, not wags.

Which meant he was here for nothing, doing nothing. He took another drag on the cigar, and blew a smoke ring into the air, contemplating randomly shooting at folks as they passed by just to watch them dance.

Then a speck rose over the crest, and he took a look with the binocs. Probably just some more greenies from Georgia, or stickies. Focusing the military glasses on the hill, he followed the roadway until reaching the tiny dot again. The cigar dropped from his mouth, and he leaned forward, nearly falling from his perch in the tree. It was them! Holy shit, it was Ryan and his gang!

THE ROAD DOWN THE HILL was covered with rocks, making driving almost impossible. The Hummer scraped bottom more than once when it rolled over broken chunks of granite. The view was spectacular, although the trees lining the serpentine road blocked most of their view of the valley below. But they could catch glimpses of a river, and seemingly endless forests of blue pine carpeting the landscape to the horizon.

Shifting gears and fighting for control, Krysty finally reached the bottom of the road and floored the wag. The Hummer surged forward in a burst of speed, and almost immediately there was a bang, the vehicle veering to the left.

"Gaia!" she spit, fighting the wag to a stop. "That tire finally blew."

"Better here than up there," J.B. said, climbing from the rear seats. "Well, we got almost fifty miles out of it. That's not bad. Time to use the spare."

Dean stepped into the bushes for a moment, while Jak stood guard at the M-60. The road ahead was level and straight, going directly to a predark bridge.

"Bridge looks in good condition," Mildred said, adjusting the focus on the binocs.

"We'll have to check for traps," Ryan commented. "This is close to Shiloh, and the blues could be anywhere."

The words were still in the air when a volley of bullets chattered across the armored chassis of the Hummer, closely followed by sound of a distant rifle cutting through the peace of the forest. Everybody dived for cover.

Lying in the dirt, Ryan worked the bolt on his Steyr SSG-70 rifle, chambering a round for immediate use. "That sounds like an AK-47," he said, sighting through the scope on the longblaster, sweeping the trees. "Yeah, it's a blue. I caught a glimpse of a muzzle-flash in the trees."

More rounds hit the wag, two impacting on the jack supporting the vehicle. The flat was lying on the ground, the new tire resting against the Hummer waiting to be attached. The jack was hit again and shook, but didn't fall.

"There seems to be only one sniper," Doc said, moving away from the wobbly vehicle.

"Only one firing," Ryan corrected him grimly. "There could more."

"Bastard's smart, too. He waited until I had the flat off, then started firing. We're not going anywhere," J.B. stated, adjusting his wire-rimmed glasses to sit more firmly on his face. Last thing he wanted was for them to slide off in the middle of a battle.

"Anybody hurt?" Mildred asked from the bushes.

Just then another wave of bullets pounded over the armored hull of the Hummer, sounding like hail on a tin roof. Several rounds hit a tire, but didn't puncture the military rubber.

"Undamaged so far," Ryan answered, as trained hands fired the Steyr and worked the bolt, loading another round. "But not for long. This guy is good."

"Too good," J.B. added, firing the Uzi twice at random trees on the distant hill. Return fire kicked up dust directly in front of him, and the Armorer dived off the road into the bushes, crawling hastily away from the spot at which he entered. Seconds later, that location shook from a hail of incoming rounds.

"Much too bastard good," J.B. muttered.

A figure appeared from the trees, holding a silvered revolver. "Want me to try a LAW?" Krysty offered, the plastic tube draped over her back.

Targeting the tops of trees, Ryan shook his head, firing again. "Don't waste it. We still have a long way to go."

"Besides, he's not going to hurt us with an AK-47,"

J.B. retorted, firing the Uzi randomly at the hilltop. "Not at this range, anyway."

"Incoming!" Dean shouted, and a split-second later, a fiery dart riding a contrail of smoke flashed by them, heading for the Hummer. A wave of heat from the exhaust washed over the companions as the rocket missed the wag by a foot and disappeared into the woods. Silence ruled the area for long tense seconds, then the forest erupted into a fireball of thundering flame.

"That was a LAW!" Ryan growled. "Okay, anybody got a gren?"

"At this range?" Krysty asked, puzzled.

"Just throw it as far as you can!"

Pulling the pin, the redhead dropped the handle and heaved the sphere with all of her strength. The ball hit the road roughly thirty yards away and rolled a few more before the charge exploded, throwing a cloud of smoke and dirt into the air.

"Camouflage," Ryan said, throwing his own slightly to the left of the first. Another huge cloud of dirt covered the roadway, completely masking the Hummer.

Sporadic fire came from the sniper as the companions used the rest of the grens to maintain the dust cloud. Resting the flat tire against his spine as protection from incoming rounds, J.B. hastily attached the new tire, using only half the nuts. But he wasted a few precious seconds making sure those were solid and tight.

"Done, go!" he shouted.

At the wheel, Mildred, the sole occupant of the wag, started the engine and rolled away, crumpling the jack still attached at the frame of the military vehicle. She cut a fast turn, throwing more clouds of dirt into the air with the spinning tires, then charged headlong into the trees and vanished among the foliage.

As if the sniper deduced their plan, another LAW streaked through the dust to violently detonate a scant yard away from where the Hummer had been parked.

"Now!" Ryan ordered, and he charged into the trees at a full run, the rest of the companions only steps behind.

Moving fast through the pine trees, Ryan curved across the sloped side of the valley, rising slowly alongside the sniper. Raising a fist, he pointed directions, and the others split into teams to converge on the sniper from different directions.

A Kalashnikov constantly chattered at the trees, the noise guiding the companions to the location of the hidden gunner. Minutes later, they found him.

The blue shirt was sitting on a hunter's box, just a few planks nailed to branches, giving him a stable platform to hide in as he waited for prey to come into view. The upper branches of the tree shook as spent brass arched from the hot breech of his blaster. Soft curses sounded, and the shooting stopped.

Creeping closer, Ryan saw the sec men rummaging frantically in a duffel bag. Then he pulled another LAW into view with a satisfied cry.

"Don't!" Ryan barked, standing and working the bolt on the Steyr. The weapon was already loaded, but the noise would drive home the point that he was armed.

The sec man registered shock, then rage and dropped the LAW, going for his longblaster. Without a qualm, Ryan fired, hitting the man in the chest, the 7.62 mm round slamming him backward into the tree trunk. Then J.B. added the fury of his Uzi, and the corpse tumbled from the trees to land on a rock with a sickening crunch. Rivulets of blood began dripping onto the ground from his hidden face.

"Doc, Dean, sweep the area for any more," Ryan ordered, approaching the corpse. There was a map sticking out of his back pocket.

But before he could reach the document, the bushes parted and two more blue shirts walked out, firing their Kalashnikovs. Diving for cover, Ryan shot the closer man in the belly with his Steyr. The other blue fired his longblaster, but then a knife sprouted from his throat. Gagging on his own blood, the sec man fell to his knees, still triggering the AK-47, shooting in every direction. Then Krysty stepped from behind a tree and fired her hand blaster into his face, finishing the job.

"Perimeter sweep, twenty yards!" Ryan ordered, rising from the ground.

Krysty, Doc and Dean moved into the forest as J.B. climbed up the crude ladder. On the platform, he stayed crouched, studying the forest around them. When satisfied, he whistled an all-clear signal and climbed back down with the duffel bag and the dead man's AK-47.

Ryan got the map as the Armorer checked the contents of the duffel. "Dark night, he had two more LAWs, and an implo gren that could have reduced the Hummer to a soup can!"

"If he got close enough," Ryan agreed, looking over the plastic paper. It was the same as the other, just a map of Tennessee. Nothing more.

A long whistle came from the forest, and Ryan answered with two short ones. The rest of the companions stepped into sight from several locations.

"Nobody that we can find," Krysty reported, holstering her revolver. "Find anything useful?"

"Nothing so far," Ryan said, turning the map over. Nothing was circled or highlighted as with the last one they had found, but there was a notation scrawled at the bottom with indelible ink. Ryan looked twice at the map to make sure he was reading it correctly.

"There's a name on this," he said, his features carved from stone. "Might mean shit, but here it is."

"Who?" Jak asked, reloading.

"Checkpoints along Timber Ridge Road, password is El Morro. Main-gate entry password...Jamaisvous."

"What did you say?" Doc whispered, dropping the LeMat from limp fingers. The man looked as if he had just been hit with a club.

"Silas," Ryan repeated, showing the map. "Silas Jamaisvous."

Without speaking, Doc retrieved the weapon, his mind lost in dark thoughts. So it was about to all begin once more.

Stuffing ammo clips from the corpse into his pockets, Dean frowned. "I thought he died in that mat-trans jump."

"We hoped he died," Krysty stated, her hair a flaming corona about her tense face. "Guess not."

"Crap! We can't go anywhere near a redoubt," J.B. grunted, slinging the duffel bag over a shoulder. "Silas knows the access codes, and could have sec men waiting for us."

"Or worse," Jak added grimly.

"So what should we do?"

"We find his base and kill the son of bitch permanently this time," Ryan said, turning on a heel. "Come on, we still have to fix that tire and get across the bridge. Once on the other side, we'll hide the wag and proceed on foot."

Chapter Seventeen

Standing alone on the top floor of the observation tower at Casanova ville, a sec man squinted at the cloudy sky and smiled.

"Almost lunchtime," the man commented aloud, his stomach rumbling in harmony. Although the sun was blocked by heavy clouds, he could still see that it was just reaching dead overhead. Noon. Soon a servant would bring him a basket of food. The sentry only hoped it wasn't rat again. They had been eating rat for the past month, and he was getting sick of the same thing every freaking day. Sure, it was better than nothing, but what good was being a sec man if you ate like a civilian?

With a sigh, he rested the heavy barrel of his muzzle-loading longblaster on a shoulder. Spare pieces of flint were tucked into loops on his belt, and his shirt pocket was neatly lined with paper cartridges for charging his weapon. It was a bloody clever invention of the baron's. Instead of counting as you poured black powder into your weapon, he had made these little paper tubes from library books. A person bit off the top and poured out the black powder inside. It was exactly enough for a full charge, always the same. At the bottom was the miniball, and you used a nimrod to stuff the paper that the cartridge was made out of down the barrel to hold the load in place. Powder, shot and wadding all in one. The sec men could fire ten times faster than before, making their crew of a hundred shoot like a thousand!

One of the servants had dared to suggest it was a predark idea from something called the Civil War, and the liar had been beaten to death right in the market square. Nobody insulted the baron and lived. Except his mud head of a son, that was.

Lightning flashed overhead, and the sentry felt a warm breeze blow over the tower. In October? Suddenly, there was a loud peal of thunder, and bright light flooded the ville. Glancing upward, he was stunned to see the sky become an impossibly clear blue color. He hadn't ever seen anything like it before! Then his eyes began to sting, and the world went totally black. Blinking to clear his vision, the sentry realized in horror that he was blind. He began to itch all over, as if a million insects were eating his skin. Dropping his longblaster, the sec man dashed for the stairs, going for help, and went straight off the edge of the roof. He screamed all the way down to the cobblestone streets and abruptly stopped as he hit.

Nobody noticed. Cooked birds were also plummeting from the sky, the leaves falling from the wilting trees. Tendrils of smoke rose from the thatched roofs of huts, people screamed, clawing at their faces, horses bolted in panic, blasters exploded, removing hands and entire arms, the fuel dump fireballed and the artesian well began to boil. Becoming hotter by the second, the thick walls of the castle started to turn reddish, then orange, and the melting stones began to sag toward the ground in thick glowing streams. Support timbers snapped, windows shattered, and the shrieking of people trapped in the dungeon rose to anguished howls.

Minutes later, silence ruled what remained of Casanova. Not a wall stood intact, not a creature moved, not a sound could be heard except for a low bubbling from the white-hot lava pool in the middle of the flaky black soil. Then a low rumble of thunder sounded as lightning flashed, and the clear sky darkened again to form a solid dome of stormy clouds over the precise circle of destruction.

THE SOUNDS OF METAL ON METAL, and metal on stone, filled the hollow expanse of the quarry. A wide road spiraled down the sides of the great pit all the way to the cutting floor, where the slaves trimmed the massive stone blocks into smooth rectangles. A sentry post was placed at the bottom of the ramp, with another at the distant top.

At the bottom of the quarry was a runoff pool to catch the rain and divert it from the workers. An electric sump pump sucked out the muddy water, a feeder pipe rising along the quarry wall and disappearing over the top. The feeder pipe was festooned with concertina wire to discourage climbing. Near the pool was a set of stocks, where an unconscious slave still stood, flies covering the bloody shreds of his back.

On the cutting floor, an APC backed near a stone block, and the driver got out. Carefully, he inspected the block for cracks, then measured it with a yardstick and finally used a plumb line to make sure it was squared off neat.

"This'll do," he announced. "Hitch the bitch, boys."

A team of slaves moved forward and began to attach long lengths of steel chains from the APC to the block so it could be dragged off to join the hundreds of others that were part of the wall ringing the complex.

"Where we at?" an overseer asked, smoking a cigarette and offering the pack. The slaves looked on with greed, but said nothing and continued to work.

"Thanks." The driver took one and lit it with a stick match. "Just starting the second course. Another month, it'll be ten feet high!"

"Shoot, what a sight. Ain't no mutie gonna get over that."

"Hell, boy, we couldn't smash through it now even with one of the rocket-tube things."

"Ain't it the truth, brother."

When the slaves were done, the overseer checked the links around the block, while the driver checked the tow bar on the APC, then climbed inside. The slaves stood nearby, savoring the moment of not doing anything.

"All set here!" the overseer called. "Roll away!"

"Back in a few!" the driver answered, waving an arm through the top hatch and driving off slowly, the mammoth stone dragging behind sounding like a baby earthquake.

"All right, break's over," the overseer called, hitching his pants. "Get your lazy asses back to the face. We want another block by sunset."

The slaves shuffled off toward the bare rock face of the quarry, joining other slaves already edging blocks and driving in wedges with heavy sledgehammers. The newcomers had been chained in pairs, Mad Dog with Cooler, Snake with Digger. The odd man out, Scarface, was paired with an old slave called Bo, probably with the notion that the whitehair would help slow down any possible trouble from the huge, burly cannie.

Dragging the length of chain between his legs, Scarface picked up a sledgehammer from a line of them and moved to a nearly finished block. Bo placed the wedge in the thin crack outlining the stone, then Scarface swung

the sledgehammer, driving the steel wedge deep into the
surrounding stone. Bo placed another wedge into position, and the cannie shifted his stance, pausing to spit
on his hands to get a better grip.

"Keep working," an overseer snarled, and flicked the
tip of a bullwhip lightly across the man's wide shoulders.

Scarface didn't flinch at the contact: he merely
grunted.

As the overseer moved on to harass another, Scarface
and Bo stepped into the cool shadows under an overhang
created by the removal of a block. The rest of the crew
was already there. Their whole shift had received a beating for making the mistake of undercutting the face, but
it had been worth the pain. The recess gave them a spot
on the floor where they could be out of sight for minutes
at a time, sometimes more.

"We can't take much more of this," Scarface said to
the rest of his chained crew. "They feed us crap and
work us like dogs. Couple more days of this, and we'll
be too weak to even try and escape."

"Good thing about the accident," Snake growled.

Bo shivered, but Scarface agreed. A slave had fallen
between a moving stone block and the wall, getting
crushed to death. The overseers wanted nothing to do
with cleaning the mess, any more than the slaves did.
However, Scarface and his crew walked to the front of
the line and offered to do it if they could have bigger
water rations. Laughing contemptuously, the overseers
whipped them to the task, which was exactly what the
cannies wanted in the first place. The dead slave was in
such bad shape, nobody noticed the body was missing
an arm and a leg when he was buried.

Cooler and Mad Dog wanted to cook the limbs, but
the smell would have tipped off the guards, so they were

forced to eat the flesh raw. The food fueled them with new strength, but they wisely continued to drag their feet like all the other starving slaves, and struggled to do work that was easy for them. Even Bo had eaten the forbidden food. He got horribly ill afterward, but ate again next time and kept it down.

"Only the leg remaining," Cooler said, watching the movement of the armed people outside the hole. "We need a plan. And to choose just the right moment."

Snake nodded. "Aye, we won't get a second chance."

"We fail, we die," Digger agreed, licking the sweat off his arms. He made a face, but kept at it. The salt kept you strong during such hard work. That was all that mattered. Only strength would give them a chance for freedom.

"So how about now?" Scarface said. "Right fucking now."

Sitting on the ground, Bo perked up his head. "In broad daylight?"

"Say the word and we follow," Mad Dog stated simply.

Scarface grunted. "You know what I gotta do," he said, hoisting the sledgehammer.

Mad Dog nodded. "I'll pay the price to get us outta here. Just do it fast!"

Digger and Snake took the man's arms, holding him motionless, while Cooler stuffed the man's mouth with a shirt. Scarface swung the sledgehammer. The lump of steel slammed onto Mad Dog's foot, crushing it flat, the bones completely pulverized. His eyes wide with pain, the cannie wildly fought to get loose, then Bo slammed a rock onto his head and the man went still.

Snake slid the shackles off Mad Dog's soft foot.

"You're free!" Bo gushed in excitement. "But how does that help the rest of us?"

"Don't help you at all," Scarface said, and the sledgehammer swung again, caving in the whitehair's head. The decapitated corpse trembled and fell to the ground. Scarface then crushed the dead man's foot, and he was free.

Swinging the length of iron chain, Scarface gauged its weight and reach. When satisfied, the two men walked from the hole side by side, as if shackled together.

Moving across the cutting floor, the men shuffled along like good slaves to the sentry shack at the foot of the spiraling ramp. The one-room shack was located on a ledge above the floor, the only access a ladder the overseers drew inside.

Snake leaned against one of the support posts, and Scarface climbed up to the man. Cresting the deck, Scarface looked about to make sure the coast was clear, then wiggled onto the platform. On the ground, Snake went behind the latrine and waited.

Sliding behind the shack where he was out of sight from the rest of the quarry, Scarface put an ear to the wall of the shack and listened. Muffled sounds could be heard, but those might be anything. Ten sec men talking business, two just telling jokes.

Going to the window, he peeked inside and smiled. A naked slave was facedown on a table, one sec men pumping at her face, the other thrusting between her legs. Easing to the door, Scarface wrapped the iron chains around his right fist and quietly entered.

Grunting and laughing, neither sec man noticed the presence of the sweaty slave until he was upon them. Scarface slammed the nearest man with the fist weighted with iron. The overseer's face caved in, pinkish brains smearing over the cannie's armored hand.

"Black dust!" the other cried out, and pulled himself free to reach for his blaster. But his pants were down around his ankles, the folds of cloth tangling around the wheelgun. Scarface tipped over the table, tumbling the girl onto the sec man. They both fell to the floor in a tangle of naked limbs.

Rushing forward, the cannie wrapped the chain around the neck of the blue shirt and pulled it tight. The sec man gasped for air, punching weakly at the massive arms of the coldheart, his struggles growing weaker by the second. Finally, he resorted to clawing at the cannie with his nails, raking bloody furrows into the tan skin.

Annoyed, Scarface jerked the chain once, and the sec man toppled over, his eyes distended and hanging loose on limp white stalks of slimy ganglia.

"Who are you?" the girl whispered, drawing her rags protectively closer. Blood dribbled down her thighs, and one eye was swollen shut.

"Just an escaped slave," Scarface said, stripping one corpse and then the other. Their clothes were ridiculous small for the giant, but he draped a gun belt over his shoulder as a bandolier and checked the load in the wheelgun. It was clean and serviceable.

"Thank you," she whispered, and rushed forward to hug the killer. "Oh, the things they did to me! I'll never feel clean again."

"Not a problem," Scarface said, taking her head in both hands as if about to bestow a loving kiss. Then he savagely twisted his grip. Her neck bones snapped, and the dead girl slumped to the floor on top of the bleeding overseers.

A peg on the wall held a ring of keys, and Scarface

easily found the one that unlocked his chains. Wrapping the spare blaster in the two uniforms, he opened the door of the shed and looked outside. Slaves were working in the quarry, the overseers watching the slaves, but not one another. The fools.

Beyond the quarry, he could see green trees, and, rising above those, was the dish, the shiny bowl dominating the valley.

Scarface looked again, wondering why it had caught his attention, then he saw the machine was moving, rotating slowly. Curious. Some sort of radio—that much he knew. But who were the whitecoats talking to?

Crawling to the edge of the platform, Scarface dropped the bundle to Snake.

Rummaging through a small bookcase in the corner, he found a pack of cigarettes, matches, a knife, a whistle and a pistol with a signal flare inside. There was also a lever-action longblaster of a type he was unfamiliar with, and a shotgun, both with extra shells sewn into loops along their straps. Mighty useful indeed.

Stuffing the weapons into a bag, he slung it over his shoulder, then paused and returned to the dead. Lifting the girl onto the table, he chose a spot and bit in deep, his pointed teeth tearing away a mouthful of tender flesh. He chewed the bloody gobbet quickly and swallowed.

"Fresh meat," he said, sighing. "Been too damn long."

There was movement at the door, and he spun with the blaster ready. Scarface relaxed as the rest of his crew came inside the shack and closed the door. Snake and Cooler were dressed as overseers. Mad Dog was pale and dripping sweat, but held on to Digger and stayed upright.

"Now what?" Snake asked.

Scarface passed over the shotgun. "Gonna get us some transport for Mad Dog. Ain't leaving him behind."

"We steal a wag, they follow us forever," Cooler warned, testing the edge on the knife. "And they got some machines like I never seen!"

"That doesn't matter," Scarface replied coolly. "Nobody can track us if they think we're already dead."

"Dead?" Mad Dog whispered.

"Not just us," Snake said, smiling in understanding. "You mean everybody is dead."

"Exactly." Working the lever on the longblaster, Scarface inspected the round, then inserted it into the side port of the breech. "Help yourselves to the meat, but don't stuff your bellies. We'll have to move fast when the chance comes."

A SEC MAN in a crisp blue shirt drove a shiny clean Hummer down the spiral ramp and onto the cutting floor. A sec man at the sentry post waved as he passed by. Rolling through the slaves, coming very close to a few and making them jump, the driver slowed to a halt near the runoff pool. Sitting before a small wooden shack was an overseer armed with an AK-47. He rose and walked to the wag.

"About time you showed," he growled. "I was about to start giving out the dynamite and have the slaves whack it with hammers to set it off. We got a bastard ton of rocks to clear before we can start cutting more blocks. The major don't like it when we fall behind schedule."

The driver climbed from the wag and reached behind the seat to lift a bulky bag into view. "Stuff it, shithead, and help me with the new explosives."

"We got explosives!" the overseer replied hotly. "What we needed is fuse, ya idiot."

"Not like this stuff, you don't," the driver retorted. Going to the rear cargo area of the military wag, the sec man released a collection of rubbery straps holding a large plastic box in place on top of a damp folded blanket. Lifting off the top, wisps of mist wafted away, exposing fifty new sticks of explosive charges nestled inside, soft sponges separating each stick.

"Color's odd," the overseer grumped. "You sure this dynamite is still good?"

"Ain't dynamite."

He scowled. "Looks like it."

"Ain't."

"So what is it?"

"Something called TNT," the driver said, easing a stick from the packing. "The major says it's much stronger, mebbe ten times, so we better use a lot less."

The overseer glanced toward the vertical rock wall hanging above them. "Ten times!"

Lifting out a single stick, the driver carefully crimped a detonator cap on the end and added a fuse.

"One stick," the man said. "Well, if it ain't hot shit, one stick won't cause us no prob. Mebbe chill a few slaves."

"What are we supposed to do with this old dynamite?"

"Boss says burn it."

"Burn it?"

The driver scoffed. "Easy as pie. I done it lots before. Slit the dynamite open like a fish, then toss on a match. Nothing to it. This TNT's supposed to be lots safer than dynamite. When that stuff gets old, it starts sweating and becomes mighty unstable, blows if you fart hard. Some damn fool slave drops a rock on it, and our dicks hit the moon.''

"Don't wanna do that," the overseer said, leering. "Found me a slut for tonight and plan to do some riding."

"Enough for me?" the driver asked hopefully. "The major been working the slaves so hard on the dish, it's like doing a corpse."

"Always room for a bud." He smiled, nudging the man with an elbow. "You like dark meat or light?"

A shrug. "Ain't choosy."

As the men grinned at each other, a sharp crack echoed across the quarry. The stick of explosive in his hand jumped, and the sec man stared in horror at the gaping hole in the paper tube.

"Nuking hell!" he screamed.

"SHIT-FIRE!" Scarface cursed, working the lever to chamber a fresh round. "The bullet didn't set it off!"

"And now they know we're here," Digger growled, wiping his bloody mouth. "Better run while we can."

"Ain't leaving just so we can get caught and dragged back here again," Scarface growled, firing another round.

The dirt kicked near the box of dynamite, and the sec man backed away, unable to think of what else to do. Then there came another crack. The box jumped, and the whole world vanished as a titanic blast ripped apart the face of the cliff, spewing out rocks and debris for hundreds of yards. The entire side of the mountain seemed to shift position when a second explosion sounded. Although muffled by the avalanche, the concussion was still louder, much more powerful, and a geyser of stone rose into the sky on a column of boiling flame.

"Well, fuck me," Scarface whispered as the concussion buffeted the sentry post with strident force.

The sides of the quarry rose and moved inward, dust filling the air as thick as mud. Then the countless tons of granite fell on top of overseers, sec men and slaves. More explosions came from the wags and storage sheds, but they were pitifully weak compared to the earth-shattering detonation of the fifty sticks of pristine TNT.

Welling from the depths of the vibrating quarry, a boiling cloud expanded over the site, obliterating everything from sight. In the nearby complex, sirens began to howl, and the great dish trembled from the quake of the blast.

Already rushing up the crumbling spiral, the cannies reached the top and dashed onto green grass seconds before the sloping road broke apart and the pieces tumbled into the smoky abyss.

Some sec man came charging out of a barracks, and the cannies gunned them down, pausing only to take their blasters. A line of trucks and a lone APC stood on a bare patch of ground nearby. Not knowing how to rig a tank, Scarface bypassed the military wag and used the stock of the longblaster to break the window of the best-looking truck. Climbing inside, he reached under the dashboard and ripped wires loose, then started touching one to another until the engine started. Twisting the connections closed, the cannie chief shoved the wag into gear and roared off at top speed.

"Where now?" Cooler asked, breathing hard.

Scarface shifted gears. "We're going home."

"Virginny is due north of here," Snake said. "Mebbe a tad east."

"Too dangerous. I heard them say they were setting traps for someone named Ryan," Digger answered, hugging the moaning Mad Dog close to his chest. "He be coming after their boss. Got the roads covered north, east and south of here."

"Remember that caravan we attacked? Heard someone yell for 'Ryan.' Mebbe that's him. Great! Let the fuckers kill each other," Scarface decided, steering into the trees, plowing through bushes and greenery. "We'll avoid both by heading west."

Chapter Eighteen

High above the polluted world, the Kite floated along through the cold vacuum of space. Tiny retro jets flared occasionally to correct the satellite's altitude, adjusting pitch and yaw against the complex gravitional forces of the Earth below and the moon above.

A thousand more satellite's moved around the world like bees buzzing about a hive. Some were large and slow, barely tethered at the extreme limits of Earth's gravitional field. Others were small and fast, beeping antiques from a bygone age. Most sported huge dish antennae, simple communications relays for television and the multinational businesses of the predark world. Both as dead as dinosaurs. A few of the satellites were of unknown purpose or origin, strange ovals whose hulls were a flat black, making them nigh invisible against the starry backdrop of space.

Several hundred miles away, a squat armored sphere bearing the design of an American flag became alive with dim lights, and spun weakly about on its vertical axis, pinhead sensors flickering as it registered the presence of the huge oncoming satellite. Radar beams scanned the goliath, and the master computer couldn't find a match within its military data banks.

A radio signal was immediately sent to NORAD Command in Wyoming. But neither the mammoth Cheyenne Mountain nor the North American Air Defense headquarters existed anymore, and the request for instructions went unanswered. The guardian satellite instantly tried contacting the Pentagon. No response. Then it tracked desperately for Looking Glass, the flying headquarters of SAC, but the Boeing 777 was nowhere to be located. Following the dictates of its programming, the guardian demanded immediate verification from the White house. There was only static. Finally the war satellite broke top secret seals and beamed an emergency signal to the armored bunker at Camp David. Nothing, only the crackle of the never ending sheet lightning from the isotope-filled clouds masking the planet.

Subprograms flared into operation, but the auxiliary routines failed to boot, so they were tried again a dozen times before the reserve files were accessed. But the long ages and steady bombardment of the solar winds had claimed a toll on the military orbiter. When reserve files were sluggishly activated, the first was filled with corrupted data, as well the second, but the fail-safe backup proved functional and the weapon systems of the hunter-killer were brought on-line within seconds.

Now a direct warning was broadcast at the intruder in international Morse code. There was no reply. The mandatory warning was tried once more with the same results. Hardwired circuits pulsed into life, and hatches irised wide. Distance was gauged, speed, vectors, trajectory, and two small missiles streaked toward the lumbering Kite.

The first went straight past the mile-wide power station, arcing off into the limitless depths of deep space. The second detonated halfway between the two machines, its chem warhead of thermite-beryllium flowering into a hellish spray of metallic flame over two thousand degrees Kelvin in temperature.

The Kite began to tilt slightly away from the guardian satellite.

Sensing the unauthorized invader was still coming, the hunter-killer activated its armor-piercing rockets and prepared to launch, when the warheads prematurely detonated inside the military satellite, blowing the orbiter apart in a silent detonation. Utterly destroyed, the crackling wreckage of the megamillion-dollar satellite began to drift toward Earth with ever increasing speed. In minutes, the friction of the thickening atmosphere rushing past its hull raised the temperatures of the ceramics way beyond their design limit, and a spectacular tail of flame stretched behind the plummeting machine, making it resemble a comet for a few brief seconds before it was vaporized.

Serenely, the colossal Kite continued its journey toward a new geosynchronous position directly above an insignificant river valley, hidden somewhere in the ragged mountains of western Tennessee.

THE MURMURING WATER was only ten feet below as J.B. wrapped his legs tighter around the wooden beam and scooted a few more inches along the trestle of the old bridge. Cross braces supported the thick planks above the man, and he moved from joist to joist, desperately grabbing anything solid to maintain his precarious perch above the river.

The spray rising from the water made everything slick and soon soaked his clothes through to the skin. Directly underneath his back, black catfish and rainbow trout darted about in the endless flow, and a winged eel broke the surface, jumping for the dancing sparkles incorrectly thinking the reflected light was food.

Scooting forward another foot, J.B. cursed as a splinter jabbed into his hand, and he bit the end, pulling it loose and spitting it away. Another eel dived for the bloody tidbit and disappeared into the river with its prize. Muttering darkly, J.B. finally reached the middle of the bridge and found the explosive charge. The flat ceramic disk was attached with steel bands bolted to the main timbers, dim telltales winking in the damp shadows.

Bootsteps sounded on the planks above, and curly black hair framing a scarred face appeared over the edge of the bridge. It took Ryan several moments before he could find the Armorer esconced within the maze of wood.

"How's it going?" Ryan asked.

"Found another land mine," J.B. replied, studying the predark device. Easing his grip on the cross braces, the Armorer rested his shoulders on the smooth butt of a joist, and traced the outline of the mine with steady fingertips. "Silas is getting really serious with these things. This model is a lot bigger than the last couple we found. Must be ten pounds of plas here. That would remove the whole bridge and most of the road on either side."

"Need anything?" Ryan asked, shaking the spray from his face.

"Yeah, turn off the river for a few minutes, will you?" J.B. grunted in reply. Hugging a cross brace with his left arm, he reached into his shirt and pulled out a pair of needle-nose pliers. A short length of string was tied from the handle of the pliers to the buckle on his belt.

An oil lantern came into view at the end of a rope.

"More light?" Krysty asked from above.

"Got enough, thanks. The problem is I don't know

this model," J.B. muttered, working on a recessed bolt. "Ah, there's the control board.... Shit!"

There was a splash as the pliers dropped into the river. Immediately, the fish nosed about the item to see if it was edible. Discovering that it wasn't, they angrily slashed fins, spraying mud over the tool, burying it completely.

"Bloody string was a good idea," he announced, reeling in the pliers on the dripping twine.

"You're welcome, lover," Mildred replied. At that angle, she could only see the man by his reflection in the flowing water.

"Everybody better move farther away," he suggested loudly. A line of color ran along the cracks between the planks. Green and red. That was power and a ground wire. He traced them into the shadows and spotted other flat disks hidden amid the timbers. "There seems to be more charges, one at either end of the bridge."

"A sandwich formation," Ryan answered. "Nowhere to run."

"Looks like. The ends are merely charges, no sensors or trips. It's when you reach the middle of the bridge that all three go. Damn good design. Best I've seen." He snipped a wire and waited for sudden violent death. When nothing happened, he snipped another.

Squatting on the shore, Dean studied the river. "So how do the blues get across?"

"Ford river," Jak said. "Not deep."

"The bottom is too soft," Doc stated knowingly. "We would be forced to abandon the Hummer. A LAV could make the transition, but not our current mode of transportation."

Levering a beveled plate out of the way, J.B. answered, "We can cross the bridge anytime, only the

Hummer can't. People, horses, most civilian wags would roll over with no trouble. But once the mine senses dense steel overhead, this whole bridge will be matchsticks in a heartbeat.''

"Can you remove the mine, let it sink in the river?'' Ryan asked, a spent round sliding from his shirt pocket and disappearing into the water. The man was annoyed he had missed the brass. It could just as easily have been a live round wasted due to carelessness. As a reasonable precaution, Ryan had emptied his pockets of anything valuable before leaning over the bridge. J.B. had done the same, his collection of items piled on the floorboards of the Hummer. And just in case the mine was tripped by magnetic fields, Ryan was stripped to the SIG-Sauer, no spare clips, and not even a knife in his boot, to keep the metal on his body to an absolute minimum.

"Not going to remove this device without power tools,'' J.B. answered, grunting with effort. "It's here to stay, bolted into position nine different ways. But I have a better plan.'' More muttering sounded from under the bridge, along some hard banging and another splash. "Shit!''

Suddenly, the birds in the trees stopped making noises, and the rest of the companions drew blasters. Straining to hear voices or engines, they waited for a patrol of blues to arrive. Tense minutes passed before a sting-wing soared from the trees with a fresh kill in its beak. The companions relaxed as the mutie flew away and the birds began to chirp once more.

Ryan eased the safety back on the SIG-Sauer, when he realized that J.B. was on the move below the bridge, wiggling quickly between the braces and joists. The one-eyed warrior retreated to the safety of the road, waiting as J.B. reached the shore and crawled backward onto the grass. Gratefully, the man stood and lifted a thick wad of grayish clay from inside his shirt.

"To hell with defusing the mine. I just removed the C-4 charge," J.B. announced with a slight smirk. "Let the damn thing ignite. It'll only make a bang that wouldn't chill a fly."

"You sure about that?" Mildred asked, handing over a backpack.

Extracting dry clothes from within, J.B. quickly changed, using stiff fingers to smooth his damp hair. Then, donning his dry fedora, he slid the Uzi over a shoulder. "Well, just in case, I'll drive the Hummer over alone," he suggested, adjusting his glasses.

Already at the wag, Ryan started the engine and stepped away from the Hummer. A stick was pressed against the gas pedal and a piece of rope held the steering wheel steady. At a leisurely pace, the armored vehicle slowly rolled across the expanse of the wooden bridge, veering a little off course toward the edge, but nothing dangerous. As the wag reached the middle, there was a sharp explosion and debris sprayed into the river, churning the surface and scaring away the fish. Smoke blew away from the support beams, but nothing else occurred and the Hummer reached the other side intact.

Sprinting forward, Ryan claimed the Hummer before it got too far away, and turned off the engine. "It's safe," he announced, untying the knotted rope and throwing away the stick. "Let's go."

Walking over, the companions piled their belongings into the rear of the Hummer and took seats. Jak took the gunner position at the M-60, and Doc stretched his long legs in the cargo area. Taking the front seat, J.B. laid the Uzi on the floor and started carving the lump of plastique into fat bricks. Gently, he wrapped each separately in a piece of a blue shirt taken off a corpse and tucked the bricks into his munitions bag.

"Can blow a lot of locks with this," he said, patting the bag contentedly. "Good for starting fires in the rain, too."

"Plas?" Jak asked, shocked.

"Sure. Most explosives will simply burn if they're not inside a container. You need a primer for TNT, or even a gunshot wouldn't set it off. An electric charge or a small explosion makes C-4 detonate, but fire only causes it to burn like coal."

Starting the warm engines, Ryan checked the fuel gauge, noting the low level, and they headed into the deadly green hills once more. So far, they had found mines on every bridge, and on a flat stretch of ground there had been a collection of bloodstained crosses lining the road, rotting corpses—without eyes or genitalia—brutally nailed to the upright timbers. Oddly, the dead were all facing eastward, toward the ville of the blue shirts. It was a clear warning about the dangers of leaving. The mines were a more direct warning about entering the valley.

"And this is the back door," Krysty said, as if reading his thoughts.

"Silas didn't believe in half measures," Ryan agreed, shifting gears. "Remember those homemade muties of his?"

"Nasty," Jak agreed.

"Maybe we should leave the roads," Mildred suggested. "Take to the woods."

"Can't," Ryan replied bluntly. "The trees are too close, the slopes too sharp. No way we could drive through these hills. Even walking would be a bitch.

We're stuck with the roads until reaching flatter country."

"Besides, there could be patrols in the hills," J.B. added, resting an arm out the window of the Hummer. "Land mines are easier to avoid then sec men."

"Prefer sec men," Jak countered, shaking the length of linked ammo to straighten a kink. "Mines always sharp, blues fall sleep sometimes."

"Only once, my friend," Doc answered, sliding a length of razor-sharp sword from his ebony stick and slamming it back inside. "And then never again."

ITS EIGHT WHEELS CHURNING out grass and dirt, the armored bulk of the LAV-25 rolled to a stop near the edge of the quarry. Sec men rushed to open the rear doors, and Silas hobbled from the war wag, stiffly walking to the ragged end of the land.

"What in hell happened here?" the whitecoat roared, standing above the abyss. "Were we attacked?"

"The damn fools must have set off the TNT," Major Sheffield said, staring at the jumble of broken rock that rose halfway to the surface. "It'll take weeks of hard work to reach the bottom again. Even longer before we can start carving blocks for the outer wall. Months lost!"

"Any survivors?" Silas demanded in cold fury, his hand clenching the cane hard.

Crossing his arms, Sheffield shook his head. "None."

"How lucky for the overseers," Silas snorted. "They would have begged for death before I was through with them!"

"Any orders, sir?" Sheffield asked.

"Yes, of course. Halt the construction of the wall," Silas stated grimly. "Assign every worker to the dish. Once done, we'll effect a clear zone around the complex.

That will afford us the security we need to finish the wall at our leisure.''

"A clear zone?'' the major asked.

Leaning heavily on his cane, Silas grunted. "We'll burn the whole Tennessee valley to ash around our base for a hundred miles. Nobody would dare to cross that.''

The orbiter could do such a thing? Amazing. It truly was more powerful than predark nukes. "How soon?'' the sec chief asked, trying to hide his excitement.

"Noon tomorrow—no, the day after. Tomorrow, I reduce Front Royal to a lava pool.'' Silas then frowned. "What are the chances that Ryan had something to do with this?''

"None at all,'' Sheffield stated firmly. "Any strangers found in the valley have been shot on sight. Our sentries report in regularly, and every passable road is heavily mined.''

"Ah, that's not exactly correct, sir,'' a corporal hesitantly offered, walking from the crowd of sec men.

Turning slowly, Silas leveled a hostile gaze at the youngster. "Explain that statement,'' he growled.

The sec man saluted. "Sir! The sentry on the west road is late reporting in, sir. We sent off his relief this morning, but no word on either of them yet.''

"The west! I should have known the coward would try and sneak up on me from behind!'' Silas glanced about nervously, feeling very vulnerable standing in the open. "Send out a LAV and squad of men immediately.''

"That is unwise, sir. We only have three armored wags remaining,'' the major reported succinctly. "We lost one during the cave-in. It must have been parked near the edge and fell into the quarry.''

"Irrelevant! I want armor on the west road within the

hour." Licking his dry lips, Silas hunched his shoulders as if braced for the killing impact of a bullet. His face felt hot, and the center of his forehead ached with a stabbing pain as if he had been already shot. A great weariness filled the man, and in horror he felt himself starting to slip into the dream state that heralded his recurring nightmare. Only this time it was happening while he was wide awake!

Through sheer force of will, he banished the delirium, but a cold certainty now gripped his heart and Silas knew that his days of sanity were almost over. Soon, madness would rule his mind, and the scientist would no longer be able to tell reality from delusion. He would probably never even know when Tanner, or the major, took his life. Breathing hard, Silas looked into the deep quarry, knowing that a single step more would end his problems forever.

Just then, a stone broke away from the ragged edge of the ground and fell into the quarry, clattering and clacking as it bounced from boulder to boulder, finally disappearing into the shadowy dust clouds far below. A few seconds later, there was a splash as it reached the runoff pool.

Shuddering at the noise, Silas stepped way from the yawning stone pit. No, not yet. His death at this time would only damn North America to endless barbarism. Democracy had failed, the anarchy of choice and the chaos of freedom combining to create skydark and nearly ending the human race. Only the iron rule of science could save humankind from extinction. The Great Project had to be completed first, no matter what the personal cost. Then and only then could he allow himself to finally die and escape the growing horrors of his own damaged mind.

Limping about, Silas started for the LAV. "Come along, Major. We're returning to the complex. That one-eyed bastard could be watching us right now through a sniper scope."

"Impossible. The nearest trees for cover are two hundred yards away. The bushes on the hillside are even farther. He couldn't hit the ground at that range. Not with a Winchester lever action, or a Kalashnikov. Told me yourself that was why you chose those specific long-blasters. Both are useless as sniper rifles."

"And what if Ryan is here with his Steyr?" Silas whispered, sweat beginning to trickle down his face. "That is designed for extreme-distance shots under tricky conditions. Perhaps I should stay inside the bunker until this matter is resolved."

"A wise move. Or tell me the entrance code to the redoubts," Sheffield urged slyly, "just in case of an emergency."

Pausing near the doors of the LAV, Silas Jamaisvous stared at the big sec chief. Proud and strong, he was the perfect human specimen, a more than worthy successor to the dying scientist.

"Maybe you are right," Silas said slowly, and started to reach into his coat. Then he stopped and stepped inside the APC.

"Not here," he said, taking a wall seat. "I will tell you in the lab. We must not be overheard."

"Of course. As you say, sir," Sheffield replied, not taking his eyes off the tiny sliver of the rainbow disk just barely visible tucked inside the breast pocket of the white labcoat.

RYAN SLOWED the Hummer as another wag appeared around a gentle curve in the road ahead of them. It was a predark truck in amazingly good condition, the tires sporting plenty of tread, the headlights intact, and not a speck of rust on the red-painted chassis. He could see two men in the front cab, and more in the rear. All of them seemed to have blasters.

"Stay loose," Ryan ordered, adjusting the SIG-Sauer at his hip. "Don't shoot unless they do first. Not everybody on this road is going to be a blue shirt."

"Mebbe," J.B. replied, pulling the Uzi onto his lap and snicking off the safety.

Moving the Hummer to the far side of the road, Ryan carefully watched the oncoming truck. The driver wasn't wearing a blue shirt. They could just be some folks leaving the area. Or sec men in disguise. The one-eyed man debated chilling the strangers purely as a precaution, and decided against it.

Maintaining its speed, the truck swung away from the Hummer, twenty feet of open space separating the vehicles. As the machines got closer, Ryan nodded and casually saluted at the other driver, and the gesture was returned.

"Big man," Krysty commented, her revolver in her hand but tucked out of sight. "Looks a bit like Ryan."

He snorted in reply. "Everybody has scars."

Almost alongside each other, the truck began to slow, and the driver pointed at the Hummer. The bald man in the passenger's seat rolled down his window and stared at the companions, first in puzzlement, then shock.

"Nuking hell, it *is* them!" he shouted, displaying pointed teeth. "Chill them all!" Instantly, the predark wag veered across the road, its engine revving with power.

"They're going for a ram!" Ryan warned, hitting the gas and sharply twisting the steering wheel.

The M-60 started chattering, and the sec men in the other wag fired back with an assortment of handblasters. The windshield on the truck exploded into pieces, while rounds ricocheted off the sides of the Hummer.

Firing one-handed, J.B. hosed the truck, but it was already too late. The hood blew off the wag, steam erupted from the punctured radiator and the truck slammed into the rear fender of the Hummer in a crash of glass and screech of metal. Jak went flying from his position behind the M-60, and the Hummer spun about from the collision, brakes squealing.

Shaking and bouncing, the damaged truck rattled to a halt, the front bumper crumpled tight onto the right tire, slicing the rubber in to shreds.

On the berm, Jak rose and started limping after the Hummer, firing his .357 steadily at the stalled truck. The driver was fighting to start the engine again, but only getting whirring noises. However, the sec men in the rear opened fire on the pale teenager with their blasters. Trapped on flat ground with absolutely no cover, Jak flinched as a hot round scored past his cheek, singeing his skin.

"Cover him!" Ryan shouted, slamming on the gas and racing forward.

The companions opened fire with every weapon they had as the war wag streaked across the road to pass straight by Jak and slam into the truck. The impact knocked the sec men off their feet, the armored Hummer almost flipping over the large truck.

Jumping from the military transport, Doc and Krysty grabbed Jak by the arms and hauled the teenager off the road. Once he was in the Hummer, Ryan backed way from the truck and spun in the dirt, guiding the wag down the road at top speed.

"Those were cannies!" Dean stated, snapping off more shots at the broken wag. The men were stumbling around the vehicle in a daze, firing their weapons blindly.

J.B. slapped a fresh clip into the Uzi and worked the bolt. "Silas hiring cannies as blues?"

"More likely they stole the truck," Doc stated, blowing flame and thunder at the men with his LeMat. A cannie with a bandaged foot recoiled from the subsonic arrival of the .44 miniball, his left arm gone from the elbow down. "And I sincerely hope they ate the previous owners!"

"Vicious old coot, aren't you?" Mildred asked.

"Just practical, madam. A dead Silas can do us no more harm."

As the truck dwindled in the distance, the Hummer rolled around the curve in the dirt road, and Ryan immediately slowed. Directly ahead of them, a flat wooden bridge stretched across a gently flowing river.

"Fireblast! How many rivers do they have here!" Ryan cursed, then ground to a halt. "There isn't time to defuse another bastard land mine!"

Munitions bag in hand, J.B. hopped from the Hummer and started off at a run. "I'll check! Mebbe it's clean!"

The companions readied their blasters, as the man rushed to the shore. Wading into the icy water up to his waist, J.B. looked under the bridge and turned toward the others.

"Triple load!" he shouted through chattering teeth. "Same as before! Ten, mebbe fifteen to defuse!"

"Do it!" Ryan shouted, gunning the engine. "We'll hold them off if they're stupe enough to try again."

Mildred gave a sharp whistle, and Jak started firing the M-60. Rattling and shaking, the predark truck appeared around the curve, the cannies steadily firing their blasters. Blue smoke trailed from its tailpipe, telling of serious engine damage. The headlights were gone, smoke poured from under the hood, but it was still moving, building speed and coming straight toward them this time.

As the companions cut loose with every weapon they had, Ryan studied the battlefield. Dense trees lined both sides, so there was no chance of driving through those. They couldn't cross the bridge, and if they tried to swim across the river they would be sitting ducks for the cannies to pick off with longblasters. Oddly, the battered truck was coming straight down the middle of the road, as if inviting the companions to try to get by, which made no sense. The Hummer was faster and armored, so no way could the cannies stop it with another sideswipe. Then the man saw the others were throwing handfuls of something out the sides of the wag. One of the objects hit a rock and loudly detonated.

"Blasting caps! Those'll blow our tires to pieces."

"But why did they come back?" Dean asked, rummaging in his clothes for another clip. Briefly, he made a mental note that he should make a vest or something with nothing but pockets for spare ammo. Yeah, that was a good idea. "We weren't chasing after them."

"It's the Hummer," Krysty stated, thumbing fresh cartridges into her blaster. "We busted their wag, so the cannies want this as a replacement."

"And us for supplies," Mildred added grimly, working the pump on the S&W shotgun she'd borrowed from J.B.

The boy registered surprise at the statement, then fierce hatred. "Let them try," he growled, for a split second sounding exactly like his father.

The truck was only fifty yards away and coming faster all the time. Spitting a curse, Ryan turned in his seat and stared hard at the bridge. Sure enough, there were small metallic dots scattered over the weathered planks. More blasting caps had been strewed about to stop anybody from following them across. Only now the small explosives might also set off the land mines and chill J.B. while he was working underneath, and there was no way to tell him of the charges on top of the bridge. They were trapped.

Having no choice, Ryan started tying off the steering wheel with the rope. "Get ready to go EVA!" he shouted, throwing the wag into neutral and shoving the stick on the gas pedal. The engine roared to life. "We've got to take them here on the road!"

"What for?" Jak demanded from the sputtering M-60. The dangling ammo belt was nearly gone, but the teenager still rode the machine gun on full-auto.

"Just do it!" Ryan shouted, throwing the Hummer into gear. The wag lurched ahead, tires spinning in the dirt.

Spewing smoke and blasterfire, the rattling truck loomed before the companions. Through the broken windshield, Ryan could see the cannie driver watching eagerly as the two wags closed with frightening speed. Then the scarred man's toothy expression rapidly changed as he realized the Hummer wasn't trying to get around, but was on a collision course.

"Now!" Ryan shouted, diving from the wag. He hit the ground hard, but managed to roll off the blow and stopped, lying on his side, blaster still in his hands. Jak and Doc landed nearby, Mildred and Krysty close behind. There was no sign of Dean.

Slamming on the brakes, the cannie driver bellowed

in rage as the two vehicles violently smashed into each other, glass shattering over the sounds of crunching metal. Every loose item in the Hummer went flying as its armored grille pushed in the front of the truck, the working engine propelled backward into the cab, crushing a man with a snake tattoo on his face.

Somebody began to scream as fuel gushed from a hole in the gas tank, pooling on the ground under the destroyed wag. Bleeding and dazed, the cannies stumbled from the truck, slipping on the shards of glass scattered on the road.

Stiffly, Ryan rose from a crouch and leveled the SIG-Sauer. "Light them up!" he shouted, and started firing.

Steady on one knee, Doc triggered the LeMat four times, and a cannie flew backward to slam into the truck, his faceless corpse sliding to the road, leaving a smear of pulped organs behind on the crumbled metal chassis.

Lying on the berm, Dean was snapping off shots, and Mildred cut loose with the shotgun, the fléchette rounds cutting a cannie in two.

Spotting his lost Colt Python in the dust, Jak dived for the blaster and came up firing, the .357 hollowpoint rounds blowing fist-sized holes in men and truck. Hit in the shoulder, a cannie dropped the ammo clip for his AK-47. In panic, he ran away but got only a few yards before reaching the blasting caps. The first blew off a foot. Crying in shock, he fell to a knee and that, too, was removed. The man collapsed to the ground and was torn into bloody pieces.

Then a large cannie lifted another as a shield and sprayed the companions with a Kalashnikov on full-auto, the machine gun fiercely chattering.

Hastily reloading, Krysty felt a tug on her bearskin coat, telling of a near miss. As she dived for cover, Ryan slapped in a fresh clip, stood and fired. The 9 mm round punched a neat hole in the forehead of the dead man, an explosion of blood and brains washing over the cannie behind him. Blind, the scarred man dropped the corpse and started to randomly shoot his blaster. Krysty hit him in the shoulder, but he didn't stop firing. Dean got him in the thigh, and Jak buried a knife in his gut. Bleeding from a dozen wounds, the cannie dropped the spent blaster, drew a knife and charged, shouting insanely. Stepping out of the way, Ryan and Mildred both put lead in his chest, and finally Doc removed his head completely with a deafening discharge from the .63 smoothbore of the powerful LeMat.

The companions stood tensely, listening for any movement, waiting for another attack. Minutes passed slowly, and the fire under the truck died away as the fuel was consumed.

"Okay, it's clear," Ryan decided, holstering his piece. "Let's gather the blasters and get going. That smoke is going to attract attention we don't want."

"Why didn't the big guy die faster?" Dean demanded, removing the partially loaded clip from his blaster and inserting a full magazine.

"Went berserk," Mildred replied, holstering her ZKR target pistol. "There was so much adrenaline pumping through his body, he could have continued fighting for quite a while. It's rare, but does happen sometimes in battle."

"He took that many slugs and stayed alive?"

"Oh, no, he was already dead. Just still moving."

"Mutie?" the boy asked.

The physician sighed. "Quite the human thing to do."

"Hey, look at this," Krysty said, lifting a bare leg.

"There are shackle scars on his ankle. These men were slaves."

"Escaped Silas," Jak replied, recovering his blades from the dead men. He wiped them clean on the clothes of one of the fallen, then on an oily cloth from the pocket of his fatigues. One blade he slid up his sleeve; the other went into a boot.

"Which means overseers could be on their trail," Ryan stated, finding the Steyr and checking the blaster for damage. It was dirty but otherwise in fine shape.

Slinging the longblaster over a shoulder, Ryan hurried to the Hummer. He started the engine and tried to drive it off the truck, but the wag seemed stuck on something underneath. Shifting gears, Ryan fought with the entangled wag, only making matters worse before admitting defeat.

"Sounds like a broken axle," he stated, climbing from the Hummer. "We walk from here."

A sloshing sound announced the arrival of J.B. from the river. As the Armorer walked onto the shore, he was holding another large lump of plastique.

"Bridge is clear," he told them wearily.

"Not yet," Doc said, pointing with his swordstick. "It is covered with blasting caps."

Turning, J.B. snorted. "We can use some branches to simply sweep them into the river. No prob."

"Unfortunately, the Hummer is out of commission," Ryan said. "The front axle is busted, and the truck is dead. We forcibly removed the engine and burned off the fuel."

"So I see," J.B. mused. "Must have been a hell of a fight. Any chance they can be pushed?"

"Pushed?" Mildred repeated.

"We move them to the bridge," J.B. said, rubbing his

arms for some warmth. He was chilled to the bone, but there was no time to change clothes now. "Hopefully, nobody will come looking for us, or the cannies, if they think we're already dead."

Understanding the plan, the companions got busy. Krysty stood guard duty while Doc cut branches off the pines trees and J.B. cleared the bridge. Then they emptied the Hummer of supplies, filling their backpacks with everything they could comfortably carry. Shoving the wag backward the few yards took all of them working together, the broken axle refusing to turn very fast. But the companions eventually got it to the middle of the bridge. The truck rolled much easier, and soon it was nose to nose again with the Hummer.

"Leave some supplies and blasters," Ryan ordered, studying the wreckage. "This has to look real. Silas is no fool."

"Can we still take along the M-60?" Dean asked. "No way they could know we have one."

"Their wags' have 'em," Jak replied curtly. "If gone, what think?"

The boy frowned. "You're right. Leave it behind."

"Better move a couple of cannies to the Hummer to make the body count balance," Mildred suggested.

While that was done, Ryan gave J.B. one of his dry shirts. Even buttoned shut, the garment still hung loosely off the smaller man, but his teeth stopped chattering and his hands ceased to shake.

Feeling better, J.B. placed the large wad of C-4 from the land mines on the bumpers of the wags, and Ryan poured the extra fuel from their spare canister over both machines. Then everybody moved across the bridge before J.B. set the charges with one of his precious predark timing pencils.

The friends headed into the trees, the bridge far from sight when the first flat explosion sounded, closely followed by a cavalcade of smaller detonations, crunching wood and multiple splashes.

"Sure hope that works," Mildred said, watching the birds take flight overhead, frightened by the noises.

"Find out soon enough if it doesn't," Ryan replied, walking into the growing shadows of the Tennessee pine trees.

Chapter Nineteen

The carpeting of pine needles underfoot made walking pleasant, and the companions put several miles between them and the ruined bridge before stopping for a needed break.

"How far away are we?" Krysty asked, sitting on a tree stump. Unfolding some silver wrapping, she popped a stick of hundred-year-old chewing gum into her mouth and started to suck the flavor from the confection. It took too long for the stuff to get soft enough to actually chew. The wrapper she tucked into a pocket to hide the fact they had been here.

"Tell you in a minute," J.B. said, sliding on dry socks from his backpack, then his shoes. His pants had dried from the quick march, and he had changed into one of his own shirts a good mile ago.

Moving to a grassy area where the branches didn't block a view of the sky, the Armorer used his minisextant to shoot the sun. "We are...yep, just south of the Shiloh battlefield, east of the redoubt and west of the ville full of those inbred crazies."

"I remember them," Mildred said, scowling, easing her med kit to the soft ground. "That's probably where Silas gets his sec men."

"Indeed, madam, sec men or his slaves," Doc stated, taking the opportunity to reload the LeMat. The bulky weapon was difficult enough to charge standing still, and impossible to do so while walking. His sure hands used a small brass brush to purge each individual firing chamber, spent black powder raining like ebony snow. An exact measure of fresh powder went in next, then the lead ball and finally a wad of cotton. He tamped down each charge with the built-in lever, then smeared a dollop of grease on the chambers as protection from wetness and a lethal chain reaction cross firing.

The physician nodded while awkwardly massaging her stiff shoulder. Mildred knew she was carrying too many medical supplies but couldn't force herself to leave anything potentially useful behind.

Screwing the cap back on his canteen, Ryan wiped his mouth and glanced at the sky. "Day's nearly done," he said. "We'll use what light there is left to head east toward the redoubt from here on. Need to make sure we have someplace to retreat in case of trouble. If it's clear, tomorrow we'll start sweeping the valley in sections and find the base."

"Then chill all blues," Jak said, rubbing the scratch on his cheek from the near miss before. There was a faint taste of blood in his mouth, and when Jak turned to spit he saw a tiny flower struggling to grow through the thick layer of needles. Hawking into the bushes, the teenager gently pushed the needles away, giving the tiny plant a fighting chance. His wife had always like daisies.

"We ace the blues and Silas. That way, we can be sure he'll never bother Front Royal again," Ryan said grimly, picking up his longblaster. "Or anybody else, for that matter."

Stealthily, the companions moved through the forest. The tall green pines were dense, the air fresh with their clean scent. There were no signs of people having ever been in these woods, not even debris from predark houses. The land was pristine, almost primordial. Occasionally, the call of a wild bird would echo through the branches, or a squirrel would race by. Dean tracked the passage of the rodents with his blaster, but didn't fire. He knew they were too close to the blue shirts to risk shooting at anything.

Forcing their way through some blackberry bushes, the companions paused at the sight of a bear tunnel going through some of the thickets. Placing a finger on the trigger of his longblaster, Ryan knelt to look inside the dim recesses of the thorny bushes.

"Nothing in sight," he announced.

Jak kicked at some dried droppings on the ground. "Month, mebbe more. Bear long gone."

"Odd," J.B. said, picking a berry off a bush and inspecting it carefully. "Animals don't usually leave a ready source of food."

"Mebbe he got chased away by a bigger bear," Dean suggested.

His father didn't reply, but chambered a round into the Steyr. A few hundred yards later, they found the half-consumed carcass of a buck deer on the stony ground, the rotting meat completely covered with busy black ants. The ripening stench was awful, and they hurriedly arced around the clearing, staying within the canopy of the trees.

Climbing over some fallen oak trees, Ryan discovered a tiny babbling brook, really no more than a creek, cutting through a tangle of underbrush. Tadpoles and crayfish were busy in the soupy mud. The water read clean on his rad counter, so he filled his canteen and moved onward. The rest of the companions hardly broke their stride, stepping over the trickle of water. A gully cut through the trees, saplings and birch standing ghostly white amid the dark pines. Climbing onto the raised land, the companions started across a sloped field of stubby grass. Soon, a river could be heard flowing nearby.

"Sounds like it's going in the right direction," J.B. said, tilting his head toward the noise. "How about making another raft?"

"Had enough of that," Ryan muttered.

Stopping abruptly, Mildred stared hard at the northern sky. "Well, I'll be damned," she whispered. "Didn't we leave the burning Hummer west of us?"

"Sure did," J.B. answered, then the man sniffed. What was that bitter smell?

Mildred pointed. "Then what the hell is that?"

A thick plume of smoke rose over the forest. The winds were thinning it across the sky until it vanished, but this close the plume was a solid black.

"Way too big to be a campfire," Dean said thoughtfully. "Mebbe the forest is on fire."

"Animals not left," Jak stated, drawing his Colt Python. "They be first."

Her hair anxiously waving, Krysty sniffed a few times. "That's coal," she stated as a fact. "A coal-burning fire."

"Plenty of coal in Tennessee," Doc said. "Perhaps it is a local blacksmith."

"Have to be a damn huge one."

"Hmm, true, madam. I stand corrected. Perhaps some local baron has built a foundry to reclaim predark metal."

"Could be anything, even a power plant," Ryan grunted. He had encountered coal-burning power stations when he traveled with the Trader. Mostly they were crude things, a rusty boiler whistling steam at a homemade turbine attached to a hundred car generators. But even a rickety machine like that made a lot of electricity. Lights, heaters, electric fences.

"Silas," Doc whispered, fingering the silver lion's head on his swordstick.

"Silent recce," Ryan declared, loosening the SIG-Sauer in its holster. "Five-yard spread. Go."

The companions spread out and started into the forest once more. After a while, they left the trees and found themselves standing on the bank of a river. The water rushed over rocks, foaming white and dangerous. On the other side was a dirt road deeply cut with rain gullies. Beyond that were thick bushes and more trees. Other than the companions, there was nothing else in sight.

"There," Jak said, gesturing with his Colt.

A short way up the river was another bridge, wider and more detailed than any of the others they had encountered so far.

"Odd," Krysty noted. "That's the first bridge with handrails. The others were just flat planks without railings."

"Doesn't look predark," Dean estimated. "Mebbe it's the first one the blues built. You always do the first of anything a bit fancier than needed."

"It does not go anywhere," Doc said, sounding annoyed. "They built a bridge, but not a road?"

"Changed minds," Jak suggested.

"Or ran out of slaves," Mildred countered.

Pensive, Ryan looked at the sky. Night was rapidly approaching. Should they continue to the redoubt, or check out the smoke? Tough choice.

"We'll recce the smoke," he decided. "But if we encounter any large groups of blue shirts, we run for the redoubt. Understood?"

All nodded their assent.

The companions stayed within the cover provided by the trees until reaching the bridge. J.B. checked underneath from the shore, and they crossed without trouble. Past the road, they went into the woods and found the pines were only a few yards deep. They stopped in a neat line, the land beyond dotted with stumps and sloping away to a valley.

"Eureka," Doc whispered, thumbing back the hammer on the LeMat.

A sprawling ville filled the floor of the mountain valley, at one end a brick building with a tall circular chimney pouring out thick smoke, insulated wires running from a battery of transformers and spreading across the valley in a black spiderweb of technology. New brick buildings stood alongside predark structures and a shiny new Quonset hut. A stone wall was being built around the enclosure, the tiny figures of sec men visible as they patrolled its top. Hundreds of people were moving about on the ground, doing incomprehensible things at that distance. Rising above everything was a huge white bowl set within a framework of steel girders and I-beams that rested on a slab of concrete. A slim pole thrust from the center of the bowl, pointing toward the cloudy sky, and tiny lights winked.

"Dark night, this is even bigger than the Anthill mock-up of D.C.," J.B. muttered, cradling the Uzi in both arms.

"Fireblast! They have a bastard tank!"

J.B. snorted. "Dead tank. See there? A couple of the sec men are hammering on the top hatch with chisels, trying to get inside."

Ryan relaxed slightly. "Good."

"What bowl?" Jak asked, squinting in displeasure. Even though the teenager used the redoubts and mat-trans units, he was no fan of technology, and this smacked of predark science on a major scale.

"That, my friend, is a radio telescope," Mildred said softly, as if afraid the people in the valley might her the words. "And it seems to be fully restored."

Ryan scowled. "A sky talker."

"Has Silas managed to launch something into orbit?" Krysty asked.

"Not here," Ryan stated. "I've seen space ports, and this has none of the right machines. No fuels tanks, or fire equipment, no bunkers." He frowned. "But it sure as hell was built to do something important."

Mildred said something that sounded like "settee."

"Come again, madam?" Doc asked.

"SETI," she repeated. "That dish antenna was an old project even before the nuke war. The search for extraterrestrial life. The government was trying to talk, or at least listen, to alien civilizations. See if we were alone in the universe."

Dean looked away from the dish. "You mean people on other worlds?" he asked incredulously. "Never thought of such a thing."

"Most considered it crazy. Even if we reached anybody, the messages would have taken dozens or even hundreds of years to get there and come back."

"We ask the question, and our great-grandchildren hear the answer," Doc intoned, easing down the hammer and cocking it again. "Indeed, that most certainly does seem like a waste of time and resources."

"Doesn't matter," Ryan said, sliding a finger under his eye patch to gently scratch. The salt from the Carolina basin had never fully washed out of the scarred hole, even with their bath in the fresh water river. "Some predark whitecoat tried to talk with another in space. Doesn't matter now. But this must be the home base for Silas and the blue shirts. Only question is, what is the bastard using the antenna for?''

"Not for talking with alien beings," J.B. said, snorting rudely, then removing his fedora and wiping the sweat off the inside. "Aliens, ha!"

Above them, the darkening sky rumbled ominously, lightning flashing from cloud to cloud.

"Satellite," Krysty suggested, brushing back her wild profusion of fiery red hair. The cascade moved about her fingers in a familiar fashion. "Mebbe he found something still in orbit and is trying to using this radio to talk to it."

"Weapon, recon?" Jak asked, straight to the point.

The woman shrugged.

"Recce would be pointless," J.B. said. "Got to be a weapon of some kind. Missiles, mebbe."

"Fabulous, just what the world needs," Mildred muttered. "Another skydark to finish the job of exterminating humankind."

"I want to get closer," Ryan said, starting down the hill. "We need to know what's going on." The ground sloped even more sharply as they walked down the hillside, the angle becoming so pronounced the companions stopped walking and slid along the seats of their pants. Any attempt at running would have sent them tumbling head over heels into the valley below. A ridge in the slope dropped five feet straight down onto a gentler angle. A few yards away, a split-rail fence extended across the slope, bare wires resting on glass knobs intertwined with the green wood.

"New," Jak stated.

Picking up a stick, Dean started forward. "I'll see if it's live."

"Don't," Ryan barked, holding out a hand. "If that is electrified, a touch might send off a signal that we're where. Live wires can be rigged like the proximity fuse of a bomb."

The boy dropped the stick and backed away.

Going near the fence, Ryan aimed the Steyr at the ville below and adjusted the focus of the telescopic sights to infinity. Pulling out his Navy telescope, J.B. extended the tube to its fullest length and did the same.

There was a quarry to the south, which seemed to have had a major collapse. Tough break for the stone cutters, but of no interest to them. Both men glanced briefly at the slaves hauling boxes to the dish antenna, then scrutinized the stone wall for weak points. The gate was impressive, but the section opposite the quarry was only two courses high.

"Six feet?" J.B. expertly guessed.

Ryan grunted. "Mebbe less. If we need to gain entrance, that's the doorway we'll use."

"Check. Lots of wags near the base of the dish."

"Might be the garage. Or their bolt-hole."

"It's a fort. There're no windows for ventilation."

Sweeping the compound, Ryan froze as he spied a LAV-25 parked near the Quonset hut. The metallic structure had bars on the windows, an armored door and was closed off with electric fencing. Whatever was inside was very important to the these people. Inside the fencing, a group of blues with blasters stood rigidly at attention around a tall, almost feline man with silvery hair, a pronounced widow's peak and bushy eyebrows. Dressed in a white laboratory coat, the thin man was leaning heavily on a wooden cane, obviously favoring his left leg.

"That's where Doc stabbed him," J.B. said.

"Wish it had been the heart," Doc grumbled, staring into the ville, unable to see anything clearly, but imagining every detail.

"It's Silas," Ryan agreed, adjusting the focus with fingertip pressure. The circle view through the crosshairs jumped into crystal clarity. "That other fellow must be the chief of the sec men. He's not saluting, and they appear to be arguing."

"Silas didn't exactly tolerate the opinions of others," Krysty added, squinting at the distant figures. The woman's vision was greater than most people's, but this was beyond even her best. "Much less that of his staff."

"Dark night!" J.B. cursed in frustration. "If we only had a weapon with good range, we could ace them both right here and now!"

"That would pay many debts," Doc stated, the wind ruffling his long silvery hair. His heart was pounding hard, but he somehow maintained an outward calm. Kidnapper, torturer, killer, what mere words could describe the lunatic genius behind Overproject Whisper and all of its subdivisions that had taken Dr. Theophilus Tanner away from his beloved wife and children.

"Emily," Doc whispered, and for the tiniest flicker of time he thought he heard her call his name in return. But it was only the cold mountain winds, moaning through the pines of the Tennessee valley.

Stepping closer, Mildred placed a hand on the old man's arm and squeezed gently. Doc started to speak, but his voice broke and he turned away from the valley.

"Chilling the bastards would be nice," Krysty agreed. "But we still need to find out what they are doing with that freaking big dish."

"True, but it would be a lot easier to recce if the baron and his top gun were both breathing dirt." Ryan worked the bolt on the Steyr, then wrapped the strap around his muscular forearm to help steady his aim. The angle was wrong, so he lay down and placed the barrel on the lowest rail of the fence. The electric wires hummed above, but he reasoned his blaster was far enough away to not set off an alarm.

"Can't do it," J.B. said, collapsing his telescope. "Not shouldn't, but you can't. It's beyond the range of your blaster."

"Beyond the effective range," Ryan corrected him, studying the wind push as it pushed a stray piece of paper along the roof of a building. The air was moving faster up here, slower down there. That meant less sheerage, but greater density. "The rounds will reach them, just not with their full force."

"What do bruises?" Jak demanded angrily.

"Means it'll only chill the mutie-maker, but not remove his entire head," Ryan said, wiggling into a more comfortable position. The short grass was itchy under him, a rock pressing into his hip. The Deathlands warrior ignored the tiny disturbances and concentrated on the silver-haired man near the APC. The element of surprise was his. But if he missed this time, Silas might stay inside until further notice, never giving the companions another clear shot. Was it worth the risk? Should he take the shot?

"Fuck, yes," Ryan growled softly to himself. Taking a deep breath and holding it, he placed the crosshairs of the scope on the whitecoat's chest, moved it a foot to the left, then six inches up, and fired.

But even before he finished pulling the trigger, Ryan remembered Overton's bulletproof jacket. Quickly, he worked the bolt and fired again, lower this time, then again, slightly to the left, and once more adjusting to the right.

"FOOL! MORON!" Silas raged, stamping his good foot and gesturing at the exposed wiring of the transformer. "Look at this mess! You have the goddamn fence wired completely wrong! I told you a looped circuit so that a break in one area will not leave us defenseless across the entire fence. Looped—don't you know the word?"

"Sir, I can handle this later," the major urged again. "We should be inside out of sight."

Silas glared at him in outrage. "Not until we have this fixed! The electric fence is our main protection from Ryan or another slave revolt, and this idiot screwed up the wiring!"

Lashing out, Silas hit the man with his cane. "Now get gloves and fix the circuits, while it's hot!"

"I'm not sure where the gloves are, sir," the sec man protested.

"Do it anyway," Silas growled.

The other sec men murmured in fear.

"While it's hot? I could be chilled, sir!" the man wailed.

Imperiously, Silas glared at the cringing man. "I have more sec men if you should fail."

Damp with sweat, the blue shirt looked to his chief for assistance.

"Do as the commander orders," Sheffield said sternly. "And next time, if you don't know what to do, ask for help before figuring it out yourself."

"B-but, sir, I—"

"Enough!" Silas shouted, hitting the trooper again. "Stop weeping like a caned child! Do your job, or die!"

Turning toward the Quonset hut, Silas took a single

step and was violently knocked backward a full yard. Gasping for breath, his lungs feeling as if they were on fire, Silas groaned and rubbed his chest in pain, fingers recoiling as they encountered the red-hot lump of a flattened bullet. Instantly, the predark scientists realized what was happening and tried to scramble under the LAV. The boom of a high-powered rifle rolled over the complex, and a second round plowed directly into his throat, clearing the vest by an inch. Blood sprayed onto the stunned crowd of sec men, the impact knocking Silas sideways, arms flailing. The second boom arrived just as the third round punched a hole below his left eye, the entire back of his head exploding into a grisly spray of brains and bones.

Even as he fell, a fourth shot slammed into his vest again, driving the corpse backward into the exposed wiring of the transformer. His arms hit the bus bars. There was a crackle of power, and eighty thousand volts of direct current flowed through the dead man in a controlled lightning bolt. His hair burst into flames, his blood boiled into steam, eyes exploded and his clothes ignited as writhing tendrils of high voltage crawled over his twisting form.

Backing away in horror, Sheffield felt a breeze brush past his face and realized what it was before the crack of the longblaster arrived. Grabbing the closest sec man, he lifted the man off the ground and swung the blue shirt between himself and the distant hills just in time. Gasping for breath, the living shield jerked and spit out a tongue and wads of brain tissue from his mouth as two more copper-jacketed rounds arrived.

Holding the corpse up, the major moved behind the nearby LAV, then tossed it aside. Safe for the moment, he could only watch as the body of Silas Jamaisvous was slowly reduced to a grinning skeleton. For a split second, there seemed to be a circuit board riveted to the man's skull, and then that vanished in a whoof of flames.

"In the wag!" Sheffield bellowed, thumping a fist on the armor. "Fire the chain gun at the hillside!"

"Where on the hill, sir?" a young voice asked from inside.

"Due south! Just above the ridge fence!" Then Sheffield quickly added, "But don't open the hatch! Stay under cover!"

Blood and teeth sprayed from the turret, followed by the rolling thunder of the longblaster.

"Damn you, Ryan," the chief blue shirt cursed, positive he knew the identity of the sniper. Who else could it be, but the man Silas so hated and feared. Suddenly, Sheffield was surprised to find a blaster in his grip, and he holstered the useless weapon. At this range he might as well throw rocks for all the good it would do. The officer wasn't even sure the chain gun could reach the fence, but it would have been worth a try.

The crackling discharge at the transformer finally ceased as the material causing the short circuit was cleaned off the fully charged bus bars. Gray ash, charred cloth and some smoking pieces of bone sprinkled to the ground.

Then a flash of rainbow from the remains caught Sheffield's attention, and he saw it was the computer disk Silas had refused to let him inspect. He started for the disk, then stopped himself. A single round from the sniper would also drive him into the transformer with the same results. The disk seemed undamaged, but was temporarily out of his reach.

Racing around a corner into the enclosure, a squad of armed sec men came into view. "Sir, we heard shots," a burly sergeant started, then stopped talking as he took in the grisly sight at the transformer.

"Holy shit," a corporal whispered, and another turned away to noisily retch.

Fists clenched, both of his hearts wildly pounding, Sheffield fought down the urge to stay where he was. But the man knew better than to demonstrate any weakness in front of the his subordinates. Victory or death. Boldly he walked from behind the transport.

"There are the intruders!" he bellowed, thrusting an arm toward the nearby hills. "Send out every man we have, use the dogs and the Bell. Find them! The man who chills them will be promoted to major and serve as my right hand. No prisoners, do you understand me? I want them dead. No prisoners!"

"Yes, sir!" the sergeant replied. Although visibly shaken, he managed a salute and started off at a run already shouting orders. The rest of the sec men closely followed, the excitement of the possible promotion wiping the shock and fear from their faces.

"You!" Sheffield barked, pointing at the sec man in charge of the transformer. "Turn the circuits off!"

Hesitantly, the blue shirt obeyed and, bracing for a shock, he threw the insulated switch. There was a snap of power, and the hum of the bus bars softly faded, but the huge copper coils continued to faintly crackle with the secondary effects of recharging the accumulators.

Moving quickly, Sheffield retrieved the disk and shoved it into a pocket. "Back on," he snapped impatiently, walking around the transformer until the southern hills were no longer in sight.

"Power is restored, sir!" the sec man shouted, excited at still being alive. "Should I summon some slaves to clean up...ah, gather the remains?"

"That won't be necessary," Sheffield said coolly. Drawing a handblaster, he aimed at the blue shirt and fired.

Shrieking in agony, the sec man fell to the ground, clutching his groin, dark blood flowing across his clothes. Ruthlessly, Sheffield fired again and again, first removing fingers, then other small body parts until the slide of his blaster kicked back, showing it was out of ammo. Reloading, the major started again, dissecting the man alive, until blood loss made the tattered lump of human flesh stop making noises and go unconscious.

Placing the weapon against the forehead of the gurgling thing on the ground, he paused, then thumbed the safety back on.

"No, you die slow," the major stated, holstering the blaster. "Unlike Silas, I don't tolerate failure."

Walking briskly to the lab, the new baron of the ville placed his palm on the wall plate, and waited anxiously until it chimed and unlocked the door. Hurrying inside, Sheffield stared through the Plexiglas windows at the sloping hills encircling the complex.

"Better start running, Ryan," he said softly, almost in a whisper. "Because you're next."

Chapter Twenty

"Let's go," Ryan said, standing. Working the bolt on the Steyr SSG-70, he opened the breech to remove the spent clip and slid in a fresh magazine.

"Did you get him?" Dean asked, shading his eyes with a hand. Sirens started to howl, something was on fire, sending black smoke wafting into the sky, and sec men seemed to be rushing about madly. The electric lights in the guard towers flickered, died away completely, then came back on again.

"Silas is dead," Ryan replied, easing the bolt home and starting up the slope.

"Can't get much more dead," Krysty agreed, walking alongside him. "He's gone forever."

"I am only sorry I did not get to pull the trigger," Doc replied, staring backward at the busy ville.

"Put a few rounds into the transformer, too. But I missed the chief sec man," Ryan said, stopping at the ridge and cupping his hands. "Bastard moved fast."

Krysty stepped into his grip, and he boosted her up onto the higher ground. Then she grabbed his arms and helped him climb the steep embankment.

Uzi at the ready, J.B. watched the hillside as the rest of the companions assisted one another, then Ryan covered him as the wiry Armorer scrambled up on his own.

"Any chance they can know the shots came from this

direction?'' Mildred asked worriedly, as they started quickly for the trees. She would feel a lot safer once they gained some cover.

"No way," Ryan replied, striding along. "I could have taken that shot from anywhere in the valley."

Just then, J.B. sneezed in warning and the companions went flat, shifting for cover in the stubby grass. A few seconds later, a sec man in a blue shirt walked out of the pine trees with an AK-47 cradled in his arms. The man gasped at the sight of the armed companions and swung the barrel of his blaster toward them. But there was a low cough, the blue shirt fell to the ground, shook and went still.

A wisp of smoke still clinging to the muzzled of the silenced 9 mm SIG-Sauer, Ryan crossed to the corpse and shot it again to make sure the man was dead. Eagerly, Dean claimed the Kalashnikov and the spare ammo. Krysty took the radio.

"We can monitor their communications with this," she said, inspecting the device. "Help us avoid any more patrols." The radio was turned on so the sentry could receive reports or instructions. She adjusted the volume to its lowest setting, so as to not give away their position.

Ryan glanced at the walkie-talkie. "Air Force model," he stated. "Very short range, these days even shorter. Probably reduced to line of sight."

"Unless they use that big antenna," Doc suggested, entering the woods. Immediately, he felt better with some protective cover around them.

Shifting her med kit, Mildred shook her head, her beaded locks bouncing wildly. "The dish antenna would have to be pointed in the correct direction. Think of it as a radio cannon. It's got to be pointed right at whom they want to talk with."

"Useless," Jak grunted, stepping over a fallen willow tree.

Ducking under a bristly pine branch, Dean asked, "We heading for the redoubt?"

"First we cross the river," his father answered. "For once those land mines will work for us. No APC or Hummer can follow."

"Sounds good," Krysty said.

Just then, the speaker of the walkie-talkie crackled loudly. "Sentry Twenty-four, any sign of the intruders?" a male voice asked.

The companions paused as Krysty pulled the device into view and the radio blared, "What is your status, Twenty-four? Are you in trouble?"

"Gaia, he means us," Krysty stated, turning off the radio with a click. "Ryan, J.B., did either of you see any female sec men?"

"Hell, no," Ryan growled.

She shoved the radio into his hands. "Then you answer quick, or else they'll know where we are."

He chewed a lip for a moment, then turned the radio back on. There came a burst of static. "—entry Twenty-four, where are you?"

Coughing raggedly, Ryan fumbling with the volume. "Raiders..." he gasped weakly into the transmitter. "Gut shot...hurts bad!" Ryan knew there was nothing more painful than a gunshot wound in the belly. He once saw a coldheart stab himself to stop the agony. Any differences in his voice and that of the younger sec man would be attributed to the terrible pain.

Biting his tongue not to speak, J.B. started rummaging inside his munitions bag.

"Where are you, man?" the radio asked urgently. "What's your location?"

Holding up the map from Georgia, J.B. pointed at the scrawl at the bottom.

Nodding in comprehension, Ryan panted heavily, "Q-quarry...."

A crackle of static. "Shit-fire! Was it muties? Tanner?"

Doc arched an eyebrow, but held his peace.

Coughing some more, Ryan whispered, "Fifty... coming...your way..."

"How fucking many?" the sec man yelled, distorting the words.

Exhaling as if dying, Ryan released the transmit button and tossed the radio back to Krysty. She made sure it was turned off and tucked the device into a pocket of her bearskin coat.

"That bought us a few minutes," Ryan said. "They'll have to check the quarry before doing anything else, just in case this was a real report."

"More than enough time," J.B. agreed, heading into the bushes.

"Fifty," Jak said. "Smart. Send all troops."

Parting some bushes with the barrel of his longblaster, Ryan grunted in reply. "That was the idea."

The sun was starting to set as the companions moved out of the band of trees. Crouching, they looked for guards, but the river and bridge seemed to be clear. Running across the bridge in pairs, the companions took refuge in the forest on the other side and waited to see if there was any signs of pursuit. The forest and river were placid and calm.

"We're in the clear," Mildred stated confidently. "Come on, I'll feel better once we are inside the redoubt and have a few feet of steel between us and the blues."

"Wait," Krysty said, tilting her head toward the river. "Motorcycles are coming our way, six, mebbe seven."

"Can't be after us," J.B. stated. "Must be going toward that quarry."

"Mebbe," Ryan said, "but we'd better make sure. Everybody take positions behind the trees."

There was a roar of engines, and a group of sleek motorcycles rolled into view along the riverbank. The riders sat inside a roll cage, an array of steel bars forming a barrier around the men, affording them tremendous protection from being clubbed or having an enemy leap on the bikes. The bars were black, but the welds were shiny. Clearly the cages were a recent addition to the machines. All of the sec men were armed with squat Ingram M-10 machine pistols, instead of the usual Kalashnikovs. The boxy blasters would be easy to wield while inside the safety cage, unlike the long barreled AK-47. Bandoliers of ammo clips hung across their chests, and each had a radio strapped to the gas tank between their legs.

Slowing at the bridge, the pack split roughly in two, three continuing toward the quarry, four rolling across the bridge. The two-wheelers separated quickly, moving to the farthest edge of the bridge, staying as far away from the midspan as possible. As they entered the woods at a crawl, branches hit the cages and snapped off at the trunks as the machines proceeded along the dirt path.

Suddenly, leaves erupted from the ground as Ryan fired his silenced weapon. A blue shirt cried out and slumped onto the handlebars. Stepping out from behind a tree, Jak jerked his arm and another sec man clutched at the knife in his throat. Ryan fired again, just as the third biker drew his M-10. The SIG-Sauer won that contest, and the dead man slammed against the protective cage, making the riderless bike topple to the ground.

The fourth sec man cursed as he fought to free the strap of his subgun, which was tangled with the lock on the cage. Shouting in rage, he walked his bike around in a circle, and twisted the handlebar throttle, preparing to run when Doc circled around a nearby tree and deftly thrust his sword between the iron bars directly into the driver's left eye.

Releasing the sword, Doc watched as the sec man stayed frozen in position, his dying brain no longer able to relay commands. The bike rolled on for another few yards, then bumped into a bush and stopped moving, the engine softly rumbling, faint blue exhaust blowing from the chrome mufflers.

Going to the trapped motorcycle, Doc placed a boot on the cage and yanked his sword free. The corpse jerked upright at the action as if renewed with life, then it slumped over, releasing the handlebars, and the engine died in perfect harmony.

Rushing out of hiding, the rest of the companions converged on the fallen machines, turning off engines before the hot casings set the dry leaves on fire. Extracting the drivers proved to be no problem. The safety cages had curved doors that locked with a simple sliding bar from the inside. The companions placed the corpses in a pile, and J.B. slid a wad of C-4 and a pressure switch under the top corpse.

"Four bikes," Ryan said, checking over the M-10. The bolt was stiff from poor cleaning, but it seemed in operational condition. "We have to balance this carefully. Dean with Jak, Mildred with J.B., Doc with Krysty. I'll ride with the backpacks."

The companions quickly piled their backpacks onto

Ryan's machine, then joined their partners. Setting the ignition switch, Mildred waited until J.B. was in position before kicking the big Harley into life. The 1450 cc engine purred with barely restrained power. Twisting the handlebar throttle, the woman gunned the engine a few times to clear the carbs, and rolled over to the others.

Krysty turned on the radio attached to her bike and heard only the hiss and crackle of static. "Odd," she muttered, checking the radio in her pocket. It was also silent. "They should be talking about the quarry by now."

"Mebbe they already figure it was a trick," Dean suggested, one arm around Jak's waist, the other holding an M-10 machine pistol. The boy knew it was a crappy blaster. The stubby two-inch barrel gave no real accuracy over any distance. However, the yard-long AK-47 was impossible to use while inside the cage, especially riding behind another person, and the subgun could shoot faster than his Browning Hi-Power.

"Could be," Ryan agreed, tapping the fuel gauge. Half-full, more than enough. "If so, they're going to come after us in force. Night will be here soon, so we'll stay in the trees until it's dark, then make a run for the redoubt across the grasslands."

"I'll take rearguard," J.B. said, the Uzi in one hand, the M-10 in the other. He was sitting reversed on the seat with his back to Mildred, legs braced against the lower bars of the cage, the buddy-bar snug between his thighs.

Dean changed position to copy the older man. The chrome steel of the buddy-bar rose to his chest and was very uncomfortable, but the stance gave him a good purchase to fight from. That was good enough.

"Mehi loricatus oportet occulte!" Doc stated in Latin,

holstering the LeMat and tying down the flap. His hands clumsily worked the arming bolt on the subgun, and he eased off the safety.

"No headlights," Mildred translated. "Bastards can't hit what they can't find."

Starting forward into the growing darkness, Ryan zigzagged the big bike past the lush growths of pine and willow. "Just shoot anybody you see," he added grimly, bent low over the handlebars. "They won't be trying to take us prisoners anymore."

IN THE LAB, Sheffield was awkwardly typing commands on the computer keyboard. Impatiently, he watched the vector graphic grow and change on the softly glowing screen. Checking the assignment integers, the man cursed in frustration when he realized that the numbers were wrong. It was aimed much too close to risk a shot. Now he would have to start all over again!

"Good news, sir!" said a voice from the intercom on the desk. "We got a report that the outlanders are at the quarry."

"The quarry?" he repeated slowly. "Who told you this?"

"A sentry reported in just before he died. We're sending most of the troops there."

"Recall them immediately," the officer commanded. "It's a trick to divert us. Send everybody to the south. That's where they really are."

Pursing his lips, Sheffield then continued, "The troops have a maximum of forty minutes to find the assassins of Dr. Jamaisvous, then recall them immediately."

"Sir?" the intercom asked puzzled.

"Just do as you're ordered, trooper."

"Yes, sir! Hail the New America!"

Cutting off the intercom, Sheffield returned to his work. Starting the programming cycle again, he typed much more carefully, and a slow smile grew as the flashing numbers on the computer screen began to take on the desired configuration.

THE QUARTET OF BIKES raced across the open fields of Tennessee bluegrass. Headlights off, it was difficult to see anything in the way, and Ryan often found himself jerking the handlebars at the very last moment to avoid hitting a large rock or some other obstacle. However, it was a good half hour since they stole the motorcycles, and they were more than halfway to the redoubt.

"How close are we?" Krysty shouted, her hair streaming in the wind.

"Just a few more miles!" J.B. yelled in reply.

"Great!"

"My dear Krysty, can you do something about your hair, please?" Doc asked. "I can barely see!"

Grabbing handfuls, she stuffed the living tendrils gently into her shirt collar and did the top button. "Better?" she shouted over a shoulder.

"Infinitely so. My thanks!"

"No prob!"

Suddenly, bright lights illuminated the field in bouncing cones of stark white light, and there came the slow chattering of subguns. A copper-jacketed round zinged off the safety cage around Doc and Krysty, another bullet slamming directly into the backpacks behind Ryan.

"It's other bikes!" he shouted, and slapped a switch, turning on his own headlights. Now able to see clearly, the man pressed the big motorcycle on to much greater speeds. The ground flashed below the wheels in a constant blur. With Ryan cutting the way, the others also increased their speed and pulled away from the oncoming motorcycles.

"Ace the leader!" J.B. shouted, cutting loose with the Uzi and subgun. Targeting the closest headlight, he put a long burst from the blasters just above the jiggling light source. There was a crash of glass, and the Harley veered off abruptly, then hit something and flipped over. Tumbling out of control, the bike rolled over and over, the screaming sec man trapped inside the cage bouncing about like a boneless rag doll.

Doc and Dean did the same, and another bike fell. Instantly, the other two drivers turned off their halogen headlights, and soon the noise of their engines could no longer be heard.

"Easy as pie," Dean said triumphantly.

"Keep going!" Ryan shouted over the roar of the Harley. "That was too easy. It's a trick to make us slow down!"

"Trap ahead?" Krysty yelled.

"Could be! Everybody, stay sharp!"

The noise started soft and low, a distant beating of drums. But it quickly increased in tempo and volume until a steady whomping sound was heard, and the companions craned their necks about to find the source. Unexpectedly, a dark shape swooped by overhead, silhouetted by the lightning flashes in the rumbling storm clouds.

"That's a bastard helicopter!" Ryan growled, buffeted by the wind of its passage. The chopper was the first flying machine the Deathlands warrior had ever seen. Silas had to have found the mother lode of all redoubts to loot. Maybe even a Deep Storage locker!

The Trader told stories around the campfires about predark vaults full of dry nitrogen gas, the temperature lowered to below freezing. Designed to keep ammo and food fresh for hundreds of years, Deep Storage lockers were supposed to be fully stocked with everything. Not the occasional box of ammo or handful of MRE packs, but literally tons of food, tanks, missiles and enough ammo and blasters for the predark Army. Silas with a Deep Storage locker—that would explain a lot.

The helicopter passed by again, lower this time.

"Why isn't it shooting?" Dean demanded, tracking its passage, but withholding fire. The boy hated to admit it, but he was terrified. Machines that flew—it was unnatural!

"He's getting our range!" J.B. shouted, firing some rounds into the sky.

"That's a Bell bubble chopper," Ryan stated. "It has no armor, and no blasters."

"Gives us a fighting chance to live," J.B. said. Dark night! A helicopter. What else did the blues have in their arsenal?

"The vehicle is unarmed?" Doc demanded. "Then it is merely here to frighten us, or track our location for others?"

"Hell, no!"

A powerful explosion ripped about the night, the ground shaking as a column of boiling flame reached into the sky.

"That's dynamite or TNT," J.B. said, sticking both weapons through the bars of the safety cage and firing, the winking muzzle-flashes illuminating the man in the darkness. "The pilot is tossing out sticks like bombs!"

Another column of strident fire blossomed directly

ahead of the companions. The concussion slapped them hard, and they fought to keep the bikes upright as they narrowly skirted the steaming blast crater, clumps of hard soil under their wheels making the bikes shake madly. A fall now meant sure death.

"Figure eight for sixty!" Ryan shouted, leading the others sharply to the left, then to the right in evasion tactics. "We go on the next blast!"

Another blast roared, and Ryan killed the headlights. The companions spread wildly across the field, only to meet again farther away.

"Volley fire," Ryan shouted. "Go!"

Doc, Dean and J.B. cut loose with their blasters, filling the sky with a hail of bullets. As a clip was emptied, they tossed it away, slapped in a fresh one and continued shooting. Speed and luck were their only chances now. A single stick landing in the middle of the bikes, and they would never hit the ground alive.

"Forest ahead!" Ryan shouted, dodging a primitive plow. A ville had to be close by. He only hoped they weren't friendly with the blues.

The subgun finally empty, Doc dropped the useless weapon and triggered the LeMat. In the darkness, the muzzle-flash reached out for more than a foot, the detonation sounding like a peal of thunder.

In throbbing majesty, the helicopter angled away and moved fast into the night until it was gone. Tense minutes passed as they waited for its thundering return on another bombing run, and then the companions broached the forest and were riding under its canopy of branches. Slowing, Ryan listened carefully for the predark machine, but only the hushed silence of the woods could be heard.

"Why did it leave?" Krysty asked suspiciously.

"Mayhap I hit the infernal contraption," Doc rumbled, studying the sky dubiously.

Sliding the last spare clip into the subgun, J.B. scowled at the clouds above. "Seems unlikely," the Armorer said. "But it's possible, and those damn .44 miniballs would punch right through a civilian copter."

Smiling with his oddly perfect teeth, Doc fondly patted the huge handcannon. "Which is why I still retain her, sir! Very few enemies, indeed, need to be shot twice with this."

"Well, the Bell would have to leave if the old coot hit the rotor," Mildred added. "A helicopter can't fly straight without its tail rotor."

"At least the thing is gone," Dean said gratefully, yanking on the bolt of the subgun, trying to free a jammed round. The misfire was caught in the breech tight and wouldn't come loose. He might have to disassemble the blaster before it would fire again.

Suddenly, the boy could see the blaster a lot clearer as a wealth of moonlight flooded into the forest, the silvery light illuminating the trees in a cool glow.

"Clouds broke," Krysty said, the hair on her head coiling tightly. "Haven't seen that happen in quite awhile."

Squinting with his good eye, Ryan rubbed his unshaved chin, making a sound like sandpaper. "You don't suppose—"

But the Deathlands warrior was interrupted as something rustled in the trees, bouncing from limb to limb to land in the bushes. The same thing happened again, and then once more, this time the object landing in plain sight on the carpet of leaves. It was a blue jay, its feathers splayed and steam rising off its body.

"What in hell...?" Ryan said.

Everybody jumped and aimed their blasters as dozens more birds fell to the ground, robins, hawks and owls, the impact of their bodies sounding almost like hail. Then a scream-wing plummeted through the foliage to hit the safety cage around Ryan. The dead mutie was only a foot away from his face, and he stared at it hard. This was the closest he had ever been a scream-wing. Steam hissed from its mouth and rectum, the eyes had burst apart and its hide was bubbly as if the creature had been dipped in boiling oil.

"The copter?" Dean asked fearfully. The boy had no idea what was going on here. Cooked birds falling from the sky?

"Oh, my God," Mildred whispered, pointing behind them with a shaky hand.

Thousands of leaves and needles were falling from the trees in a heavy wave, the bare branches darkening, and some of the small growths bursting into flame. The bushes began to smolder, and the grass withered. It was as if the forest were dying before their very eyes. There was a sharp line of the approaching destruction, green plants on this side, withered death on the other.

"Sweet Jesus save us, it's a Kite!" Mildred fumbled twice in her haste to kick the motorcycle into life. "That's what the bastard Jamaisvous was talking to, a goddamn freaking Kite!"

"Silas ace plants?" Jak demanded.

"It kills everything!" the woman shouted, and twisted the throttle to the last stop. The wheels spun wildly in the loose leaves, spraying out debris, then contacted dirt and the Harley roared forward, almost crashing into a tree. The cage slammed into the trunk, ripping off bark and making J.B. drop the subgun.

"Hey!" he cried out, nursing a wrist. There was a sharp pain inside as if a bone had been broken.

"Fuck it!" the physician screamed, plowing through a bush. "Run, run for your lives! And for God's sake don't look up!"

Starting their bikes, the others took off after the woman, not exactly sure what was happening. Doc watched as the oncoming line of destruction approached to within only a few yards of the rolling motorcycle, when he began to twitch uncomfortably. It felt as if a million insects were crawling over his skin, and the grip of the LeMat started to grow warm.

"Faster, madam!" he shouted, almost throwing the blaster away. "We have to go faster!"

Ahead of them, the forest was cool and green, the thick foliage starkly lit by the full October moon. His left eye socket itching madly, Ryan fought to control the Harley as he drove full tilt through the woods, sometimes the trees so close he thought the safety cage would jam tight between the trees. But the bark scraped loose, giving scant inches, and the Harley roared onward.

Glancing behind, Krysty saw the crumbling forest was steadily gaining on the bikes. "It's gaining on us!" she yelled, tears flowing down her cheeks. It felt as if her hair were on fire, the pain almost beyond endurance. She had a hard time thinking clearly, and more than once the bike nearly toppled over from her clumsy driving. Silently, she prayed to Gaia for the strength to live.

Their bikes riding side by side, the companions crashed through a wall of thorny rosebushes, the safety cages holding most of the stems at bay, but still their clothes snagged and trickles of blood flowed from a dozen small cuts.

Ryan glanced into his rearview mirror. "We're not going to get away!" he shouted grimly.

"We have to!" Mildred answered, then shrugged and dropped her heavy med kit. "Heave the baggage! Lose everything!"

Stunned for a moment by the incredible act, Ryan resolutely reached behind himself, grabbed a backpack and stuffed it through the warm bars of his safety cage. When there was only one left, his speed noticeably increased. The man hesitated for a heartbeat, then also threw away that pack. Mildred knew her stuff, and whatever it was that was after them, he didn't want it to reach them for the sake of a few pounds.

Dropping the subgun, J.B. watched the weapon fireball as the crackling wave reached the blaster. The man hesitated for a tick, then tossed away his precious accumulation of explosives and primers.

"Brace yourselves!" he shouted just as the bag thunderously detonated, the blast toppling over the dying trees, bushes flying, shrapnel zinging through the air in every direction.

Struggling with one arm at a time, Krysty got out of her heavy bearskin coat and stuffed it through the cage. Dean dropped his canteen, then the newly acquired Kalashnikov and the ammo clips. The coat burst into flames, and the ammo exploded as the grass turned brown underneath the items.

The brown line in the soil streaked after them, coming closer by the second. Frantically, the companions emptied the pockets of MRE packs, spare knives, extra ammo and everything else they could find.

"Radios!" Jak shouted, ripping the transmitter free and casting it away.

With the motorcycles moving at top speed, the companions raced through the forest in a nightmare of dodging trees and crashing through bushes. Unstoppable, the death wave from the Kite swept onward, getting closer and closer with each passing moment.

Chapter Twenty-One

Their load lightened, the companions began to pull away from the wave of death, the crackling of the leaves slowly fading into the distance. Soon it was gone from sight, and living green plants surrounded them once more. The itching eased, and the metal of their blasters started to cool. But the riders didn't slow their frantic pace through the Tennessee woods. Soon, the trees began to thin, and the companions broke out of the woods and onto smooth rolling grasslands again. An hour passed in silent speed, clouds forming overhead to mask the eternal stars and moon. Thankfully, there was no sign of the pools and streams that had surrounded the redoubt before. The waters must have receded over time and the land was alive again. But not for long.

"We should be safe now," Dean said hopefully. The boy held his Browning Hi-Power and a single clip in sweaty hands, ready to lose both should it prove necessary. He had tried unlacing his combat boots, but it was plainly impossible to do that on a moving bike.

Shaking her head, Krysty released her hair from its confines, and the fiery cascade flexed freely once more. "Thank Gaia that's over," she exhaled. "My hair was in agony!"

"Nobody stop until we reach the redoubt!" Mildred countered, still hunched over the handlebars. "And watch the clouds! The Kite might be skipping ahead of us, so we race straight into its beams.''

Maneuvering his bike closer, Ryan shouted, ''What was that?''

The open spaces allowing her to relax a notch, Mildred bit a lip and tried to figure a way to explain what they had just faced. ''In the kitchens of the redoubts,'' she replied, ''you've used the microwave oven to boil water, and once we baked a potato. Same thing.''

Ryan frowned as the engine of his bike sputtered, and he revved the throttle. The Harley was dangerously low on fuel. ''You called it a Kite,'' he called out. ''That a war satellite?''

She shrugged. ''Not originally, but I guess it is now.''

The quivering needle of the fuel gauge stopped moving as it reached the empty mark, and Ryan concentrated on squeezing a few more miles out of the gas vapors in the tank. Silas had found a microwave satellite and gotten control with an old SETI dish. Good thing he had aced the old bastard on sight. But if Silas was chilled, then who was operating the Kite?

The landscape began to take on a familiar shape, and Ryan began to remember details of the last visit there, the fights, desperate running, a bloody ambush and the endless chilling. It had been one of their worst jumps, and the redoubt itself was as bare as a spent round. There wasn't a can of beans, or anything useful inside just an armored vault filled with predark works of art—bronzes statues and antique oil paintings. Why would the Pentagon waste valuable space storing those things away from the ravages of a nuke storm? That was just another of the endless mysteries about the redoubts, and one he had no desire to solve.

Just then a familiar shape rose from the ground in the

glare of the headlights. The front of the redoubt was as Ryan remembered, battered and charred from the nuke blasts of skydark. But the armored door was as sturdy as ever, and the companions would be safe once they got inside.

"The redoubt!" Krysty shouted, slowing her speed.

Taking the lead, Ryan rolled his bike around the outcropping until reaching the front of the underground base. Massive black doors stood untarnished and immutable in a small recess, an armored keypad set into the burnished jamb of the portal.

Braking to a halt, the companions turned off the engines and set the kickstands. Silence greeted them, a soft wind blowing from the direction of the distant forest.

"Thermal currents from the Kite," Mildred said to the unasked question, as she stiffly climbed from the cage. For a second, she looked for her med kit, then memory flared, and she grimly walked toward the redoubt. They physician could assemble another kit over time. More important, safety was only a few yards away.

Ryan was already standing at the door, tapping the entry code onto the keypad when the ground underneath the man heaved and he was thrown sprawling yards away.

Spitting curses, the companions drew their blasters as a nightmare crawled out of the soil directly in front of the door. It was a twisted mutie unlike anything they had ever seen before. The grotesque creature possessed a misshapen head covered with different-sized eyes and multiple ears. Its drooling mouth was filled with fangs, and a forked tongue lolled over pale leathery lips. The long serpentine body was covered with spotty fur as if it suffered from mange or rad poisoning. However, massive muscles rolled beneath the leathery skin as the mutie shambled closer on four powerful legs, two tiny shriveled limbs dangling impotently from its hideous chest. Sharp claws ripped apart the hard soil as the slavering beast started to crawl catlike toward the companions.

"Silas!" J.B. cursed, working the bolt on his Uzi. "He knew we'd try for the redoubt and left one of his DNA experiments for us!"

Rising to one knee, Ryan leveled the Steyr SSG-70. He was down to only a few clips, but there was no time to waste with this mutie. They had to get inside before the Kite returned. "Chill it!" he commanded, triggering his longblaster.

In unison, the companions opened fire in a ragged volley, the barrage of rounds tearing the screaming animal apart. It slumped to the ground, bleeding from a dozen wounds.

"See any more around?" Ryan demanded, standing and chambering a fresh round. He glanced at the ground for any suspicious movements, then at the sky. The clouds were still thick and heavy. Good.

"Looks clear," Doc reported, studying the fields around them while waving away the smoke from his LeMat.

Colt at the ready, Jak dropped to one knee and placed the flat of his hand in the cold soil. "No vibrations," he reported.

"Nasty-looking bugger," J.B. stated, then stared in astonishment as the dead mutie began to stir.

Sluggishly, the thing rose on its hind legs, the holes in its skin closing into dainty puckered scars.

"By the Three Kennedys," Doc whispered as he switched the selector pin on his LeMat from the .44 miniballs to the smoothbore .63 shotgun. There was only a single load, but at such close range it should remove the creature's head.

Hastily, Krysty thumbed fresh cartridges into her revolver as a rill of porcupine quills extended protectively along the neck of the snarling mutie. "Gaia protect us, it's regenerating," she said, dropping a few rounds but reloading the blaster in record time. The redhead closed the cylinder with a snap of her wrist and fired again immediately. The soft-nosed bullets hit the creature in the chest and neck with less effect this time. The wounds closed without scars after only weeping a few drops of the weird semi-transparent green blood.

"How the hell are we going to chill something that can do that?" she demanded, backing away.

"Don't have to chill it," Ryan yelled over his booming rifle. "Just have to get past!"

Furiously working the bolt on his Steyr, Ryan pumped two rounds from the longblaster directly into the beast, stalling for Doc until he was ready. The long 7.62 mm cartridges each took out an eye, which started to regrow. J.B. added a burst from the Uzi, concentrating on the chest. Greenish blood spurted with every hit, the wounds closing faster as if the mutie were accelerating the healing process.

Stepping closer, Doc ducked under a lashing tail and fired the LeMat at point-blank range. The massive blackpowder weapon vomited flame and smoke from the wide muzzle, the shotgun round slamming the beast backward against the door of the redoubt. But as the companions watched, the growling mutie rose again. The gaping hole in its chest, leaking a greenish ichor, began to close and the bleeding stopped.

Dodging to the left, then darting to the right, the mutie

came ever closer, a forked tongue running hungrily along its mottled jaws.

"Dark night!" J.B. snarled, releasing the Uzi and swinging the S&W shotgun into play. Only four shells remained, and the Armorer knew he had to make every one count.

Working the pump, he fired two shells at the creature, the spray of fléchettes tearing its head apart. But the bleeding pieces of flesh slid together again, and a pair of scorpion tails arched from its mottled back, the barbed tips glistening with moisture.

"Poison!" Mildred warned, targeting its face with her ZKR pistol. Several of its eyes exploded from her soft lead rounds, and the hissing mutie started directly toward her, the other orbs extending on pale stalks.

Suddenly, clear moonlight flooded the battle scene.

"The Kite!" Krysty yelled, her flexing hair already coiling protectively.

"Go for its head!" Ryan shouted, moving forward and firing with each step. The companions aimed and unleashed a ragged volley, the beast screaming in agony, the barrage of lead and steel tearing apart its writhing form. But their weapons achieved only the same meager results.

The roar of an engine shook the night, and Jak raced away from the redoubt on one of the stolen Harleys. The noise of the engine caught the mutie by surprise, and it arched its back as if about to leap upon the cowardly runaway. But the humans understood, and maintained their useless blasterfire to hold the beast in place, as Jak turned the bike and charged forward, gunning the big engine to top speed.

The engine coughed and died mere feet away from the snarling creature, but continued rolling. The safety

cage slammed into the mutie, crushing it against the
nuke-proof door of the redoubt with a sickening crunch.
Howling in pain, the bleeding creature clawed at the
metalwork, struggling wildly.

"Not dead? Try this!" Jak yelled, and fired his Colt
Python directly into its exposed brain, pink goo splat-
tering onto the door and rocks.

Convulsing, the mutie jabbed the barbed tip of its
scorpion tail through the openings of the cage. Struggling to undo the lock of the cage, Jak dropped his
empty blaster and slashed at the creature with a knife. It
shook the wreckage in unbridled rage, and, incredibly,
began to shove the motorcycle off its trapped form.

"Cover fire!" J.B. shouted, emptying the shotgun as
more pink brains blew out of its smashed skull.

Only a second behind, Doc lunged forward, skewering
the beast through the chest, then twisting his sword, so
the blade opened wide the wound. Emerald blood poured
from the gash, quickly slowing to a trickle. A tail lashed
at the old man, and he nimbly ducked out of the way,
slicing off the barbed tip.

A crackling sound could be heard from the distant line
of trees, withered leaves raining to the ground by the
thousands.

Climbing on the wreckage, Krysty and Mildred emptied their blasters at the creature, as Dean got Jak loose.
They hastily retreated, and seconds later Ryan crashed
into the beast with another bike. A wash of greenish
blood vomited out the mutie's mouth, and Ryan fired his
handblaster at the beast. Ichor pouring from a dozen
wounds, the mutie spit sticky phlegm at the one-eyed
man and demonically tried to rise again.

Grinding gears, Ryan rolled the bike backward a few
yards, then hit the throttle and slammed into the creature

again, driving the safety cage of the first bike into its body, dicing the mutie into pieces. Legs and claws wiggling, it began to reform once more, but it was pinned helplessly to the wreckage.

"Stay close!" Ryan ordered, wriggling past the bikes and managing to reach the keypad. It was covered with greenish blood, so he wiped the alphanumeric pad clean with a bare hand and tapped in the entry code.

Avoiding the claws and whipping tail of the mutie, which were stretching for them, the itching humans waited impatiently as the massive doors cycled open, the brown grass sweeping closer by the second.

"In!" Ryan commanded, and squeezed through the widening crack. As the last person rushed through, the one-eyed man keyed the sequence that would close the door.

Cutting away from the mouth of the access tunnel, just as a safety precaution, J.B. paused as he looked over the garage of the underground base. It seemed cleaner than he remembered from their last visit, and there were tools on the walls. Dimly, he recalled the place had been completely stripped, but they had been in so many redoubts it was easy to get them confused occasionally.

"By gad, I hate Tennessee," Doc spit, holstering his nearly spent LeMat. "There are always traps of some kind at this accursed redoubt!"

"Check your ammo," Ryan said, checking his own blasters. The Steyr was out, the SIG-Sauer down to six rounds.

"Out," J.B. snapped. "Haven't got a thing left."

Scowling, Dean dropped his clip and slapped it back in the butt of his blaster. "Four rounds."

"One round," Mildred stated, patting her pockets. She had six speed loaders for her target pistol, but none of them held a single bullet. Just the casings she used for combat reloading.

"Same here," Krysty said, closing her revolver, then added, "You want to drop that now, or are you keeping it as a souvenir?"

Jak stared at her, confused, then saw a ropy length of forked tongue clenched tight in his grip. In disgust, he threw it away and wiped his fingers clean on his pants. The teenager started to speak when alarms cut loose all over the base, bells clanging, and Klaxons howling in deafening volume.

"Fireblast! There must be leakage through the armor somewhere!" Ryan cursed, looking about quickly. Nothing seemed out of the ordinary, but then microwaves were invisible. "Head for the mat-trans chamber!"

Bypassing the bank of elevators, the companions raced down the stairs. With each level they passed, the itchy sensation of the microwaves lessened a little bit. Getting off at the fourth landing, they raced down a long corridor lined with doors and slammed aside the wooden door at the far end. Charging into the control room, the companions slowed for a moment in spite of the horrible sensation on their skin. The bodies of the dead from years before were gone, the bullet holes in the consoles patched, the computers humming softly with their lights twinkling. The spent brass covering the floor was gone, and the walls looked freshly painted. Everything was clean and seemed in proper working condition.

"Silas has been here." Krysty frowned, forcing herself not to cringe from the growing misery of her living hair.

"Touch nothing!" J.B. warned, going to the door that led to the mat-trans unit. He ran fingertips along the jamb and lintel before opening the heavy portal.

"Clear," he reported. "Let's go!"

Rushing into the chamber, Ryan saw that the armaglass walls had also been painted, the deep purple identifying this as Tennessee now painted over with a deep military green. However, the paint was peeling from the armaglass. But the disguise might fool a casual observer.

"Hiding his location," Dean said, scratching at his forearms. "Smart son of a bitch."

"Dead son of a bitch," Mildred corrected, then paused before stepping onto the platform. "Damn. Think he might have jimmied the controls?"

"Only one way to find out," Ryan said, and, pulling out an empty clip for the Steyr, he tossed it the chamber. The companions closed the door and waited in mounting pain, then hastily opened it again. The metal-and-clear-plastic clip lay in plain sight on the cold floor on the chamber. Nothing had happened.

"He did something, or the microwave is affecting it," J.B. said woodenly, the alarms screaming in the background.

Touching her quivering hair, Krysty winced slightly. "It doesn't hurt as badly here in the mat-trans unit," she said. "Mebbe we can ride out the attack. The blues can't keep the Kite focused on us forever."

"Yes, they can," Mildred replied coldly. "And this is only buying us time. We're still being chilled, just slower than outside."

"What do?" Jak asked, rubbing his itchy face.

"It seems that we are to die today," Doc said, bowing his head in finality. "Microwaves are seeping in, and the mat-trans unit is deactivated. What other course do we have?"

"Fuck that. We're trapped, not aced," Ryan spit, rubbing a fist in the palm of his hand. "Mebbe..."

"What?" Krysty barked impatiently, her hands tucked under her arms, to keep from clawing her skin off.

His empty socket feeling as if it were filled with hungry ants, Ryan scowled. "There's a fission reactor in the basement. The extra shielding might help protect us."

Tossing away his hat, J.B. wiped the hot sweat from his face. "Mebbe," he panted in agreement. "B-but for how long?"

"Till we starve to death, or they fucking turn it off!" Ryan growled, a red fury growing inside the man. "And then we'll go back and smash that bastard machine just like we did Silas."

"A chance for life is all I ask," Doc said weakly. "Lead on, my dear Ryan."

Turning for the door, Ryan braced himself for the pain waiting outside the chamber. Then, closing his good eye tight, the man charged into the control room, blindly stumbling through the maze of the redoubt for the faint hope of survival deep within the radioactive bowels of the military base.

Epilogue

Alone in the laboratory, Major Sheffield sat the computer desk and carefully turned on predark machine. It cycled through the boot programs in a few seconds, and the screen lit with a picture of a hundred tiny icons. Reaching into his shirt pocket, the sec man pulled out a CD-ROM, wiped some blood off the disk, then inserted it into the little tray as he saw Silas do once. The device pulled the drawer back inside, made soft noises, then cleared into a picture of Silas.

"Hello, Major," the whitecoat said without a smile. "If you are listening to this, then I am dead, most likely from my own hand to stop the nightmares. If so, now you are charged with the all-important task of purifying North America, and the saving of the human race from the growing threat of the muties."

"Think again, norm," the major said softly, his two hearts beating hard. "And now it's Baron Sheffield."

The laser-disk ghost of Silas Jamaisvous went on undisturbed, "...and thus the redoubts were originally conceived during World War II as haven against the crude nukes of the time. However, upon creation of the mattrans unit, several interesting possibilities became evident and the Pentagon decided to implement a particularly bold plan called Overproject Whisper...."

The voice went on for hours, and Sheffield stayed through the night, drinking in the most amazing story he had ever heard, all the more so because he knew it to be completely true.

Almost unnoticed in the background, the computer that controlled the Kite blinked steadily as the orbiter poured gigawatts of raw power onto an insignificant patch of grasslands in the hills of Tennessee.

When the disk eventually finished, Sheffield turned the machine off and walked to the barred window to watch the sun rise over the craggy mountains of the valley.

"My mountains," he whispered, and slowly began to smile. "My valley, my continent!"

There was a crackle from the intercom. "Sir?" a voice asked in concern. "I heard a shout. Is everything all right, Major?"

"Everything is fine," the mutie replied. "And the next time you call me 'Major,' I'll rip out your guts and feed them to the dogs!"

"S-sir?"

"I am Baron Sheffield!" he roared. Then he added softly, "The new ruler of North America."

The Great American Empire is no more....

STONY MAN™ 43

ZEROHOUR

A new strain of anthrax is developed for a vicious madman bent on bringing the Western world back into the Dark Ages. The Stony Man commandos race to find the conspirator and deliver swift justice—before zero hour arrives!

Available in November 1999 at your favorite retail outlet.

Take
2 explosive books
plus a
mystery bonus
FREE

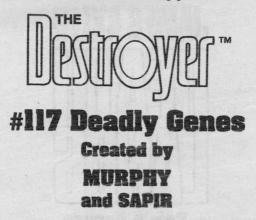

An old enemy poses a new threat....

JAMES AXLER
DEATH LANDS®
Gaia's Demise

Ryan Cawdor's old nemesis, Dr. Silas Jamaisvous, is behind a deadly new weapon that uses electromagnetic pulses to control the weather and the gateways, and even disrupts human thinking processes.

As these waves doom psi-sensitive Krysty, Ryan challenges Jamaisvous to a daring showdown for America's survival....

Book 2 in the Baronies Trilogy, three books that chronicle the strange attempts to unify the East Coast baronies—a bid for power in the midst of anarchy....

Beyond diplomacy...

DON PENDLETON's

MACK BOLAN®

Code of Conflict

A group known as the Nevada Minutemen stumble onto an old Army cache of poison gas and decide to use it to trigger anarchy. It's up to Bolan to put the lid on this terror and save the lives of thousands of innocents.

Available in October 1999 at your favorite retail outlet.

Journey back to the future
with these classic

titles!

#62535	BITTER FRUIT	$5.50 U.S.	☐
		$6.50 CAN.	☐
#62536	SKYDARK	$5.50 U.S.	☐
		$6.50 CAN.	☐
#62537	DEMONS OF EDEN	$5.50 U.S.	☐
		$6.50 CAN.	☐
#62538	THE MARS ARENA	$5.50 U.S.	☐
		$6.50 CAN.	☐
#62539	WATERSLEEP	$5.50 U.S.	☐
		$6.50 CAN.	☐

(limited quantities available on certain titles)

TOTAL AMOUNT	$
POSTAGE & HANDLING	$
($1.00 for one book, 50¢ for each additional)	
APPLICABLE TAXES*	$ _____
TOTAL PAYABLE	$ _____
(check or money order—please do not send cash)	

To order, complete this form and send it, along with a check or money order for the total above, payable to Gold Eagle Books, to: **In the U.S.:** 3010 Walden Avenue, P.O. Box 9077, Buffalo, NY 14269-9077; **In Canada:** P.O. Box 636, Fort Erie, Ontario, L2A 5X3.

Name: _____

Address: _____ City: _____

State/Prov.: _____ Zip/Postal Code: _____

*New York residents remit applicable sales taxes.
 Canadian residents remit applicable GST and provincial taxes.

GDLBACK1